Annette Roome

Annette Roome started writing in response to early-onset mid-life crisis. Her first novel won the Crime Writers' Association's John Creasey Award for the Best First Crime Novel of the Year.

She is married, with one daughter, and lives in Guildford. *Deceptive Relations* is her fourth novel.

ANNETTE ROOME

DECEPTIVE RELATIONS

HarperCollins*Publishers*

HarperCollins*Publishers*
77–85 Fulham Palace Road, London W6 8JB

The HarperCollins website address is:
www.**fire**and**water**.com

This paperback edition 2000

1 3 5 7 9 10 8 6 4 2

First published in Great Britain by
HarperCollins*Publishers* 1999

A catalogue record for this book
is available from the British Library

ISBN 0 00 651029 9

Set in Meridien and Bodoni

Printed and bound in Great Britain by
Caledonian International Book Manufacturing Ltd, Glasgow

1

The lock-up garages at the rear of Marjoram Mews are approached via Redbourne Road, a narrow, winding cul-de-sac within walking distance of the High Street, and you have to think that it's awfully inconsiderate of anyone to die in one of them. When I arrived in Redbourne Road, an ambulance was trying to squeeze through the gap between a Volvo estate parked on a bend and a large white van with somebody's brand-new windows strapped to the side of it. It was a Tuesday afternoon in January, the sales were in full swing, and pedestrians laden down with carrier bags were grimly heading for the cars they'd parked illegally on double-yellow lines, mercifully oblivious to the proximity of a still-warm corpse.

I followed the rear bumper of the ambulance as though attached to it by an invisible thread, but as soon as we arrived on the garage forecourt a young constable loomed out of the gloom and inserted himself rather unwisely in front of my right headlamp. When we'd both got over the shock of my emergency stop, he motioned for me to wind down my window.

'You'll have to turn round and go back, madam,' he said stiffly, his breath steaming past my window. 'There's been an incident and this area's restricted access only at the moment. Quick as you can, please, there are police vehicles behind you.'

There was a terrible smell of petrol and overheated engine oil in the air.

'I'm from the *Tipping Herald*,' I protested, but he affected not to hear, so I shot forward with a terrifying squeal (I'd

1

only had my new Golf for a few weeks, and hadn't quite got the measure of its clutch) and launched into a laborious seven-point turn. I'd no intention of turning round and going back. There was a minute parking space between the rear end of a police car and an old van propped up on bricks in front of one of the garages, and the moment the constable took his eyes off me I stopped pratting about with the gears and reversed straight into it.

I got out of the car. The door of the third garage on the left was open, a single light bulb illuminating a large black car half draped with a dustsheet, and on the floor behind the rear wheels lay a man, face down, his body rumpled into an awkward arc like a recently vacated sock. He was wearing an unpressed blue suit and white shirt. A semicircle of police officers and ambulance men were gathered round him, prodding at him as though he was some as yet unidentified piece of flotsam washed up on a beach. In the centre of his head was a bald, shiny spot, with strands of greasy-looking dark hair standing upright on either side of it, unmoving in the still, cold air.

I bundled a handkerchief to my nose. A miserable, damp afternoon, a middle-aged man in a dated suit, and a dirty concrete yard littered with Kentucky Fried Chicken boxes. I was beginning to get a sinking feeling in the pit of my stomach.

A vaguely familiar voice interrupted my thoughts. 'Well, really, if this isn't the absolute end! I was in M and S when my bloody mobile went.' It was Linda somebody-or-other from the *Hudderston Advertiser*. 'I'd just found this pair of black velvet trousers, size fourteen – *half price*! I'll bet they're gone when I get back. What on earth do we do this bloody job for – you tell me that?'

Of course, we all know Marks and Spencer would never reduce anything by as much as fifty per cent, not even a pair of trousers with one of the legs missing, but in the circumstances a bit of exaggeration seemed fair enough.

'Oh, dear,' I sympathized. 'What a shame. How are you? Good Christmas?'

'No, not really. Is there any such thing? Oh God, I'm not

standing around here all afternoon. I think I know that sergeant over there. Come on, hold this – let's do ourselves a favour.' She thrust a Jacques Vert carrier bag into my hands and made a beeline for a group of policemen in front of the garage. 'Hallo, Sergeant, I'm Linda from the *Advertiser* and this is Chris from the *Herald* – remember me? I'm the one who got your picture on the front page when one of your men rescued a dog from Dollis Pond. You're not going to make us wait for a statement from your press officer, are you? Go on – fill us in on a few details so we can go home and get our husbands' tea.'

The sergeant, who had been stooping over the body, retrieved something from an inner pocket and straightened up.

'Well, well!' he exclaimed affably, winking at Linda. 'Come on, love, you know the score. Push off before the monkey suits turn up or you'll get me into trouble.'

'But it's only a suicide!' protested Linda. 'Go on – give us his name.'

The sergeant opened the wallet and pulled out a card. 'Only a suicide?' he remarked, ironically. 'Tut, tut – and they say it's us men that are emotionally stunted.' He glanced at the card. 'Go on. Michael Henry Irons, Director, Irons Executive Services Limited. Oops, you didn't get that from me.'

I dropped Linda's carrier bag and found my notebook.

'Thank you, Sergeant!' exclaimed Linda. 'I'm sure you'll go to heaven for this. Any idea how long he's been dead?'

'Oh, not long – he's still warm.' He bent over Mr Irons again. 'He made a right dog's dinner of it, you know. Changed his mind at the last minute, I'd say. Look at the hands.' I didn't. 'See what I mean? He's almost ripped his fingernails out trying to pull the door up to get out. Looks like he was sat in the driving seat with a picture of the wife and kids when he had second thoughts. Choked on his own vomit in the end.'

'Oh God, that's awful!' I muttered involuntarily.

'Not nice,' agreed the sergeant. 'I can think of better ways to do it. He had a nice car, too.'

We all glanced towards the rear end of Michael Irons's Mercedes.

Linda sighed. 'Well, I'm off,' she said, seizing her carrier bag. 'Thanks again, Sergeant. Bye, Chris, see you around –'

'Yes. Thanks, I owe you a favour!' I called, but her heart was already in Marks and Spencer's separates department.

I went back to the Golf. Michael Henry Irons, ex-human being, ex-company director. Two lines, bottom of the front page. I was halfway into the passenger seat when a woman wrenched the door out of my hand and leaned into the car.

'You a reporter? I want to talk to you!'

'What about?' I enquired nervously, immediately fearing that some ghastly printing error had transformed one of her relatives from a prominent local Mormon into a prominent local moron, as had happened recently to another Tipping resident.

'About Philip Chandler!'

'Who?'

'Oh, Christ!' She was in her mid-thirties, with short brown hair, a lot of make-up and two gold hoops in each earlobe. Her breath smelt a bit stale. 'Philip Chandler! Of Tuck Woodford and Chandler the solicitors!'

'Oh!' Of course I knew Tuck Woodford & Chandler. My ex-husband had used them when we got divorced. 'And were you a friend of Mr Irons?' I asked, indicating the garages.

'Oh, I wouldn't say that exactly. I knew him – all right? Anyway, who cares about him! Which paper are you from?'

'The *Tipping Herald*.'

'OK, then, I've got a hair appointment at four. My car's at the end of the road. Do you know the Garden Coffee Shop on Kingsmead? If you're interested in the story, meet me there in ten minutes! Got that? If you're not there in ten minutes, forget it!'

I watched her run off into the gloom. She was wearing a thin red blazer of the sort sales staff who work in electricity-board shops and mobile phone salesrooms are forced to wear, and she looked like the kind of person who wouldn't rest until she'd got your signature in several places on a set of forms that included a direct debit arrangement with your bank. I decided it probably wouldn't be a good idea to keep an assignation with her in the Garden Coffee Shop: even if

4

she *was* able to fill in a few details on the late Michael Irons, I could get these with considerably less hassle from other sources, and Mr Heslop, my editor, wouldn't be interested in some titbit of gossip about a local solicitor, no matter how salacious. I decided to take extra care getting out of the space so she'd be long gone by the time I made it to the end of the road. Except that when I got there, she wasn't gone. I could see her as I approached the junction, holding up traffic in an old blue Fiesta with a white stripe down its side, craning over her shoulder to look for me. As soon as she saw me she shook her fist angrily and pulled out peremptorily into the path of an oncoming taxi. All I could do, when things had calmed down, was wince and follow.

By the time I arrived at the coffee shop she was already ensconced at a table in an alcove surrounded by white plastic trellising, with a cappuccino and half a large doughnut in front of her.

'You took your bloody time!' she snapped.

I ignored this. 'Can I get you anything?'

'Yes – you can get me another doughnut. I haven't had anything since breakfast and I'm starving. I've got five minutes!'

I didn't much care for her manner, but I ordered coffee and two doughnuts and sat down.

'I'm Chris Martin,' I said. 'What's this story you've got for me?'

'You'll get that in good time. First I want you to do something for me.' She rubbed her hands together, scattering sugar in all directions, and delved into her handbag, which was made of soft black leather and had a little gold motif on the flap. She'd stuffed it overfull with cosmetic bottles and sheafs of paper that looked like invoices with delivery notes attached to them. 'I'm Janet Cox, by the way, and this is my husband, Lee,' she said, pushing a photograph towards me. 'We're separated – OK? Just over a year ago. I won't bore you with the details, but we sold the house and sorted things out financially and now I just want to divorce him. OK? He's gone missing and I want *you* to find him.'

I did a double take. 'What?'

5

'Oh, come on, it's not difficult. You've got the facilities. Newspapers are always tracking people down! All you have to do is find out where he's living – that's all. I'll do the rest. Come on, what do you say?'

Of course, local newspapers don't actually have the facilities for full-scale manhunts, and in any case, there was no way my editor would agree to such a thing, but I decided it would be diplomatic to string her along for a bit. I picked up the photo and studied it obligingly, and my pulse rate immediately tweaked upwards. Lee Cox possessed the sort of looks that are bad news for any woman's blood pressure, even one in her forties with a semipermanent headache: he had well-muscled shoulders, blue eyes, light-brown wavy hair you could imagine running your fingers through and a nice smile. In the picture, Janet was standing next to him looking vaguely bad-tempered, which, from what I'd seen of her so far, was probably about as good as her mood ever got.

She registered my lingering stare, and smirked. 'He's quite a looker, eh? And a right bastard too, but that's none of your business. OK, all right, I lied. He's got money and I want it. I know he's got money, because the last time I saw him he told me he was on to the deal of a lifetime and if his number came up I wouldn't see him for dust. Well, more fool him for having such a big mouth – we're still married and what's his is mine.'

'I see. What business is your husband in, exactly?'

She frowned and shook her head irritably. 'What does that matter? This and that – buying things, selling them – cars mostly. *Business*.' She reached into her handbag again, produced a notepad and said, 'This is the address of his house in Hudderston. I've already been through it with a fine-toothed comb and I can tell you he didn't leave a forwarding address so don't waste your time on it. He's had the place all boarded up, and the phone disconnected. I saw him last about the end of June, but that doesn't mean anything because the swine never returned my calls. I'm going to write down another number you could try –'

At that moment my coffee and two doughnuts arrived and

Janet seized one of the doughnuts without being invited and bit into it eagerly.

'Just a minute,' I interrupted quickly, while her mouth was still full. 'Before we go any further, what is this story on Philip Chandler you think I'll be so interested in?'

She frowned. 'What do you mean – are you stupid or something? Look, Chandler is rich and middle-class and successful and a *bloody lawyer* – wouldn't you like to print something about him that'd wipe the smug grin off his face? You find my husband, *then* you get the story – that's the deal.'

I laughed nervously. 'Actually, I'm afraid my paper doesn't print gossip about people, no matter how rich and middle-class and successful they are.'

'Oh, for God's sake!' She banged her cup down into its saucer, displacing all the froth from both our cappuccinos. 'Look, all right then, forget the story – I'll *pay* you! How about that? Payment on delivery. I tried a private detective but he wanted to charge by the hour plus expenses whether he found Lee or not. Two hundred quid on delivery! What do you say?'

I was so surprised I didn't say anything, and Janet appeared to mistake my silence for compliance. 'Right. Good,' she said, immediately mollified. 'I haven't got much time, so if you need anything else you'll just have to ring me. I've put my address and phone number on here as well. I want you to get on to it straight away and ring me the minute you've got anything. All right? But I don't want you approaching Lee or talking to him or mentioning my name – I just want you to find out where he is and report back to me. And do it quickly, because this is an emergency.'

'Why?'

'Never you mind, it's none of your bloody business!' She climbed awkwardly to her feet and leaned across the table. 'Look, are you going to help me or not?'

'I'll try. I'll ring you.' I didn't like her much, but I could see she was desperate. I tried to back away from her stale breath and manic gaze without appearing rude. 'I'll give you a ring tomorrow.'

'You'll try,' she repeated, with heavy sarcasm. 'Oh, good,

that makes me feel so much better!' And she picked up her handbag, slung it across her shoulder and stalked out of the café into the cold in her ten-denier tights. I watched her stop traffic as she marched across the street to the hairdressing salon opposite.

After she'd gone, I sat at the table and stared into her husband's eyes. I could see why an ex-wife might not want to give up on him. Then I ate my doughnut, but somehow it had lost its sweetness.

2

I was late into work the following morning, because we got embroiled in a Bathroom Row. Julie's alarm clock had failed to go off, and Pete – who will, according to Julie, never really be her stepfather until global warming reverses itself and the second Ice Age cometh – usurped her turn in the shower. This led to the usual hurling of personal insults, everybody refusing to eat their breakfast, and ultimately to Julie accidentally slicing herself in the armpit with Pete's razor. By the time I'd found sticking plaster, Germolene, and a new razor blade, Julie had missed her bus and I had to drop her at school. Unfortunately, Mr Heslop was already in a bad mood. It had been a very slow news week, and he was agitatedly sifting through lost cat stories, looking for something resembling a sinister pattern. Unless we struck lucky, our lead story was going to have to be 'Into the Millennium: details of the town's long-awaited Millennium project to be announced shortly'. He'd managed to get someone who was good at such things to produce a computer-generated view of Councillor Draycott's proposed riverside park as it would look in about 2050 when the trees had matured and the hedging round the bowling greens had filled out. They hadn't included a depiction of the adventure playground as it would undoubtedly appear after fifty years of graffiti, or futuristic shopping trolleys up to their handles in the shallow waters under the footbridge, but readers could presumably use their own imaginations on that score.

By the time his afternoon tea arrived, he was on the verge of desperation. 'That suicide of yours. We're just going to have to pad it out and put it on the front page. Have you got hold of the widow yet?'

'No. The phone rings and rings.' The last thing I wanted was to be dispatched to ask Mr Irons's widow how she felt. 'But listen, I met this woman at the 'scene yesterday – her husband's gone missing and she wants us to help her find him.'

'Oh? Suspicious circumstances?'

'Not really – but it seemed very odd. First she said she's got some story about a local solicitor for us, and then, when I said we don't do gossip, she offered me money to look for the husband!'

He rolled his eyes. 'Don't tell me, he's a bastard and he's walked out leaving her to cope with the kids and the mort-gage, and you – because you still believe in all that seventies sisterhood crap – want to track the poor bloke down for nothing.'

'No, actually –'

'Well, forget it! If you want to do social work, you can do it on your own time. Go on, go out and find this Mrs Irons and don't come back without something we can use. You know, the man's parrot died and it pushed him over the edge – or he lost a winning lottery ticket, something like that.'

I got up reluctantly.

'Try and make it the parrot, Chris,' he added. 'Tipping people empathize more with parrots than with lottery tick-ets.'

I didn't want Mrs Irons to be in, so when I got to Marjoram Mews – which was just round the corner from the lock-up garages where her husband had died – I was relieved to find a large envelope and a handful of adverts for takeaway pizza protruding from the letterflap of the Ironses' neat little terraced home. I rang the doorbell though, and after a few moments, when nothing had happened, I pushed their mail through and tried to peer into the house. But they'd got one of those brush things to exclude draughts and all I could see was a chink of green carpet.

I turned to go back to the car, and a woman from across the street came out, hugging herself against the cold.

'Her husband just died,' she whispered urgently, as though such things should not be spoken of aloud. 'I think she may have gone away but I don't know where.'

I decided if I didn't say anything, she would have to get it off her chest.

'Gassed himself in his garage, apparently. It's awful, isn't it? You don't know what to say, do you? He must have been nearly fifty, but even so –' She was only about twenty-five, so I forgave her this remark. 'She's terribly upset, of course.'

I made sympathetic noises. 'Did you know them well?'

'Oh, no! They haven't lived here long.' She hesitated. 'Perhaps I shouldn't say this, but *apparently*, Trish – that's Mrs Irons – told Nina-on-the-corner this morning that her husband couldn't possibly have committed suicide! She said he would never do anything like that and it must have been some sort of accident. Nina says Trish is really upset with the police for the way they're handling things.'

'I see –'

'And apparently there's been an insurance adjuster round already about the damage to the garage where the police had to force the door open, and *he* says deliberate damage isn't covered by the policy so Trish will have to pay for the repairs. Isn't that awful?'

'Yes! It's terrible!' I didn't know what to say.

She shivered suddenly. 'Well, I must go in, just thought I ought to tell you what's going on.'

I waited till she'd gone and then rang Nina-on-the-corner's doorbell. I wasn't quite sure how you could sit in the front seat of your car with photos of your wife and children on your lap and gas yourself by accident, but I thought perhaps I should try and follow this up. Unfortunately, though, Nina-on-the-corner wasn't home.

When I got back to the car, my mobile was ringing.

'There's a body on Nuthurst Hill,' Mr Heslop announced excitedly. 'It's in a layby off the Rudgeleigh road. Do you know where I mean? If you're coming from Tipping you go up on to the dual carriageway as if you're heading south, then take the first exit on the left. The layby is just beyond where the slip road joins the Rudgeleigh road.'

'Oh – you mean the little road you can use as a short cut to the new Sainsbury's?'

'Yes, that's it. Hurry up, will you? We may have to rearrange the front page and I'm playing bridge this evening.'

I didn't want to have to go up on to Nuthurst Hill and look at another body. 'But what about the suicide? Apparently the man's wife says –'

'Bugger the suicide! Come on, don't waste time – get straight over there and ring in as soon as you've got something,' he snapped, and disconnected me.

On a clear day, as you bowl along the dual carriageway that winds round Nuthurst Hill, you (or your passengers, unless you have a death wish) can marvel at the splendid vista of downland, telegraph poles and golf courses spread out as far as the eye can see. Today, though, the sky was sitting greyly almost on top of Nuthurst Hill, and a pool of mist had collected at the turn-off to the Rudgeleigh road. I put on my fog lights and windscreen wipers and carefully followed the serpentine coils of the slip road. I couldn't remember ever having noticed a layby along the Rudgeleigh road, and, as following directions has never been one of my strong points, I had a nasty feeling I might have misunderstood Mr Heslop's instructions. But I spotted the police cars as soon as I came off the slip road. A potholed track ran parallel with the road for a hundred yards or so, partially obscured by a row of trees, and then rejoined it. I remembered it now. In the summer, lorry drivers sometimes stopped there to clean out their ashtrays.

A policeman wearing yellow armbands showed me where to park. There were rows of bollards across the ends of the track, and fluorescent police tape all over the place. I pulled up behind a Land Rover belonging to a TV crew.

'What's going on? Have they said anything?' I enquired, doing my best to look as if I was used to tripping over expensive pieces of sound equipment.

'Not really. Some woman with her head bashed in, that's all – we were on our way back from an anti-bypass demo. They said robbery to begin with but now they've changed their minds, and we've already missed our deadline. You local press?'

'*Tipping Herald.*'

His eyes glazed over. 'Oh. So, would you know if there's a pub round here anywhere? We're freezing our bollocks off.'

'Er, there's the Rudgeleigh Arms at Rudgeleigh, but they're quite posh,' I ventured, and then wondered if he would take this as an insult. 'What I mean is –'

'How far's Rudgeleigh?'

'It's just down there – about two miles, I think –'

'Right. Alex!' He turned to his companion. 'Get on to 'em and order steak, chips and peas for five. No – hang on – three steaks, a vegetarian alternative, and I'll have –'

'Actually, the Rudgeleigh Arms is a very smart restaurant. It's owned by the chef Stefan Andre,' I protested, but the entire crew was in the process of withdrawing, so I got out of their way. When they'd gone, I had an uninterrupted view through the trees of the roped-off area, which included a little polythene tent, a small blue car, and several men in navy overalls with hoods. The track was littered with paper and various small objects, and one of the men in overalls was photographing these, while others patrolled the area in loose formation, heads down, arms akimbo, apparently looking for something. The whole scene was calm, businesslike and efficient. People were talking in normal voices with normal resonances, as though taking part in a well-rehearsed working procedure.

I leaned over the tape to get a better view of the polythene tent, half hoping for a glimpse of the body, and at that moment the small group of officers who had been examining the car suddenly dispersed. The car, I noticed for the first time, was also draped in polythene. It was an old-style blue Fiesta with a white stripe along its side.

Something flipped over inside my stomach, but I ignored it. There must be lots of old blue Fiestas around with white stripes down their sides, and this one was quite possibly a different blue to the one I'd seen Janet Cox in yesterday. You couldn't be sure in the gloom. I got out my notebook and began to make notes. 'Blue Ford Fiesta', 'coloured papers and other items scattered around near the car'. I pushed anxiously against the loose tape to get a better view. The 'other items' were cosmetics – lipsticks, bottles of nail varnish, mascara wands, a sachet of cotton buds. And next to the car lay a black leather handbag, upside down, with its insides turned half out.

My stomach did another flip. I didn't want Janet to be dead. When people die soon after you've met them, no matter what the cause, you can't help feeling involved. I called out to the men in overalls. 'Excuse me! Could I speak to somebody? I'm not sure, but I think I might know the victim.' And then suddenly I thought, perhaps it isn't Janet under that tent at all – perhaps Janet's not the victim, but the *perpetrator*. Remembering our conversation, and her manner, who could tell?

One of the men in blue stood up, his knees stained with mud, and they all stared in my direction. I recognized DI Carver of Hudderston CID, and I tried to part my lips in a friendly smile, but the lower half of my face was numb with cold so it came out as a sort of rictus grin. Worryingly, the inspector seemed to recognize me instantly.

'Ah, Mrs Martin,' he said. 'The *Herald*, isn't it?' Then he started. 'Oh, good God, this Cox woman's not one of yours, is she?'

'No, no. I only met her yesterday. It *is* her then, is it?'

'Well, you tell me. Early to mid-thirties? Short hair? Bad legs?'

My heart sank. 'It sounds like her.'

'Right. Like to take a look for us?'

'Not really – I told you, I only met her yesterday –'

He ignored this, and ushered me under the tape.

'Wait here a second,' he said, when we got to the polythene tent, which now had a powerful light set up inside it. He lifted the tent flap. 'Neville, I've got a woman here who may be able to confirm whether or not this is Cox. Ready, Mrs Martin?'

Reluctantly I stooped to look inside. Two bodies in two days: it was too much.

The woman was wearing a heavily bloodstained red jacket,

short black skirt, and sheer tights that were holed just below the right knee. The back of her head seemed to be missing.

'Is it Mrs Cox?' asked the inspector.

I backed hastily out of the tent. 'I don't know. I think so.' The last thing I wanted was for him to tell me to go back in and have another look, so I did my best to sound positive. 'She's certainly wearing the same clothes she was when I saw her yesterday afternoon.'

DI Carver looked disappointed, but at that moment a uniformed officer appeared on the scene, urgently brandishing a notebook.

'Sir, we've just had Wickham Road on. That address is a block of flats. Mrs Cox's name is on the door, but there's no one home.'

'What – not in any of the flats?'

'No, sir.'

'Tell them to try again. Any luck with the agency number?'

'Yes, sir! They're a marketing agency in the West End. They've got a Mrs Cox who works for them on a freelance basis doing in-store product demonstrations and special promotions. Apparently she was supposed to be doing a demo at Army and Navy in Guildford this morning and the store called to complain she hadn't turned up. But I'm afraid they're not keen on sending anyone down, sir.'

'And what about the husband?'

'Nothing, sir. The house is boarded up. One of the neighbours says he's away but she doesn't know where –'

'Excuse me, *I* can tell you about the husband! His name's Lee and they're separated,' I interrupted, reaching into my handbag. 'I've got a photo of him somewhere. Mrs Cox said he went missing several months ago and she wanted my paper to help her find him.'

'I see.' DI Carver paused to consider this. 'Right. Well, you heard, Potter – get back on to Wickham Road and tell them to stop pissing about. I need someone over here *now* who can positively ID the body.'

'Yes, sir!' agreed Potter, and departed.

Infuriatingly, I couldn't find either the piece of paper Janet had given me or the photo.

'Don't bother with that now,' said DI Carver. 'I just need to know when and where you had this conversation with Mrs Cox.'

'About four o'clock yesterday, in the Garden Coffee Shop. I think she had a hair appointment at the salon opposite.'

'Good. Do you remember if she had anything to eat?'

'Er – a cup of coffee and two doughnuts. Look, I don't know if it's relevant, but she said she'd got a story for me on Philip Chandler, the solicitor.'

DI Carver raised his eyebrows and wrote this down, but before I could elaborate, another uniformed officer appeared with a young woman in tow. 'Sorry to interrupt, sir – I think I've got a witness!'

'A witness?' DI Carver didn't look as if he thought this very likely.

'Yes, sir. This is Elaine. She says she witnessed an incident here yesterday between a man and a woman.'

'What incident, love?' asked DI Carver, taking in the woman's multicoloured leggings, uncombed hair, and the whimpering toddler attached to her shoulder, and transparently looking unimpressed.

'A woman in a red coat being attacked by a man!' exclaimed Elaine, her eyes bulging. 'They were arguing about her driving – it happens all the time! They do eighty up there and there's never a police car in sight!'

'I see. You mean on the dual carriageway?'

'*Yes*! It's the short cut to Sainsbury's. People don't like it when you get on the road in front of them and they have to slow down. You indicate to go off at the next exit just round the bend and they have to slow down again and they go *berserk*!'

'I see –'

I got out my notebook and began making furtive notes.

'Well, you ought to put up cameras or something!' went on Elaine. 'You ought to give us a special lane! A few minutes earlier and it could have been me! What did he do to her, for God's sake? It could have been anyone! Oh my God, I wish I'd stopped –'

'Hold on, Elaine, can we go over this from the beginning?'

He flipped over to a new page in his book, still looking unimpressed. 'What time was it when you say you saw this happen?'

'About five-thirty. I was on my way back from –'

'Could you give me a description of the couple?'

'Yes – she had short hair and a red coat and that's her car over there. I could do a picture of her if you like!'

'And the man?'

'He had his back to me – he had a black car and it was behind hers with its door open.'

'Age?'

'I'm twenty-eight.'

'Not you. Him.'

'Him? Oh, *him*! Oh, I don't know! I'm doing my best!' You could see she was close to the end of her tether. 'Oh God, I know I should have stopped, but she was giving him as good as she got. Oh, what kind of world are we bringing children into!'

At that moment, inside my coat pocket, my mobile let out a sudden warble.

'Right, I'm going to have to ask you for a statement,' DI Carver snapped grimly. 'You'll have to come down to the station so one of my officers can go over the whole thing with you, but in the meantime – What *is* that bloody racket?' he added furiously, as my mobile let out another warble.

Hastily I withdrew from the group and answered the phone.

'Well?' said Mr Heslop.

'It looks like it could be road rage.'

'Road rage! Are you sure?'

I walked back towards the car, thinking this over as I dodged puddles. 'It's the woman I met yesterday – the one I was telling you about who wanted me to find her husband, and I can personally testify that she was a very bad driver. This witness saw her in the layby arguing with a man, and apparently lots of people get into fights with other drivers near the Rudgeleigh turn-off. That was at half past five. I last saw her at four –'

'Good – that's great,' interrupted Mr Heslop. 'That'll have all our readers shuddering over their cornflakes and twittering,

"No, after you," at roundabouts. And you say you knew this woman?'

'Well, I met her once –'

'Good! Wonderful! At last we're ahead of the rest of the pack when it counts! Do all the usual and have something on my desk in the morning. Thank Christ,' he added fervently, presumably referring to the Lord's bountiful intervention vis-à-vis our front page.

I unlocked the car and climbed in. 'Doing all the usual' in the case of a suspicious death meant interviewing people who had known the victim and garnering stories about their delightful, warm personality and great value to the community, and I had a feeling it was going to be no easy task in Janet's case. And since tomorrow was deadline day, I hadn't got much time to do it in. I tipped the contents of my handbag on to the front seat, and immediately Lee's photo and the paper with Janet's address on it tumbled out of a recess. I peered at them in the gloom. *Janet Cox, 6 Springfield Court, Chatfield Way, Hudderston*, and then she'd written her husband's address and a mobile phone number. There didn't seem much point in visiting Lee's house, since the police had already tried this, but on impulse, I dialled the mobile phone number. If he answered, I'd have to find some way of telling him that his wife was on top of Nuthurst Hill with her head bashed in, and this would not make me popular with the police, who always like to be first in with this sort of news. There was complete silence for several seconds, and then a female voice cut in: 'You have reached the mobile phone of Claire MacInnis. I'm afraid I can't take your call just now, but please leave a message after the tone, or if it's really urgent you can try me at the restaurant. Thank you for calling.' I disconnected hastily. What restaurant? And who on earth was Claire MacInnis? I could ring Hugh Burton-Cooper, our occasional restaurant critic, and ask him if he'd ever heard of a Claire MacInnis, but it had better wait till I got back to the office.

I got out a street map and looked up Chatfield Way, expecting to find it on the southern outskirts not far from the new Sainsbury's. But it wasn't. It was on the *northern* side of Hudderston, which meant that Janet hadn't ended up on the Rudgeleigh turn-off on her way home. Unless of course she'd decided to make a detour to Sainsbury's. I took a last look at the polythene tent glowing eerily in the middle of the layby, and set off to look up Janet's neighbours.

Springfield Court was a purpose-built block of flats with a small landscaped area in the front which might have looked quite attractive in spring when the prunus trees were in flower, but that afternoon, littered with greasy chip bags from the takeaway just up the road, it was bleak and uninviting. There wasn't even an officer from the Wickham Road police station camped out on the doorstep, as I had half expected. I examined the name-board and rang a few doorbells. Janet's just said 'J. Cox'. I got the feeling that Springfield Court was probably occupied by young professionals on their way up in life, the sort of people whose dinner parties came straight from the chill cabinet of the nearest supermarket and who hadn't got the time or inclination to argue with their landlord over what colour wallpaper went best with the carpeting in the communal areas (cream and a nasty shade of orange, as it happened). If so, this was bad news from my point of view.

A male voice suddenly crackled through the intercom in response to my desultory bell-pushing. 'Yes?'

I thought quickly. You can't explain to a person over an intercom that one of their neighbours has been murdered.

'Cable television!' I shouted.

'What?'

'Cable television! Can I talk to you about Flat Six?'

There was a short pause, some clicking, and the front door buzzed open.

I stepped into the warmth of the foyer and waited for a few moments. When no one appeared, I tried knocking on the door of Flat 1. Flat 2 still had a full bottle of milk and a small Hovis on the step, so I gave up and began climbing the stairs.

Unsurprisingly, there was a bottle of semiskimmed languishing outside the door of Janet's flat. There was also a new Yellow Pages and a sportswear catalogue too big to go through the letterbox.

Cautiously, I tapped on the door. It seemed unlikely, but there was always the possibility that Janet had a flatmate who did not take milk in his/her coffee and who was too drunk, drugged or depressed to bring the mail in. No one answered, and I was just about to approach the door of Flat 5, when a thought occurred to me. Even single people bent on furthering their careers and having relationships with other single people need to get their plumbing checked over occasionally. Perhaps opening the front door to service personnel was a mutually agreed practice. Perhaps it meant that residents like Janet who were out at work all day habitually left spare front door keys under their doormats in case of emergency.

It was getting pretty dark on the landing, so I pressed the switch to bring on the landing light. But there was nothing under Janet's doormat, not even a note instructing a caller to enquire at Flat so-and-so. I stood up on tiptoe and felt along the top of the doorframe. Nothing. Then I spotted the ashtray stand under the window. With considerable difficulty, I manoeuvred it out of the niche it had dug for itself in the carpet, and there, side by side in the centre of a flattened circle of Axminster, lay not one but *two* front door keys. Of course – one for each flat on the landing. Scarcely able to believe my luck, and certainly not thinking of the consequences, I picked up the key nearest to Janet's door and tried it in the lock. It turned. The door opened. I stumbled triumphantly into the flat and shut myself in before anyone could turn up to stop me.

3

I was immediately plunged into a total, sticky, musty darkness. A tiny red flickering light was marooned in the blackness
a few feet away at waist height, but it illuminated nothing. I
took a step forward, groping along the wall for a light switch.
The room smelled of sour drains and Janet's hairspray. At
last I found the light switch, and as I leaned to turn it on
something sharp hooked itself enthusiastically into my right
shin. I whirled round frantically, fearing a vengeful cat, but
it was only a staple protruding from the corner of a cardboard
box that had caught on my tights. I gave the box a kick to
make myself feel better.

All the doors opening off the small hall – there were four of
them – were slightly ajar. I pushed open the first door on the
right to discover a bathroom littered with balled-up towels
and underwear. You're supposed to be able to tell a lot about
people from their bathrooms, but I didn't know what to look
for and I didn't dare turn on another light, so I opened the
vanity unit and examined Janet's choice of soap (the Body
Shop, dewberry fragrance), and her toilet rolls. At the back,
behind her bath oils, there were two men's disposable razors
and a canister of shaving foam.

I began to feel rather bad at this point. This had been Janet's
home: it reeked of her; everything in it had been touched by
her, looked at by her, positioned by her. When she died, a
picture of this flat as it was now, exactly as she had left it,
had probably flashed before her eyes. I'd got no business
going through it. And anyway, the police might arrive at
any minute.

With my heart pounding, I peered first into the living room, then the kitchen. Janet's kitchen was in a much worse state than I ever let mine get into, even during a very bad week. Her wastebin was overflowing with cans and bottles, and there was a nasty smell of something decomposing in the bottom of it. I'm afraid I couldn't resist putting on the light to have a gloat. Janet's sink was full of water with brown scum and vegetable peelings floating about in it. It looked as though, instead of washing up on a regular basis, she just dumped things into the water to get them out of the way. Her draining board was piled high with dirty cups and glasses.

I knew I ought to get out of the flat – and fast – but I had the distinct feeling that the kitchen – despite its state of disarray – was Janet's favourite room. A single chair stood next to the table with a worn cushion on the seat, and an old woolly cardigan tossed over its back. The chair was angled as though someone had just got out of it to leave the room for a moment. There was even a pair of very un-Janet-like fleecy slippers on the floor under the chair.

I sat down in the chair. The table top was covered in crumbs, specks of congealed tomato sauce, and used cotton buds. Janet must have sat here, morning and evening, eating, reading her mail, and dealing with her make-up while watching the news on her portable TV. A tottering pile of opened mail sat on the right-hand corner of the table, and I picked up an envelope and pulled out its contents. It was a letter from a property agent about the flat, asking Janet to sign a statement of service charge arrears so these could be reclaimed from her mortgagee. I riffled steadily through the pile, doing my best not to disarrange it. There were bills from the electricity board and British Telecom, and letters containing such phrases as 'no alternative but to resort to legal action'. Poor Janet – no wonder she'd been so anxious to find Lee and sue him for whatever she could get out of him. But then I came across her latest bank statements – and to my surprise these showed she had over a thousand pounds in her current account and nine thousand seven hundred and two pounds in a deposit account.

Why risk having your flat repossessed when you've got ten thousand pounds in the bank? It didn't make sense. I picked up a small piece of paper anchored in place by an empty coffee mug. It was a page torn from a last year's pocket diary, and it said, 'Holly Cottage, Gooserye', and 'St Martin's Court, in small neat handwriting that wasn't Janet's. On the back in the same hand was written, 'Dentist, 12.50', against April 12th.

I replaced the diary page. This wasn't going to advance the story Mr Heslop wanted me to write about Janet one iota. I made a note of the two addresses in my book, just in case they meant something, turned out the light, retreated to the hall, and put my ear to the door. Outside, all was quiet. I took a last look round – and that was when I noticed the answerphone with its little red light flashing and the Yellow Pages open next to it. The Yellow Pages was open at the entry for solicitors, and there was a ring round the name Tuck Woodford & Chandler. I thought about the answerphone. It couldn't do any harm, no one would ever know. I found a tissue in my pocket and used it to press the 'Message' button so the police wouldn't have to wonder whose prints they were on the machine.

'Hallo, it's me,' said a male voice, amid static. 'I've only got a minute.' Short pause. There was a muffled thump in the background and the sound of a female voice calling out someone's name, too distantly to distinguish for sure, but it sounded like Denny or Lenny. The speaker breathed heavily into the phone, and said, 'Look, come to the flat tonight between six and eight. Before eight anyway. Speak to you soon.' The line disconnected noisily. An electronic voice rasped, 'Tuesday, two-fifty p.m.,' and then, 'No messages.'

By now I was beginning to expect the howl of police sirens at any moment, but I couldn't help wondering why the caller hadn't rung again when Janet didn't turn up at his flat the previous evening. Or maybe he had. I picked up the phone, dialled one-four-seven-one, and got the 'We do not have the caller's number' message for a call timed at nine-thirty. This probably meant that Janet had been phoned by a telesales firm touting someone's double glazing; it didn't necessarily mean the previous caller hadn't phoned back earlier.

I made a note of the gist of the phone message in my book, gave the table top a quick wipe with the tissue, and made for the door, skirting carefully round the cardboard box with the staple sticking out of it. The staple had already pulled a large hole in my tights, just below my right knee. I stared at it for a moment, and I got a sort of creepy feeling. Janet's tights had been holed in exactly the same place when I saw her on Nuthurst Hill – but of course she couldn't have damaged them on the box, because she hadn't had time to come back to her flat between leaving the hairdresser's and meeting her end in the layby at five-thirty. It was just a nasty coincidence. I snapped off the light and let myself out of the flat.

It was pitch-dark on the landing, but I didn't put on the light. I began groping my way towards the ashtray.

'Did you sort it?' enquired a voice.

Various parts of my anatomy threatened to burst through their membrane covering. I reached for the light switch and slammed it on.

'Sorry, did I make you jump?' He was leaning against the door of Flat 5, smoking a cigarette. 'Didn't mean to. Did you sort the problem with the television?'

'With the television –' I wished I had died. 'Er, yes. It's sorted.'

'It's just that I was thinking' – he contemplated the end of his cigarette – 'it's a wonder she ever finds time to look at the thing. I bet she watches that channel where they sell you stuff.'

'What?' Any minute he was going to ask me some terribly technical question about cable television and I wouldn't be able to answer it.

'Yes – you know. She's very acquisitive, our Janet – very possessive. You wouldn't want her to catch you nicking her milk, I tell you. Not that I'm nosey, but you can't help noticing people's little foibles in a place like this.'

I manoeuvred the ashtray back into position.

'She must be raking it in, all those promotions she does – she's hardly ever home,' he went on. 'Don't know when she finds time to switch on. I thought she was trying to get started up in business.'

'Oh.' Two cars had just pulled up on the forecourt of Springfield Court. 'Was she?'

'Apparently. She's always looking for free advice. I'm going to put her on to my accountant.' He stubbed out his cigarette in the ashtray. 'Still, you never know, she's a funny woman.'

The drivers of the two cars were now in the lobby. We could hear muffled noises echoing up the stairwell. They couldn't be police, or they'd have come straight up. 'In what way?' I prompted.

'Well, she keeps funny company. I probably shouldn't tell you this – you got a couple of minutes? – but I was coming up the stairs just after Christmas and there's this guy on the landing – right where you are now. Big bloke he is, about six foot tall, and suddenly he takes a swing at Janet. And when I say a swing, I mean a real *Mike Tyson*, you know? – straight from the shoulder. Luckily he misses, and Janet starts screaming. She's scared shitless, and who can blame her – and I'm thinking, what do I do? What do I do?'

'Goodness!' I managed, after a pause.

'OK, I'll tell you what I did. I don't know where it came from, I really don't, but I tapped the guy politely on the shoulder and then when he turned round I gave him this straight-leg kick like you see in the martial arts films. Right in the nuts! So that was that – he staggered off down the stairs. Look! You can see where I dropped my chicken tikka in the heat of the moment,' he added proudly, indicating a stain on the carpet.

'How exciting!' My heart was going into overdrive again. 'What was it all about?'

'Oh, God – who knows? I don't know anything about her love life. This bloke looked a bit poncey – you know, long hair and Gucci aftershave, that's all I know. Do you reckon I saved her from a fate worse than death?'

At that moment the landing light snapped off suddenly, making us both jump. I gritted my teeth. 'Nice chatting to you – must go or I'll be late for my next appointment,' I said, and ran off down the stairs and out of the building before he could start wondering about me. I sat in the car for a few minutes, wondering if I ought to phone DI Carver on my mobile and alert him to the fact that only a few weeks ago someone had attempted to assault Janet in her own home

– but then a police car with its blue light flashing pulled on to the flats' forecourt. I started up the Golf and made my departure.

The following morning I wrote up my story on the Janet Cox murder under a banner headline, 'Local woman murdered on Nuthurst Hill: Is it road rage?' and showed it to Mr Heslop. He wasn't at all pleased.

'You haven't got any personal details,' he complained. 'And this photo makes her look like a criminal. Where's the human interest?'

I didn't want to have to explain to him what had happened at Springfield Court or why I didn't want to go back there to chat up the rest of Janet's neighbours.

'We're lucky to have the photo!' I retorted, aggrieved. 'It's not my fault she wasn't the sort of person to have friends. And listen, to be honest – I'm not sure it *was* road rage. Someone apparently tried to beat her up at her flat a couple of weeks ago – and there's this story she wanted to sell me about the solicitor –' I just stopped myself in time from telling him about Janet's Yellow Pages being open at Tuck Woodford & Chandler's entry.

'OK, I get it – a bit of a psycho. What a pity! Well, we just won't use the photo. I'll get on to Sainsbury's in a minute and see if they'll give us a quote. All right, given the material, not a bad attempt,' he added, grudgingly.

'Thank you!' My headache immediately began lifting. 'Shall I keep on to it?'

'If you think it's worth it.'

I went back to my desk. By lunchtime tomorrow, the story of Tipping's first apparent road rage victim would have sold out every copy of our early edition, and I felt rather guilty about this. I tapped into our new Archive programme and typed in the name Tuck Woodford & Chandler. To my surprise (our Archive programme doesn't always work) up came a piece on the firm's fiftieth anniversary celebrations held in the summer of 1996, and there was even a blurred photograph of the firm's senior partner, Philip Chandler, shaking hands with Tipping's mayor on the office steps. It wasn't a very good photo, but you could tell Chandler was middle-aged and quite distinguished-looking, not the sort of person you'd expect to be the subject of gossip. I wondered what possible connection there could be between him and Janet. The article said that the firm of Tuck Woodford had been started by Robert Tuck and Henry Woodford in 1946, and had soon acquired a reputation for combining legal acumen with Christian ethics. Philip Chandler (educated at Oxford, following a comprehensive school in Darlington) had come on the scene in 1972 as a trainee solicitor and in 1978, not long after he'd married Anne Woodford, only daughter of Henry and Mary Woodford and heir to the Woodford family's modest South African holdings, he'd become a partner. The firm handled all kinds of domestic and commercial matters, including wills, injunctions, litigation and a long list of other things one hopes never to become involved with. They seemed particularly proud of the free advice clinic they'd pioneered in the early seventies when most local solicitors weren't interested in giving anything away. In fact, all in all, Philip Chandler looked like being a totally unpromising subject for investigation, but there must have been something behind Janet's story. And I couldn't think of any other way of finding out what it was than by going to his office and asking him.

Philip Chandler's offices were located in a large, regal old house at the top end of town. The firm had had their name painted on all the downstairs windows in black and gold lettering so you couldn't mistake it. I parked in their car park, despite the strict notices about clamping, and ventured into reception, where a girl sat at a switchboard with a phone tucked under her ear.

'But do you have a *reference*?' she enquired patiently of the phone. 'I'm sure they'll have given you a reference, otherwise we can't tell who's dealing with it . . . Yes. In the top right-hand corner . . .'

On the wall behind her desk was a photo of the porch of the office building with three men standing in it. The photo was captioned, 'Mr Tuck and Mr Chandler welcome the Bishop of Hudderston to Edinburgh House.' In very old suits, I thought, rather unkindly – but of course the photo could have been taken at a time when lapels big enough for jumbo jets to land on were fashionable.

'I'm sorry to keep you. Can I help you?' said the receptionist, replacing the phone.

'Yes, I'd like to speak to Mr Chandler, please. I'm from the *Tipping Herald*.'

'I'm afraid you've just missed him. He's taken an early lunch. Is he expecting you? Or could someone else help?'

'Not really. I'll wait, shall I?'

At this, the girl, who was about twenty, began to look a bit flustered.

'They don't see anyone without appointments.'

'Don't they? Oh dear. Well, why don't I just ask *you* a few general questions about the firm then? It's for an article we're doing. What's it like working here?'

She frowned. 'I'm sorry?'

'It's for our Local Profiles series,' I explained, gushingly.

'Oh.' She looked blank, which wasn't surprising, because our Local Profiles series appears once a month squeezed in between our Around and about the Villages section and Classifieds, and is read only by its subjects' mothers. 'Well, it's all right – *you* know.'

'Just all right?' I got out my notebook. 'Have you been here long?'

'About nine months. Um, I don't know if I really ought to answer questions –'

'What are Mr Tuck and Mr Woodford like?'

'They're dead, I think. We've got four new partners now,' she added, and reeled off their names and the areas of the law they specialized in. '. . . and Mr Chandler does matrimonial and family work,' she finished.

I pretended to write all this down. 'And how do you get on with Mr Chandler? What's he like to work for?'

She looked puzzled. 'Well, he's a solicitor – you know.'

'I see.' This didn't seem to be working. I snapped my book shut. 'All right, not to worry. I'll wait for Mr Chandler. Will he be long?'

'I don't know. Um, look, I suppose you could talk to Alison.'

'Alison?'

'Yes. She used to be Mr Chandler's secretary. She retired before Christmas. I'm sure she could tell you more about Mr Chandler and the firm than anyone else here because we're all new.'

'Oh, that's great!' I exclaimed, and did my best to look grateful. Obviously, Alison would have more sense than to reveal anything meaningful about her former employer, but it didn't look as though I was going to get a better offer.

When she'd copied the address from her computer, I said, 'There is one more thing I'd like to ask you, if you wouldn't mind – does the name Janet Cox mean anything to you?'

She looked taken aback. 'Sorry?'

'Janet Cox,' I repeated. 'Do you know her? I'm afraid Mrs Cox was found dead yesterday evening at a place called Nuthurst Hill. Didn't you hear about it on the news?'

Her hand flew to her mouth. 'Oh my God,' she said. 'Was that Mrs Cox?'

Encouraged, I produced the photo of Lee and Janet and held it out to her, but she didn't even bother to look at it. 'I didn't say I'd ever met her. I just remember a woman called Janet Cox kept trying to ring Mr Chandler and I wasn't supposed to put her through. Oh, dear!'

'Why weren't you supposed to put her through?'

'I don't know.' At that moment, two lights started winking on her switchboard. 'I'm sorry, you'll have to excuse me now,' she said haughtily. 'I have to answer the phone.'

I thanked her, and ran back to my car. From where I was parked, I'd got a good view of the entrance to the Tuck Woodford & Chandler building, and I was sure I'd be able to recognize Philip Chandler from his photographs. *Janet Cox kept trying to ring Mr Chandler and I wasn't supposed to put her through* . . . If only I hadn't been so sniffy with her when she offered me the story on Chandler, Janet might have given me some clue what it was about. She was quite attractive in her own way. Perhaps she'd had an affair with Chandler; perhaps she'd come to him as a client and had an affair with him and then he'd dumped her. I opened up my egg and watercress sandwiches and tried to imagine this scenario as I bit into them.

At ten to two, a motorcycle courier and Philip Chandler arrived almost simultaneously in the forecourt, and I nearly didn't notice because I was dealing with a spilt yogurt. Fortunately though, they got involved in a little embarrassed shuffle round one another on the steps, and I was able to leap out of the car and place myself in front of Chandler before he could let himself into the building.

'Mr Chandler? Chris Martin, *Tipping Herald*!' I said rather breathlessly. 'I wonder if I could have a word with you about Janet Cox –'

'I'm sorry?' He stopped with his hand on the door, and his breath steamed out across the porch and disappeared in a swirl of rain. I think he looked shocked, but given my sudden and dramatic appearance this was hardly to be wondered at.

'Janet Cox,' I repeated. 'She was found dead yesterday on Nuthurst Hill. Did you know?'

He frowned and put down his Boots carrier bag and a briefcase on the step. 'I'm sorry – would you mind telling me what this is all about? You're from the local paper, you say?'

'Yes. We're trying to put together a story on Mrs Cox and I wanted to give you a chance to explain. You see, I met Mrs Cox a couple of days ago and she said something rather strange about you.' I waited for him to react, but of course solicitors spend years and years in front of mirrors practising deadpan expressions, so he didn't. I decided to plough on as best I could. 'I'm sorry, Mr Chandler, but I'm afraid Mrs Cox alleged you'd been up to some sort of – well – impropriety. She didn't say what because I didn't ask her – naturally my paper doesn't print that sort of thing!' I added, with a high-pitched giggle I immediately regretted.

He nodded slowly. His hair, which was silver, fell forward in a not unattractive wave over his forehead. He wasn't reacting at all.

'And?' he prompted coldly, when I'd got over the giggle.

'*And* – I just wondered if you'd like to make a statement. We're trying to put together a story on Mrs Cox. *Did* you have any sort of relationship with her? Your receptionist said she kept phoning and you wouldn't take her calls. I was just wondering if you'd like to – you know – sort of clarify things and prevent speculation.'

'I see.' He had a habit of squinting at you as though you made his eyes hurt. 'Well, there's really nothing to clarify, Mrs Martin. Obviously, I've no idea what Mrs Cox said to you. I was consulted some time ago by *Mr* Cox in the matter of their divorce, but I had no relationship with *Mrs* Cox whatsoever. It's standard practice that one doesn't speak to both sides in an action. I can only add that sometimes, in a divorce case, people take things very personally and start slinging mud indiscriminately. I'm sorry, but you'll have to excuse me now,' he added, holding up his hand politely. 'I know you've got a job to do, but I really can't discuss clients' affairs, and I have an appointment in four minutes. Good afternoon to you, Mrs Martin.'

I went back to my car. Philip Chandler had told me next to nothing about the Coxes, when actually he need have told me nothing at all, and I wondered if this was significant. I started up the engine, put the car into reverse and took a cursory look over my right shoulder at the condensation trickling down the back windows. I couldn't see anything so I pulled out. Immediately there was an outburst of hooting and a black thing appeared in the drip trails on my window. In the nick of time, I slammed on the brake, changed gear and went back into my space.

The black thing jerked into the space next to me and a man leapt out of it.

Worse than that, it was my ex-husband, Keith.

I switched off the engine and got out of the car. Keith's expression ran the full gamut of emotions from anger through surprise to discomfort. We had contrived not to meet for several months.

'Oh, it's you,' he said at last, glancing at the Golf in surprise. 'What happened to that Mini I got you?'

'Its header gasket went, or something. It was ten years old.'
My heart began to pound uncomfortably. Keith was wearing
a new and expensive suit and he'd had his hair cut in a subtly
different way.

'*He* chose this for you, did he?' He hopped from foot to
foot, chortling to himself. 'Christ – is he having an affair
with his insurance broker or something? Your premiums
must be astronomic! And by the way, I've got a bone to
pick with you. Why didn't you invite me to your wedding?'

I did a double take. He couldn't be serious. 'You can't be
serious!'

'Of course I am. We shared *twenty long years* before you
sent me packing. You'd think you could have afforded me the
pleasure of watching you make the biggest bloody mistake of
your life.'

Now, of course I could have told him that he'd already
witnessed me make the biggest mistake of my life, twenty-
three years previously, when he'd said, 'Oh go on, nobody
uses a contraceptive *every* time,' but it would have hurt me
more than it hurt him and there wasn't any point.

'Oh, come on, I was only joking!' he snapped, giving me
a pat on the arm. 'Well, come on then, how're things?'

It suddenly occurred to me that we were standing in the
car park of the firm of solicitors Keith had used when we got
divorced. What was he doing here?

'Fine, thanks,' I said. 'How about you?'

'Oh, fine! Do you remember me telling you about Sandra,
the woman I met on holiday?'

'Yes –?'

'Well –' He glanced at his watch. 'Shit, I'm already late –
sorry. How about meeting up for a proper chat sometime so
I can tell you all about it?'

'Good idea.' All about what? I felt a pang of alarm. I didn't
want Keith to be in any kind of trouble.

'OK. I'll give you a ring. Bye now.'

He turned to go.

'Wait! You haven't got an appointment with Philip Chandler, have you?' I called after him.

'Good God, no, he's too expensive! Why –' He swivelled to a halt, his eyes glinting. 'That who you were seeing?'

'Yes – about a story.'

'Oh.' He grunted and walked off.

4

Mr Heslop emerged from his office looking exhilarated. For an awful moment I thought someone had found another corpse somewhere.

'We're all set up for next week's front page! I've got you an interview with Dave Ormond – he's going to give you chapter and verse on the Millennium project. Seven o'clock this evening – at his home.'

I pulled a face. It was Friday, and I like to do my weekly shop on a Friday evening. In fact, I was already surreptitiously working on my list.

'But I thought you said *you* were going to handle our coverage of the Millennium project personally. I thought you were a personal friend of Councillor Ormond.'

'Well, I wouldn't be so presumptuous as to put it quite like that, but as it happens the wife and I have got something on this evening we can't miss. Look, most people would jump at the chance of an interview with Dave. You've never been out to his place, have you? He's turned it into quite something. How the other half live, eh? But just watch him when he refills your sherry glass – remember you've got to drive back.' And then he said, because he couldn't resist it, 'If my memory serves me right, your husband never used to pass up the chance of a drink with Dave – but then I don't suppose he ever passes up the chance of a drink with anyone!'

I decided to ignore this. Pete had once been Mr Heslop's senior reporter: that was how I met him, before he moved on to supposedly finer things on one of the tabloids. He and Mr Heslop had never exactly seen eye to eye on the need to supply refreshments to interviewees.

'What's supposed to be the point of this interview?' I asked.

'I told you, he's going to fill us in on the Millennium scheme. The Millennium Committee made their final decision this morning, apparently, and it's going to the full council on Monday evening, but it's just a question of rubber-stamping, so I'm told.'

'I see. But don't we already know –'

He was beginning to get annoyed. 'Look, if you can't fit this in between the shopping and ironing lover-boy's shirts, just say so, but this is a once-in-a-lifetime opportunity. Doesn't the Millennium mean anything to you? For God's sake – it's a turning point – a milestone! *Two thousand* years of history – two thousand years since the birth of Christ –'

I could tell he'd been reading the *Daily Mail*.

'But won't everything just go on as before, except that for a while we'll all be wearing new improved Millennium trainers and watching Delia Smith's Millennium recipe collection, and some of us won't be able to spell it?' I suggested.

He sighed and handed me a slip of paper. 'Sometimes you're a big disappointment to me,' he muttered. 'You should be grateful it's Dave I'm sending you to see, and not our friend George "Fifty years in public service" Draycott. I expect he's too busy preparing his acceptance speech for the OBE he hopes to get.'

After he'd gone I felt a bit out of sorts: I don't like being a disappointment to people. I called up Dave Ormond's biographical details on our computer. I'd seen him a few times in the council chamber and he was quite dishy, but our computer didn't have a photograph of him, unfortunately. It said: *Ormond, David: First elected 1980. Has served on the Planning and Arts and Recreation Committees. Born 1948 in Tipping, a descendant of Matthew Ormond, the founder of Ormond's Biscuits. Travelled extensively and turned his hand to various activities, including a spell working on a 'Dude' ranch in Arizona, before settling down at Harewood Farm in 1978 and opening the Harewood Garden Centre in April 1984. Appeared in an amdram panto at Hatchley Heath Village Hall as an Ugly Sister Christmas 1988 and got rave reviews. Lists his hobbies as sailing, keeping fit, and the appreciation of fine wines*. I reached for our big local street directory and opened it at the page showing Councillor Ormond's address, Harewood Farm. Of course I already knew roughly where Harewood Farm was, but snow had been forecast for the evening and I didn't want to find myself doing a three-point turn in some silage depot when I'd gone the wrong way.

I was just about to put the directory away when I noticed that on the very edge of the Harewood Farm page, beyond Harewood Common, was a tiny piece of Gooserye Common, and this naturally reminded me of the addresses I'd seen on the diary page in Janet's flat. I checked my notebook. 'Holly Cottage, Gooserye, and St Martin's Court'. I flipped over to the next page in the directory. Gooserye Common covered quite a large area: several tracks crossed it, and a dozen or so dwellings were marked on it, so Holly Cottage must be one of these. As far as I could remember, the common consisted of a rather dense piece of woodland with smallholdings and riding stables carved out of it. Then I checked the index for St Martin's Court, but there wasn't an entry for it. There was a St Martin's Church, and a St Martin's Primary School, but definitely not a St Martin's Court. Of course, it might be a very new development – our directory was two years out of date.

I was hesitating with my pen poised over the two names in my notebook, wondering whether to strike them out as having no significance, when my phone rang.

'Hi. You doing anything?' It was DS Wayne Horton from Hudderston Central, who I like to think of as my police informant. 'I was just reading something rather interesting and I thought I'd give you a ring.'

I don't know why, but I immediately assumed he was referring to my piece on Janet Cox's murder.

'Oh, thank you!' I exclaimed, beaming with pleasure. 'How kind of you to take the trouble to phone!'

'Oh. That's all right. As a matter of fact, I was hoping you'd do *me* a favour. It's the wife's birthday and I'm in Debenhams. Do you think you could pop down and give us a hand choosing a present?'

I stopped smiling. 'But I don't know your wife. Couldn't one of the women from the station help?'

'You must be joking! You ever met any policewomen? They give their husbands a night out at the dogs for their birthday. Oh, go on, it'll only take you half an hour and I'll fill you in on the PM as we go.'

'The what?'

'The postmortem on that woman on Nuthurst Hill. I told you, I've got it in front of me.'

'Oh.' This sank in, and I squirmed uncomfortably on my seat. 'All right then. Give me ten minutes.'

Wayne was slouching against the Lancôme counter of Debenhams perfume department when I arrived, chatting up an assistant. He is quite good, in a gauche sort of way, at chatting women up, but I don't think he realizes this. The assistant looked very disappointed when she saw me.

He took my arm. 'Come on, let's go and look for something sexy in silk. She's either a twelve or a fourteen depending on the fit, apparently. I want you to help me pick something classy.'

I had once seen a photograph of Wayne's wife. She was a rather tough-looking blonde who would not take kindly to being presented with a size-fourteen dress chosen for her by another woman. I allowed him to lead me on to the escalator without comment. 'So what's the latest on the Janet Cox murder?' I enquired, as we soared majestically over a display of half-price Christmas gift packs of body-smoothing lotion.

'Well, the latest – and you won't like this, because I read your story this morning – is that Mrs Cox wasn't murdered on Nuthurst Hill.'

He was striding on upwards, nodding to people as he nudged them out of the way, and I had to follow as best I could. 'How on earth is that possible?' I demanded.

'Well, there's some brain tissue missing, which means she can't have been murdered where we found her body – and there isn't nearly enough blood at the scene either. Sorry, love.' Several shocked-looking shoppers were reeling about on the steps, staring at us, and Wayne had the good grace to apologize to one of them before he pushed past her. 'Ah, look – "Classics",' he remarked, gazing at an overhead sign. 'That ought to do us!'

I followed him round a display of blouses. This didn't make sense. 'But there was a witness,' I protested.

'Yes, I know' – he examined a white blouse with a lace collar – 'but the thing is, according to the PM, Cox was still alive for at least an hour – maybe two – after this alleged road rage incident of yours in the layby.'

'How do you know?'

'Because of her stomach contents. She died with a plateful of undigested egg and chips in her stomach.'

I didn't get it.

He put back the white blouse and picked up a black one. 'Look – Cox ate two doughnuts just before she went to the hairdresser at four and she hadn't eaten anything all day. You told us that and the PM confirms it. She left the hairdresser just after five and it would have taken her twenty-five minutes to drive from the hairdresser's to the layby, so –'

'All right. I see.'

'Plus, on top of the egg and chips, she'd drunk enough Scotch to put her over the limit for driving if it had all got into her bloodstream, which it didn't – at least two doubles. Did you smell alcohol on her breath? And anyway, the pathologist reckons the doughnuts had been in her digestive system for at least three hours before she died, because –'

'All right, I see what you're getting at.' I was now off doughnuts for good. 'You're saying Janet didn't die until seven o'clock at the earliest.'

He turned over the black blouse and inspected its label. 'Yes, that's about it. Apparently, she was hit twice around the head with a heavy blunt instrument which smashed her skull, and the pathologist reckons it would have made quite a mess. It *could* have been some sort of club hammer, or a wrench – or just about anything heavy and metal. Anyway, we showed Elaine a few photos and she couldn't pick out Cox, so right now we're at square one. We don't know whether the woman she saw having the set-to in the layby really was Cox or not.'

I tried to get my head round this. 'Are you saying you think Elaine seeing someone in the layby who looked like Janet was just a coincidence?'

'It would be a whacking great big one, but it's possible. Look, love, I'm telling you all this in confidence, right? At the moment we don't know what to think. Someone's suggested Cox drove to the layby to meet a boyfriend, went off somewhere with him for a meal, and then he killed her and took her back to the layby to dump her. But you tell me – would you pick that layby to meet your boyfriends in?'

'I might if they were married, I suppose.'

He handed me the blouse. 'The only boyfriend we know about isn't married. Hang on to these. I'm going to look at trousers.'

'Who is this boyfriend?' If he meant the boyfriend who'd left the message on Janet's answerphone then the meeting in the layby theory didn't hold up: 'Denny' or 'Lenny' had been expecting to meet Janet *at his flat*.

Wayne grinned. 'The boyfriend, you just won't believe. We got his name from her address book – the hairdresser picked it out as the boyfriend's. As a matter of fact, he's not the sort we usually get down at the station unless they've got a Hoover attachment superglued to their private parts.'

A woman inspecting a purple waistcoat on the display behind Wayne dropped it and moved hastily away.

'You know what I mean – the sort that thinks it's funny to get his best mate drunk on his stag night and leave him tied up naked across the bonnet of his mum's Audi. Too much education and too little to bloody do, that type. He's only about twenty-two. Not really Cox's sort, you'd think, but there you go. Anyway, he claims they were just friends – I won't bore you with the explanation he gave us for the message he left on her answerphone, asking her round to his flat.'

'Ah.' I managed to look impassive. 'Have you arrested him?'

'God, no. He says Cox didn't turn up and he doesn't know why.' He hesitated over a particularly nasty pair of trousers in a shiny mock-lizard skin fabric of some description. 'According to the hairdresser, she was in a tearing hurry for them to finish her cut and blow-dry so she could get off to meet someone, but she couldn't confirm it was the boyfriend.

Apparently Cox used to ring home a couple of times a day to access her messages, so she should have got this one. Who knows? Oh, and then there's the husband, of course. Now he's a bit of a lad. We've had him in our sights a couple of times over the years but somehow he's always managed to wriggle off the hook.'

I don't know why, but this took me completely by surprise. 'What – are you saying Lee Cox is a *criminal*?' I demanded, shocked.

'Definitely – we've just never managed to pin anything on him.' He held the trousers up at arm's-length. 'What do you think? I reckon I could fancy her in these.'

'Er – I'm not sure I like them, to be honest. What do you mean? What sort of criminal?'

'Well, if you ever meet him, and he offers to sell you a Merc or a Roller – don't buy it.' He sighed and put the trousers back. 'This is a right bugger. Now I remember why I usually stick to chocolates.' He seized a skimpy little black dress off a rack. 'On the other hand, this is more like! This is definitely more like. What do you think?'

'Um – it's nice. Have you questioned him?'

'We will when we can find him. According to one of Cox's neighbours a guy who looked a bit like Lee threatened to punch her lights out a couple of weeks ago, but he couldn't give us a proper description.' He lowered the dress dejectedly. 'I can't make up my mind about this. Have you seen the price? She'd slaughter me if I gave her something this cheap! It's on sale!'

'Oh, dear.' I examined the dress desperately. It was actually quite nice, and I didn't think I could stand another tour of the separates department. I glanced back through my notes. 'Have you spoken to Philip Chandler yet?'

'I don't think so. I haven't seen a report yet.' He turned towards the dress display. 'You know, this just won't do –'

'Yes, it will!' I had a sudden brainwave. 'Look, why don't you buy her some perfume as well? You could get them to giftwrap the perfume and the dress together in a box, book some tickets to a show or something, buy her a bunch of –'

'God, you're brilliant!' He suddenly hugged me so violently

40

and unexpectedly that the dress hanger nearly went up my nose. 'You're a marvel! If our first kid's a girl, I'm going to name her after you!' He let go of me. 'Did I tell you we've decided to try for a family? I reckon it's the answer, it'll put everything into perspective – you know, all that other rubbish I was telling you about,' he added, and my mouth fell open, because only a few weeks ago he'd been asking me how much it cost to get a divorce. 'Right – come on, let's go and get this perfume sorted out.'

Still in shock, I followed him towards the 'down' escalator. When we got to the perfume counter, he said, 'It's a bit early for lunch, isn't it – I'll have to owe you. Fancy a stroll round Mothercare?'

'No, thanks.' The thought of it made me feel a bit peculiar. 'I tell you what, though, why don't you give me the name and address of the boyfriend? Then we'll be – you know – quits.'

He raised his eyebrows. 'What – so you and some of your mates can ring him up every few hours and ask him how it feels to help the police in a murder enquiry?'

'Of course not!'

'No? You disappoint me. Sometimes people confess all to us just to get rid of you lot. Give me your book.'

I said goodbye to Wayne and left him negotiating with the assistant over wrapping paper and ribbon. Mothercare was two doors down. I hastily averted my eyes from its window display, which was already being decked out with a selection of babygros and toy rabbits in pretty spring pastels, and made a dash for the office. If I'm not careful, I can sometimes get all nostalgic for little wriggling fingers and the smell of milk.

When I got back to my desk, there was a letter on fine parchment paper in my in-tray, signed with the unmistakeable flourish of Hugh Burton-Cooper, our restaurant critic. It said, 'Dear Mrs Martin, My profound apologies for not responding sooner to the message you left on my answerphone. I have only just returned from my Somerset address of which you might like to take note . . . In answer to your query, I believe there is a very charming lady by the name of Claire or Clara MacInnis on the staff at the Rudgeleigh Arms, although as you know, unlike many restaurant critics I prefer to remain anonymous and have therefore not been introduced. My best wishes to all on the news team. P.S. Whilst writing, I should be very grateful if you would point out to Mrs Dixon in Accounts that I have still not received reimbursement for the sum of £4.83 short paid against my November 1997 expenses . . .'

The Rudgeleigh Arms? I felt a prickle of excitement at the back of my neck. I rang down to Mrs Dixon in Accounts about the £4.83, then dialled the Rudgeleigh Arms.

'Could I speak to Claire MacInnis, please?'

'Ah – I'm afraid Mrs Andre isn't here at the moment. Can I take a message or get her to call you back?'

'Mrs *Andre*?' The Rudgeleigh Arms had been taken over about a year ago by a semi-famous chef called Stefan Andre; to the chagrin of Hugh Burton-Cooper, Mr Heslop had personally covered their opening night. 'Hang on – are you saying Mrs Andre and Claire MacInnis are one and the same person?'

'Of course. Do you want to leave a message? Mrs Andre's got a mobile phone but I'm not supposed to give the number out.'

'That's all right. I've got her mobile number. Oh, wait! Do you have a Lee Cox there?'

'Who? I'm sorry, I don't know anyone by that name.'

I thanked her, and rang the mobile number. It rang for what seemed a long time, and then a blast of static took over.

'Hallo? This is . . . Can I . . . ?' queried a female voice. 'It's . . . innis.'

'Hallo? Can you hear me? Is that Ms MacInnis?'

'Yes!'

'Look, I'm sorry to bother you, but I've been given your number as a contact for Lee Cox. Could I just ask you a few questions?'

There was a sudden and complete silence, following what could have been either a blip on the line or a sharp intake of breath. I wasn't sure which, or if the phone had gone dead.

'Hallo?' I tried again.

'Who gave you this number?' Suddenly the line was as clear

as a bell. 'Who are you? You've got the wrong number! I'm warning you, don't ever ring this number again!'

And then she hung up on me. I waited a few minutes before dialling her number again, but she'd switched her phone off.

I was sure of one thing: whatever Claire's connection with Lee Cox might be, I hadn't got the wrong number.

5

The rain was trying to turn to snow as I drove across Harewood
Common that night, hurling itself against my windscreen in
piercing white rods. The Harewood Garden Centre loomed
suddenly into view, a sign inviting you to 'Drive in for Xmas
Trees with roots in pots' still flapping about on its gate. Tipping
people were quite fond of the Harewood Garden Centre,
even though most of them went to B & Q to bulk-buy
their bedding plants. It was the sort of place where you
could always find someone to explain to you the purpose
of a dwarfing rootstock, and where dandelions just like the
ones you've got at home grew behind the greenhouses. In
fact, a lot of people in Tipping were quite fond of David
Ormond himself. He was known for his unstuffy attitude and
approachability, although, of course, he had a few detractors.
Some people said he'd funded the repairs to the old Civic
Hall roof after it was damaged in the hurricane out of his
own pocket, and that he was a really good bloke, and
some people said he was a bit of a playboy because he'd
been married twice. Well, that's Tipping for you. And of
course there were a lot of people who resented him because
he came from a privileged background. The Ormonds had
owned Tipping's one and only factory, Ormond's Biscuits,
which had, it was said, employed most of the town's older
generation at some time or another, and there was even
an Ormond Arms public house where you could appreciate a series of portraits of long-dead Ormonds and admire
the Ormond family tree. Some of Dave Ormond's detractors said he would never have had the resources to be a
'really good bloke' if he hadn't been an Ormond, so you

shouldn't be too impressed by this. I think I was probably one of them.

They'd left a light on for me in the farmyard, which had been paved over with genuine Victorian paving stones, and its barns converted into garages and a guest cottage. In the centre of the yard stood a twenty-foot Christmas tree held in place by guy ropes, and I couldn't help wishing that its lights had been on because it would have looked very romantic with the snow swirling round it. In fact, I was so carried away thinking about this that I narrowly missed running over a guy rope and had to swerve the car sharply into a corner, bringing it to rest millimetres from a stone trough planted with variegated ivies. Then I sat still and practised deep-breathing to stop myself imagining the horrors of David Ormond's Christmas tree crashing in through my sun-roof.

A blonde woman answered the door.

'I'm so sorry about the tree,' she said, and I knew immediately that she'd witnessed my near accident. 'Dave was going to get the men to take it down this afternoon but the weather was so awful – do come in. I'm Carol, by the way. Let me take your coat. Dave's still in the gym.'

I glanced at my watch. I wasn't early. 'Oh dear, when will he be back?'

She laughed. 'Actually, we had the bakehouse converted to a gym. Dave should have been finished ages ago but he was late back from London this afternoon because of the wretched trains. Come this way.'

She led me through a glass door, along a rather plain, cold corridor, and through another glass door into a large wood-panelled room that smelled pretty much as I've always imagined Sweden must smell – piney, with a touch of anti-septic and sweat.

Councillor Ormond was splayed out on some sort of torture machine, working an enormous bar back and forth. He disen-tangled himself, reached for a towel, and extended a tanned arm, complete with natty little sweatband.

'Thanks so much for coming. Now, tell me something before we go any further. Am I right – are you the lady who married my old mate, Pete Schiavo? So what should I call you – Mrs Martin, or Mrs Schiavo?'

Actually, this was a bit of a sore point. 'Well, I call myself Mrs Martin professionally, and Mrs Schiavo personally,' I explained. 'But it's Chris.'

'There – told you.' He gave Carol a smug look, and I felt a bit flattered to think they must have been talking about me before I arrived. 'I win, so you get the glasses,' he added mysteriously. 'Come on, let's go through to my office.'

He pulled on a pair of tracksuit bottoms, and I followed him back along the corridor to his office. He had curly dark hair evenly flecked with silver, and – I couldn't help noticing – a very nice body without a trace of superfluous padding.

'Take a seat, make yourself comfortable. This is the best bit about exercising,' he added, sinking back into a leather recliner. 'Relaxing afterwards. No – actually it's the large gin and tonic that's coming. But don't tell Carol I said that.'

I laughed. I still wasn't sure if I liked him or not.

'Anyway, you haven't come all this way to talk about me. Let me put you out of your suspense, if you're in it. The committee have finally decided to go for a multifunction entertainment centre on the riverside site.'

For a moment, I couldn't think what on earth he was talking about. 'What? For the Millennium – an entertainment centre? But I thought we were going to have a park –'

'We were, up until a few months ago, but after a lot of thought we came to the conclusion that the entertainment centre offers more long-term benefits than the park, and personally I think it's more appropriate. Don't you? The park would have been lovely, of course, and I know a lot of people will be disappointed, but long term, it wouldn't have been able to provide the benefits the entertainment centre will, and even in the short term it would have very little to offer our young people – who after all ought to be the point of the whole thing, don't you think?' He held up the fingers of his right hand and began to count them off. 'The entertainment centre will provide jobs, a wide range of entertainment – of course – *and* it'll provide a boost to the arts. Let me tell you about it. There's going to be a multiscreen cinema, a bowling alley, two or three small theatres, a purpose-designed library, cafés, a restaurant –'

There's no other word for it: I was gobsmacked. This was Big News and I was the first to hear it.

'*Really*? But isn't all this going to be expensive? How can we afford it?'

'Actually, it's going to cost us almost nothing at all. We've negotiated a complicated lease agreement with Fairlands Leisure – you'll have heard of them, of course, they're part of the Fairlands Bellchamber Group. Basically, they lease the site and build the centre, *we* fund part of the running costs and set up some community-based schemes to get the ball rolling. I'm particularly excited about a drama-for-all group that's in the pipeline. Anyway, when you take into account the amount we'd budgeted for ongoing work on the park over the next ten years, and the anticipated return on the council's investment in terms of profit-sharing. Oh, don't worry,' he added, as I struggled with my shorthand. 'You don't have to write all this down. I'm going to give you a mass of paperwork later.'

'Good. Thank you!' I decided to stop pretending I wasn't impressed. 'This is amazing! Did you say the centre was going to include a *library*?'

'Yes. Obviously, the idea is to pull as many people into the centre as possible, but considering the state of the current library it's an added bonus. In case you're interested there are similar schemes in' – he reeled off the names of three towns in the Midlands I'd vaguely heard of – 'and they all seem to work very well. I do assure you we've checked them out.'

'I see.' I was still gobsmacked, but I managed to pull myself together. 'A bowling alley, a cinema and a *library*? But surely the sort of people who go to libraries won't be the same ones who go to bowling alleys and cinemas.'

He laughed. 'Now, if I may say so that's the sort of remark that goes with sun-dried tomatoes and designer-beige aubergines. "*We* don't go to bowling alleys, *we* don't visit the cinema – *we* are library users. And in fact we are really happy using our run-down, shabby facilities, because – actually – we like to suffer for our culture."'

I blushed, and at that moment Carol came in with a tray.

'David, don't be so mean. I heard you. Give the poor woman a chance, she's only doing her job.'

'I'm not being mean! As a matter of fact, it's exactly what I thought when I first had the scheme explained to me. But the thing is, Chris, as I'm sure you can see, we've got to bring libraries back into the community. At the moment, who uses them? Pensioners, the unemployed – a few kids who aren't on the Internet? That's all. If we want to keep the libraries going we've got to find some way of tarting them up and making them sexy, it's as simple as that.' He folded his arms and gazed thoughtfully out across the slowly whitening fields behind his house.

'Never mind all that. What will you have to drink?' interrupted Carol briskly, setting a tray with glasses on it down on the desk. 'We've got all the usual, plus some very nice Armagnac Dave brought back from Honfleur a couple of days ago.'

'Or I could open a bottle of Margaux,' added Dave. '1994. You'd like it.'

I remembered what Mr Heslop had said about sherry. 'The Margaux would be fine,' I said nervously.

'Good! A woman after my own heart. Will you do the honours, Carol? Chris – any questions?'

Of course, all my carefully worked-out questions had had to do with the riverside park.

'What will happen to the old library?' I enquired, eventually.

'Oh, we'll keep it open for a while as a sub-branch. Until people get used to using the new one.'

'And what about the riverside park? I mean, Councillor Draycott was very keen on it, wasn't he? Is he very disappointed?'

Dave Ormond hesitated. 'Off the record? He's a bit sick, actually, but – and this is definitely off the record – I think you'll find the next town plan will include a Councillor Draycott bowling green of some description. Anyway – cheers! What do you think of the wine?'

'It's lovely.'

'Good, but be warned! A bottle of Margaux will set you back a small fortune in your average wine shop this side of the Channel. Do what I do – hop across to the other side and restock your cellar with good stuff from time to time. I'm lucky because I've got the perfect excuse of having to visit a nursery in Honfleur occasionally to restock on azaleas as well.'

I thought, how on earth does he think we all live, but I said, 'Thank you, I'll remember that. So – er – when do you think the new centre will be finished?'

'Well, the plan is to lay the foundation stone as part of the Millennium celebrations – it'll be called the Millennium Centre, of course – and it *should* be at least partially open to the public within a year – but let's say eighteen months, shall we? It makes us look such prats if it's not finished on time. I don't mind telling you, I'm really quite excited about it. I only wish there'd been somewhere like it here when I was young.'

My eyebrows flicked wryly skywards before I could stop them.

He frowned. 'Look, just because I may have been slightly privileged doesn't mean I'm completely out of touch with what goes on in the world. Being born with a silver spoon in one's mouth isn't all it's cracked up to be,' he added, rather crossly.

I blushed. 'Oh, no, I'm sure you're right about the centre. It's very important for young people to have somewhere to go. If–' If there'd been a Millennium Centre in Tipping when I was young, it wouldn't have changed my life one iota. 'If there'd been a Millennium Centre in Tipping when I was young, it would have been so much easier to avoid temptation – you know, drugs and things. Oh! Not that I – you know –'

'No, no, of course not!' He laughed. 'Nor me – better things to do with one's life. Anyway, I expect you've got children of your own, haven't you? I know old Pete had quite a few.'

I could feel the blush deepening. 'He's got three. I've got two, but only one lives with us, actually,' I said, and found myself thinking this over.

'Goodness, you do awfully well to cope with an extended

family *and* to work full time in such a *demanding* job!' remarked Carol, in a deeply patronizing tone.

Luckily, I was too busy thinking about the fact that Pete and I had five children altogether and that only one of them lived with us to react to Carol. I suddenly had the feeling that my life had gone wrong somewhere, but I suppose wine on an empty stomach will do this to you. I hastily finished my glass and stood up. 'You've both been very kind, and I'm sorry to dash off, but I really ought to be going before the snow gets too deep. Thank you so much for letting the *Herald* be first with the news,' I added gushingly.

The councillor got up too. 'My pleasure. But I'm sorry you're dashing off. I was going to suggest Carol give you a quick run-through in the gym.'

Carol managed a wooden smile. I decided I wouldn't fancy being run through anything by her under any circumstances.

She collected my coat and they showed me to the door. 'Thank you so much,' I said again, as he presented me with a thick plastic folder full of press releases and pictures of entertainment centres.

'Well, if you need anything else – anything at all, just give me a ring,' he said. 'I've put my card in there. You ought to be able to get me any time on my pager. Just keep mum about the whole thing until after the council meeting on Monday.'

I was halfway out of the door, aglow with the Margaux, when I suddenly thought of something. I pointed vaguely into the blizzard. 'That's Gooserye Common over there, isn't it? I was just wondering – have either of you ever heard of a place called Holly Cottage?'

'Holly Cottage?' Carol looked blank. 'Oh, Dave'll know it, won't you, darling?'

He was still in his T-shirt, standing back from the wind. 'No,' he said sharply. 'I hardly know Gooserye at all, I'm afraid. Why?'

'Well, it's just – you know that woman who was murdered the other day? On Nuthurst Hill? She had a – um –' Oh, God. 'She had a piece of paper with the names Holly Cottage and St Martin's Court written on it and I'm trying to find out something about them to see if they've got any connection with her death. I'm sorry, I shouldn't have bothered you with it,' I added, suddenly embarrassed.

'That's all right. St Martin's Court? You'll draw a blank there, I'm afraid. It was demolished in the early eighties. It was a block of council flats at the top of Market Street.'

'Oh.' If St Martin's Court had been demolished in the early eighties, why on earth would anyone write its name down in a diary in 1997?

'Anyway, I thought this poor woman was the victim of a road rage attack?'

'No. We got that wrong, I'm afraid.'

'So what was it all about then?'

'A crime of passion, the police think. You know, the usual thing – they're looking into her personal life and trying to find her husband. He's disappeared, apparently.'

'Oh, I see. Of course. It's always the husband, isn't it?' He laughed rather mirthlessly. 'What a fascinating life you lead.'

I said goodbye to the Ormonds and went out into the snow, clutching to my breast full details of twenty-first-century Tipping and hoping the car would start. On the whole, I'd liked David Ormond. The next time Mr Heslop sent me out to interview him, I wouldn't offer any objections.

By Monday I was itching to get down to writing a vivid account of Tipping's new Millennium plans, but of course I couldn't, not until the council had done their rubber-stamping. Instead, that afternoon I drove along Sutton Road in search of the address Wayne had given me for Janet's boy-friend. The snow had already melted and all but vanished in a scouring cold wind straight off the Siberian steppes, leaving behind the ghosts of abandoned snowmen on people's front lawns. I found the house easily enough. Daniel Kerr-Dixon's flat was in a Victorian residence built at the turn of the century by a wealthy Tipping family to celebrate their rise up the social scale. All the houses in Sutton Road had been built at the same time, for the same reason, and all had since been converted into flats, business schools and clinics.

At first, though, I couldn't find Flat 2b. A grubby card was pinned to the doorframe beside the bell for Flat 2. 'Flat 2b is *at the rear* of the building' it warned, 'Do not ring Flat 2's bell for 2b'. I withdrew my finger and wondered how you got to the back. After a few moments I set off along a bleak passageway between The Grange and the house next door, and almost ran into a young man in a duffel coat coming from the other direction.

'Sorry,' I said, as we sidestepped one another awkwardly. 'I'm looking for 2b.'

He hesitated, gave me an odd look, and sprinted off without comment, which I suppose was better than the '2b or not 2b' joke I'd been half expecting. I wasn't quite sure what to do, so I carried on till I got to the top of a steep flight of steps that led down into a small yard, and straight ahead, to my relief, was a newly painted door marked '2b'. As you went down the steps, you could if you wanted to peer right into the flat over the top of the net curtain at the window.

After what seemed a long time a man in his early twenties, dark, tousled and unshaven, opened the door. He had it on a chain.

'Daniel Kerr-Dixon?'

'Yes. Sorry – I haven't got the money for double glazing or anything at the moment. You'd have to speak to my father. He arranges all that.'

'No – I'm doing a story on Janet Cox,' I said quickly, showing him my press card before he could shut the door, 'and I've been given your name. I just want to ask you a few questions, that's all. Can I come in? It's freezing out here. It will only take a minute.'

'But –' He looked startled. 'I don't know her – I don't know the woman!'

'Are you sure? But I've been given your name by the police. They said you were helping with enquiries.'

'Did they? Well, OK – I just helped out, that's all. I don't know anything about it and I don't have to talk to you!'

'All right, if you feel like that.' I was a bit sorry for him actually. 'I can just say that the police are questioning you in connection with Mrs Cox's death. Don't worry about it.' I turned to go.

'Hang on – you can't put that, my parents would have a fit!' He undid the chain and came out after me. 'Look – please – I've *explained* all this to the police! This isn't fair! All right, you can come in if you want but you're wasting your time – I'm *not* a suspect!'

For a moment, I was tempted to warn him that he was, but I managed not to. I followed him inside.

'Look, I told the police – I hardly knew the woman. I met her through an agency and it didn't work out. I haven't seen her for months and I don't know anything about what happened to her, OK?' Like most of his generation and class, he had a confusing tendency to miss off the ends of words as though they weren't worth bothering with. I found myself struggling to keep up.

'What agency?'

'You know – I filled in one of those forms in the paper for a laugh and they matched me up with these women.'

'A *dating agency*? Really?' It seemed incredible that someone of Daniel's age and – after a bit of a wash and brush-up – undoubted good looks, would need to resort to a dating agency to attract women. I think he must have read my thoughts because he blushed and said, 'Look, I was bored – all right? I wanted something to do.'

'So what happened with the others?'

'What others?'

'The other women you met through the agency. You said "these women". Did you get on better with one of the others?'

'No! Does it matter? Look, I don't want to discuss this, I've *explained* it all already to the police! I met Janet three times for drinks, OK? We didn't have anything in common so that was it. The only reason we kept in touch was because she worked in department stores and she used to have first pick of the sales. Sometimes she rang me up if she saw something she thought I might like, sometimes I rang her if there was something I was after. I expect she did the same for all her friends. Right?'

'I see.' His flat consisted of one large room with an L-shaped kitchen in one corner and a platform with a bed on it in the other. He had a rather nice leather-covered three-piece suite in the centre that looked as if it might have come straight off display at Allders.

'So Janet was just a platonic friend. Someone you got in touch with occasionally and bought things from.'

'Yes! I was thinking of getting a couple of rugs or something and I rang her up and left a message on her answerphone the day she died, that's why the police came and interviewed me,' he went on. 'They shouldn't have given you my name. They know I've got nothing to do with it.'

'Are you saying she didn't turn up?'

'No, she didn't turn up. How many more times – I'm *not* her boyfriend, and I don't know anything about her – all right?'

I met his gaze and tried to hold it, but he looked away quickly before I could lock on.

'Can you prove she didn't turn up?'

'What? Look, I've got to be at work in half an hour –' He fiddled a cigarette out of its packet. 'Yeah – I can prove she didn't turn up. My parents were here all evening. My dad fixed my leaky shower. They were here from seven till about ten-thirty – all right?'

I thought about this. It seemed an awfully long time to take over changing a washer. 'They were here for three and a half hours fixing your shower?' I queried.

'Yes – my dad's a stockbroker, not a plumber. Anyway, we had some wine and a takeaway, and if you don't believe me you can ask Neil in Flat Four because he had to come down to ask Dad to move his car so they could get theirs out.'

'Why shouldn't I believe you?'

Daniel drew angrily on his cigarette and said nothing.

I got my notebook out. 'Look, I know this is a nuisance, and you've been very helpful, but I wonder if I could ask you a couple more questions about Janet? I just want some background info on her, that's all. If you first met her on a date, she must have –'

'It was last summer! It was *ages* ago, I can't remember! Come on, I told you I wasn't interested.'

I was beginning to think Daniel was protesting a bit too much.

He took another deep drag on the cigarette, as though he was trying to suck the lifeblood out of it. 'OK. She said she was separated – right? She was nuts about her husband but he was a bastard who went off with other women, all that stuff. She said he wanted a divorce but she didn't, and she was hoping they'd get back together eventually. She filled in the newspaper thing on an impulse because she was lonely. Christ, what do you expect me to say? I'm not a psychiatrist!'

This seemed rather an odd remark to make in connection with someone you hardly knew, but Daniel didn't look in the mood to expand on it. I put my notebook away. 'That's a nice picture,' I said, indicating a painting hanging over the bed. It was a beach scene in rather odd colours – yellows, browns and pinks – and depicted two bodies (light purple) writhing à la *From Here to Eternity* in surf (tan and lemon). I had no idea what the colouring signified, or if I liked it, but it went quite well with his bed covering. The initials D.K.D. were entwined in one corner. 'Oh, did you do that? Are you an artist?'

'No – it's crap!' He stepped between me and it. 'Do you want to discuss art with me now? I told you, I've got to be at work in half an hour.'

'Where do you work?'

'Dino's.'

'Dino's?' Dino's was a burger bar in the High Street. 'Is that your full-time occupation – or are you a student or something?'

'It's my full-time bloody job – all right?'

He showed me to the door, and slammed it behind me without a second glance. As I walked up the steps, he turned on an REM track at full volume, and immediately a little nostalgic shiver ran down my spine. I couldn't count the number of times when while we'd still been a family, Richard, my son, had slammed his bedroom door on me and turned on REM at full volume. In fact, Daniel reminded me a lot of Richard as he'd been until he met Becky a few months ago: twenty-something, with a whole life in prospect, and no idea what he was going to fill it with or if he cared enough to bother.

I got in the car. There were one or two things about Daniel that didn't quite gel, but you wouldn't be twenty-something if everything gelled. Maybe it was just the resemblance to Richard, but I couldn't imagine him bashing anyone over the head with a blunt instrument.

I sat in the car for a moment, thinking about Janet. She obviously had a definite tendency to involve herself with very good-looking men. Perhaps she'd met someone else through a dating agency. I could try ringing round a few to see if she was on their books. There had to be another man in Janet's life somewhere. And then I suddenly remembered Michael Irons. Now of course from what I'd seen of him, Michael Irons seemed nothing at all like Janet's type, and having predeceased her by several hours he wasn't up to much as a murder suspect. But still, there was no getting away from the fact that Janet had said she knew him, and that when I ran into her outside the lock-up garages she must have been on her way either to or from his house. She'd parked her car in Redbourne Road. Redbourne Road was a cul-de-sac leading nowhere except to the lock-up garages and to Marjoram Mews. I hadn't thought of it before, but there was obviously some kind of a link between Michael Irons and Janet Cox – and now both of them were dead.

6

As I turned into Marjoram Mews, I could see immediately that there were lights on downstairs in the Ironses' house. I found my notebook and pen and ran eagerly up the front path.

The door was opened by a woman in her early fifties in a smart grey suit and well-cut shirt set off by a deftly positioned silk scarf. She looked as if she'd just got home from the office, and I was pleased about this; I don't cope well with grief.

'Mrs Irons?'

'Yes.' In her hand was a 'Mr Happy' mug full of steaming tea.

'Chris Martin from the *Tipping Herald*. I don't want to intrude, but I wondered if I could talk to you for a moment?'

Her eyes rounded. 'Are you the reporter who's been round before? Oh dear, if you've come because of what I said to that girl on the corner about it being an accident you've had a wasted journey, I'm afraid – I made that up. I'm so sorry!' she exclaimed. 'I just wanted to stop her waffling on about aromatherapy and her aunt in the Samaritans. I'm dreadfully sorry, I hope I haven't made you go out of your way.'

'No, I –'

'It was so silly of me! I do try to make people understand what it feels like to be fifty, and on the verge of bankruptcy for the second time, and a laughing stock among your friends, but they don't seem able to get it. I am sorry,' she said again.

I managed to get my arm in the way of the door before she could shut it.

'Mrs Irons, please could I ask you one question? I'm dreadfully sorry, but I really have to ask it. Did your husband know a woman called Janet Cox?'

'Who?'

'Janet Cox. Tall woman, short hair. She was murdered last week – maybe you've heard about it? She told me she knew your husband.'

This piece of information passed Mrs Irons by without impact. 'Oh. Did she? Well, I know she rang Mike a couple of times just after Christmas but I don't think he ever met her. It was her husband, Lee, that Mike knew. At one time they were involved in some sort of business venture together, although it never came to anything.'

'Were they? What sort of business?'

'I don't know exactly. I'm sorry.' She hesitated. 'Do you want to come in? I don't mind.'

I thanked her, and she led me into a tiny hall and opened a door which banged on to the back of an armchair.

'I'm sorry there's not much room. We moved in a year ago but we never really got things straight.' The living room was furnished with oversized chairs and the various constituent parts of an enormous outdated stereo system, none of which looked to have been positioned with any regard for either aesthetics or convenience. 'Do sit down. My name's Trish, by the way.'

We shook hands, and I said, 'You said Janet phoned your husband – do you know why?'

'She was trying to get hold of Lee's address, I think. They were separated, and he'd moved on without leaving a forwarding address, apparently. Not that that came as any surprise to me,' she added darkly.

'What do you mean?'

'I didn't like the man. I didn't trust him. He was all gold medallions and fast cars – that type. He and my husband were as thick as thieves for a while last summer but it didn't last. Just as I was thinking I'd have to tell Mike what I thought of Lee before he got in too deep, the whole thing seemed to fizzle out. In fact Mike was adamant he'd never have anything to do with Lee ever again.' She frowned. 'Actually, that was when Mike started drinking again.'

'I see.' I thought for a moment. Michael Irons the down-on-his-luck car-hire operator, and Lee Cox, the dealer in second-hand, slightly dodgy, executive cars. A marriage not exactly made in heaven, but close. 'Lee was going to supply your husband with cars for his business at discount prices, was he? Do you think your husband found out some of the cars were stolen or clocked or something? Was that what happened?'

Trish Irons shook her head in surprise. 'Good heavens, it had nothing to do with cars! Mike used to be a property developer – didn't you know? I'm pretty certain they were negotiating a property deal. Mike was very successful in the early eighties, before the market crashed. He had three companies, two buying different sorts of property for development, and one in construction. We lived in a lovely farm-house over at Manning Green, the children had ponies, Mike –'

'*Property*?' I interrupted. 'Are you saying Lee Cox and your husband were going to buy land and build houses on it, that sort of thing?'

'Yes. Why not? The market's really picking up these days, although you have to know what you're doing, of course. Finance is the key to everything, you know. I expect they had in mind a nice cheap piece of land belonging to someone who didn't know its value. Mike got very angry when I asked him about it – you know what men can be like. He was at a point in his life when he'd have done anything to get back into the swing of things. He and Lee spent a whole evening going through old plans, and Lee took some files away with him. Oh, and I know what you're thinking. You're thinking, if only this woman had been more sympathetic, everything might have been different. But I *did* try to talk to him. It was just that he resented me being the main breadwinner, just like he resented being a glorified chauffeur. In a way I was the last person on earth he could talk to.'

'I see.' I suddenly had an unpleasant flashback of Michael Irons lying in the lock-up garage with bits of hair standing on end and his fingernails torn out.

'And if you want to know why he killed himself,' said Trish, apparently divining my thoughts, 'it was because he got done for drunken driving a few weeks ago so that was the end of the car-hire business, too. They were coming to repossess the Merc next week. Oh, but if only you'd known him in the old days, he was a different man! Look, I've got some pictures here – let me show you what he was really like –'

I didn't particularly want to look at her photo album, but before I could think of a way of telling her this that didn't sound callous, she'd handed me the album. Unhappily, I began turning over the carefully captioned pages. 'Mike and Trish in the Algarve', 'Trish and the girls on Dartmoor', 'Manning Lodge before the builders move in' . . . Then, suddenly, I stopped turning the pages. The captions were written in a small, neat, upright script – and I'd seen that handwriting before. In Janet Cox's flat, on the diary page on her kitchen table.

'Mrs Irons, did your husband write any of the captions in this book?'

'The captions? Yes, of course. He wrote all of them. He was devoted to the girls. In fact, I think that was why –'

'Did he keep a pocket diary?'

She gave me a sideways look, as though she was beginning to wonder if I came from the sort of place where they don't put a handle on the inside of your bedroom door.

'Well, just for appointments and birthdays and making notes. Why?'

I studied the writing again to make sure. 'Look, I know this is going to sound like a very odd question, but do the names Holly Cottage and St Martin's Court mean anything to you?'

She frowned. 'Well, I've heard of Holly Cottage, but not the other place. Holly Cottage was a site on Gooserye Common Mike was hoping to redevelop.'

'Was this the deal he and Lee Cox were working on?'

'Oh, goodness, no! This was years ago – *ten* years ago at least. The landowner approached Mike, but Mike couldn't get the finance. Would you like me to get the papers?'

I could scarcely believe my luck. 'Oh, would you?'

She ran upstairs and began rifling a filing cabinet. I could hear her pulling open drawers, scraping hanging files along their runners and banging the drawers shut.

When she returned she handed me a manila file labelled 'Holly Cottage, Gooserye'. It looked very promising, but there was nothing in it apart from a rusty paper clip.

'It must have been one of the files Lee Cox took away with him,' she said, looking puzzled. 'How odd! As far as I can remember, the landowner's plan was to demolish the old house and build four luxury bungalows in its place, but Mike couldn't raise the finance to do it all in one go, so he came up with the idea of renovating the old house, selling that – and then building the three new houses one by one. Anyway, the whole thing fell through because the owner – or whoever it was – wouldn't agree to it.'

'What do you mean – whoever it was?'

'Well, it could have been another developer or a speculator. There used to be lots of people who knew nothing at all about property but who still managed to make a lot of money out of it, just by knowing how to spot an opportunity. Anyway, whoever he was, he obviously wanted the old house demolished and the whole development built and sold as quickly as possible because that's how you make the fastest profit – so he found someone else who could raise the money, I suppose. Mike was desperately upset because it seemed such a good deal.'

I was intrigued. 'So what on earth would Lee Cox want with old plans?'

'Well, I know Mike went as far as employing an architect and getting plans for the bungalows drawn up. I suppose they were hoping to use them on the new venture. Is it important? I'm afraid I'm not being much help, am I? The doctor gave me quite a lot of pills, you know.'

'No – you've been *very* helpful.' I didn't really know whether she had or not. 'Thank you so much for talking to me.'

Trish Irons looked shocked. 'But I didn't give you any tea. Shall I put the kettle on now?'

This was the last thing I wanted, but I felt immediately guilty. 'Well, if it won't take too long that would be nice. My daughter will be wanting something to eat –'

'Oh, you've got a *family*! In that case, of course I mustn't keep you. How thoughtless of me!'

61

'Oh, no, not at all! My husband's due home early tonight and he's really very good about the house –'

'Don't worry, dear, you go!'

When I arrived home twenty minutes later I was amazed to find that Pete's MGB really was pulled up on the pavement outside our house. I let myself in quietly, expecting to surprise him in the kitchen lovingly preparing something with too much pepper in it, but when I peered round the kitchen door a horrifying scene met my eyes. The grill pan, awash with grease, was suspended from the grill, a tomato ketchup bottle, ketchup-stained fork and open packet of butter complete with ketchup-stained knife stuck in it at a jaunty angle lay on the worktop, and the smell of bacon gratuitously cooked by someone who had not bothered to turn on the cooker hood fan was so strong it immediately permeated my hair from roots to split ends.

I went straight to the living room, from whence emanated the Simpsons' theme tune at full volume.

'What on earth do you think you're doing!' I demanded angrily, throwing open the door.

Pete and Julie were sprawled on the sofa in front of the television with their feet on our new glass-topped coffee table, eating bacon sandwiches. They both stopped dead in mid-bite, and grinned companionably at one another, which made me even more angry.

Pete removed his feet guiltily from the coffee table, and Julie held out my best Italian fruit bowl upon which slithered a mound of sandwiches. 'Go on, have one. Sit down! We did loads –'

'My God, you haven't even got plates! Or napkins!'

'We're being careful,' Pete protested, weakly.

'Oh, don't be ridiculous! You're the one who's always reminding us this sofa isn't paid for!' I seized the remote control and snapped off the television. 'I've had an awful day! I've just been talking to this poor woman whose husband killed himself. I feel really terrible.'

'What woman?' asked Pete.

'Do we care?' interrupted Julie, snatching back the control unit and reinstating the Simpsons on screen.

'Trish Irons, the woman whose husband killed himself in a lock-up garage the day Janet Cox was murdered. I didn't even ask her anything about her husband – you know, anything personal. What must she think?' Pete's eyes had slid back towards the TV screen and he was trying not to chuckle at a joke. I kicked him. 'Come on, aren't you even going to listen? Do you remember I told you that Janet Cox and Michael Irons knew each other? Well, apparently it was because last summer, Lee Cox and Michael Irons were working on a business deal. Mrs Irons seemed to think it had something to do with buying a piece of land and building houses on it – and her husband's file on Holly Cottage, the address on the diary page I told you about – which incidentally was in Michael Irons's handwriting – is missing. She thinks Lee Cox took it.'

'Oh.' He turned away from the screen with an effort. 'So?'

'So – I'm trying to work out what this has got to do with Janet's death! Have you got any ideas?'

Pete reached out absent-mindedly towards the sideboard, probably hoping his fingers would connect with a drink. They didn't, and he withdrew them hastily, hoping I wouldn't notice. 'I'm afraid nothing comes immediately to mind,' he admitted nervously. 'So what's happened to this Lee Cox, then?'

'I don't know. All I know is that Michael Irons fell out with him and he was a pretty shady character. Oh, and he'd consulted this solicitor Janet wanted to sell me the story on about getting a divorce.'

'Hmm,' said Pete. 'Well, then –'

'Can't you two shut up, or talk about this somewhere else?' interrupted Julie angrily. 'I just want to watch this *one* programme, that's all, and then I've got two bloody essays to finish!'

Pete jumped to his feet and rubbed his hands to get rid of the crumbs. 'She's right. Go and get changed. Have you got an address for Lee Cox?'

'Yes – but I told you, he's been missing since last autumn. What's the point of going to his house when we know he's not there?'

'We'll see.' He waved a sandwich under my nose. 'Go on, eat this, get changed, and we'll pay his neighbours a visit. Oh, and whatever you do, don't go in the kitchen.'

I gave him a hard stare, to indicate that I already had, but it was too late because his gaze had strayed back to the television. When I'd eaten the sandwich and taken some paracetamol, we looked up the address Janet had given me for her husband on the street map. Lee's house was situated in an area I vaguely knew on the outskirts of Hudderston, a less than salubrious area where semis huddle together too closely for comfort and 'For Sale' boards jostle for attention. In fact, it's an area of Hudderston not unlike the part of Tipping where Pete and I live, but of course Tipping has a picturesque High Street and once won a Most Beautiful Town award, so it's not the same thing at all.

We found a parking space between a skip and an old Sierra sporting a 'Police Aware' sticker, and walked up Lee Cox's front path. If there was one thing the house didn't resemble, it was the home of an incipient property developer with friends in high places. And you could tell no one had lived there for some time, because the porch was ankle deep in litter blown in by the wind – sweet wrappers, leaflets advertising Christmas special offers, assorted garden debris and old Coke cans. And something had happened to the downstairs bay window, because the central pane was boarded up. I climbed on to a frozen flower bed and peered inside, past a dingy net curtain. I could just make out some unremarkable furniture, a shirt hanging on a hanger in the doorway, and newspapers and glasses on a coffee table.

I stepped over the remains of a fence into next door's garden and rang their bell.

'There's a car in here,' called Pete, who was inspecting the garage. 'Looks like an old Rover.'

At that moment a sulky-looking teenage girl opened the door. 'What do you want?' she demanded aggressively. 'I already told the other bunch, my dad won't give to anything Christian.'

'We're not collecting. We're looking for your next-door neighbour, Mr –'

'Oh, *God*! *Dad*!' She opened the door wide, letting out a warm gust of chip-fat odour. 'It's another one for him next door!'

Her dad appeared behind her and scowled at us menacingly. 'What do you want?'

'We're press.' Pete thrust forward a hand. 'Hi, I'm Pete. We're after the story on him next door, and there's a drink in it for you, if you're interested.'

'Oh, yeah?' His beer gut was seeking an escape route over the top of his trousers. 'Steve. What story's that then?'

'Well, you tell me. For a start, do you know where we can find him?'

Steve made a rude noise. 'You must be joking! I wish I did, mate. We've had 'em all round here – electricity board, gas board – the flaming building society! *Police*. We're flaming sick of it. You heard about his wife, is that why you're here?'

'Yes. Come on then, what do you think – did he kill her?'

'*What*? *Him*? Never in a million years!' He settled himself comfortably against the doorframe. He wasn't going to ask us in. 'Poor bloke used to hide from her behind the sofa, pretend he was out! He reckoned he was going to get his locks changed to keep her out, but I don't think he ever did. Matter of fact, she was round here a couple of weeks ago poking her nose in – that car of hers was out front for hours. He reckoned he'd never be free of her till she got her hooks in some other poor sod. Anyway, I told you, he's gone – did a runner months ago. You want to know what I think? *I* think he's in Florida!'

My heart sank. Pete looked unimpressed. 'Are you sure? What makes you think he'd want to do a runner?'

'Well, I don't know, it's none of my business, is it? All I know is he told me once he fancied taking off to Florida as soon as he'd got some money together. He's got a mate there who runs a motel. You ever see that film, *Midnight Cowboy*? Well, he was a dab hand with the ladies. I told him he'd make a good – you know, what's the word? Not a juggler, the other one –'

'Gigolo?'

'Yeah! That's it. He had two women on the go that I knew

about – probably more when he was off on his trips. It was driving around in all them flash cars, I reckon.' He leaned forward confidentially. '*I* reckon he used to clock those motors, you know – I saw him doing something funny with a BMW in his garage. He said he could make a couple of grand on the right motor just by making a few phone calls. Jammy so-and-so.'

'I see. So did you know any of these women friends of his? Do you think he might have gone off with one of them?'

He shrugged. 'He could've,' he agreed, thoughtfully. 'I don't know, I never thought of that. I suppose he could've. They were both blondes. There was the one that come round on Sundays sometimes with the champagne – the wife reckoned she was that Cherie Jackson that used to work at Radley's doing the dispatching.'

I got my book out. 'Radley's?'

'Yeah, on the bypass – Radley's Road Haulage. But it was years ago when the wife knew Cherie – I don't reckon it can have been her. She was a scrubber then – she'd be well past it by now.'

'And the other one?' prompted Pete.

'Oh, I didn't know her from Adam! Tall, classy looking – legs up to her throat – know what I mean?'

The teenage daughter, who had been hovering in the background shovelling dry cornflakes into her mouth straight from the packet, giggled.

'Oh, shut up, Sammie!' Steve snapped.

'So, when do you think was the last time you saw Lee Cox?' asked Pete.

'Well, I've been thinking about that. The wife and I didn't really notice he wasn't around until just before Christmas, when there were all these leaflets sticking out of his door. I reckon it must have been August Bank Holiday, while I was out front cleaning the car. We had a bit of a chat.'

'What about?'

Steve hesitated. 'Oh, nothing.'

There was a moment's silence. Sammie started dancing on the spot. '*Dad*!' she hissed. 'Aren't you going to tell 'em? Go on – tell them about his accident.'

'What accident's that, Steve?' asked Pete.

'To his house!' exclaimed Sammie, jumping up and down excitedly. 'Haven't you seen it? He got a scaffolding pole through his window, didn't he! You should've heard it! There was this big crash like an explosion in the middle of the night! Mum thought it was the IRA come for Mr Jenkins 'cos he used to be in the army –'

'Shut up, Sammie!'

'It smashed his telly and everything! And it wasn't an accident either because Emma's brother Darren saw this man coming up the road in a lorry with a map looking for his house! At three in the morning!'

Steve suddenly grabbed his daughter by the waistband of her tiny skirt and threw her inside, cornflake packet and all.

'Get inside and do as you're told!' he yelled after her angrily, slamming the door and holding it shut. 'Bloody kids! Sorry about that, mate – don't take any notice of her.'

Pete and I exchanged startled looks, then turned to examine the boards at the front window of Lee Cox's house. 'So are you now saying this *wasn't* an accident?' asked Pete. 'When did it happen – was it around the time Mr Cox disappeared?'

'No, mate. It was about a month previous. Of course it was an accident! Bloody hell, you don't want to take any notice of her! That kid Darren does drugs! It was just some halfwit in a lorry – they get lost looking for the industrial estate – that's why he had the bloody map.'

'I see. So was this what you talked about the last time you spoke to him? What did he say, exactly?'

'Oh, nothing really. He said he was trying to get his insurance claim sorted out and the insurance company were being funny because he hadn't got a police report. You know what these bastards can be like.'

'But why didn't he report it to the police?' I asked.

'*What*? Well, that's obvious, isn't it?' Steve gave me a pitying look. 'He didn't want the police sniffing around his place, did he? Not with all them cars he'd been clocking and so forth. If you ask me, there's some dead dodgy gear in his garage.'

'I see.' Pete nodded. 'All right, Steve – hand on heart. Have you got a forwarding address for Lee Cox?'

'Sorry, mate – no.'

'All right. Never mind. Here –' He reached into his inside pocket. 'Buy the kids a couple of ice-creams. Come on, Chris. Good night, Steve!'

When we got back to the car, I said, 'What now? What do you think?'

'Like the man said, I think Lee Cox is in Florida.'

'Do you?' I did up my seatbelt and shivered slightly. 'Don't you think there could be a connection between the accident and Lee's disappearance?'

'Oh, of course there's a connection! Lee lives in a crap street with crap neighbours, and the insurance company won't pay up to repair his front window and replace his TV set. I think Florida sounds very attractive in the circumstances.'

Of course, he'd got a point. I watched pair after pair of semis scud shoulder to shoulder past my window as we roared off up the road. 'So what do you think Lee was up to with Michael Irons then? Do you think he really was going into property development?'

Pete laughed. 'Well, I'd say the words "bull" and "excrement" come to mind. Believe me, there isn't a bank manager in the world who'd even sit down at the same table as those two. A used-car salesman and an ex-bankrupt? You must be joking!'

7

The following day, when I got to reception, our windows were already emblazoned with posters for this week's edition. 'Tipping – the Millennium dawns. Shock as council opts for luxury entertainment centre. See this week's *Tipping Herald* for full and exclusive details of the town's stunning plan for the Twenty-first Century'. I went straight to my desk and tossed my notes on Lee and Janet Cox and their rather squalid lives into my bottom drawer. Mr Heslop dispatched Ernst, our photographer, to the abandoned timber yard where the centre was to be built to take a few 'before' shots, and chose an artist's impression to show the 'after'. Everybody in the newsroom was working on some aspect of the story, but I was doing the main write-up.

It took most of the morning, and when I'd finished, I felt like jumping on the desk and performing a quick rhumba. I was about to ring Pete – rather unwisely, I suspect – to give him the benefit of my prose, when my phone rang.

'It's me,' said Keith. 'You said to phone.'

'Oh, hallo! How are you?'

'Fine. Fancy lunch tomorrow?'

'Yes, that would be lovely! I'd really like that.' I tried to think of something else to say to him that didn't have to do with the paper, but couldn't.

'Good. Well, suggest somewhere then. Somewhere out of town. Do you know, the last time I came into Tipping at lunchtime . . .' He launched into a rambling story concerning the multistorey car park and an argument he'd had with a traffic warden over use of disabled parking bays.

'How about the Rudgeleigh Arms?' I said, when he'd finished.

'Good choice. About one? Leave you to book, shall I? Look forward to it. Bye.'

I put the phone down and immediately started to think about what I'd wear tomorrow. Something sexy – but also something that had gravitas. My black trouser suit, perhaps. I'd be able to tell Keith all about the Millennium Centre, and for once he wouldn't sit there looking bored and remarking irritably that he knew all about it – and I was sure I'd lost enough weight to look quite presentable in the trousers.

Still pondering over the cut of the trousers, I dialled Councillor Draycott's number. As a footnote to the Millennium Centre story, I thought it would be a good idea to write a brief summary of rejected Millennium schemes. I knew Mr Heslop would like this, because he was very keen on balance, and since Councillor Draycott's riverside park plan had been favourite right up to the finishing line, I thought he might like to make a comment. I suppose it did occur to me that Councillor Draycott was one of Tipping's more reclusive councillors, rarely giving interviews and never opening fêtes or shaking hands with a constituent if he saw them coming, but I was too busy planning my wardrobe to worry about it.

'Mrs Draycott? Could I speak to your husband, please – it's Chris Martin from the *Tipping Herald*,' I said, finally dismissing the black trouser suit on the grounds that it showed up my pallor.

The phone was banged down on to a hard surface without apology.

'Yes,' said Councillor Draycott, a few moments later, just as I was selecting a shirt.

'Oh! Councillor, I'm sorry to disturb you. We've just got details of the Millennium Centre which we're publishing this week and I wondered if I could ask you for a reaction.'

There was a long silence.

'Fuck off,' said the councillor.

I retrieved the phone, which had slipped through my fingers on to the keyboard and scored a line of k's across the screen, then looked round to see if anyone had noticed my blush. 'I'm sorry? Do you want me to print that?'

'You print it, I'll see you in court.'

I didn't know what to say, so I apologized again. 'I'm terribly sorry – have I offended you in some way? I was just ringing to ask how you feel about the entertainment centre, since your scheme for a riverside park was one of the ones rejected by the committee. I mean, we were all expecting a riverside park, and I believe you felt quite strongly that Tipping needed some green space near the town centre. Not to mention a bowling green. Isn't that right? Would you like me to say you're pleased there's a small landscaped area included in the new scheme?'

There was a short pause. 'Look, *dear*,' said the councillor, 'I'll make this as simple as I can for you. Get a piece of paper and draw yourself a diagram.' I reached obediently for a sheet of A4. 'Ready? Now envisage that landscaped area, all of it – are you doing that? Especially the bit with the little uncomfortable-looking knobbly trees on it – and *shove* it, the whole thing, as high as you can get it, right up your –'

Hastily, I slammed down the phone. I went straight to Mr Heslop's office to tell him about it, and ask his permission to print an edited version of the conversation on our front page, but he'd left for an early lunch, so I went back to my desk, punched my password into the computer and looked up Draycott, Councillor George. Naturally, as Tipping's elder statesman, he had a huge entry. *Elected 1967, South ward . . . served as mayor 1983–6 . . . Special interests: countryside issues, bowling . . . Interviews by prior arrangement only.* Of course, I should have checked this first. I scrolled dementedly up and down through the cuttings section and to my surprise a headline containing the name 'St Martin's Court' flickered into view. 'Councillor Draycott at opening of St Martin's Court,' it said. I did a double take. *Councillor Draycott officiated yesterday at the opening of Tipping's first tower block, built on the revolutionary new Broxham system, which will provide modern, convenient homes close to the centre of town for three hundred council tenants. Councillor Draycott said he was delighted with the standard of accommodation achieved, and proud to have been instrumental in introducing the Broxham system to Tipping.* The item was dated 9th April 1970. All but forgetting my run-in with Councillor Draycott, I decided to try a random search on

St Martin's Court. After a brief pause a piece headed, 'Town centre block of flats to bite dust,' appeared on-screen. It was dated 10th September 1982, and detailed arrangements for traffic rerouteing during the demolition of St Martin's Court. So Dave Ormond had been right. I didn't know what to think. What possible reason could Michael Irons have had for jotting down in his diary the address of a building demolished sixteen years previously? I closed down my computer and went back to Mr Heslop's office, hoping he might have sneaked back in while I wasn't looking. He hadn't, so I got my coat and went out for a breath of air.

It was still only a few degrees above freezing, and I decided to skip the air. I got in the car and drove down to the top of Market Street. And as soon as I got within sight, I remembered what St Martin's Court had looked like – a concrete-and-steel block with a blue fascia that had either loomed over southern Tipping like a dire warning of things to come, or presented its breathtaking, unbroken lines to the sky in a dazzling display of modern engineering prowess, depending on your viewpoint. Its site was now occupied by a council-owned multistorey car park and a very smart office building, both of which blended into their surroundings as if they'd always been there.

I pulled over alongside a bus stop, got out my notebook, and looked back at the notes I'd made in Janet's flat. The name I'd written down was definitely St Martin's Court, and the page had definitely been torn from a 1997 diary. Which didn't make sense. Unless there was some sort of connection between the court and Holly Cottage I couldn't think why anyone would have written both names down on the same page and at the same time. Perhaps it had something to do with both buildings having been demolished during the eighties? I glanced at my watch. I could afford to take a full hour for lunch and still finish the Millennium piece on time. If I asked Mr Heslop first if he'd like me to investigate Holly Cottage, he'd tell me not to bother.

Unlike Harewood Common, which is mainly deciduous wood-land entered at intervals by clearly marked private roads leading to houses whose owners park an assortment of Porsches on their drives, Gooserye Common is coniferous, and the track that crosses it looks gloomy and uninviting. The sign said 'Gooserye. Leading to Gooserye House, Hunter's Lodge and Brown's Cottages, etc'. I decided to give it a try. The road meandered apparently pointlessly through dense woodland, relieved here and there by small fields where horses shivered under blankets, past the elegant Gooserye House and a vast ugly modern edifice incongruously called Skylarks, until it finally finished up abruptly in a turning circle outside Brown's Cottages. I looked around for another way out, but there wasn't one, so I parked the car and left it in the turning circle with the engine running.

A woman in a painting smock answered my knock at the door of One Brown's Cottages.

'I'm sorry to trouble you, but I'm trying to find out where a house called Holly Cottage used to be – I think there are about four houses built there now. If I show you the map, do you think you could point it out to me?'

She looked blank. 'Holly Cottage? Well, I can show you where it is if you want.'

'Are you saying it's still there?' I demanded eagerly. Of course, if Holly Cottage was still there, Trish Irons might have been right about Lee and her husband embarking on a redevelopment scheme.

'Well, it was this morning! Can I ask who you are? Are you a friend of the Suttons?'

'Er, no. Actually I'm a local reporter.' I couldn't face going through the whole thing. 'I'm thinking of compiling a series of stories on old houses –'

'Oh, I *see*! Oh, how marvellous! What a wonderful idea. You know, I've often thought of doing something like that myself – Holly Cottage is about a quarter of a mile beyond Hunter's Lodge, on your right. You must have missed it.'

'Oh. I don't remember seeing Hunter's Lodge either.'

'Don't you? It's the newish-looking place with the solar panels. Oh no, of course – all the signboards are down, aren't they?' She suddenly ripped off the painting smock to reveal a clay-stained fisherman's sweater beneath. 'Hang on – I'll take you! I'm Faye, by the way.'

'Oh! Don't worry –'

'It's no trouble! I'm in the middle of painting thirty-six parsley pots for the craft centre and I could do with a break. And I've *always* wanted a good look round Holly Cottage –'

Before I could stop her, she'd jumped into my front passenger seat and was doing up the seatbelt.

'It's such a wonderful old place,' she went on, as I got in. 'Victorian. Of course, it needs a lot doing to it, but so worthwhile when you've finished! These woods used to be full of lovely old cottages, but I'm afraid a lot of them have gone now and there are these ghastly modern things in their place.'

We started off, and by the time we'd bumped down the lane, taken the turn-off I'd failed to spot on the way up, and negotiated an ever-narrowing track into the woods, I had learned a lot more than I cared to about the delights of doing up old cottages and the pitfalls of life at the potter's wheel.

The track came to a muddy end just short of a once-gravelled drive. Two empty mailboxes were nailed to a gatepost, and beyond these and a mountainous growth of rhododendrons you could just make out bits of a house. It was built of mellowed yellowish-grey brick, and roofed with greenish-grey slate.

Frankly, I could see the appeal of knocking it down and starting again.

I got out of the car. There was an almost total silence apart from the sighing of the wind through the trees.

'Anyway, I think this new kiln will solve all my problems,' Faye announced, running after me and raising her voice so I wouldn't miss anything, 'because I shall soon be up to date with my back orders and of course the market for hand-thrown pots has never been so buoyant. Wait –' She pushed in front of me and pounded the door knocker with gusto. 'Let *me* introduce you to the Suttons. They're very elderly, and you know how funny old people can be. Ellen! Ellen, it's me, Faye! *I brought you the vegetables last summer,*' she added, through the letterflap.

After a few moments, Ellen opened the door on a chain.

'Are you all right, dear?' asked Faye, and then hurried on without waiting for an answer. 'This lady is from the *local paper*. She wants to do a story about your lovely old house! Can we come in?'

'A story about the house?'

'Yes. It's very cold out here – you don't want to keep the door open for too long in this weather!'

Ellen took the chain off obediently and let us in. She was wearing several cardigans and a quilted waistcoat. 'My husband's in the kitchen. About the house, you say? From the papers?'

'Yes. Oh, gosh, this is the original *tiled floor*, isn't it?' Faye peered round the draughty hall and kicked up the corner of a worn piece of matting. 'Good heavens, you're so lucky.'

'I'm afraid you haven't come at a very good time,' Ellen said unhappily as she led us across the hall. 'We do our best but we live in the kitchen when it's cold because of the boiler. Did you speak to Hardings first?'

'What's Hardings?' I asked.

'The agents.' She pushed aside a faded nylon sheet and a pair of long johns suspended on a rack from the kitchen ceiling. 'We rent the house through Hardings. Edward, we've got some visitors to see the house –'

'Oh, my goodness! An *original washing rack*,' interrupted Faye, fighting her way through the sheet.

Edward was seated over by an ancient Ideal Standard boiler with one leg propped up on a stool. He stared at Faye and me for a moment, his right eyelid flickering fitfully, as though we were unexpected supernatural phenomena, then struggled to his feet with the aid of a stick and thrust out his hand. 'Edward Sutton. Good Lord. Sorry about the mess.'

I shook his hand obligingly. 'Chris Martin. Look, I didn't realize you were renting. It's really your landlord I need to speak to. Do you have his or her name and address?'

'Oh – ah.' He frowned. 'Now I did have that once. Oh, dear. Let me think, where might I have put that – Ellen?'

'Oh, dear,' quavered Ellen, looking anxious. 'Is there a problem with the house?'

'No, not a problem – it's just that I heard a rumour there were plans to redevelop the site, and I –'

'*Redevelop the site*?' said Faye furiously, halting her loving examination of some stained-glass insets held into the window by Sellotape. 'What a *terrible* thing to suggest! What sacrilege! This house is *priceless*!'

'Redevelop the site? What does that mean?' echoed Ellen.

'*Hold on a minute*!' I interjected, just in time, because Faye was obviously working herself up to an explanation that would involve bulldozers and shattered fitments. 'Let me explain. The people who were involved in the plan have – well – changed their minds. I just want to talk to your landlord about it – and of course about the cottage's history – that's all.'

'Oh, my goodness, we've been here for fifteen years,' said Ellen. 'We love it here. We couldn't *bear* to leave –'

'We've been here for *twenty* years, almost to the day, I think you'll find –'

'We had a lovely house in Tehran but we had to leave when the Shah went. We tried living in a flat but we didn't like it. We're just so *used* to this place. Do you really think they're going to knock it down?' Ellen insisted, miserably, and I wished heartily that I hadn't come.

'I'm sure they're not, but if you could just give me your landlord's name –'

'Ah, yes. On the tip of my tongue,' said Edward, unfazed. 'A lady, I think, lives in Australia. I'm afraid we always deal with Hardings. Ah, now, the lady at Hardings knows all about the cottage's history!' he added, brightly. 'You ought to talk to her. She had a quiet word with me when we first moved in in case someone else started telling tales. Been there years, she has.'

I thought over what he'd just said. 'She had a quiet word with you about what?'

'Oh, of *course* the *tragedy*!' put in Faye. 'I'd almost forgotten. Oh, you'll have to put that in if you're writing the history of the cottage! Now, according to the story I heard, there was a young man who lived here in the seventies – a writer – and he committed suicide *right here*, in this very room, because the BBC rejected one of his plays!'

'Oh!' I had no idea what to say.

'Shot himself,' said Edward.

'Yes! Now there were one or two other rumours doing the rounds about that young man, but we won't go into those.'

'Why not? What sort of rumours?'

'Well, that he used to grow cannabis plants in the back garden – but really, I can't see it myself.' We exchanged glances, and I knew she knew as well as I did that you can't grow cannabis plants in a cold back garden in Southern England. 'Anyway, I expect this woman who bought the cottage after he died got it *very* cheaply,' she added, disapprovingly. 'I think we're all lucky it's still standing.'

'Marjorie!' Edward exclaimed suddenly, as though tearing the name from his very bowels with a seam-ripper.

I got my book out eagerly.

'Lady at Hardings,' he went on. 'That's her name – Marjorie!'

'Yes, Marjorie,' agreed Ellen. 'That's who you should speak to – not any of the others. When we had our burglary last summer their Mr Blackmore said we'd have to pay for the damage to the door ourselves and get the money back from the insurance company, but we couldn't afford it, so dear Marjorie sent one of those – you know – facsimile things to our landlord, and within a week we'd had a cheque and it was all sorted out. It was *so* kind of her!'

'I didn't know you'd had a burglary!' exclaimed Faye, before I could say anything. 'When was it? Was anything taken?'

'Some of my mother's jewellery, I'm afraid. And two pictures and a clock that belonged to the house, and Edward's Iranian silver goblets. It was the twenty-first of June, in the middle of the afternoon –'

'Good heavens! We should all have been told! The police should have told *everybody*, in case we *all* got burgled –'

'They made an awful mess. They went through everything. They even went up in the attic. Edward was at physiotherapy and I was out for a walk. We think the picture they took from

77

the attic may have been valuable. Someone else came here before hoping to get their hands on a picture, and we think that might have been the one.'

'*Really*?' demanded Faye. 'What – one of these shady antique dealers, you mean?'

'We think so. It was the very first week we moved in, while we were still unpacking. This very smart young man knocked at the door and asked if he could have a look round. He said he was a relative of our landlady and he'd come to collect an extremely valuable picture. He got very agitated when he couldn't find it – I don't mind telling you I didn't like the look of him at all! Anyway, Marjorie said he was obviously some sort of con man. It was just lucky she'd put some pictures and things up in the attic to give us more space or I don't know what would have happened. Marjorie said she didn't think any of the pictures had any value, but I'm not sure she's an expert,' she added, shaking her head thoughtfully.

I leapt into a break in the conversation.

'I'd be very grateful if you could just give me Hardings' address and phone number and then I can leave you in peace,' I said firmly.

'Oh, of course!' Edward said. 'Let me find a pencil –'

I handed him my pad and pen.

'Now, where's the address book –'

'Ooh, have you got a cellar?' demanded Faye, stamping on the cracked lino.

'A what, dear?' enquired Ellen.

Instead of answering, Faye pounced on a door in the corner of the room. It was thickly enrobed in cream paint and had an old shawl hanging from it on a hook. 'I'll bet *this* is the cellar!' she exclaimed, and without further ado wrenched at the door handle.

There was a brief moment of silence before the door opened, to reveal the back of an ironing board and about half a dozen brooms and mops. And then, one by one, with increasing speed, the ironing board, four brooms and two mops toppled forward and thundered to the floor, to be followed – after another brief pause – by three canisters of wax, two bottles of bleach, a box of empty glass jars and a shelf. At least one of the glass jars rolled out of the box and smashed itself noisily against the skirting.

'My kilner jars!' shrieked Ellen, horrified. '*My kilner jars*!'

There was a shocked silence.

'Ah. My fault. So sorry. Should have mended the damn shelf,' said Edward. 'I do hope you're not hurt. Get some water, Ellen.'

For once, Faye was almost speechless. 'Oh, my goodness!' she murmured. 'I was so sure –'

'I'm so sorry, this is all my fault,' I interrupted. 'Just send your bill to the *Herald* marked for my attention – here's my card.'

Faye was very quiet as I drove her home. She got out of the car muttering something about ninety per cent of Victorian houses of equivalent size and status having cellars, and didn't invite me in to look at her pots. For the price of a few kilner jars, this seemed like a bargain.

I had scarcely seated myself at my desk with a mug of hot chocolate and a surreptitious sandwich when the phone rang.

It was Wayne.

'I wanted to let you know how it went,' he said.

My mind went blank. 'Sorry?'

'The wife's birthday! Remember? Well, I took her up West for the night – taxis door to door both ends – dinner, champagne, and a double room at the Kensington Hilton. Cost a bloody fortune, but who's counting? Oh, and she loved the dress.'

'Oh. Good!'

'But the thing is, she's a bit suspicious about it. She keeps telling me I've got such crappy taste she can't imagine how I picked it, so if you run into her one day, for Christ's sake don't let on you know anything about it.'

I laughed. 'Don't worry, if she ever wins first prize at the Women's Institute for one of her sponges, and I'm sent to interview her, I promise I won't say a thing.'

'Oh, fat chance!' He sounded relieved. 'By the way – strictly off the record for the time being – we've got Daniel Kerr-Dixon downstairs.'

'Have you? *Why*?' I reached for a pen.

'Well, we checked out the staff in that burger place where he works, and according to them, he definitely had a thing going with Janet. She used to call him Bunny, and ring up and leave soppy messages for him to pick up when he got in. We checked with BT. She made calls either to his home or the bar at least once a day. In other words, he lied.'

'Oh.' I was shocked, but then I thought it over for a moment. 'Actually, it doesn't necessarily mean he's lied. It just means Janet fancied *him*. Perhaps he didn't reciprocate but she wouldn't take no for an answer.'

'Oh, come on!'

'And have you thought of checking the dating agencies? I expect you know Janet met Daniel through filling in a computer form. Perhaps she'd met someone else the same way.'

'We've checked all the agencies, she wasn't registered with any of them. I'll let you know when we get a confession.'

'Wait!' I could imagine Daniel's small frame huddled into one of those ugly wood and metal chairs they have in interview rooms. 'Is the only reason you suspect Daniel the fact that you think he's lied? Someone attacked Janet in her flat a few weeks ago – I remember you saying. And anyway, hasn't Daniel got an alibi –'

'Hang on, Chris. When we've got a confession, I'll fill you in on all the details. It depends how much forensic evidence we can get on him.'

'What does?' I began to get an awful feeling in the pit of my stomach. Sooner or later, unless Wayne picked up on things himself, I was going to have to tell him about my visit to Janet's flat. And perhaps it had better be sooner.

'How quickly we can get him to confess depends on how much forensic evidence we can chuck at him! That's the way it works. I've got a team going over the flat. So far they've already picked up some hairs that look like Cox's. So –'

'Wayne, there's something I'm not sure if I mentioned to you,' I interrupted desperately. Personally, I was going to confess slowly. 'When I met Janet that time – remember? – she said she had a story she wanted to sell me on a local

80

solicitor, and she gave me her address and some info on her husband, and I was supposed –'

'Ah, yes, I'm glad you reminded me,' said Wayne. 'Hang on, I've got a statement here from Philip Chandler. He was the husband's solicitor – right? He says he wrote one letter to Cox on Lee's instructions, then Lee absconded without paying his bill. He never met Janet – I think she was having you on. Sorry – where were you going with this?'

'Er – I was telling you what she told me about her husband. Did you know Lee Cox knew Claire MacInnis, the wife of the owner of the Rudgeleigh Arms?'

He was silent for a moment. 'Sorry, I don't get your point,' he said finally.

'Well, the Rudgeleigh Arms is only just up the road from the layby where Janet was found. Surely that's significant. And' – I took a deep breath – 'I'm afraid there's something else. I –'

'Oh, shit!' Wayne exploded suddenly. There was a hubbub of noise in the background. 'Sorry, I'll have to go. Look, I'll give you another ring, OK? Watch this space!'

8

Mr Heslop stirred his morning coffee carefully and then examined it for undissolved lumps of skimmed milk powder. 'What on *earth* were you thinking of? A murder victim's flat, for God's sake?'

I winced. 'Look, Mr Heslop, at the time it looked like open-and-shut road rage, the key was there, I just didn't think. What do you think would happen if I went to the police now, and told them everything I've found out about Lee Cox and Michael Irons and Holly Cottage? Do you think –?'

'I think you'd better like prison food and high jinks in the shower if you're thinking of doing that!' he interrupted, horrified. 'You must be mad! Are you sure this neighbour you spoke to didn't catch on?'

I hesitated. 'Positive. He thought I was a cable television engineer.'

'Good God. Well, that's all right then. Think yourself lucky and put it down to experience. Now get on to Hudderston Central and find out if Kerr-Dixon has confessed. If he has, so much the better. And hurry up, will you, we'll have to rejig the front page if he's been charged.'

'Right.' I reached for the phone and dialled Wayne's number. A DC Hunt answered his phone.

'Sorry, love. All I can tell you is that the men in white suits going over his flat with their tweezers scared the shit out of the little sod – but he kept all his other orifices shut so we had to let him go.'

'Oh.' I wasn't sure whether to be relieved or disappointed. 'Does that mean he's been eliminated from the enquiry?'

'No, of course it doesn't. Sorry – which planet did you say you were from?'

I put the phone down hastily and repeated what he'd said to Mr Heslop.

'Right, you'd better keep on to it then,' he said. 'Have you got any other leads, apart from the ones connected to this diary page you're not supposed to have seen?'

'Well, there's the MacInnis woman at the Rudgeleigh Arms – I don't know how she fits in or if she does – and I didn't finish checking out this solicitor Janet offered me the story on.'

'OK, but *be careful*. Especially with the solicitor, for God's sake.'

I nodded. 'And there was something else that happened yesterday I didn't tell you about . . .' I said, and filled him in on the details of my skirmish with Councillor Draycott.

His eyes rounded. 'Oh, my God, I hope you apologized!' he exclaimed immediately.

I did a double take. '*Apologized*! *Me*!'

'Yes! How many times do I have to tell you, this isn't the *Guardian*! We *need* to keep on the right side of people like Councillor Draycott. We've got a limited readership, for Christ's sake! Do you think we're going to win friends by telling people they've elected officers who are foul-mouthed sexist pigs?'

'But he –'

'I don't care! It won't do us any good to point out that some of our councillors think the people of this town are idiots and are only in the job so they can get their names up on plaques! Even if that's true – and I'm not sure it is. So no smart-aleck retaliation. Have you got that?'

'I suppose so,' I agreed grudgingly.

I went back to my desk. Mr Heslop was right, of course, about both Councillor Draycott and my plan to give myself up to the police – I felt relieved about the latter at any rate. I reached for the phone book and looked up Philip Chandler's home address. It was listed simply as Ravenswood – not Drive or Crescent or Avenue – and in Tipping this translates as 'private road of really expensive houses with absolutely no through traffic'. I wondered whether any of the other

Chandlers in the book were related to him – there were lots of them, too many to ring on the off-chance. I decided I'd got no choice but to try the ex-secretary. I checked her address in the street directory. I'd just about got time to fit in an interview with her before keeping my appointment with Keith at the Rudgeleigh Arms. I got my coat, and set off.

Alison Carter's house was tucked away in a small cul-de-sac on the outskirts of a large sixties-built estate, its tiny paved front garden dotted with stone troughs full of alpines, and its gaping picture windows discreetly netted. On the step, freshly washed milk bottles glinted in the morning sun.

A large person in shabby trousers and some sort of baggy top answered my knock. At second glance I recognized this person as an elderly woman.

'Mrs Carter?' I enquired.

'*Miss*,' she corrected, frowning behind thick blue-rimmed glasses.

'Sorry. I'm Chris Martin from the *Tipping Herald*.' She ignored my hand. 'I've been asked to write a piece on Philip Chandler for our Local Profiles series, and I was wondering if –'

'Stop you there, it's my sister, you want. Alison,' she interrupted. '*Alison*! Are you there? For you!' She opened the door a few inches. 'Well, come on, come on – you're letting the warmth out.'

I squeezed past her into the house, the temperature inside which was, if anything, marginally colder than without.

'This woman's here about Philip,' she announced, showing me into the front room. 'From the *Herald*. They want to do a story for their Profiles spot. Like that blasted awful thing they did on old Mother Pringle from the cake shop when she retired, I shouldn't wonder.'

I began to suspect things weren't going to go according to plan, but I shook hands with Alison, who looked exactly like her sister, except that she was wearing a neat blue dress with self-covered buttons and had had her hair restyled within the last decade by someone not armed with a pair of hedge trimmers.

To my surprise, Alison smiled. 'Oh, what a lovely idea!' she exclaimed, hastily pushing an old sock she'd been darning out of sight behind a cushion. 'Do sit down. I'd love to help. Jane and I do a bit of writing ourselves from time to time – although we're hardly the Brontës, I'm afraid, are we, Jane?'

'Hmm,' said Jane.

I sat down and opened my book at a clean page. 'Well, what I'm really after is a personal insight from someone who knows Mr Chandler well, and his receptionist suggested you. I already know he joined the firm in the early seventies and he's married to Mr Woodford's daughter, all that sort of thing, but I want to know what he's like to work for – is he a stickler for detail – is he bad-tempered in the mornings? During the time you worked for him, did you ever hear any rumours about –'

'Oh, well, I can tell you *all* about Mr Chandler, in that case!' interrupted Alison, delightedly. 'I was really sorry to leave, but Jane and I – we're twins – we always said we'd retire at age sixty, and we did. Jane was in the NHS. I do hope this new girl is looking after Mr Chandler properly. You simply couldn't ask for a better boss. Mind you,' she leaned forward conspiratorially, 'when I was first assigned to him I was horrified. I put in a complaint – didn't I, Jane? There he was, this brash young man in a ghastly suit that hadn't been properly pressed, not at all the sort of person one wanted to be working for in a Tipping solicitor's office.'

'I see –' I moved to make a note.

'Oh, but it wasn't his fault! You should never judge people by appearances. Mr Chandler was the perfect gentleman. I took him in hand, didn't I, Jane? I brought an iron and a board into the office so I could do his shirts for him. He was living in all sorts of ghastly digs, you see, he couldn't look after himself properly. He'd come down from somewhere up North –'

'Darlington.' I didn't really want to discuss Philip Chandler's laundry.

'Darlington – yes. His poor mother went down with Alzheimer's, you know.' She exchanged a glance with Jane and they gazed silently into space for a moment. 'It was so sad.

She never knew that all the sacrifices she must have made for him had paid off. Still, I always think it's because he's had to struggle so hard for everything that he's such a caring person – and of course, this is why he fitted in so well with Mr Tuck and Mr Woodford. You see, Mr Tuck and Mr Woodford were both –'

'God-botherers,' put in Jane. 'Mr Tuck and Mr Woodford were both God-botherers.'

'– *committed Christians*,' insisted Alison, turning her back on her sister crossly. 'But I expect you know that already. Mr Woodford used to say that respect for the law and its procedures provided the underpinnings for a Christian society. He believed that honour and reputation were more important than making vast amounts of money . . .'

At this point I remembered what Keith had said about Tuck Woodford & Chandler's final bill for our divorce, and somehow managed to stop my eyebrows hitting the Artex.

'. . . and although I don't think Philip's exactly a Christian – I think he only went to church to please Anne – in his own way he's always followed Mr Tuck's and Mr Woodford's principles. I'm sure, wherever they are, they're looking down on the firm now and smiling.'

'Hmm,' said Jane.

'Oh, stop it!' snapped Alison suddenly. 'You don't know what you're talking about.'

'Yes, I do. I ought to – it was Mr Tuck *this* and Philip *that* for thirty-five years – I certainly ought to know what I'm talking about! Do you see that there?' she demanded suddenly, pointing at a cut-glass fruit bowl on the sideboard. '*That's* what Philip Chandler and the firm gave my sister for thirty-five years' service. We had a labrador, Molly – died when she was eleven. We spent more on burying Molly in the remembrance garden than Philip Chandler spent on my sister's leaving present!'

'Oh, stop it! That's all you think about – what things cost!'

Jane scowled furiously. 'Indeed! Well, if there's one thing I can't stand it's hypocrisy! I don't like people who pretend to *care* – in inverted commas – when really the only *caring* they're doing is for their own reputation.'

'That's a terrible thing to suggest,' said Alison, and they glowered at one another in silence.

I stood up. Obviously, this wasn't going to be any help at all. 'Well, thank you, you've both been very kind. I'm sure I can use some of this. Er, I don't suppose you can think of anyone else who might be able to contribute?'

Alison smiled. 'Oh, yes – you *must* talk to the Reverend Marston at St Mary's! Mr Tuck set up a free advice clinic through St Mary's, and Philip worked *so hard* on it – even if he wasn't a Christian!' she added, glaring meaningfully at her sister.

'Hmm,' snapped Jane. 'Well, come to that, she ought to talk to Lola Champion. Don't you think?'

Alison frowned. 'Oh no – I don't think that would be fair. Poor Mrs Champion.'

'Who's Mrs Champion?'

'Who's Mrs Champion?' repeated Jane. 'Mrs Champion is Philip Chandler's *good cause*! She lost her family, you see – through several faults of her own, it has to be said – being a drunk, and falling in with the wrong sorts of men, mainly. Philip met her through the advice clinic and helped her find her children through the proper channels – this was in the seventies when all that sort of thing was so frightfully difficult. Apparently she'd lost two of her children to social services and two to I don't know what – I think that's pretty careless, don't you? Anyway, he seems to have got himself stuck with her. Whenever she's down on her luck she turns up on his doorstep wanting a handout!'

'Oh, that's not very fair!' repeated Alison. 'I'm sure Mrs Champion is very grateful. She's almost a totally reformed character now –'

'Huh! Just don't get downwind of her in Tesco's, that's all!'

Alison sniffed. 'I don't care what you say, I'm sure she's completely dried out. She's looked after Philip's house for him since Anne died and I'm sure he'd keep her on the straight and narrow.'

'I see.' I pretended to write down the names of the Reverend Marston and Lola Champion. 'Well, thank you very much again. We would prefer it if you didn't mention this interview to Mr Chandler – just in case the article doesn't come off.'

I hurried out to the car, threw my notebook on to the back seat, and reached for my make-up bag. In twenty-five minutes Keith would be sitting waiting for me in the bar of the Rudgeleigh Arms. Or rather, he'd be sitting waiting in the bar of the Rudgeleigh Arms for his familiar old wife of twenty years' standing: I wanted to waft in on a breath of Fifth Avenue and lipgloss and take him by surprise.

I arrived at five to one, and was disappointed to find the patrons' car park half empty. The Rudgeleigh Arms – complete with its timber framing, ancient tiled roof and tiny uneven windows decked out with fairy lights – has always looked as if it has just stepped off a Christmas card. The cotoneaster bushes clinging to its walls were delicately edged with frost, and a plume of blue woodsmoke wavered in the air above ornate chimneys. Stefan Andre had taken it over a year ago, and since then it had become The Place To Go, but there's no point in going to The Place To Go if there's no one there to see you. Still, I couldn't wait to drool over the menu. Stefan Andre (real name Stefan Andreyevitch, a name too Russian-sounding to inspire gourmet interest, apparently) had transformed the restaurant from a cosy rendezvous for family celebrations to a superior venue for business lunches and assignations between middle-aged, middle-class men and much younger women to whom they wish to demonstrate their grasp of popular culture. I had never in my wildest dreams expected to be coming here to meet Keith.

As I'd hoped, he was already in the bar.

He didn't give me a second glance. 'Hope you don't mind,' he said, before I'd sat down, 'but I've gone ahead and ordered us the chef's recommendation to save time because I'm in a hell of a rush. Want a drink? The food'll be about fifteen minutes.'

I began to get a sort of *déjà vu* feeling. I declined the drink, and followed him to the restaurant.

When we'd sat down and got our coats off, I said brightly, 'Well, well, what a lovely table! How're you? How's work?'

'Frantic. I've got an important tender to finish by four. Still – you look nice.' He looked me up and down. 'Your hair's longer. Same style, of course, but curlier and looser. I like it. Julie tells me you're getting the house sorted out at last.'

'Yes. We are.' 'At last' was a bit unfair. 'So what about you? Julie just keeps telling me you're fine.'

'I am fine, as a matter of fact.' His gaze flickered over the wine list. 'Chardonnay all right with you? You don't think it's a bit – you know – passé, do you?' he added anxiously.

'I don't know.'

'Oh, well, it's only us.' He called the wine waiter over.

I contained my curiosity until the wine waiter had gone. Then I said, 'By the way, what were you doing at Tuck Woodford and Chandler's the other day?'

'Ah, I was coming to that. Actually, I had an appointment with this new chap they've got there, Michaelson. He does prenuptial agreements.'

There was a long silence, as Keith allowed this piece of information to sink in, followed by the bit I could work out for myself.

'I see. You mean you're getting married.'

He beamed. 'Yes, that's right.'

'To Sandra?'

'Well, of course to Sandra.' He was really enjoying this. 'I wanted to tell you myself before someone else did.'

Oh, I'll bet you did, I thought, my heart pounding like an arrhythmic pile driver. 'Well, I am pleased,' I lied, because for some reason I wasn't at all. 'And when is the big day?'

'As soon as possible! You and Pete are invited, of course. Probably the first week in April, I should think.'

'Look forward to it,' I lied again. 'But what do you want a prenuptial agreement for?'

Before he could answer, our starter arrived. Two elegant-looking plates of a prettily striped terrine garnished sparsely with *frisée* and pine nuts.

'Well, we live and learn, don't we?' said Keith, picking up a fork.

I felt my jaw go rigid. 'And what do you mean by that exactly?'

'Well, what do you think I mean?' He hesitated. One of the reasons he is still alive is that he always knows when he's pushed me too far. 'Oh, come on, it's nothing personal. If you must know, I'm putting some money into a business venture with Sandra and her brother and I wanted to get one or two things checked out, that's all.'

'So it's not really a prenuptial agreement at all then, is it?' I stabbed a pine nut. 'You're trying to wind me up.'

'No, I'm not. Why would I do that? Anyway –' He summoned up one of his most patronizing smiles. 'Enough about me. What exciting things are going on in Tipping that we unfortunates who don't work at the *Herald* know nothing about?'

Of course, I made up my mind immediately that wild horses on amphetamines would not drag out of me the details of Tipping's new Millennium Centre.

'Well, you'll just have to wait and see, won't you?' I hissed, through clenched teeth.

We finished our starters in silence, and no sooner had we relinquished our forks than the waiter appeared with our main course.

'Roast monkfish with lentil salsa,' he announced, standing back so we could give it a round of applause.

'Excellent,' said Keith, motioning for him to go ahead and serve it up. He glanced at his watch for at least the third time since we'd sat down. 'Good. Thank God they're not keeping us hanging about. Do you know, we haven't had so many tenders on the go at once since the eighties – I think the economy is about to take off again. It's really quite exciting . . .' I allowed him to regale me with his views while I dug around in the lentil salsa.

When he'd finished, I said, 'So you think we're on the verge of a boom, do you? Does that mean now would be a good time for a property developer to try and buy up a piece of land to build houses on? Only I'm working on this story, you see, about an old cottage on Gooserye Common.' Keith's firm sometimes designed bits of buildings: he just might have some expertise it could be worth tapping into. 'It's owned by someone who lives overseas –'

'*Really*! Well, if it's owned by someone who lives over-seas they might not know the value of it. There you are, there's your story – some poor old sod tricked out of a fortune by a wicked property developer!' He dug into his monkfish. 'Nothing illegal about it, of course, but there you go.'

I thought about this. 'It'd be unethical though, wouldn't it?'

'Well, what do you think? Sometimes I think I went into the wrong line, you know. That's why now I've got this opportunity to go in with Nigel, Sandra's brother, I'm seriously tempted.'

'I see.' I didn't take this in. I was still thinking about Holly Cottage and St Martin's Court. 'Keith, do you remember that block of council flats at the top of Market Street? St Martin's Court? It was built on something called the Broxham system, and they demolished it after it had only been up for a few years. You wouldn't have heard anything about it, would you?'

He shook his head irritably. 'No, of course I haven't. It's not my field, is it? I've heard of the Broxham system, though. Do you want me to find out something about it for you? Some of these systems were seriously flawed, you know – that's why they stopped using them.'

'*Really*?'

'Yes.' He put his fork down suddenly. 'Now listen, I'm trying to tell you something.'

'What?'

'I'm trying to tell you that I'm thinking of jacking in the job and throwing everything in with Nigel. I know it's a risk, but sometimes you have to take risks, don't you?' He hesitated. 'I didn't tell you, did I? About Sandra.'

'What about Sandra?'

'She's pregnant.'

I was in the middle of a mouthful of Chardonnay. It immediately turned to battery acid on my tongue, but some-how I managed to swallow it.

'Is she? Good heavens.'

Keith frowned angrily. 'What's that supposed to mean?

Did you think I wasn't capable? Sandra's thirty-four! She's still young!'

'I didn't really mean anything –'

'And as a matter of fact I'm really looking forward to being a father again. It's a second chance, isn't it? I bet Julie'll be thrilled at the thought of having a new baby half-brother or sister.'

'Ah. Um, yes. Er, perhaps you'll leave it to me to give her the news.' I didn't know whether Julie would be pleased or not. I helped myself to more battery acid and took a large swallow. 'Look, I'm really happy for you both. Would you excuse me? Must dash to the loo – weak bladder these days, I suppose.'

In the foyer, someone had left open the front door, and I gulped in cold air gratefully like a goldfish taking in water after a brief shimmy across the mantelpiece. Keith with a new baby? And happy about it? After Richard's birth he had suffered the most terrible postnatal depression, alleviated only by frequent trips along the A30 on his motorbike, and when Julie appeared his allergic reaction to anything bearing a Mothercare logo had kept him out of the house on an almost permanent basis. If Sandra was expecting help with the nappy-changing, she was in for a shock. Ought I to warn her? *Keith* with a new baby. It didn't seem fair –

I was distracted from this unexpected dilemma by a minor commotion in the doorway. Two women in what looked like kitchen uniforms were assisting a man in from the car park.

'Ooh – your arm, Stefan –'

'– mind your head –'

Their charge was wearing a chef's apron splattered with blood, and his head was aggressively bald. I guessed, of course, that he was Stefan Andre.

'Thank you, ladies, thank you very much!' He clapped his hands as if to scatter them like chickens. They scattered.

'Oh, Stefan, are you all right?' demanded the receptionist, flying out from behind her impressive desk and almost sending me sprawling across two chintz sofas. 'Did they stitch it?'

'Of course they stitched it. Where's Claire?'

'I'll get her!'

He let out an explosive snort and marched across reception towards the door marked 'Staff Only' through which the kitchen staff had already disappeared, his head glinting shockingly in the glow of the fairy lights. He was about thirty, tall, with a fair complexion, strikingly long eyelashes and vivid blue eyes.

'Don't bother my wife if she's busy! I thought she'd be here! Just tell her I'm OK and everything's OK and I'm in the kitchen,' he said, and the door shuddered in his wake.

I resumed my search for the Ladies, but before I could investigate the recesses beyond the bar, the front door burst open again to admit a tall blonde woman in a figure-hugging suede trouser suit.

'Where is he?' she demanded, hurling herself melodramatically at the desk. 'Is he all right?'

'Yes, Ms MacInnis, they stitched it.'

'They stitched it–' She took a deep breath and sagged over the desk-top for a moment. 'And everything was all right – no problems?'

'No, Ms MacInnis. Stefan said to tell you everything was fine.'

She let out another sigh of relief, and her manner suddenly changed. 'So why wasn't I informed?'

'Sorry?'

'Don't you "sorry" me!' She'd got her back to me, but I could tell from her voice that her teeth were clenched. 'I've told you before, Caroline – I want to be told *straight away* if anything happens to my husband. What were you thinking of, sending him to Casualty with those stupid girls from the kitchen?'

'Why? It was only a *nick*, for heaven's sake – it just wouldn't stop bleeding. You weren't here, Miss MacInnis, I didn't know where you were.'

'*Wouldn't stop bleeding* –' For a moment, her knees seemed to buckle, but she quickly pulled herself together. 'Don't be ridiculous! Of course you knew where I was! Are you sure everything's all right?'

Caroline, who was in her early twenties, looked totally

unfazed. 'Look – I took the decision not to bother you,' she remarked, calmly.

Claire was furious. 'Well, don't you *ever* take that decision again! Not if you want to continue working here. *You* don't take responsibility for my husband's health – I do!'

'Yes, Ms MacInnis,' agreed Caroline, as though she couldn't care less, and Claire turned round angrily and trampled over my foot with her steel-tipped boots.

'Oh, I'm so sorry,' she apologized. 'I wasn't looking where I was going. My husband had a bit of an accident. I'm so sorry.'

'That's all right. Is Mr Andre OK?'

'Yes, he's fine, apparently, thank you.'

'Actually, I'm from the *Tipping Herald*, Ms MacInnis,' I said, as she turned to go, and she immediately executed a swift about-face. She was a cool, Nordic blonde with skin the colour of pale winter sunshine, and she wore blue topaz and silver earrings that matched her eyes. She towered over me by a full head.

'Oh, are you?' Suddenly she was all smiles. 'I do hope you're enjoying your meal? Can I get you anything? I do rather fuss over my husband, but when people are very creative they need to be cosseted or they can't function. He's fine, really. Have you seen today's menu? The monkfish is a new creation of Stefan's – I hope you'll give it a try.'

'Yes, actually, I –'

'And I do hope we're not going to see in the paper that Stefan's out of action or suffering from some terrible health problem or something – it really is just a minor cut and I'm sure he's already back at work. Goodbye now – do enjoy your meal.'

It suddenly occurred to me that Claire perfectly fitted Lee's neighbour's description of the tall classy blonde with legs up to her throat who'd visited Lee's house.

'Wait –' I stopped her in mid-stride. 'Actually I'm here because I believe you know Lee Cox and I'm trying to trace him,' I said boldly.

She frowned. 'I think you must be mistaken. I don't know anyone of that name.'

'Are you quite sure? I was given your mobile phone number to contact him on, and I'm told your staff don't give out that number to anyone.'

Claire ignored this and retreated towards the 'Staff Only' exit. I followed doggedly. 'Is he a client, Ms MacInnis? Can I ask what business you're in?'

'I'm an interior designer. Ah! *Lee Cox*. I remember now. I believe he was the person I bought our Audi from last January. I expect I gave him my number to arrange for delivery of the car. Yes, that'll be it. I'm afraid I haven't seen him since. Sorry.'

'Wait a minute.' She had bluish veins in her temples. 'If you bought this car a year ago, and you haven't seen Mr Cox since, why would his wife still have it as a contact number? You know Janet Cox is dead, don't you, and that her body was found just down the road from here?'

'What? Oh, wait – hang on a minute!' Her jaw tightened, elongating her smile unpleasantly. She glanced across at Caroline, who seemed to be watching us but was now safely out of earshot. 'Look, this is very awkward. I *do* know Lee Cox but I haven't seen him since last summer. That's the truth. I certainly know nothing about his wife and I have absolutely no idea where he is now. Anyway, I can't possibly talk to you about it here.'

'I see.' I felt a little tingle of excitement in the back of my neck. 'Where could you then?'

'Oh, for goodness sake, this is a complete waste of time and I'm terribly busy! I suppose I could come into your office when I'm in Tipping on Friday if you really think it's necessary.'

'That would be fine. Thank you.' I turned on my heel and went straight back to the restaurant so she couldn't chase me into the Ladies to say she'd changed her mind.

Keith had given up on his monkfish and was seeing off the wine. I felt a bit guilty about this, because I should have known that any reference to a bladder would put him off his food.

We had coffee, and the waiter brought the bill.

'Let me get this!' The words rose unbidden to my lips. 'My congratulations present.'

'Oh, thank you very much. I'll do the tip then,' said Keith.

I opened up the bill, and made a mental note that if in the future I ever do develop a bladder problem, I must at all costs avoid unexpected bills from the Rudgeleigh Arms after the consumption of liquid.

We parted in the car park. 'My very best to Sandra,' I said. 'Make sure you take good care of her.'

'I will.'

I climbed into the Golf and took a long look at myself in the rear-view mirror. It had never occurred to me before that Keith might have other children. I don't know why, but I knew I didn't want him to. The more I thought about it the more, for some reason, it started to hurt. I watched as my breath slowly steamed up the mirror, mercifully obscuring my wine-flushed complexion and tousled hairdo. I looked about as appealing as a single sock in the bottom of a tumble dryer. But then I had a brainwave. I'd worn my hair in the same style – a sort of shaggy bob – for years. I could have it cut. Not exactly a new lease of life, but a start. And I'd go to *Janet's* hairdresser to have it done. Quite why I hadn't thought of this before, I don't know, but Janet had obviously had a good stylist with whom she kept regular dates. If Janet's stylist could make my hair look only half as good as Janet's I'd be very pleased – and everyone knows that hairdressers act as part-time confessors to their clients, so, as an added bonus, I could have it done on the paper's time.

I parked my car in the side turning off Kingsmead parade, exactly where I'd parked it when I met Janet in the Garden Coffee Shop. The salon window had a variegated rubber plant trained around it, and through its leaves and the condensation trails running down the glass I could make out a comfortable-looking salon with two elderly women sitting under hoods and a bleached blonde in a bright-green overall pushing hair clippings around with a broom. It was a bit more downmarket than I'd expected, but in the light of the credit card bill I'd just run up at the Rudgeleigh Arms, this was all to the good.

As I entered, the blonde put down her broom and settled herself behind the desk.

I decided not to beat about the bush. I wasn't really in the mood for it. 'I'm hoping you can fit me in right away for a cut and blow-dry. I'm a reporter for the *Tipping Herald*, and I'd particularly like to be done by Janet Cox's stylist.'

The blonde's mouth fell open, revealing a dental brace that looked as if it might serve as a cattle fence in its spare time, and she said she'd have to go and ask Mandy. She returned a few moments later with a green cape over her arm and almost before I knew what was happening – and this could have been due to the Chardonnay – I found myself pinned backwards over a sink with her pouring water over my head and releasing powerful deodorant fumes up my nostrils from the recesses of her armpits.

She ushered me to a chair. 'If you'll just wait here – If you'll just sit forward so I can put this towel round you – This is Mandy.'

The woman who appeared in the mirror in front of me was middle-aged, wire-thin in black top and leggings, and her hair looked to have been sculpted in to her rather stringy neck with a razor. I said hallo to her reflection.

She examined me wordlessly for a moment. 'Hmm. You're growing out a previous style, I take it?'

'Yes,' I lied. 'I'd like you to do exactly what Janet Cox had,' I added rashly.

'All right. Let's see what we can do. I think it will really suit you.'

Our eyes met in the mirror and we both smiled insincerely.

'Can I ask a few questions about Janet while you're doing it?'

'Well, you can ask, but I'm telling you what I told that Detective Sergeant Horton who came round here thinking he was such a hotshot – it's not true that customers tell hairdressers their innermost secrets. You have to treat everything they say here with a pinch of salt – especially when there's an audience.'

'I see.' She tipped my head this way and that, distorting my disappointed expression into pathos. 'Well, could you at least tell me what you told him?'

'Yes. I don't mind telling you that.' She lifted up my hair and let it fall through her fingers. 'Not too badly split really, considering. I told him Janet was late turning up for her appointment, she was in a bad mood, and she left before I'd finished with her – I don't think I tonged her, did I, Sophe?'

'No, you never,' agreed Sophie, handing her a clip.

'So there you are,' said Mandy, putting the clip on half my topknot, and chopping ruthlessly into the rest of it.

I stared in horror as about a year's growth of hair flew in all directions.

'Did he ask you anything else?' I whimpered, eventually.

'Yes. 'Course he did. He wanted to know all sorts of things. He wanted to know where Janet was going when she left here. We said, we don't know. Was she meeting her boyfriend? We said, we don't know. Did her boyfriend beat her up? Did they have kinky sex? We said –'

'OK – I get it.' All I could think about was my beautiful hair hitting the vinyl.

'She could be a right moody cow,' put in Sophie, spluttering slightly through the brace. 'She never gave us a tip that day, and she gave Mandy a right earful because she left her for a couple of minutes to finish off Mrs Ellis. I said to her, if you're worried about being late for your boyfriend or something, you can borrow the phone, but she just gave me one of her looks.'

'I see.' I thought about this. 'What sort of a look exactly? Did you get the impression she was in a bad mood because she was late, or was it because of something else?'

Mandy suddenly let go of my hair and stepped in front of me, so that for the first time I was face to face with her crow's feet. 'Now look,' she said grimly. 'I've already told you, I don't mind you asking questions, but don't go trying to put words into our mouths. Sophie doesn't know why Janet was in a foul mood or why she didn't want to use the phone – how could she?' Mandy went back to her place and resumed her deft snipping. 'I've got a nephew – right? He's a bit of a tearaway, but he's a good boy at heart – he once did three months for a mugging he didn't commit because the police got some stupid woman to think she'd seen something she couldn't have done. I know how the police twist things. So if you think me and my staff are going to make something up just to help you out you've got another think coming.'

She pulled my head back sharply, and I found myself gazing up into the intricacies of a light fitting, just as an alarm bell went off at the back of the shop. I jumped, but neither Sophie nor Mandy missed a beat. 'Go and see if Mrs Brown is done, will you, Sophe?' said Mandy. 'If she is, neutralize her!'

'Right,' said Sophie.

'Right!' said Mandy decisively, combing out my topknot vigorously and pushing my head forward so she could attack the back. 'Now don't get me wrong. I did Janet's hair for ten years – I did it for her on her wedding day – I'd *really* like to know who killed her. First they said it was road rage, and then Sophie says they said on the radio that it wasn't. Have you got any ideas?'

'I wish I did.'

Mandy worked on in silence for a moment, then she said, 'Well, if you ask me, Janet was the sort of person who was always in the wrong place at the wrong time. There's some funny people about these days. I think she had very bad luck, poor soul. Do you know, this time last year she was in here crying her eyes out because Lee wanted them to split. And then along comes this other creep. You have to feel sorry for her, don't you? I put in some highlights for her, that cheered her up.'

'I see.' I held my breath in horror as endless scatterings of hair floated past on either side of my head. 'Why did you call Janet's boyfriend a creep? Do you mean Daniel?'

'That's right – the posh bloke with the double-barrelled name she met through the dating agency. Mind you, I reckon she used to delude herself where men were concerned – do you know what I mean? When she was married to Lee she used to go on about what a perfect husband he was and how he'd never look at another woman, when we all knew he was the sort that'd go for anything in skirts. I was worried this one was taking her for a ride, but she reckoned he was the love of her life. A real whizz kid, apparently.'

'*A whizz kid*?' My head tried to jerk upwards in astonishment. '*Daniel*?'

'Yes. The next Damien whatsit, according to her – you know, that one that cuts animals in half.'

'Oh, I see.' Poor Janet. She must have been really in love.

'She used to go on and on about him being a tortured genius and just needing a break and so on. I don't know anything about art. Do you? I don't think Janet did either. I told her to be very careful. I mean, it's one thing getting your heart broken, but risking your money starting someone up in business – that's another thing.'

This time, my head made it to the vertical. 'Starting someone up in business? What do you mean?' I met Mandy's eyes in the mirror. 'Is that what Janet told you she was doing – starting Daniel up in business?' The words 'Daniel' and 'business' didn't seem to go together at all. But suddenly I thought of all those unpaid bills piled up on Janet's kitchen table, the ten thousand pounds in her bank accounts . . . 'What sort of business? Have you told the police?'

'No, of course I haven't. It was just something she mentioned, *once*, when I was telling her about this problem I've been having with the Inland Revenue. I expect she was just showing off – she used to do that a lot. Where would Janet get the money from to set someone up in business? Do you know how much I had to borrow to get this salon started? It doesn't bear thinking about,' she added, crossly. 'Now come on, take a good look – what do you think?'

She nudged my head forward, and suddenly I was face to face with the mirror.

'See? I was about your age when I had my hair cut short. It's an instant face-lift – right?'

I was dumbstruck. I forgot all about Janet and Daniel and the murder, and stared at myself in disbelief. Suddenly I'd got ears and eyebrows and funny wispy sideburns, and this wasn't at all what I'd expected. Then, my new face started to grow on me.

'You're right!' I exclaimed. 'Oh, my God!'

'Of course, it doesn't last. Take it from one who knows – the day will come when you need a sling to keep your chin out of your soup. Still, you've got a few years yet. What do you think?'

I thought, it's a pity you're a bit short in the tact department, but I said, 'I think I'd better make the most of it. Thank you!'

9

By late afternoon the following day, my thrilling feature on the Millennium Centre had been printed in glowing colour and was on its way to news stands across Tipping. I could hardly wait for tomorrow, when the phone would start ringing off its hook with surprised plaudits from people who'd recognized my name and thought there must have been some mistake. I got myself some tea from the machine, put my feet up on the radiator, and admired the silhouette of my new cheekbones against Tipping's skyline as the lights came on on the dual carriageway. I'd come a long way since the days when I used to admire Tipping's skyline from my kitchen window and wait for the children to get home from school. A very long way.

I picked up my phone and dialled Wayne's number. I was toying with the idea of asking him to meet me for a drink so I could stun him with my new face and make a clean breast of my illegal entry into Janet's flat and all the rest of it at the same time, but at the last moment I chickened out and disconnected the call. Instead, I looked up Daniel Kerr-Dixon's number in the book and dialled it. His phone rang and rang, so I looked up Dino's burger bar and tried that instead.

'Hallo, Dino's? I'm sorry to bother you. Do you think I could have a quick word with Daniel Kerr-Dixon?'

'He's not in.'

'Are you expecting him in later?'

'No. I think he's got a couple of days off. Who's that?'

'It's Chris from the *Herald*. Do you know any other number where I might be able to contact him?'

'Well, he could be at home with Mummy,' remarked the speaker, in a tone sour with sarcasm.

'Oh, really? You wouldn't happen to have the number by any chance, would you?'

'No, I wouldn't.'

'Oh, well, if I give you my mobile number, perhaps you could give it to him when you see him and ask him to call.'

I hung up and looked up the name Kerr-Dixon in the phone book. There was only one entry, for a G. A. Kerr-Dixon at an address in Tipping's leafy outskirts, so I tried it. It didn't answer. I was beginning to get a very bad feeling about Daniel. The police were right: he'd lied. You don't go into business with someone you hardly know. But *Daniel* – and *business*? I reached for a discarded copy of the *Daily Telegraph*, and looked up 'Business Opportunities'. Most of the adverts seemed to want you to sell something, and I couldn't imagine Daniel selling anything. There didn't seem to be any opportunities appropriate to an aspiring artist.

I closed my eyes and imagined myself back in the Garden Coffee Shop with Janet. 'Lee's got money,' she'd said, 'and I want it.' But all Lee had was a dilapidated three-bedroom semi in need of structural repair and an old Rover. What could Janet have been thinking of? Some sort of 'hot' money, perhaps? I thought about this. I wasn't quite sure what constituted 'hot' money – where you got it from or what you did with it, but Lee Cox – would-be gigolo and dodgy Merc salesman – seemed just the right sort of person to have acquired some. I grabbed the phone book again and looked up Hardings. If Lee Cox and Michael Irons had put in a bid for Holly Cottage, it would prove Janet had been right about Lee somehow acquiring a large sum of money. And if there was a large sum of money at stake, it was bound to have something to do with Janet's murder. Hardings's offices were in the Upper High Street. If I hurried, I'd just got time to get there before they closed.

I parked illegally in the little staff car park behind the library and ran up the High Street in the pouring rain. Hardings occupies first-floor offices over a dingy little shop selling made-to-measure curtains at cut prices, squeezed in between an employment agency and an accountant's, and that evening their reception area smelled strongly of stale cigarette smoke and wet umbrellas. I rather suspected that it always smelt of wet umbrellas, even when it hadn't been raining. Their slogan, 'Tenants and Landlords, relax and let the Professionals take care of you', is etched in gold on a large board listing a hundred or so addresses in the Tipping area.

'Can I help you?' asked the woman on the desk.

'Yes. I'd like to speak to someone about a property you manage on Gooserye Common – Holly Cottage. I'm hoping you might be able to put me in touch with the owner.'

'Oh?' She reached for a large, well-thumbed ledger with post-it notes and bits of paper sticking out of it. 'Why – is there some sort of problem with the property?'

'No. But I believe someone may have approached the owner last summer about redeveloping the site and I'd like to talk to them about it.'

'I see.' She gave me a suspicious look, propelled her chair noiselessly across the worn brown carpeting with the ledger clutched protectively to her chest, and put her head round the door of the office behind her. 'Marjorie, could you come out here for a moment, please? There's someone to see you.'

After a few moments, Marjorie, a woman of pensionable age with a penchant for dangly earrings and primary colours, duly trundled out of the office, one hand on her walking stick and the other occupied with a half-inch of cigarette.

'Yes? Can I help you?' Deftly she reorganized the stick and cigarette and offered me her free hand. 'Marjorie Di Carlo, Property Manager.'

'Chris Martin, *Tipping Herald*.' I shook her very warm hand. 'All I want is the name and address of the owner of Holly Cottage so I can talk to them about their plans for redeveloping the site.'

'Redeveloping the site – good God!' She stopped squinting at me through her reading glasses and took them off. 'I don't know where you got that from – we got the go-ahead only last week from the owner's solicitor to extend the tenants' lease for another twelve months! Who told you that?'

'Of course, I didn't want to go into this. 'Well – it was last summer, actually. Both the people involved have since dropped out – one way or another.'

'Oh. Well, I don't know anything about it, but I'd be very surprised.' She sucked the last gasp from her cigarette and stubbed it out in an overflowing ashtray on the counter. 'The place is owned by a woman in Australia, owns a fruit farm or something. Went out there from England just after the war and made a fortune, apparently – bought Holly Cottage to retire to. Of course, I don't think she'll ever come back here now – she must be knocking on a bit.' She chuckled asthmatically. 'But I don't reckon she'd want to go to the bother of selling up either. *Where'd* you say you were from? The *Herald*?'

'Yes. We're – um – doing a piece on how the countryside's being redeveloped. You know – the changing face of Tipping – for the Millennium,' I added, inspired.

'I see.' She looked wary. 'Well, I can give you the owner's name and address, if it'll help, but she's never seen the place, you know. Bought it because it was going cheap,' she added, and collapsed suddenly into a paroxysm of coughing. When she'd finished, she carried on as if nothing had happened. 'I wrote to this woman when we took on the let, told her she ought to spend a few bob on the place if she wanted to collect a decent rent, but she said she didn't want to be bothered. She said just to rent it out on short lets as it was – tatty old furniture and all – until she could come over and take a look at it. We were lucky to find anyone to take it on.'

'I see. So she wouldn't have any idea what the property was worth at today's prices, would she?'

Marjorie shook her head, the multicoloured globes suspended from her ears flying around independently in their own orbits. 'No, she wouldn't have a clue. Like I said, she must've bought it for a song, and she's never spent a penny on it. The previous owner died, you know. If my memory serves me right it never even came on to the open market. Some friend of the deceased advised her to snap it up and the family wanted shot of it as quickly as possible. Property prices were just starting to rise,' she added, nodding sagely.

'So you're the owner's only representative in this country, are you? I mean, if something goes wrong at the house you arrange to get it fixed? Or if somebody wanted to buy the cottage they'd have to come through you to get the owner's name?'

'Yes. I suppose they would. Mind you, now you come to mention it, about ten years ago we got a letter instructing us not to relet the place because it was going to be sold. But then, when the time came, we got the usual renewal notice, so she must've changed her mind.'

'About ten years ago?' Perhaps this was when Michael Irons had his original plans drawn up. 'But you don't know who the purchaser was?'

'No. You'll have to ask her. Our job is to manage the property and oversee the let – that's what we do. Oh, we've been very lucky with the Suttons. I think they hope they can live out their days there. I don't know if we could find anyone else to put in there the way it is at the moment. I mean, it's not just its history, that's all forgotten now, of course.' She gave me a significant look.

'You mean the young man who committed suicide because the BBC rejected one of his plays?'

'Yes.' She laughed, a sound like gravel swirling round in a concrete mixer. '*If* that's what it was all about, of course. I mean, if *you* were writing plays for the BBC, would you be messing around with drink and drugs?'

I had no idea whether I would or not. 'Is that what he's supposed to have done?'

Her eyes glinted. 'They say he used to go up to London on Saturday nights and come back on the milk train on Sunday morning with some bit of skirt he'd picked up. He woke people up revving his engine as he went past Stringer's Cottages – they're not there now, of course – otherwise no one would ever have known what went on up there, would they? It was like the local dosshouse, apparently, you never knew what drop-outs and riff-raff he'd got staying with him. Shot himself that very hot summer – seventy-six, I think – it was probably in your paper.' She studied her cigarette-end speculatively. 'As I say, we were very lucky to find tenants for it. I think the old bat's lost interest in the place now. I think we'll have it on our hands till she dies, and then we'll have the problem of finding somewhere else for the Suttons.' She sighed. 'Sometimes you have to be a flipping social worker in this job. Lorna, give me the book, will you.'

Lorna handed her the book, and she opened it at a well-thumbed red marker. 'Here we are, Mrs Violet Gladstone. I'll write it out for you, but I'm telling you, you're wasting your time. I think she's gone a bit *doolally*. We only ever hear from her solicitors now and *they're* not going to take it on themselves to sell the place, are they? Here.' She found a card, flipped it over, and started to write the address on the back. 'You know what *I* think you should be doing? Something about haunted houses. You wouldn't believe some of the stories we hear!' she remarked, jerking her head towards the address board. 'Mind you, it'd be more than my job's worth to repeat them!'

I followed her glance to the address board.

'Is there a finder's fee for ghosts?' cackled Marjorie. I laughed half-heartedly, but then I noticed something about the address board.

'What a lot of places called something "Court"! I don't suppose you'd know anything about a place called *St Martin's Court*, would you?'

Marjorie shook her head, but Lorna looked up from her keyboard.

'What – that council place? Yes – it got knocked down. I had an aunt who lived there. It wasn't a bad place really. It had hot-air heating.'

'Oh. So why did they knock it down?'

'I don't know. My aunt ran off with the man from Sun Alliance and we haven't spoken to her since 1985.'

She shrugged and turned back to her keyboard, and Marjorie handed me the card. 'Here,' she said. 'Give my love to Lillian in Classifieds!'

'Thank you,' I said. 'I will.'

When I got downstairs it was raining hard, so I bundled up my coat around my newly exposed ears and made a dash for the nearest shop doorway where I could examine the card

Marjorie had given me. She'd written out an address and a fax number. First thing tomorrow I'd send off an urgent fax asking for information on any offers made for Holly Cottage. Of course, there was no guarantee I'd get an answer, but it was the only thing I could think of.

I hurried back to the car in the rain, still wondering about Lee and his mysterious assets. Of course, there was one person who'd know all about Lee's assets – his solicitor, Chandler. You don't lie or prevaricate to your solicitor about your circumstances – that's what you pay them for.

Philip Chandler's address, Ravenswood, is a wide avenue that meanders between broad pavements nobody ever walks along, and is overhung in a well-mannered sort of way by the branches of large trees. In the faint orange glow from the occasional streetlamp it was hard to determine where the grounds of one house ended and those of the next began, so I wound down my window and cruised slowly along, looking for Chandler's house. It was halfway down, where Ravenswood looped back on itself, a small mansion built on top of a rise and half hidden from view by a row of beech trees. The driveway curved between fine lawns, and came to a graceful halt at the foot of an elegant flight of steps which led through a rockery to the porch. This is what you get if you persevere with your law degree.

There were lights on in the house, and also in a flat over the garage adjoining the house. I climbed the steps to the front door and rang the bell in the porch. From the garage flat, I could just hear the ghastly strains of the *Neighbours* theme tune.

After a long pause, the front door was opened by an elderly woman. She put on the porch light and stared at me in its glare.

'Hallo. Is Mr Chandler here? He does know me – I'm Chris Martin from the *Herald*.'

She opened the door another inch for a closer look at me, and a large ginger cat dashed out and disappeared into the darkness on the rockery. 'Oh dear, Mr Tiggywinkle, come back!' she exclaimed, grabbing at him and missing by several feet. 'Oh, *Mr Tiggywinkle*, what *are* you doing there? Come back at once! He's got a dead mouse or something over there, you know. He's been eating it all week and he'll be sick on the carpet.'

She reached absently for my card, and I detected about her person the faint odour of brandy. She was small, rotund and sixtyish, with horn-rimmed glasses and thinning hair.

'Is he in? Are you *Mrs* Chandler?' I enquired, knowing full well she wasn't.

'Oh, no – oh goodness, no!' she exclaimed, and giggled. 'I'm Mrs Champion. Mr Chandler's not back yet. Is he expecting you? He didn't say anything to me. Help me get Mr Tiggywinkle back, will you – he's not supposed to go out at night!'

She lurched out on to the step, and it occurred to me that if Philip Chandler thought he'd got her dried out, he was wrong.

'Oh, Mrs Champion, *of course*!' I gushed. 'I think I've heard about you. Are you the lady he met through the church? Mr Chandler helped to reunite you with your children – isn't that right?'

She gave me an odd sideways look.

'No – the girls never forgive you,' she said, and the remark went through me like a kebab skewer, because I'd just spent twenty-four hours avoiding telling Julie about her new sibling.

She lunged past me to teeter perilously on the edge of the rockery. 'Here, Tiggers, *naughty Tiggers*, I've got a lovely lamb chop in my pocket!' she called enticingly, and to my amazement, she produced a large piece of burnt meat from her cardigan and began waving it towards the cat. 'He's such a naughty boy, but you mustn't give in to them, you know. You have to make them dance to your tune or one day you'll turn your back and they won't be there!'

'Ah. I see.' I began to look on Philip Chandler with new eyes. If he was prepared to allow this woman to rummage through his laundry you couldn't really question his altruism. 'Well, perhaps I could just ask you a couple of quick questions about Mr Chandler while I'm here –'

I turned towards the light to look out my notebook, and a

heavy hand clamped the back of my neck in a vice-like grip. 'Don't move!' she hissed. 'He's right there. Come along, Mr Tiggywinkle, here you are – just let old Granny take care of you –' She let go of my neck and scooped up the bewildered cat into the folds of her cardigan. 'There!' she exclaimed. 'Got you – in you go.' And she bundled him into the house along with the chop and closed the door on him.

I hoped she'd got her key.

'Right. Now what was it you wanted?' she demanded briskly.

'Well, just to ask you a few questions about Mr Chandler.'

'Oh, really!' She folded her arms across her chest in an oddly menacing manner. 'And why's that then?'

'Because – because I'm interested in him, that's why.' I felt compelled to back off slightly towards the top of the steps.

'Oh, you're *interested* in him, are you! I know your game!' Without warning she raised an arm, and if some instinct hadn't alerted me, I'd have been flattened by a right hook.

For a moment, I was too stunned to say or do anything. Then I decided the time had come to discontinue our conversation, and I started off down the wet steps at top speed.

By the time I got to the bottom, Mrs Champion, who obviously knew the steps like the back of her hand, was catching up fast. I flung myself off the last one and made a sprint for my car, just as a black BMW swept into the drive and pulled up behind it. Philip Chandler immediately leapt out and made a beeline for Mrs Champion.

'Is everything all right, Lola?' he demanded. Then he looked at me and did a double take. 'Ah – Mrs Martin from the *Herald*, isn't it?'

'Yes –'

'Good. Fine. I know this woman, Lola. Why don't you go in and I'll deal with it.' In the light spilling down from the porch I could see the worried look on his face.

'No! I'm all right! I wasn't going to do anything!'

'I'm sure you weren't, but please go in,' he said firmly. '*Now*! Put the kettle on for me, will you?'

She hesitated on the step, scowling at me. Before time and

alcohol had taken their toll she'd had fine, strong features – you could tell.

When she was out of earshot, he said, 'I must apologize for Mrs Champion. She can be a bit eccentric – the legacy of a rather tragic life, I'm afraid. No harm done, I trust?'

I was still in shock. 'No – but what was all that about? She just went for me!'

'Oh dear, I am sorry. I will talk to her, I promise. She's very protective, I'm afraid. I've rather taken her under my wing and now she sees it as her mission in life to ensure my welfare. She lives in the old granny flat and keeps house for me after a fashion. You are all right, are you?'

'I suppose so.'

'Good. Good.' He relaxed slightly. 'Look, it's late and I'm tired. Are you here about Mrs Cox again? I've already told you – *and* the police, who incidentally are quite satisfied – I never met or communicated with Mrs Cox and my only contact with Mr Cox was a consultation regarding the possibility of a divorce. I have nothing to say to you. Good evening, Mrs Martin.'

He tried to sidestep me, but I stood my ground. 'Mr Chandler, please – couldn't I just ask you one question about Lee Cox's financial situation? Do you know if he had a large sum of money hidden away somewhere that Janet might have been trying to get her hands on? I'm thinking of – you know – *hot money*.'

'*Hot money*? What on earth are you talking about?'

I blushed. 'I don't know exactly.'

'No. You don't, do you? Will you get out of my way, please?'

He made another attempt to push past me, and this time I decided to let him go, but somehow I wrong-footed myself and ended up almost headbutting him instead.

'Oh dear, I'm awfully sorry,' I exclaimed, in case he rang Mr Heslop. 'I'm afraid I'm really not used to doing this sort of thing. It's only that I met Janet just before she died and I feel personally involved. Did you know that Lee seems to have disappeared? Apparently someone put a scaffolding pole through the front window of his house.'

Philip Chandler looked mildly shocked. 'A *what* through his front window?'

'A scaffolding pole.'

'Good heavens.' He said this in a light, almost flippant, tone, and shook his head, and I came to the conclusion that he wouldn't have cared much if it had been a telegraph pole with the entire exchange system for South-East England attached to the back of it.

'I think Lee may have put in a bid to buy a place called Holly Cottage,' I went on. 'Would you happen to know anything about that?'

'I *beg* your pardon?'

'Apparently the owner lives overseas and doesn't know its value. Couldn't you just sort of give me a hint – has Lee Cox got a large sum of illegally acquired money?'

There was a long silence. After a while I become convinced that Philip Chandler was putting together in his head a particularly virulently worded complaint against me that would be on Mr Heslop's desk in the morning. He'd certainly got no intention of answering questions. I decided to give up.

'I'm sorry, Mr Chandler. Good night,' I said, and I went back to my car, switched on the engine and turned up the heater to maximum. I had the vague feeling I was on to something; I just wasn't sure what it was.

10

Wayne rang me at half past nine on Friday morning, just as I was getting my coat off. He sounded excited. 'Just to let you know, we may be getting a spot on *Crimewatch*.'

'Really!' I was excited, too. 'You mean, for the Janet Cox murder?'

'Yes. We want to appeal for the man and woman who were in the layby to come forward so we can eliminate them from the enquiry.'

'Oh! Gosh. Are they going to do a reconstruction and everything – with proper actors? Will you be on it?'

'I don't know. They're deciding between us and a serial rapist at the moment, apparently. By the way, Kerr-Dixon now admits that Cox had the hots for him, but he says he did his best to discourage her. He's sticking to his story about their relationship being platonic, but I don't believe him for a minute. Some of those hairs we found in the flat were Cox's – they were all tangled up in the headboard of his bed.'

'Ah. Oh.'

'Exactly. You want to hear the latest? Forensics found traces of Cox's blood and bits of grit on the back seat of her car, so we know her body was moved in it. What we think happened is this. Cox went straight to Kerr-Dixon's flat from the hairdresser's. They had tea together, and then they had some kind of a row which ended with Kerr-Dixon bashing her over the head – probably in his yard, because there's a big patch by the bins that's been scrubbed with disinfectant. Then he drove her up to the layby and dumped both her and the car. He must have hitched a lift back to his flat – probably from the petrol station on the dual carriageway about a quarter of a mile away. We're hoping to eliminate the possibility that the man and woman in the layby had anything to do with the murder – and hopefully turn up the motorist who gave Kerr-Dixon the lift. Then we'll be home and dry.'

I didn't follow this at all. 'But what about Elaine? I mean, surely you can't think Janet went straight from the hair-dresser's to Daniel's flat, when –'

'Ah. Elaine. Well, I told you, she couldn't positively identify Cox as the woman she saw. I questioned her for an hour last night, and all she's really sure about is that this woman was wearing something red. She said she *thought* the woman's car might have had a white stripe down the side, but when we showed her a photo of a car – in the dark, in the rain – with a headlamp beam trained on it from the angle Elaine's headlamps would have shone on a car parked in the layby as she drove up to it, she said that could have been what she saw too.' He waited for this to sink in. It sank in, but all I could think of was how upset Elaine had been when she saw the little polythene tent in the layby.

'Elaine seemed really certain to me.'

'Witnesses always are when they're trying to help, love, it's a known phenomenon. That's why the force spends a fortune on improving interview techniques. Look, we know Cox wasn't killed in the layby at five-thirty, it's as simple as that.'

I backtracked hastily through my notes. 'But Daniel says he was with his parents at his flat from seven until ten-thirty. Are you saying they're in on it, as well?'

'No, not exactly, but the only independent witness we've got to corroborate the parents' story is a neighbour who says the father's car was blocking the forecourt at nine-fifteen. Come on – wouldn't you lie to give one of your kids an alibi?'

'For murder?' I shuddered. I'd need time on that one.

'Oh, come on, why are you so determined to find this bloke innocent?' demanded Wayne, irritably.

I didn't want to admit that this was partly because when I'd first met Daniel, he'd reminded me of Richard. I said, 'Look, I know Daniel lied about his relationship with Janet, but there could be *lots* of reasons for that – couldn't there?' Offhand, I was unable to think of one. 'Anyway, what about this – Janet was apparently talking about starting Daniel up in a business. You wouldn't kill a person who was going to lend you money, would you?'

'What?' There was a shocked silence. 'Where the hell did you get that from?'

'From Mandy, the hairdresser. I don't know if it's true, but what do you think?'

'I think Kerr-Dixon's a lying little shit, which we already knew! *Jesus*! How did you find *that* out? Those women in the salon said they knew zilch about Janet's personal life!'

'Well, you should've let them retouch your roots.'

'*What*?

'Never mind.' I had a feeling I had just made things a whole lot worse for Daniel. 'By the way, will it be OK if I ask Daniel a few more questions?'

'Yes. Ask away!'

'Thank you.' I wondered briefly if my part in Janet's last hours would be shown in the reconstruction, and if so, who they'd get to play me. Someone incredibly attractive, I hoped.

'Anyway, the super says I ought to get myself a new suit, just in case I have to go in front of the camera,' said Wayne. 'So I'm off to M and S. Oh, what was it you wanted to talk to me about the other day?'

'Er –' I thought quickly. 'Oh, *that*! It was nothing really. It was just – you remember I told you Janet offered me a piece of gossip about Philip Chandler? Well, Chandler's got this really strange housekeeper called Lola Champion. I just wondered if you've got anything on file on her.'

In the brief silence that followed, I could imagine the face he pulled. 'I don't know. What's her address?'

'Same as Philip Chandler's.'

'All right. Don't forget to watch next week!'

I said goodbye, breathed a sigh of relief, disconnected Wayne and rang down to Dawn in reception.

'Has a Daniel Kerr-Dixon phoned for me at all?'

'No,' said Dawn. 'But Mr Heslop's looking for you.'

At that moment Mr Heslop emerged from his office, looking harassed.

'Ah, there you are!' he said pointedly, as though I'd been missing for a week. 'Look, I'm going to have to put some of these calls through to you or I'm not going to get anything done. My phone's been ringing off the hook about the Millennium Centre.'

'Why?'

'Well, calls seem to be evenly split between people who want to know when the centre is going to open so they can get their kids down on the waiting list for the youth theatre, and people who want to know how much their council tax is going to go up to pay for it. Oh, and everybody is upset about Councillor Draycott's riverside park. I don't think anyone's read your piece properly. Don't waste too much time on individual callers, just try and assess which way the wind is blowing so we can decide how to react.'

'Oh. All right. Mr Heslop – guess what, Tipping's going to be on *Crimewatch* next week!'

'Oh, great! That's wonderful! What – the Janet Cox murder?'

'Yes. And listen . . .' I told him what I suspected about Lee Cox, his hot money and Holly Cottage. His eyes glazed over about two sentences in to my explanation, but he patted me affectionately on the arm, so when he'd gone back to his office I composed a fax to Mrs Gladstone's solicitors in Brisbane. I asked them to get in touch as soon as possible to explain why the plan to redevelop Holly Cottage ten years ago hadn't been taken up, and whether two men had made an offer for the site last summer. Then, on the off-chance, I tapped into Archive and did a random search for references to Holly Cottage. After a long wait – during which I answered three calls from people who wanted to know when the council would start interviewing for staff for the Millennium Centre, and in one case whether there'd be weight restrictions on applicants – a page from July 1976 appeared on screen. I found myself staring back at the then mayor of Tipping with his enthusiastic sideburns and lapels the size of Manchester. Good God, and that was the mayor. The Holly Cottage item was under the headline, 'Suicide verdict'. It said:

The Coroner today returned a verdict of suicide on twenty-four-year-old Miles Anthony Lloyd, of Holly Cottage, Gooserye, who was found dead at his home with shotgun wounds to the head last Saturday. It is understood that Mr Lloyd may have been suffering from depression. His body is to be flown out to the family home in St Helier, Jersey, for burial.

My phone rang again. I ignored it for a bit, fearing another reader might be on the end of it, but this time it was Claire MacInnis.

'That matter we talked about,' she said tensely. 'I've changed my mind. I'm not coming in to your offices. If you want to meet me, I'm in the phone box in front of the post office. And if you're not here in ten minutes, I'm leaving.' She banged down the phone.

I looked out of the window. It was raining. I grabbed my coat and umbrella and ran down the stairs to the street.

Claire was waiting next to a white van which had her name painted on its side. The van was parked on double-yellow lines, and she was shivering under a large black and white umbrella, her face stark and vengeful beneath a black wool hood.

'I was about to go,' she snapped. 'I've only come to tell you you'd better not bother me at the restaurant again. I know my rights. I can get an injunction against you.'

'Why would you want to do that?'

'Never mind. I don't know where Lee is, all right? I met him when I bought a car from him, and I saw him socially a couple of times after that and that's all – so just *leave me alone*!'

'Socially?'

She blushed slightly, which meant that her cheeks took on all the richness of economy magnolia emulsion. 'Oh, sod off, will you? I've got an appointment in half an hour the other side of Hudderston!' She snapped her umbrella shut, opened the passenger door of the van and tossed her handbag on to the front seat.

'Please wait a minute!' I protested, jumping into the gutter and making a grab for the door, but without a word, Claire hit me in the chest with her umbrella. I think the blow landed more solidly than she intended, because she looked almost as shocked as I was. This didn't stop her running round to the driver's door to make her escape, though.

I followed, keeping a wary distance between us.

'Ms MacInnis, I think there's been some sort of misunderstanding. Honestly, all I want is to find Lee before the police do so I can get the story on him and Janet.'

'Tough!' She jumped into the van and slammed the door.

I would have given up at this point, but she'd caught my left breast with the metal cap of her umbrella and it was beginning to throb. 'Fine – I'm giving your name to the police as a contact!' I shouted angrily, and leapt out of the way as she started her engine. Unfortunately a passing pensioner, apparently oblivious to this drama, chose that moment to step off the kerb and somehow or other Claire jumped the van forward and stalled it against his leg.

There was a horrified silence.

'Oh, my God,' said Claire, springing out of the van. 'I'm so sorry! Are you all right? Oh, my God!'

The pensioner muttered something about women drivers and limped off, red-faced, and I decided the time had come to leave, but Claire caught me by the coat sleeve.

'Wait a minute. This is your fault! I've told you a dozen times I don't know where Lee Cox is and I don't care! If that man is hurt it's your fault!

'He isn't –'

'Well, no thanks to you! For the last time, I haven't seen Lee since last August. *Please* don't go to the police and give them *my* name. I *did* have a fling with Lee! It was just –'

A sudden gust of wind blew the rain round the corner of the post office in almost horizontal sheets. We both stood our ground.

'– it was just a stupid, stupid thing!' she gasped, water streaming from the wisps of hair protruding from her hood, and cascading down her nose. 'I saw him less than a dozen times and I've paid for it, oh God I've paid for it! Right – *now* will you get out of my way?'

She made a move towards the van, and I stayed at arm's-length.

'What do you mean, you've paid for it – does your husband know?' I asked.

'That's none of your business!'

She opened the van door and started to climb inside.

'Was Lee Cox *blackmailing* you?' The thought formed itself and tripped off the end of my tongue before I'd had time to consider it. 'Did he threaten to tell your husband unless you paid him off?'

'What did you say?'

Suddenly I was struck by the fact that I was standing outside Tipping post office, from whence not so long ago I used to collect my Child Benefit, demanding to know the intimate details of a perfect stranger's marital problems. A wave of embarrassment overcame me.

'I'm sorry. I just – you know – wondered if Lee tried to make you pay for his silence. Sorry. It was an awful thing to say.'

'Oh, come on – you're enjoying this, aren't you?'

'No, honestly, I –'

'You lead a perfect, boring, blameless life. You have sex every Friday night with some boring man who's been doing it to you just the way you like for twenty years –'

'No, actually –'

'Well, lucky you! OK, you're *right*! Does that make you happy? When I tried to break things off with Lee he threatened to phone Stefan and tell him the whole story unless I paid him. So I *paid* him, all right? And I haven't seen him since! Now leave me alone! If you don't, I'm calling the police!' And she jumped into the van, started up the engine and drove off blind, despite what had happened before, with the door still half open and her windscreen wipers not on.

I stood in the High Street and watched as she weaved off. I hadn't noticed it before, but I was soaked to the skin.

11

Mr Heslop sat at his desk, looking grim, surrounded by readers' letters. I could read the words, 'Sir, I have never written to a newspaper before but I feel I must tell you what I think of the Millennium Centre . . .' from the doorway.

'Nice weekend?' I enquired politely, as he slit open another envelope.

'Not particularly. I'm decorating.' He pulled a letter out of the envelope and glanced at it. 'Damn it – against,' he said, adding it to the biggest pile. 'Dear, oh, dear, I should never have let you give the centre such a glowing write-up. I don't know what Dave's going to think. He's put a lot of work into this and now we're stuck with it. He's not going to like it one bit.'

'What – are you saying they're all against it? But it seems like such a good idea! I mean, the centre's got everything and it's not going to cost anyone anything!' I couldn't believe my carefully crafted prose had failed to enthuse the people of Tipping. 'Oh dear, I hope it's not my fault. What's the matter with everyone? Don't they want to move into the twenty-first century?'

'Apparently not. I blame that bloody Dome. Anyway, I'm going to have to think about this and come up with a strategy. I don't know what we're going to do. Was there something else?'

I sat down. Compared with the crisis facing my Millennium story, it no longer seemed important. 'Well, it's just I've been thinking about Lee Cox. Apparently he was blackmailing Claire MacInnis over their affair, and I was wondering – perhaps he was blackmailing other people as well.'

He wrinkled his brow in distaste. 'Oh dear, how very unpleasant.'

'He could have been blackmailing the other woman he was seeing. Her name was Cherie Jackson, according to the neighbour.'

'Hmm.' He sighed, then settled back in his chair and began to gaze at a hole in the ceiling plaster that had been made by someone ripping down tinsel too enthusiastically on Twelfth Night. 'It's just so depressing, isn't it? Do you know I was talking to an American the other day – at that bridge do I told you about – and he said that what disturbs him most about England today is that when you pick up a newspaper – even a little local newspaper like ours – the news in it could have come from Los Angeles, or Oklahoma City, or – anywhere. Stabbings, blackmail, drugs, child abuse. What's happened to us, Chris? What kind of a nation are we taking into the next millennium?'

I waited patiently for him to get back to the point. Instead he pushed aside a stack of unopened letters and reached for a notepad. 'Whatever happened to the sleepy English market town? Whatever happened to jolly old men selling you hot chestnuts on street corners – to the crime of the month being the local policeman getting knocked off his bike by a cheeky young lad with a snowball? Just because we've moved into a high-tech age, do we really have to forfeit our national soul? Oh dear – I feel an editorial coming on . . .'

I nodded sympathetically as if I'd taken this in. 'So what do you think I should do? Do you think I should try and track down Cherie Jackson and see if she was being blackmailed too? Perhaps there are other women that we don't know about.'

Mr Heslop muttered something about people who'd lost touch with their roots. Then he said, 'The trouble with stories involving blackmail is that you can't print anything about them without a raft of writs arriving on your desk. Wait and see what happens after this *Crimewatch* thing, will you? We've got enough problems at the moment as it is.'

'OK.' I went straight back to my desk and wrote out a note

to remind myself about Cherie Jackson, then dialled Daniel's number from memory.

This time, he answered.

'Hallo, it's Chris Martin from the *Herald*. I'm sorry to bother you so early.'

'What do you want?' He sounded half asleep.

'Well, I just wanted to ask you how it's going. I mean, you obviously know you're now the police's prime suspect.'

There was a shocked pause, during which I thought I heard a bedspring creak violently and a faint scratchy sound, like two people whose heads were close together, whispering.

'Did you know Janet's murder is being featured on tomorrow's *Crimewatch*?' I prompted.

'*What*?'

'You didn't know?' And I wondered for a horrible moment if I'd given away a secret. If so, it was too late now. I pressed on. 'Look, you really ought to tell the truth before things go any further. Do you know what I mean? The police already know you lied about your relationship with Janet – that's why they suspect you. Why don't you tell *me* about it? Perhaps we could print your story in the paper –' Now I could definitely hear whispering. At half past nine on a Monday morning, Daniel had someone else in his bed.

There was a click and the dialling tone hummed in my ear like an angry bee.

I replaced my receiver and made a note of our conversation, then reached for the phone again to redial his number, because I felt a bit concerned about Daniel. I'd got a nasty feeling I'd made things a whole lot worse for him with Wayne. Before I could get to it, though, it rang by itself. I leapt on it.

'Daniel? Is that you?'

'No – it's me!' said Keith, aggrieved. 'I came in early this morning to look up the Broxham system for you –'

'The what?'

'The Broxham system – *St Martin's Court* – remember? Look, I haven't got time for this sort of thing. Do you want it or not?'

I reached for my notebook.

'Right. It was manufactured under licence in Finland although the designer was actually an Australian. It consisted of preformed flat-packed sections made to order at the factory in Turku under rigorous quality control, thermal-wrapped and . . .' My pencil faltered over the shorthand outline for 'Turku'. '. . . Apparently their machinery was geared for accuracy to the nearest point-five of a millimetre, so obviously . . .' I wondered if Daniel was trying to ring me back, and what he would do if he couldn't get through. '. . . and once it had been correctly pre-tensioned *theoretically* the system should have been foolproof, but of course it still relied on the sections being properly handled by the people assembling them. Well, you know what British building contractors are like.'

'Right!' I agreed.

'Anyway, to cut a long story short, I've managed to get hold of some information on seven blocks of flats which were put up in in the early seventies. How many others there were I don't know. Anyway, one developed serious problems with stress fractures within its first year and had to be taken down. One had to be demolished after a gas explosion, and another one was taken down because the foundation housings were defective and it was too expensive to repair. The rest are OK as far as I know.'

I wasn't sure what conclusion I was supposed to draw from this. 'I see. So –'

'So – *obviously*,' he interrupted irritably, 'there's nothing wrong with the system provided the buildings are properly assembled, but unfortunately they often aren't. I hope you've got all that.'

'Yes! That's great. Thank you!' I glanced down at my one and a half lines of badly written notes. 'So – did you come across anything specific about St Martin's Court? Do you know if there are any other buildings in Tipping built on the same system?'

'How could I possibly know that? I just told you everything I found out. Look, I've got someone coming in to see me in a couple of minutes. Did you tell Julie about the baby yet?'

I didn't want to tell him I was still trying to get used to it myself. 'Er, no, not yet. I've been – you know – waiting for the right moment.'

Keith sighed. 'I don't know why you're making such a big deal of this. And you'd better tell her soon, 'cos Sandra's started to buy baby stuff. You know, a cot and a sort of mobile thing to hang over it.'

'Oh.' I swallowed a small lump in my throat. 'And how is Sandra?'

'Very sick in the mornings. I must go, I'm keeping people waiting.'

He went. *Very sick in the mornings*. It was definite, then. I redialled Daniel's number so I didn't have to think about the cot with the mobile hanging over it, but now there was no reply. I let it ring for a long time, just in case. Perhaps he wasn't there, sitting on the sofa Janet had got for him at a discount with his new girlfriend – perhaps he'd gone out. I looked up the number I'd found before for a G. A. Kerr-Dixon and dialled that instead. This time, a woman answered.

'Oh, hallo, I'm awfully sorry to bother you, but could I speak to Daniel please?'

'*Daniel*? He don't live here no more. He hasn't lived here for years. First he was at university, then he chucked that in and they bought him a flat.'

'Oh. I see. Is *Mrs* Kerr-Dixon there then? Could I speak to her, do you think?' I had no idea what you were supposed to say to the mother of a murder suspect, but I knew I ought to try.

'She's not here. She's at her shop. You know – that Yesteryear Boutique place on Church Street. Do you want the number?'

'No, it's all right. I'll find it, thank you.' My heart sank. If Mrs Kerr-Dixon ran a shop, she'd have to let people in. I'd got no excuse for not calling on her and enquiring how she felt at the prospect of weekly body searches in Wormwood Scrubs visitors' wing. I tried to dream one up, but couldn't, so I reached for my car keys and went reluctantly down the backstairs to the car park.

When I arrived at the Yesteryear Boutique, it was devoid of

customers. A woman stood at a small counter at the rear of the shop, shouting at someone down the telephone. She was dressed in a navy-blue suit with white piping round the lapels, and wore her hair in a style with all the fluid, ethereal qualities of a motorcycle helmet. My hopes of empathy flew out of the window, but I did my best to be amenable, studying her displays of fifties kitchen appliances and thirties china, and pretending to admire a set of dismal yellow sherry glasses, circa 1960, while she finished her phone call.

'Can I help you? Those are absolutely charming, aren't they?' she boomed, crossing the shop with one bound and interposing herself between me and the glasses. 'They've just come in from my supplier, and I haven't priced them up yet, but there's a lot of interest in that period at the moment, I can tell you!'

I stepped back and bruised my shin on a very nasty early Habitat coffee table. 'Mrs Kerr-Dixon? I'm Chris Martin from the *Tipping Herald*. I wonder if you could spare me a few moments to talk about your son.'

'About my *son*?'

'Yes – Daniel. You do have a son called Daniel, don't you?'

'Yes.' Her expression went from alarm to suspicion through puzzlement and back again, and at this point, my guilt threshold got the better of me. 'Look, I'm awfully sorry,' I said. 'I know just how you must feel. I mean, if it was my son, I'd be terribly upset and I certainly wouldn't want to talk to complete strangers about it either. But I'm trying to help Daniel. You see, I've got myself very involved in this story.'

For a moment, Mrs Kerr-Dixon looked totally baffled and I began to think there might be two Daniel Kerr-Dixons in Tipping and that I'd got the wrong one's mother, but then she exclaimed, 'Oh, this is about that dreadful Cox woman, isn't it! I should have known! Who gave you my son's name? The police, I suppose! Good God, this is an absolute outrage!'

I tried to apologize again. 'If you would just let me explain –'

'No wonder law and order in this country is in such a state if the police are wasting their time hobnobbing with journalists!' she roared. 'I suppose you've got some sort of a – a *snitch* or something, have you? Gives you tip-offs, does he? Well, you'd better get this straight once and for all. My son is *not* a suspect in Mrs Cox's murder, he was never a suspect. He was interviewed *once* by the police because they found his name in her diary and he helped them as much as he could and that was the end of it. So your *snitch* has told you wrong! Write it down. Go on – write it down.'

I opened my book and fumbled for a pen. I had just realized that I'd heard Mrs Kerr-Dixon's strident tones before – on the background of the answerphone message Daniel had left for Janet.

'Good. Make no mistake – if I so much as see Danny's name in your newspaper *on the same page* as Mrs Cox's you and your editor will be hearing from our solicitors!'

Her eyes met mine briefly. They were aflame with righteous indignation, and I thought, *she doesn't know*. She's got absolutely no idea the police are still investigating Daniel and that he's now their prime suspect. How can she not know? If he's innocent, why hasn't Daniel told his parents what's been happening? After all, they're his alibi.

I pretended to write down what she'd said. I'd got a prickling feeling at the back of my neck. 'Are you close to your son, Mrs Kerr-Dixon?' I asked.

'Of course I am! What kind of a question is that?'

'Well –' I made eye contact with a sad-looking china dog. 'It's just, I'm surprised he hasn't told you. That he's a – you know – a prime suspect.' I tried not to giggle apologetically. 'The police had him in for questioning for a second time and they sent a forensic team round to his flat.'

'What?' Her mouth dropped open. 'What for?'

'Oh – er, well, you know. To look for evidence – hairs and things.'

Mrs Kerr-Dixon slowly turned an interesting shade of puce. *Hairs and things*? How could there be hairs and things in my son's flat? That's absurd! How could the police possibly imagine he killed her?' Her expression lightened, and she wagged her finger accusingly. 'I think you're making this up!'

'I'm not – honestly!'

'Well, in that case this is an absolute disgrace! How dare

they? I've already told the police, Daniel couldn't possibly have had anything to do with the murder because he was with us the whole evening. I had a detective in here for an hour taking my statement. That means they doubt our word! *How dare they*?'

'Well, they say there are no independent witnesses to corroborate your story, apart from a neighbour who saw your husband's car outside Daniel's flat some time after nine, and, you see, the murder took place between seven and eight –'

'*No independent witnesses*! I'm a *magistrate*, for God's sake!' She was beginning to look worried. 'What do they want independent witnesses for?'

'I'm afraid it's because you're Daniel's parents and they think you might lie to protect him.'

'Oh, how *ridiculous*!' She snorted vigorously, and began repositioning china ornaments on the table next to her, knocking some of them over. 'Danny stopped seeing that woman months ago. Surely they can see she's not his type! I don't believe this! It's to do with that silly message he left on her answerphone, isn't it?'

'Yes, that and –'

'Well, there you are! How ridiculous! Danny wanted her to get a carpet for him, that's all, he told me –'

'– that and the fact that she was still ringing him almost every day at Dino's. *She* didn't seem to think their relationship was over.'

'Well – more fool her! My son can't be held responsible for what other people think, can he? He did his best to discourage her.'

'By inviting her round to his flat?'

Her eyes flashed. 'But I told you, that was –'

'And did you know she was trying to raise the money to start him up in business? That doesn't sound like he'd dumped her, does it?'

For a moment, she was stunned into silence. 'What on *earth* are you talking about? Who told you that? Janet Cox had absolutely nothing to do with the gallery!'

'The gallery?'

'The gallery in Brighton Danny wanted to buy into so he

could show his work – isn't that what you're talking about? Who told you Janet was involved in it?'

'One of her acquaintances.'

She gasped in exaggerated disbelief. 'An acquaintance of *Janet*'s told you this and you believed it? Good God, what a suggestion! If this gallery idea isn't as stupid as it sounds, my husband will raise the finance for it. He's looking into it. Where do you think that woman would get twenty-five thousand pounds from, may I ask? She was just a jumped-up sales assistant. For goodness sake!' And she let out a sudden derisive laugh. 'Do you know, I don't know why I'm even listening to this. Nobody with any sense is going to believe any of it! This is some ploy, isn't it – to make me say something you can print. Well, I'm not falling for it. I know who I believe – I believe my son. There was never anything going on between him and Janet – he didn't even sleep with her, *so there* – he told me! He met her through some stupid prank and she's been pestering the life out of him ever since. I warned him about her, and thank God he listened! My son is a perfectly normal young man with perfectly normal desires. He's been going through a bad patch since he dropped out of university and he's made a few mistakes, but I assure you he'll want to settle down one day and it won't be with the likes of Janet Cox! Have you got that? Right! Now I'd like you out of my shop!'

I made a quick note about the twenty-five thousand pounds for the gallery in Brighton and put away my book. I had a sudden urgent desire to get Richard on the phone and tell him how much I loved him. Of course I wouldn't, though.

'Thank you for talking to me,' I mumbled, and weaved round the china displays to the door.

'I don't know what kind of parent *you* are!' Mrs Kerr-Dixon roared, as a parting shot. 'But I stand by my son!'

I hurried out into the street, buttoning up my coat against the wind. Whatever else Daniel Kerr-Dixon was, the police were right – he was an accomplished liar.

12

Julie paced across the living room again and opened the curtains a crack.

'Nope! It's not him!' she announced, with obvious relish. 'He's forgotten, Mum! Why don't you try phoning him again?'

'I told you, he's got it switched off.' I glanced at my watch anxiously. *Crimewatch* would be starting in an hour, and I didn't want to miss it.

'Well, let's just go then, shall we? Come on – you promised. You don't have to go and interview this bloke tonight, do you? Leave it till tomorrow or next week.'

'I can't. I told you, we've got to do it tonight, while *Crimewatch* is actually on. Pete says it'll give us a – you know – a psychological advantage. It could be my big breakthrough.'

'Oh, my God, your big breakthrough!'

Another car droned up the road and disappeared. 'All right,' I said, 'we'll give him another five minutes and then we'll go without him. I don't suppose it'll matter. Daniel wouldn't answer the phone all day – tonight he probably won't answer the door.' An excited shiver ran down my spine. I hadn't meant to, but I was beginning to wind myself up. I got up and started blowing dust off ornaments. Then I heard myself say, 'Julie, there's something I've been meaning to tell you about your father.'

'My father? Oh, you mean that other bloke we used to live with before we got the one who keeps his vodka in our fridge? I didn't know you were speaking to him these days.'

'Don't be silly! You know perfectly well I met him for lunch

129

in the Rudgeleigh Arms last week. Anyway, it's about him and Sandra. Apparently they're going to get married.'

'Oh.' She sounded relieved. 'Well, I knew *that*! I told *you* that, remember?'

'No, you didn't!'

'Yes, I did! Dad and Sandra were acting all soppy one afternoon, and I said to them, should me and Mum start saving up for a toaster, and Sandra giggled. I *told* you.'

'No, you didn't, and anyway – it's not just that. It's –'

'God – Dad took you to the Rudgeleigh Arms! That must have set him back a packet!'

'No, actually, it set *me* back a packet. Why – how come you suddenly know so much about the Rudgeleigh Arms?'

'Oh, there was something in the *Telegraph* magazine about it, that's all – well, not really about the restaurant – it's about this chef that owns it.' She dived under the sofa and pulled out a heap of magazines. 'See? "The twenty chefs most likely to be at the cutting edge of British cuisine into the Millennium". I told you, Sam wants to be a chef. He says the Rudgeleigh Arms is the only restaurant in the area he'd ever eat at. He reckons chefs are going to be the rock stars of the next decade.'

'Oh, really?' I glanced at the magazine. At the bottom of the page, underneath several much larger photographs of his better-known counterparts, was a small picture of Stefan Andre wearing a black silk shirt and sporting curly chestnut hair. He looked quite dishy.

'Anyway Sam says that article's crap, and Pete reckons some of the journalists on the *Telegraph* couldn't write their way out of paper bags,' observed Julie.

'Does he?' I snapped back to attention and looked at my watch. It was nine o'clock. 'All right, get your things. I'll take my mobile and give Pete another call when I get there. Come on, let's go.'

We got in the car and headed for the main road. Julie turned on the radio, and began flicking from channel to channel, which didn't help my jitters. I told her to stop. She snapped the radio off and we drove round the block to Sam's house in silence. 'By the way,' she said, as she opened the car door. 'What was this other thing you wanted to tell me about Dad?'

I didn't want to tell her now. I handed her her books. 'Nothing. We'll talk about it another time.'

'*Why*?' Her eyes rounded. 'Oh, God – is he *dying* or something? What is it? Tell me!'

'It's nothing! Of course he isn't dying. It was just something about him and Sandra and –'

'Oh, *God* – this is about that boring holiday in Wales they want me to go on! I suppose *you* want me to go too so you and *him* can have the house to yourselves for a weekend!'

'No. We –'

'Well, you can *forget* it!' she exclaimed triumphantly, flinging herself out of the car. 'If you think I'm spending three nights under a damp tent just so Dad can show off he can carry me up mountains when I get tired, you've got another think coming! How old does he think I am – *three*?'

At that moment, the front door of Sam's house opened and his tall lanky figure loped out on to the step. Julie's manic glare dissolved instantly, and she ran off up the front path into his arms without a second glance at me. I had no idea what she was talking about. I breathed a sigh of relief and drove off.

Sutton Road, at this time of the evening, was parked bumper to bumper with cars belonging to residents. I drove up and down it, twice, then managed to insinuate the Golf into a small gap on a corner and left it with its rear end sticking out. If anything wider than a Mini passed by, I'd lose my entire rear-bumper assembly. Then I tried Pete's phone again, and managed to get through to his message service. I left a brief message and set off, my heart making a noise like a foetal monitor and the minestrone soup I'd had for tea swirling round uneasily in my stomach. The sky was overcast and starless. I tried not to, but I couldn't help imagining Janet parking her car exactly where I'd parked mine and heading for the alley that led to Daniel's flat, the wind whipping round her exposed knees. In fact, as I crossed the road in the dim glow of the streetlamps I had the awful feeling she was right behind me.

The alley was in pitch darkness, and by the time Janet's

ghost and I had groped our way to the end of it, I was beginning to have more than second thoughts. I hesitated on the top step. To hell with psychological advantages. I could come back later – or tomorrow – with Pete. I turned to go, and something grated sharply under my left foot.

Grit.

Suddenly, the whole thing began to look very nasty. I couldn't wait to get back to the Golf and turn on the engine and the radio. I cast a last nervy glance across the yard towards the flat – and my eye was caught by a sudden movement. Through the gap over the top of Daniel's net curtain, I could see two men leaning against the stripped-pine dining table, one of them clad only in a pair of underpants, and the other in jeans and an overcoat.

And they were kissing. Passionately.

I think I must have sculpted myself to the handrail, stunned into inactivity. After what seemed like a decade the man in the underpants – who I now recognized as Daniel – pushed the other one away and disappeared from view. Daniel then reappeared in the window in a bathrobe, and before I could second-guess what was going to happen next, there was a loud click, the front door opened, and a bright light snapped on. It was one of those three-thousand-watt security lights that instantly illuminates everything this side of the Channel and it caught me bang to rights.

The man in the overcoat stared at me.

'You've got a visitor, Dan,' he said.

All I could think of – and I'm ashamed to admit this – was that I'd been wrong about Daniel. He wasn't anything like Richard at all.

Daniel's thin white hands flew to his mouth. 'Oh, Jesus – it's that reporter I told you about from the local paper! The one that's been on to my mother!'

I immediately turned to go, but it was too late. The friend took the steps two at a time, pushed past me and blocked my retreat along the alley.

'What do you want?' he demanded, aggressively. 'Is this a professional thing – this spying on people – or do you do it for kicks?'

Daniel was now barring my escape down into the yard.

'Will you please let me pass?' I said, with as much hauteur as I could muster. 'My colleague will be here any minute.'

A look passed between them, and I made the decision to count to three, kick the friend hard in the crotch, and then run for it along the alley. I got to two, raised my foot, and in the last nanosecond he moved out of the way. The adrenaline was coursing through my veins like a power shower. 'Dan, you're a real arsehole,' he said, the words coming out like missiles. 'This is your mess, *lover-boy* – you sort it,' and he disappeared into the alley, his footsteps fast and angry.

Daniel jumped on to the lower step. I dived for the alley and somehow in the sudden darkness ran straight into one of the side walls. The trouble was, I wasn't sure which one. Before I could reorientate myself Daniel's hand clamped on to my shoulder. He pulled me round to face him. 'Where are you going?' He sounded aggressive, but then he let go and backed off with both hands raised in a gesture of nonviolence. I think he must have seen my knee come up. 'All right – I'm sorry – OK? No harm done, right? I can explain what you just saw if you give me a chance.'

'No – I have to meet a colleague.'

'What – you get your story and you just go? You said you wanted to hear my side of things. This isn't fair!'

Right on cue, my mobile rang. I managed to retrieve it and answer it.

'It's me. I'm on the train,' said Pete. 'Where are you? Don't do anything till I get there.'

'I'm at the address, talking to the interviewee.'

'What?'

'I said, I'm with Mr Kerr-Dixon. How long will you be?'

'I'm just passing through bloody Weybridge!' expostulated Pete, and I could hear all the fitments rattling as the train hit a bend.

'I see. You're on your way then. Good.' I hesitated. If Daniel had been toying with the idea of bashing me over the head, he would surely think twice now he knew he'd only got a few minutes to dispose of the evidence. 'Well, Mr Kerr-Dixon wants to talk so I might as well get on with it.

You know where the flat is. See you in five minutes,' I said coolly to the phone, and disconnected Pete before he could respond.

Daniel looked for a moment as though he might have changed his mind about wanting to talk, but he led me down to his flat and showed me inside. The television was blaring out the end music to the nine o'clock news. I had a quick look round to check on the proximity of blunt instruments, and there were lots of them, all easily to hand, but I sat down anyway and got out my book. I was beginning to feel a bit sick.

'All right,' said Daniel. 'So now you know – I'm gay. It took me twenty-three years to find that out for certain, and *you've* got it in one.'

I blushed. I was so taken aback I had no idea what to think or what to say. 'I'm sorry, but I'm afraid I don't understand,' I said finally. 'First you say you hardly knew Janet, then it turns out you did. You say you didn't sleep with her –' I glanced towards his bed with its ornate brass head. 'But apparently you did. *You* say you had no relationship with her – *she* told people you were the love of her life and she was going into business with you. *Now* it turns out you're gay –' I stared at him in disbelief. 'So, what I don't understand is this, if you're gay –'

'Oh, you want to discuss my sexuality, do you?' Daniel interrupted angrily. 'Well, I don't! I've been talking about it to idiots like you – teachers and agony aunts and so-called counsellors – since I was sixteen! I've read the leaflets, seen the video, got the T-shirt. If anybody else wants to discuss it with me they can take a ticket and get to the back of the queue!' He drew savagely on the cigarette he'd just lit. 'Look, I only met Trevor just before Christmas. Before that, I didn't know I was gay – not for sure. Yes, OK, I did have a relationship with Janet. She was crazy about me, and I was flattered. I needed somebody, OK? Then I tried to cool it off, but things got – well, sort of complicated. Then one night Trevor walked into Dino's, and my life suddenly fell into place. I wanted to come straight out with it and tell everybody, but I knew my parents would have had a fit and

I thought I could – you know, let Janet down gently. Then this happened –' He shrugged in a gesture of helplessness, then added sharply, 'What did you want me to do – tell my parents, hey, guess what, you remember that woman I used to sleep with, I'm a suspect in her murder enquiry and by the way, I'm gay?'

'I see.' I took this in slowly. 'So you're saying all the lies started because of Trevor. You lied to your parents because they'd have had a fit and to Janet to spare her feelings – is that it? This money you're hoping to borrow for the gallery didn't have anything to do with it then?'

He immediately turned scarlet, and I knew I'd struck home. After a moment, he said, 'Look, I don't expect you to understand, and I don't care. All right, I'm a shit.'

I was still trying to make sense of it. 'So who is lending you the money? Was it going to be Janet? Or is it your father? Your mother said your father was going to finance you.'

'Oh, yeah, *right*!' He banged his hand down on the table. 'You don't know my dad. He's still pissed off with me for dropping out of university, and he thinks painting is for wankers! He's pissing about with accountants and lawyers – and the guys want the money by the end of February, latest! Look, this is my big chance to make a career out of painting, which is the only thing I've ever wanted to do. Can't you understand that? The plan was to keep my mouth shut about Trevor and take the money from whoever came up with it first – preferably Dad, of course. But if it was Janet I'd've drawn up a proper legal agreement with her – I wasn't trying to screw her, if that's what you think!' He leaned forward. 'The gallery is in Brighton, in The Lanes. It's going to be a sort of co-op – you know, we all share everything and nobody tells anybody else what to do. The location's perfect and I don't care if I have to do crappy stuff for a while to sell to tourists. I'm still hoping Dad will come through – that's why I don't want any of this to come out.'

It sounded like a project doomed to disaster, but I decided not to point this out, because Daniel's eyes were gleaming as though he could already see the canvases parading across the walls with his signature scrawled in their bottom right-hand corners.

I also decided that Daniel had been right about something else: he *was* a shit, but fortunately before I could tell him so, the *Crimewatch* theme tune thundered out threateningly from the fingermarked TV set on the kitchen worktop, rattling the beer bottles in the sink, and Nick Ross appeared on screen. Daniel reached for the switch and fiddled with the volume control, and I dropped my pen and leaned forward eagerly. There was a brief pause, and then Nick Ross smiled his kindly smile, wished us all good evening, and began reciting the roll-call of crimes last month's programme had helped to solve. It crossed my mind briefly that at this moment up and down the country law-abiding citizens everywhere were sighing smugly over their Cadbury's Highlights and thanking God they'd resisted the temptation not to pay for that pack of Polo mints they picked up in the newsagents the other week when no one was looking – and that if I wasn't sitting next to a prime suspect in a murder case I would be one of them. I glanced at Daniel. He was biting his fingernails, riveted to the set.

'. . . *We begin with a murder that has got police baffled,*' said Nick, shaking his head and contriving to look baffled himself. *'This really is a very puzzling case and the police are desperately hoping for some help on this one.'* Suddenly, a headshot of Janet appeared on the screen and Daniel and I let out spontaneous gasps. *'The victim, Janet Cox, was found lying next to her car in a layby just outside Tipping. The postmortem later showed she'd died of head injuries, but contrary to stories circulating in the local press at the time, it's now not thought she died as a result of a road rage incident. Now, at this stage Hudderston police don't want to reveal too much about the case, but they would like anyone who can give them any information about a man and a woman seen in the layby at about five-thirty on the evening of Tuesday January the twentieth . . .'* Janet's face was supplanted by a photograph of the layby swathed in police tape. *'. . . to get in touch with them immediately. I think we've got a map coming up to show you exactly where the layby is.'* The map came up. *'Good. Now if it was you, please do come forward. It's absolutely vital that the police establish as quickly as possible whether this couple have any connection with the enquiry. Hudderston police's phone number is coming up on screen now, or you can as always speak to one of our researchers. Now, crimes involving the elderly are particularly unpleasant and I'm afraid our next case . . .'*

Daniel let out an involuntary yelp, and I leapt to my feet in astonishment, as on screen the faces of unidentified pensioners in National Health spectacles flashed up in quick succession. Surely there must have been some awful mix-up at the BBC. No Wayne! No DI Carver! No establishing shots of Tipping High Street with people one might be able to recognize in freeze-frame coming out of Boots –

'*There*!' exclaimed Daniel, switching off the set with a flourish. '*Nothing* about me! That means I'm off the hook! Doesn't it?'

I stopped wondering what had happened to Wayne and his new suit. I got up, and we faced each other across the table. I decided on a stab in the dark.

'If you're innocent, why did you get your parents to lie to the police to give you an alibi?'

'What? That's rubbish! My parents would never lie to the police! Mum's a magistrate!'

'But she did – and the police know it. And I can prove it.' This was a bit of an exaggeration, but I'd been thinking about it while I paced the living room waiting for Pete and I'd got a theory. 'That message you left on Janet's answerphone – the one you said was about carpets – you asked her to call on you between six and eight. I think that's because you weren't really expecting your parents until *after eight* – not at seven, like they said. I think they lied to give you an alibi for as much of the evening as possible. I'll bet if I checked I'd find that your father gets home from work every evening at seven.'

His blush spontaneously combusted for the second time that evening. 'But that makes it sound as if my parents think I killed Janet, and they don't – I *didn't*! Is that what the police think? Look, Mum didn't want me getting mixed up in an enquiry, that's all.'

'Why not, if she knew you were innocent?'

'Because she didn't like Janet, she said she wasn't *"our sort"*.' He produced an exaggerated impression of his mother's accent. 'It was my day off, OK? I phoned Janet from Mum's shop to warn her my parents were coming round. I didn't have time to explain.' He hesitated. 'Mum thought I wasn't seeing Janet any more. That's why I made up the story about the carpets in the first place. For her. I suppose that's really how the whole thing got so tangled up.'

'I see.' I put my book away. I'd had about as much as I could take of Daniel with his damp bathrobe and matted chest hairs. I almost felt sorry for his mother, even though she'd mistaken me for the sort of woman who'd want to display a set of 1960s-style sherry glasses on her sideboard.

He didn't try to stop me as I made for the door.

'What am I supposed to do now?' he demanded, bleakly.

'You ought to go to the police and tell them the truth as soon as possible. Really, it would be the best thing.'

'You think they'll believe me?'

Since he obviously didn't expect an answer to this I decided not to depress him with one. Then, on the step, I thought of something.

'Your friend Trevor – did he go round to Janet's flat a few weeks ago and threaten to beat her up? Was he jealous?'

'What? Oh, p-*lease*!' said Daniel, and slammed the door in my face for the second time in our acquaintance.

I ran up the steps and into the alley. Halfway along the alley a throaty roar accompanied by the rattle of loose exhaust pipe bolts echoed between the walls like a precursor of doom, and when I emerged on to the forecourt of The Grange, Pete's MGB was hurling itself to a halt in the gateway. We only just stopped short of a messy collision.

'You all right?' he demanded, leaping out of the car, accompanied by a scattering of old car-park tickets. 'I thought you were going to wait for me – there was a power failure on the bloody tube and I've been stuck in a tunnel under Green Park for two hours with a bunch of claustrophobics! What happened?'

I told him.

'Jesus!' he exclaimed, pulling a face. 'What a little shit! I hope you told him to take his toothbrush when he goes down to the station. Do you believe him?'

I still wasn't sure. 'Sort of. What do you think?'

Pete leaned against a brick pillar with a precarious-looking concrete ball on top of it and appeared to be thinking the matter over. Finally he rubbed his eyes and produced one of his best smiles, of the sort that had first reminded me there's more to life than a freezer with perfectly labelled contents. 'Actually, darling, all I can think of at this precise moment is how sweet you look with the new hairdo, and how much I'd like to be at home having this discussion with you over a bottle of wine. What do you say?'

He walked me to my car.

'Pete, how do you think a woman like Janet Cox would be able to raise twenty-five thousand pounds by the end of February?' I asked, as he opened the door for me.

'I don't know, how would a woman like Janet Cox be able to raise fifteen thousand pounds by the end of February?' he repeated mechanically, as though it were a joke.

'Well' – I got into the car – 'how about by taking over where her husband left off with his blackmail victims?'

'Uh huh.' He reached in to help me with my seatbelt. 'I see where you're going with this, darling, and I don't want to dampen your enthusiasm, but in real life women don't usually kill people to stop their husbands finding out they've had affairs.'

'No. I know. But supposing Lee Cox wasn't just blackmailing women he'd had affairs with – supposing he'd moved on to something bigger.'

'Such as?'

'Well – something Michael Irons put him on to. Perhaps what Michael Irons and Lee Cox were involved in together wasn't a property deal but a blackmail plot. I'll bet it's got something to do with those old files that belonged to Michael Irons. And maybe that's why Janet was in Marjoram Mews that day – to try and get Irons to help her!' I added, excited now.

'Ah. I see. Some long-forgotten scandal from the greed-is-good eighties, you mean, when nobody was anybody unless their salary looked like an extract from the New York phone book.'

'Yes. Exactly. Because there was definitely something peculiar about that Holly Cottage deal back in eighty-seven –' I just stopped myself from repeating Keith's remarks on the ethics of property development. 'And then there's St Martin's Court, which I haven't found out anything about yet, except that it was system-built and the council took it down in a hurry.'

'Oh.' Pete looked mildly interested. 'You know, quite a few councils got their fingers burnt over system-building. You could be on to something there.' He shivered. He was only wearing his thin leather jacket, the one I bought him for his birthday last autumn, over a shirt. 'How much did you say Lee Cox took this MacInnis woman for?'

'I don't know. She didn't say.'

He shrugged. 'Oh. Well, you ought to find out. There's all the difference in the world between playing games for pocket money and being in the grown-up league.'

'Yes, I see what you mean.' I thought about this. 'I do see what you mean. I could try and find this other woman – perhaps she'll be more forthcoming.' I kissed his cold nose. 'Why aren't you wearing that coat I bought you in the sale? I spent hours choosing it. Don't you like it?'

'Of course I like it. You bought me this too. I like this.'

'But you're cold! What's the point of having a coat if you don't wear it?'

'I'm only cold because you're making me stand here and listen to all this.'

I gave up. 'All right. Let's go home.'

The following morning I made my way through the usual snarl of rush-hour traffic to the semiindustrial outskirts of Hudderston, and, after several slow-motion laps with a street directory, finally found the site occupied by Radley's Road Haulage. It consisted of a squat, ugly office building, two cavernous workshops and a large bleak area parked up with the front parts of lorries, the back parts of lorries, and sort of container things decorated with rust streaks.

I parked in front of the office building next to a brand-new red MG that Pete would have given his eye teeth to own, and got out on to the forecourt. The office building had two unmarked doors at either end, and no windows on the ground floor. In fact, only the presence of a copy of Yellow Pages at one of the windows suggested that it might be the office building. I've had some very nasty experiences in paint shops and builders' yards where there are no 'Reception' or 'Toilets' or 'Entrance' signs, from which I've learnt that if you're not careful you can find yourself accidentally stumbling across a urinal that won't have been flushed since well before cars were fitted with radios as standard. I huddled against the Golf in the Force Nine gale blowing over the tarmac, and a lorry thundered past at thirty miles an hour to screech to a halt outside the workshop with a tremendous rattle and squawks of protest from its braking system. The driver jumped out lithely, leaving his cargo to carry on clattering slowly to a halt, and disappeared into the workshop without a second glance at me.

There was no one else around to ask, so I opted for the door on the left, climbed a flight of uncarpeted concrete steps, pushed open another unmarked door, and found myself in a large neon-lit room furnished haphazardly with desks, computers and filing cabinets, all seemingly linked together by a lethal web of multicoloured, dusty-looking cables. A woman of about fifty with aggressively auburn hair seemed to be the only occupant of the room, seated at one of the terminals. 'Yes?' she demanded, peering at me in surprise over the top of her glasses.

'I'm sorry to bother you. I'm looking for a woman called Cherie Jackson, who I think used to work here. Can you help at all?'

'Cherie *Jackson*?' Several of her chins dropped even lower. 'Do you mean Mrs Bolt?'

'Oh! I don't know.' I took in the gleaming male pin-ups on the partition behind her. 'Do I?'

'Well, that's the only Cherie we've got that I know of.' She took the glasses off and let them dangle on their gold chain. 'She's Mr Bolt's widow. Do you want to see her? What's it about?'

'Well, it's personal, actually. Hang on a second!'

Before I could stop her, she'd grabbed her phone and dialled a number, her face aglow with intrigue and Max Factor Lasting Performance. 'Cherie? It's Jan. I've got a woman here to see you, says it's personal ... What? ...' She clapped her hand over the mouthpiece. 'She says what's it about.'

'Er – tell her it's about Mr Cox.'

'It's about a Mr Cox!' exclaimed Jan, spinning round on her chair. 'Yes, that's it – Cox! You know, like the apple. Shall I ask her ... Oh! All right.' She dropped the phone back on to its cradle in surprise. 'Well! She says you can go in! Lucky you! Down the end, second door on the right.'

'Ah. Thank you. Is – um – is Mrs Bolt –?' I couldn't quite make up my mind what question to ask, so I didn't bother. 'Thanks. Second door on the right.'

The door had an impressive patina of handprints on its fingerplate and, at last, a sign. It said, in neat gold lettering, 'Managing Director'. For a moment I thought I must have taken a wrong turn at the filing cabinets. I glanced over my shoulder at Jan, and she nodded enthusiastically, so I knocked and went in.

The room contained a large desk cluttered with files, phones, and paper cups. Seated at it was a petite, pretty blonde in a very nice suit who at first appeared to be in her late thirties. Then you noticed the thinning hair, the permanently startled expression, the taut, curveless limbs.

'Er – excuse me, I'm looking for Cherie Bolt,' I said hesitantly. 'Have I come to the right place?'

'I don't know about that.' She had a hard voice. 'You are?'

'I'm Chris Martin from the *Tipping Herald*.' In my wildest dreams I couldn't have expected to come across Cherie Jackson/Bolt as easily as this so I hadn't worked out my pitch. 'Oh dear, this is rather awkward. I've been given your name as a friend of Lee Cox's.'

Her eyelids remained half closed. She looked at me along the tip of a too-perfect nose. 'Who by?'

'By one of Mr Cox's neighbours. I'm investigating the possibility that Mr Cox has relationships with women and then blackmails them,' I said, and looked away hastily so neither of us need be embarrassed. 'I mean, *obviously* none of this is going to appear in print. I'm not even really interested in the blackmail. I'm following up the story of *Mrs* Cox's death.'

To my surprise, when I looked up, one corner of Cherie's mouth had tweaked into a smile. She sat back in her chair and crossed her legs with a little silken swish. 'Let me ask you something,' she said. 'Do I look stupid?'

'Sorry?'

'Come on, I've got a man coming in in five minutes to sell me two hundred and fifty thousand quids' worth of forklift trucks. Believe me, it would take someone a lot smarter than Lee Cox to play silly buggers with me!'

'Oh!' I didn't know what to say. 'I'm awfully sorry. I didn't mean to offend you. There's been a misunderstanding, obviously.' A flush started at the back of my neck and worked its way forward. 'I'll see myself out.'

I turned to go.

'Oh, for God's sake!' she snapped. 'Come back and sit down! I never said you'd offended me. Come on, any idiot with half a brain could see what sort of bloke Lee was. Do you really think I'm stupid? I didn't mind paying for my pleasures.'

'Oh.' I hesitated in the doorway. 'But I thought you said –'

'I said he wasn't *blackmailing* me, I never said I didn't pay him for his services.'

'Oh. Ah.' I hovered over her desk uncertainly.

'Well, what's the difference?' She reached out impatiently, snatched my handbag and dropped it on her desk. '*Sit down*! You pay for everything else in this life, don't you? You needn't look so po-faced! Listen, I was married for twenty years to a bloke twenty years older than me who couldn't get it up most of the time, and I never complained – it was part of the price. Well, he's gone now, and I've had a gut full of men who think they're Casanova, whingeing on about their wives and wanting their egos massaged. I'd rather write out a cheque.' She smiled sweetly, and pushed an untidy stack of papers and old Christmas cards to one side so that we were face to face across the desk. 'So what's all this about then? Are the police looking for Lee, or what?'

I tried to banish the image of Cherie in a silk negligée, discarded underwear in one hand, casually writing out a cheque. 'For his wife's murder, you mean? No – I don't think they think he's got anything to do with it. Actually, they suspect the boyfriend.'

'I see. And what about you? What do you think?'

'Me?' I was flattered. 'Well, as a matter of fact I've got a sort of theory. I think Janet tried to blackmail one of her husband's blackmail victims.'

'Oh, right. So in other words, you had *me* down as a suspect –'

'Oh, *God*, no!'

She leaned forward. 'Well, I hope you know what you're doing. Do you? I suppose you realize there are some very unpleasant people in this town.'

And I knew immediately she wasn't talking about the sort of yobbo with no trolley etiquette one meets in Tipping supermarkets. I laughed.

'Christ!' snapped Cherie, angrily. 'What are you – retarded, or something? I don't know why I'm bothering with you. Show yourself out and ask Jan if my forklift-truck bloke has arrived yet, will you?'

Of course, I stopped laughing straight away. 'I'm sorry – what do you mean?'

'*What do I mean?* What do you think I mean? Haven't you seen what happened to the front of Lee's house?'

'Yes. But that was an accident, wasn't it? His neighbour said a lorry ran out of control –'

'Oh, don't be ridiculous! Do you think I don't know what I'm talking about? I'm telling you, that wasn't an accident – it was a contract job.'

'A *contract job*?' My mouth fell open indecorously. 'But that's – I mean –' I began to wonder if Cherie was quite all right in the head, or if the last chin-tuck had gone a bit too deep. 'Well, I suppose it would explain why Lee decided to do a bunk,' I said, just to humour her.

'Decided to do a bunk –' She raised her eyebrows. 'Who told you that? I suppose they also told you he'd gone to Florida, did they? Well, dream on. Oh, it's no skin off my nose,' she added quickly. 'If you must know, the bastard bummed a couple of hundred quid off me the last time I saw him and I'd like it back, that's all. As it happens, I know someone who knows someone who knows this mate of his in Miami – the one he reckoned he was going to join up with – so I checked.'

'I see.' Our eyes met briefly. 'So you think –'

'Oh, no! *I* don't think anything. That's down to you.'

For a moment I said nothing. I couldn't quite make up my mind about Cherie; I couldn't work out what her agenda was or if she had one. 'So someone takes a contract out on Lee, and then he disappears,' I suggested finally. 'Because of the blackmail, you mean?'

'Well, so *you* say. I'm telling you what I know, which is that *somebody* delivered a message to him in a flat-bed truck – and four weeks later he's not answering his phone. You work it out.' She flicked back her jacket sleeve to examine her watch. 'Now come on, that's it. You've had all you're getting. If you do happen to run across Lee at any time and he's got his wallet on him, tell him I want my cash back. Go on – this bloke'll be here any minute and I've got to make myself look presentable.'

But you are eminently presentable, I thought enviously, as she opened a drawer and produced a mirror. 'You haven't told me anything!' I protested, getting up. 'What about Janet? I told you, according to my theory –'

'And *I* told *you*' – she interrupted, reaching for my handbag and tugging irritably at its clasp – 'that my relationship with Lee was strictly business. I know nothing about his wife! See yourself out, and make sure you don't come round here again asking questions, because I don't want my staff thinking they know all about my private life. Understand? Because the next step from that is they want us to be all-girls-together, and then I have to fire them, and then I have to go to tribunals to explain why I've fired them – and I really haven't got time for all that. Got it?'

I got it. I shook her hand, taking care in case I crushed it, and wondered if I dared point out it was *my* handbag she was going through, looking for cosmetics.

'Er, I'm sorry, but I think that's my handbag you've got there . . .'

Cherie muttered something under her breath and pushed things back into it without apology.

In the doorway, I said, 'By the way, can you remember exactly when was the last time you saw Lee?'

'No. I haven't got my cheque book with me.'

'Oh.'

'Wait!' She called me back as I was shutting the door. 'Matter of fact, I *do* remember when I last I saw him. It was here, in the office. The first Tuesday in September – I was in the middle of a meeting so I told him to sod off.'

'Oh.' I thought this piece of information over. 'But wasn't that a bit unusual, him coming into your office? I mean, I thought you said your relationship was –'

'Look, just push off, will you? You asked me a question and I've answered it. *Bugger off*!' She picked up her phone. 'Jan? Where's that forklift fucker?'

13

I rang Hudderston Central as soon as I got in and asked to speak to Wayne, but they wouldn't put me through.

'Is it about the *Crimewatch* programme?' enquired the operator chirpily. 'We've got a team of officers taking calls, but I'm afraid they're all busy at the moment. You can either leave your name and number now, or ring back later if you would prefer to remain anonymous.'

'Oh!' I was intrigued. 'Are you getting a lot of calls then?'

'Yes. And if you were going to point out that the BBC map showed Tipping with one "p", we know that already, thank you. We had nothing whatsoever to do with the production of the map.'

'I see. Well, could you just tell DS Horton that Chris from the *Herald* rang, and the next time he talks to Daniel Kerr-Dixon he should ask him about Trevor. Got that? *Trevor.*'

'What? Trevor who?'

'I don't know. Just tell him and say it came from Chris.'

I hung up. Mr Heslop's door was closed, so I rang through to Classifieds.

'I want to put an ad in under "Personal", please,' I said. 'And I know it's past your deadline for this week but this is the newsdesk here and I'm afraid it's urgent.' There was a furious silence, so I rushed on quickly: 'We want you to put, "St Martin's Court. Ex-residents, please contact Chris Martin at this newspaper as soon as possible in connection with confidential investigation."' I waited through another silence. 'Have you got that?'

'Yeah – who's paying for this?' asked the girl suspiciously.

'We will,' I said rashly. 'Oh, and you'd better put in my home phone number for p.m. calls.'

Next I rang Tipping Council and asked to speak to someone who could give me some information on the untimely demise of a block of council flats. After about fifteen minutes of being passed via Housing, through Building Control, Planning, and back to Housing, I finally got hold of someone who was able to give me a name and reference number to write in to. I dashed off a letter, marked it 'urgent', and took it down to the post room for dispatch by fax and first-class mail. Of course, I knew I'd eventually have to resort to trawling through reams of council minutes, but it helps if you know where to look.

Mr Heslop's door opened just as I finished with the letter.

He scowled at me. 'What happened with the programme last night? A bit of a let-down, wasn't it?'

'I know,' I agreed. 'My video recorder missed it completely because the clock was three minutes slow. But listen, I've got a new theory –'

'Oh, for God's sake, Chris, we haven't got time for it now! There's a major row brewing over the Millennium Centre. As far as I can tell, things are running at about sixty-forty against –'

'*Against*?' I was aghast. '*Why*?'

'Oh, lots of reasons.' He dumped a fat file on my desk. 'Mainly, people don't want the library to move. Then there's traffic. They don't want the bottom end of town blocked off by giant cranes and traffic diversions and scaffolding for months or years on end. When push comes to shove, people just want to be able to drive their daughters to their ballet classes and get there on time without having to make detours via Portsmouth. In fact, to most people, the Millennium is just a sort of big Christmas and they don't see why they should have to have their lives disrupted because of it. I find it most depressing,' he added, with a sigh. 'Anyway, you're meeting Councillor Ormond at two o'clock this afternoon to get some answers. Make sure you tape the interview, too, so we can pin him down on it later if we have to. This is going to be a very messy business.'

'Oh, God!' I murmured, terrified. 'What sort of answers do you want me to get?'

'Well, read the letters, for God's sake, and find out! I warn you, if we get this wrong, we'll all be going into the Millennium with salary cuts.'

When I arrived at Harewood Farm that afternoon, the Christmas tree had gone from the yard, and half a dozen rather nice cars were parked in its place. A new red BMW, a Toyota Celica, that sort of thing.

Councillor Ormond answered the door himself. He did a double take when he saw me.

'Oh!' he exclaimed, taking my hand in both of his and shaking it warmly. 'It *is* you! The new hairstyle – sorry, it took me by surprise. Gosh – I like it. Turn round.'

I blushed and shuffled round in an awkward circle.

'Hmm. Don't take this the wrong way, but it makes you look quite different. More – I don't know – sophisticated and dynamic. I really like it. It's amazing how changing just one aspect of a person's appearance can have such a dramatic effect. Anyway, come in and let me take your coat.' And at that moment, somewhere at the back of my mind, something peculiar happened. A half-formed thought let out a loud shriek for attention and then dived for cover in the shadows without letting me have a proper look at it. I couldn't for the life of me work out what it was, but I knew it had something to do with someone changing their appearance . . .

'Sorry, have I embarrassed you?' enquired David Ormond, taking my coat. 'Oh dear, I didn't mean to do that. Let's go straight to my study. Carol's got some of her buddies over this afternoon. I think she wants to show off the ring I've just given her for our anniversary.'

I followed him to his study. We could hear squeals of female laughter issuing from the other end of the corridor, and the words 'husband' and 'pathetic' being bandied about with malign relish.

He seemed to wince slightly. He pulled out a chair for me and I declined a drink. I had already worked out a headline for my piece – 'The Millennium Centre – the questions *you* want answered', and accepting a drink from Dave Ormond wouldn't really have been in the spirit of things. 'Well, well –' He settled back in his chair. 'So what's the latest from our esteemed electorate? Is it true you've been getting whingeing letters about the centre?'

I immediately felt slightly offended on behalf of Tipping's electorate.

'Well, I don't know about "whingeing". A lot of people just feel the scheme is a bit over the top for us. Didn't you get that impression from the calls we referred to you?'

'Well – you always get a few dissenters. But don't forget it's usually only the people who want to complain who bother to get in touch. The vast majority of Tipping residents *haven't* responded so I think it's safe to assume they're in favour.'

'Oh.' I wasn't quite sure I followed the logic of this. 'Or perhaps they just can't be bothered to express their opinions?'

He smiled slightly, and of course I remembered then that people not bothering to express their opinions is mainly how democracy works.

'Well, go on, then – shoot!' he urged.

I got out my tape machine and set it up. 'Sorry, but Mr Heslop thought it would be a good idea.'

'I bet he did. You carry on.'

'OK. Firstly, lots of people seem to be worried about the library moving to the other end of town. They say it doesn't matter how wonderful the new library is if people can't get to it because of the buses.'

'Oh. I see.' He gazed out of the window for a moment. 'You know, I suppose when you've got a couple of cars standing by all the time it's easy to forget what it's like having to rely on public transport. All right, I'll try and get some input from the bus company.'

'What – you mean ask them to lay on special buses? Really? Can you get them to do that?'

'Of course I can't! And it'll be up to the Highways Department as well.' He reached for a pad. 'But if I can convince the bus company they'll make bigger profits by tinkering with a few of their routes, we'll be halfway there. Leave that one with me. Go on, next point.'

Ten minutes later I'd put to the councillor all my questions on traffic congestion, disruption to residents during building, and cost, and he'd addressed them all and come up with quite a few answers. Except on the issue of traffic, of course, but then he isn't God.

I was impressed. I began to feel a whole lot more optimistic about the centre.

I switched off the tape.

'Right,' said Dave Ormond. 'I think I'm going to insist you have a sherry. They're awash with some sort of punch down there but I don't recommend it.'

'No, thanks – really. I must be off.' I started to collect up my things. Further down the corridor, the talk had turned to an exuberant discussion of men's habits in the bathroom, and I felt a bit sorry for the councillor. More to drown this out than in expectation of an answer, I said, 'Councillor, do you remember the last time we met we talked about the Janet Cox murder and I mentioned to you a place called St Martin's Court, and you told me it had been demolished? Well, I know this seems an odd question, but I don't suppose you'd have any idea *why* it was demolished, would you?'

He frowned. 'It is an odd question. What on earth do you want to know that for?'

I didn't want to have to explain the whole thing. 'Well, it's a long story. It's got to do with something Janet Cox's husband was involved in. Anyway, I consulted a structural engineer about the Broxham system – which is the system they used to build St Martin's Court – and he says it had lots of flaws in it. Well, they weren't flaws in the system itself, apparently, but sometimes the parts weren't put together properly, and a couple of buildings had to be taken down to stop them falling down, or blowing up – or whatever. So I just wondered if the reason St Martin's Court was taken down in such a hurry was because there was something wrong with it.'

The councillor looked seriously alarmed. After a short pause, he said, 'I can tell you this – if there was something wrong with St Martin's Court, we on the Planning Committee weren't told about it! Dear God – what did you say the name of the system was?'

'Broxham.'

'*Broxham*.' He wrote it down. 'Are you trying to give me a heart attack or something?'

'Sorry?'

'Well, haven't you thought this through? If one building was put up in Tipping using this system, there could be others!'

'Oh, no! Do you think there are?'

'I don't know.' He got up and went to a filing cabinet in the corner, then changed his mind. 'No – I won't have anything much in here predating when *I* joined the Planning Committee, and I know *we* haven't sanctioned anything like that. Let me think –'

I watched him drum his fingers on the filing cabinet for a moment. I decided to admit to my lack of understanding of the situation. 'Er – I'm not really sure I understand how these things work. Are you saying there could have been something wrong with the building that nobody on the Planning Committee was told about? So why would they have agreed to demolish it then?'

'Oh – that's easy. Because everybody hated it, and most people thought the whole area needed a revamp. I'd only just joined the committee, and I seem to remember that taking down the Court was one of the few decisions we made that I wholeheartedly agreed with.' He pulled open a drawer and selected a file. 'Yes, here we are. Minutes of a Planning Committee meeting held on the sixth of January 1982. Where are we? Blah, blah, blah – *recommendation that the Court be demolished to make way for future development* – blah, blah – *and that that future development should more fully comply with the aesthetic constraints of the area* – Well, there you go. I think what it means is that we all agreed the Court stood out like a sore thumb. It doesn't say anything about –'

At that moment Carol burst in, looking dishevelled and a bit drunk.

'Darling, Yvonne's got to go now and there's an old car

out there blocking her in,' she complained. 'Do you think you could get someone round to shove it out of the way? Someone's locked the bloody thing!'

'What old car?' demanded Dave.

'A battered old Golf with a stupid anti-fox-hunting sticker in the back!' she exclaimed, and I knew immediately that I must have parked an awful lot closer to the Toyota than I'd intended. 'David, Yvonne's got a hair appointment in –'

'*Darling*,' Dave interrupted, meaningfully, before I could say anything. 'This is Chris – Chris from the *Herald*. Remember?'

Carol got the message. 'Oh, God, I'm so sorry! Me and my big mouth – I didn't see you there! We bought an old car once, didn't we, Dave, for Mother to knock about in – you just have to take whatever rubbish they come with, don't you? *Would* you mind moving it?'

'No, I'm just going anyway –'

'Nonsense! You haven't had that drink!' interrupted Dave. 'Darling, come and sit down and show Chris your ring.'

Carol leaned rather too heavily against his desk and waved her left hand at me vaguely. 'It's a sapphire –'

'It's lovely!' How much do I love thee? Let me count the carats. I hid my small diamond discreetly behind my back. 'But I really must go. Thank you very much for seeing me, Councillor.'

'My pleasure.' He showed me to the door. 'If I turn anything up on this Broxham thing I'll let you know. By the way, I saw *Crimewatch* the other night about that poor woman. They didn't give away much, did they? Are they still looking for the husband?'

'The husband? No, they're not. I think they should, actually, but not for the murder. He had a very strange accident –' I decided against boring him with the details. 'Anyway, thank you very much, Councillor, for all this.'

'Dave,' corrected Dave.

'*Dave*,' I agreed. We exchanged smiles. 'I'll keep in touch.'

As soon as I got back to my desk, Dawn from reception rang.

'Woman down here to see you,' she said, 'says she knows you. Shall I send her up, or what?'

During my time as a receptionist back in the dim and distant past, no one would ever have dreamed of saying 'or what' to a person on a higher salary than they were (even if it was only very marginally higher). I decided not to argue the point though, and asked her to send the woman up, and a few moments later a blonde girl appeared at the top of the main stairs. I was quite sure I'd never seen her before, but I abandoned my Dave Ormond tape reluctantly and intercepted her.

'You're not looking for me by any chance, are you? I'm Chris Martin. Can I help?'

'Yes – Caroline. Remember? I sometimes work at the Rudgeleigh Arms.'

'Oh, of course!' I didn't remember her at all. 'Come through and sit down!'

She followed me to my desk, gawking unashamedly at our battered photocopier, dusty monitors, untidy in-trays and filing cabinets with drawers that wouldn't shut. When we'd sat down, she said, awestruck, 'So this is what it's really like in a newspaper office! I've got a degree in media studies and I'm waiting for something to come up at the BBC.'

Suddenly, I felt about a hundred years old. 'Good idea,' I agreed.

'Yes, it'll be absolutely brilliant, I can hardly wait! Anyway, I've come about the *Crimewatch* programme on Tuesday night. You know, the Janet Cox murder.'

I immediately snapped to attention. 'Yes?'

'Yes. Well, actually, it's not really to do with the murder, but I was in reception when you were asking Ms MacInnis if she knew a *Mr* Cox, and when I saw *Mrs* Cox's picture on the television I sort of put two and two together.'

'I see.' My heart sank. She was going to tell me that the entire staff of the Rudgeleigh Arms knew that Claire had had an affair with Lee – that the only person who didn't was Stefan.

She hesitated. 'Well, I don't suppose this has got anything to do with anything,' she said again. 'I mean, I wouldn't want to go to the police and cause trouble for Claire and Stefan, but since you were asking about this Mr Cox, I thought you might be interested. The thing is, Claire and Stefan – well, it's the talk of the restaurant.'

I smiled resignedly. 'What is, exactly?'

'Well, they don't sleep together – never have done since they moved in. They've got separate rooms. They're all hearts and flowers on the surface, and Claire's always fussing over Stefan as if he's made of eggshells or something, but they never seem to touch each other. Nobody can figure out what makes them tick. He's so fiery, she's so cool. I mean, they're both quite attractive! They're young, they're –'

'You're going to tell me Claire had an affair with Lee Cox,' I interrupted, before she could regale me with the prevailing view of the kitchen staff on the state of Claire and Stefan's sex life. I reached into my drawer and showed her the photo of Lee and Janet.

She studied it with an enthusiasm that bordered on rampant lust. 'God, is that him? It was last summer, wasn't it? Go on – I bet it was! We all *guessed* she must be seeing someone because she started being nice to people. Wow! He's really nice!'

I took the photograph back to stop her drooling on it. 'Isn't that what you were going to tell me – that you'd seen this man and Claire together?'

'Oh, no, I've never seen him before – it's *her* I know! Janet Cox – the one who was murdered. I recognized her picture on the programme. She came to the restaurant, twice.'

'*Janet* came to the Rudgeleigh Arms? Why? To eat, do you mean?'

'Oh, no. She came to see Claire.'

'When?'

'Well, she first turned up in early December. We were really busy with Christmas parties and she asked to speak to Claire on *an urgent personal matter.*' Caroline's eyes sparkled. 'Well, Claire was out that afternoon and she made an awful fuss. She said I was to tell Claire if she ever put the phone down on her again she'd be sorry. Anyway, one night about a week later she turned up again just as we were closing. She and

Claire went into one of the private rooms for a few minutes and then she stormed out. This Janet Cox, I mean. She didn't even pay for a drink she'd ordered from the bar, but Claire said not to worry about it.'

'I see! Do you know what she wanted?'

'No, but one of the waitresses – Pat – was hanging round waiting for her lift afterwards, and *she* said Claire and Stefan had a huge row. She said you could hear them screaming at each other all the way across the car park. Stefan was *hysterical*, apparently. He kept saying it was the end of the restaurant, and that it was all Claire's fault. Pat thought we were all going to lose our jobs!'

I was so stunned I couldn't think of a thing to say.

'Anyway, she never came back,' said Caroline. 'What do you think – do you think Janet found out about Claire and came round to slag her off? Wow! I mean, Claire can be a right cow at times, but I still feel sorry for her. I had a bit of a thing with a married man once,' she added, wistfully. 'It was a stupid thing to do, but you know how it is. Oh well, I'd better go. I was just passing and I thought I'd look in.'

Obviously, she couldn't wait to get back to the restaurant and report. She got up, extended her hand – and as she did so the odd half-thought I'd had earlier when Dave Ormond greeted me at Harewood Farm – the one about someone dramatically altering their appearance – suddenly shifted into sharp focus. Supposing Stefan had been the man with the long hair and Gucci aftershave who attacked Janet in her flat?

'Just a minute! I know this is an odd question, but – Stefan – do you remember exactly when he had his head shaved? Was it fairly recently, do you think?'

Caroline halted in her precipitate dash for the stairs. 'Oh, Stefan's always doing things to his hair. Sometimes he dyes it weird colours to go with his clothes. He had it all shaved off just after Christmas. *We* think it's all to do with his background. You know, coming from a country where you're supposed to conform and everything. Oh, and by the way – you won't ever tell Claire it was me that told you all this, will you? I'd hate to have to go back to temping in grotty offices!'

'Well –' Fortunately, before I could tell her that I had no idea whether I'd be able to keep her identity secret or not, she was already halfway down the stairs.

14

I went straight to Mr Heslop's office and told him all about it.

'What do you think?' I demanded. 'Do you think I should ring the police? Do you think the Andres murdered Janet Cox? The layby is only a few minutes' drive from the restaurant! Do you know, I think Elaine was right after all! I think what she saw was *Stefan* meeting Janet –' Suddenly, I remembered my conversation with Wayne in Debenhams 'Classics' department, and a whole new scenario began filling itself in for me like one of those magic painting books you go over with a wet brush. Lee and Claire meeting in the layby during their affair – Stefan meeting Janet there with the promise of money. 'But I wonder why he took her somewhere else to kill her. Perhaps it was because it was the rush hour and there was a lot of traffic on the road. Do you think he took her to the restaurant?'

Mr Heslop frowned. 'Now hold on a minute. Let's not get carried away here. Your contention is that this wretched Cox woman tried to blackmail Claire Andre, Claire Andre told her husband the whole thing, including the part about her having had an affair, and in order to stop the story coming out Stefan Andre beat Janet Cox to death with a blunt instrument?'

'Yes. Well, sort of.'

'But why? You're not making any sense, Chris. Apart from Stefan Andre, who's going to give a brass farthing if Claire Andre has an affair? Are you suggesting Stefan killed Cox to stop her going to the tabloids? Come on! "Chef's wife sleeps with car salesman" – I doubt if many tabloid readers have ever heard of Stefan Andre. And even if some editor did use the story to pad out the bottom of page two on a slow news day, so what? How could it possibly lead to *the end of the Rudgeleigh Arms*? Face it, Chris, people don't boycott a restaurant because its owners sleep around.'

Of course, he'd got a point.

'So what do you think Stefan could have meant?'

He shrugged. 'Search me. Maybe the waitress misheard. I can't for the life of me think of anything this wretched Cox woman could say or do that would be a threat to the restaurant – *ergo*, I can't see that the Andres had a motive for murdering her.' He pulled a face. 'But frankly, she's beginning to get right up *my* nose. Still, you'd better tell your sergeant friend just to be on the safe side.'

I went back to my desk and reached for the phone. I didn't see how the waitress could possibly have misheard. *It'll be the end of the restaurant and it's all your fault . . . it's all your fault, it'll be the end of the restaurant . . .* How could you mishear something like that? But surely the only thing that could lead to the end of the restaurant would be a lack of diners, and Mr Heslop was right, people wouldn't be put off their food by the chef's wife's sexual peccadillos. Or the chef's, come to that. Stefan Andre was young and healthy and striking-looking; he was vital and talented and glamorous. As a matter of fact, you'd imagine that he and Claire would have a pretty healthy sex life – but apparently they didn't. According to Caroline, they didn't even touch each other. I replayed in my head the moment when I'd almost run into Stefan in the restaurant foyer; he'd had a cut finger and Claire had been making a production out of the fact that a member of the kitchen staff had accompanied him to Casualty to get it stitched. Was this for show, an attempt to convince staff and guests that they were a loving couple? *It wouldn't stop bleeding*, said Caroline, and Claire almost fainted. *Are you sure everything was all right?* she asked. At first, the idea forming itself at the back of my mind seemed ridiculous, but the more I thought about it, the bigger and more ominous it looked. Why had Claire been so insistent that Stefan had 'no ghastly health problems'? Unless he had.

I forgot about phoning Wayne. Perhaps Stefan Andre was

suffering from some sort of disease – some sort of blood-borne disease. Haemophilia? I wrote this down as a possibility. Hepatitis? HIV? Aids? If Stefan had one of these, it would explain why Claire had been so anxious that no one but she should accompany him to hospital; it would explain her queasiness at the possibility of his bleeding profusely; it might explain why they chose not to sleep together. If Stefan was a carrier of HIV or hepatitis, and word got out, who could tell how many people might stop patronizing the Rudgeleigh Arms?

And if Lee and Janet Cox had known about Stefan's affliction, it could certainly have posed a threat to the restaurant.

'Oh, my God,' said Mr Heslop, reaching into his drawer for a mirror so he could examine his tongue. '*I* ate there just before Christmas.'

I decided to ignore this. 'What shall I do? Shall I tell the police?'

'Oh, *shit*!' he muttered. 'Shit, shit, shit! If you're right, this raises all sorts of ethical dilemmas – the public-health angle, an individual's right to – *Shit*!' He glared at me, as if it was my fault. 'No – for God's sake don't tell the police – not without some sort of concrete evidence. The next thing is it's leaked out and we've got a libel suit on our hands. I'm going to have to think about this. Look, just forget it for now and we'll talk it over in the morning when I've had a chance to think.'

'But how am I supposed to get hold of concrete evidence?'

'I don't know. Look, I don't even want to think about this at the moment.'

I could see he meant it, so I went back to my desk and tried looking up blood-borne diseases on the Internet. But I'm not very good with the Internet, and there were literally dozens of references, mostly offering help and advice for sufferers of various conditions. And of course, since I didn't know which condition Stefan had, there didn't seem much point in looking any of them up. In the end I gave up and got out my Millennium Centre papers. There was only one way to find out about Stefan: I'd have to go to the restaurant and ask.

*   *   *

There were lights on in the foyer of the Rudgeleigh Arms when I arrived, even though it was still early, and through the small, irregular windows of the restaurant itself I could see people moving slowly from table to table adjusting flower vases. I peered at my watch in the darkness – it was half past six. There'd be plenty of members of staff about, but no customers. I parked the car on the forecourt and went straight in.

No one was manning the reception desk, so I headed for the bar. It was open. Two men in suits glanced up disinterestedly as I entered.

'Nasty night,' remarked the barman automatically, although it wasn't particularly. 'What can I get you?'

'A gin and slimline, please. Are either Mr or Mrs Andre around?'

'Find out for you, madam.' He selected a glass from the overhead rack, gave it a final polish, and placed it glinting on the bar. 'Gordon's or Booth's?'

'Er, Gordon's. It's very urgent I speak to one of them.'

'Ice and lemon?'

He didn't seem to be getting the point. 'No – look, any way it comes!' I snapped, as he reached for a lemon and a knife and started looking for the chopping board.

The two men in suits gave me a pitying look.

'As you wish, madam.' He handed me the drink, minus lemon and ice and I pushed some coins into his hand and told him to keep the change.

By the time he returned, a few moments later, with Claire, I'd consumed the drink.

She took one look at me and ground her teeth unpleasantly, but she said, 'Would you like to come through?'

I followed her out of the bar to an untidy office stacked with boxes of stationery and roller towels. My heart was beginning to pound uncomfortably.

'I thought I told you not to bother me any more,' she said as she shut the door behind us. 'What do you want now?'

'I've just come to ask how your husband is.'

'I beg your pardon?'

161

'I've come to enquire how Stefan is – bearing in mind his condition.'

And even as I spoke I decided that if she said, 'What on earth are you talking about – my husband isn't in any sort of condition', or something like it, I would immediately apologize and make a hasty exit from the Rudgeleigh Arms, never to return to it until a change of management had taken place. And probably not then, either.

But she said no such thing. There was complete silence, apart from the faint hum of a computer processor in an adjoining room. In reception, a telephone rang, and a sudden burst of eager voices announced the arrival of customers on their way to the bar.

'Who told you? Oh, the hospital, I suppose! Well, let me tell you what the position is – if you print one word about this, you'd better be able to prove it. And if you can prove it – if someone's given you access to confidential medical records – I promise you, you and your source and your editor will face some very serious charges under the Data Protection Act!' She'd obviously had this little speech ready for some time, just in case, but all the same, her shock was evident.

'I'm sorry, Ms MacInnis. I didn't get it from the hospital, but obviously there's a public-health issue here, and my editor –'

'Oh, don't give me that! You know as well as I do there's no public-health issue! You *bitch*!' She was losing her Nordic cool completely. 'How dare you come on to me with all this sanctimonious crap! What do you care? I ought to call the police and get you thrown out of here!'

I didn't like the look of her expression, so I started backing towards the door. 'Actually, my editor is expecting me to call in within the next few minutes. If I don't, he'll be ringing the police himself.'

'What on earth for?'

I hesitated. First rule of journalism according to Pete: if you haven't got any proof, bluff. 'To tell them it was you and Stefan who murdered Janet Cox. To stop her exposing Stefan's condition. We wondered if you'd like to make some sort of comment.'

162

'I *beg* your pardon?' She glared at me in astonishment. Out in reception, a cultured female voice could be heard to observe, 'Table for four, Saturday the fourteenth . . . I'm *awfully* sorry, we're *terribly* booked up. I can't *possibly* give you a table, but I could put you down for a cancellation . . .'

Her astonishment slowly turned to horror.

'Wait a minute, wait a minute!' She shook her head until her earrings spun into crazed flashes of light. 'I see what you're getting at, but you've got it all wrong! You've been talking to my staff behind my back, haven't you? My God, when I find out who – Someone's told you that woman came here and made a scene, and you've put two and two together and made five! Janet Cox didn't know about Stefan being HIV – how could she? She only wanted her wretched husband's address, which I haven't got! I've told you that already!'

I could hardly wait to tell Pete that I'd put his theory into practice and it had worked. 'So why did Stefan go to Janet's flat and threaten her then?' I demanded.

'He didn't! That's a lie! He was just trying to make her see she was wasting her time! I don't know where you're getting all this nonsense from. Look, I've already admitted that that bastard Lee tried to blackmail me –'

'What do you mean, *tried* to blackmail you?' I interrupted.

'All right – he *did* blackmail me then! For God's sake, does it matter? He wanted a thousand pounds not to go to you people and I told him I couldn't get that much cash out of my business in one go, so he agreed to have it in two instalments. I was desperate, I didn't want Stefan to find out! I gave him the first five hundred – and that was it, he never came back for the rest.'

I had a sudden flash of inspiration. 'Why not – did you get a friend with a lorry to deal with him for you?'

'What? What on earth are you talking about? I haven't *got* any friends with lorries! Look – I've already told you, I only paid Lee off because of Stefan. I'd have given him the second five hundred if he'd asked for it, but that would have been it. I know exactly what our legal position is – do you want me to explain it to you again?'

'No, thank you. But I don't believe you weren't worried

163

about being blackmailed. There are lots of other ways of spreading malicious gossip than through newspapers.'

She frowned, and bit back an angry response. 'All right – all right. But I can prove that Stefan and I had nothing to do with Janet Cox's murder. I don't see why I should, but I can. All I ask is that you don't put Stefan through the ordeal of having to go over all this with the police. He shouldn't have to suffer any more.'

'What do you mean, you can prove it?'

'Well – write this down. It's the phone number of the producer of the BBC's *Food and Drink* programme.' She recited a London telephone number which I took down. 'Have you got it? Ring her – go on. You'll find that Stefan and I were in the studio all that evening, doing a live item on Cape gooseberries.'

For a moment I was so stunned I didn't know what to say. It's not often you find someone who's got three million witnesses to their whereabouts.

'Well, go on!' She thrust the phone at me. 'I'm telling you, we had nothing whatsoever to do with the murder. I met Janet twice, that's all – once in the layby, and once when she came here. And Stefan certainly never laid a finger on her.'

'You met her in the layby?' I interrupted.

'Yes. She kept phoning and phoning when I was with clients so I thought if I met her face to face I could convince her she was wasting her time. But you couldn't reason with Janet. After that she turned up here, hoping to intimidate me. I don't know what makes you think she knew about Stefan. And for your information, not that I care what you think, but just to put the record straight – Stefan got the virus from a blood transfusion. He was involved in a car accident in Rumania a couple of years ago. He's not ill – we only got the test done to be on the safe side because we read somewhere about the danger from blood transfusions – and I'm perfectly all right. Do you understand? He's no danger to anyone. Other people are more of a danger to him, as a matter of fact.' She folded her arms and glowered at me. 'It's none of your business, but I love my husband. I shall stand by him to the end. I made one mistake and I won't be repeating it. If you've got any conscience at all you'll leave us alone – and if you haven't, I'm warning you –'

At that moment, the door burst open to admit Stefan, dazzling in his white uniform, his bald pate bouncing back rays of neon.

'Claire!' he exclaimed dramatically. 'Those bastards, I'm going to kill them! I ordered tuna *steaks* and they've sent me a whole bloody tuna! I've got Rico filleting the venison, Steve is down with flu – and now I've got a bloody tuna!' He was carrying a nasty-looking meat cleaver in his right hand.

The door to reception was open. I fled without waiting to find out what would happen next.

When I got home, Julie was in the kitchen, surrounded by empty tomato tins and an assortment of utensils.

'I'm making spaghetti "Al Sugo",' she announced, indicating one of my cookery books propped against the kettle. 'I'm not following the recipe exactly, but you have to cook the tomatoes down until all the liquid's evaporated off.'

'Yes, so I see,' I observed, eyeing the tiling at the back of the cooker with horror. 'Do you want any help?'

'No, thanks. I'll bet Pete will say it's not how his grandmother used to make it – but who cares? Where've you been? Why're you so late?'

'I went to the Rudgeleigh Arms.' I instantly regretted mentioning this. If I told Julie about Stefan, she'd be bound to tell Sam, and he might tell someone at catering college . . . I shuddered, and hurried on. 'I think I've worked out what Janet Cox was doing in the layby just down the road from the Rudgeleigh Arms. I think she went there to meet the person she was blackmailing, and the reason she chose the layby was because she'd already met – well, she'd met someone else there before.'

Julie carried on stirring her sauce without comment. I took off my coat.

'Anyway, I think this person intended all along to kill her, but he couldn't do it in the layby because of the traffic, so he persuaded her to meet him somewhere else later. He probably promised to go to a cashpoint to get money for her. So –' I began filling the kettle with water for the pasta. 'So Janet must have popped back to her flat for something to eat, and – *of course*! That'll be when she got the hole in her tights!' I added excitedly.

Julie turned round and gave me a hard stare, but I ignored this.

'Oh, dear – I've already thrown away my own tights with the hole in! Anyway, if Janet met this person in the layby at about half past five, went home – say at about six-fifteen – cooked herself egg and chips and drank some whisky –' I thought about the egg and chips. 'No, hang on. She died between seven and eight. Oven chips take at least half an hour –'

'You can get microwave chips,' remarked Julie, dully.

'Oh, can you? Oh, good. So if she died between seven and eight – say half past seven – then the meeting place has to be no more than twenty minutes' drive from her flat, assuming she left at about seven immediately *after* drinking the whisky but *before* most of it got into her bloodstream! Let me get a map –'

'*Mum*!' snapped Julie, suddenly. 'For God's sake! My *friends* don't have to put up with this! *Murder*! *Bloodstreams*! For God's sake, can't we talk about something else for a change?'

'Oh. *Oh*.' I felt guilty and a bit hurt. 'I'm sorry. I didn't mean to bore you. What do other mothers talk about then?'

She scowled. 'Don't try to be funny because you're not.'

'Oh. Oh, all right.' I plugged in the kettle. 'Actually – actually, I have got something to tell you.' I bit my lip. I didn't want to do this, but it was now or never.

'What?'

'Well, it's about your dad and Sandra. It's good news really,' I added desperately.

'*What*?'

'Well, apparently Sandra is pregnant.'

Julie dropped her spatula. 'Sandra,' she repeated finally, not rescuing the spatula from its messy plunge into the cutlery drawer. 'Sandra's going to have Dad's baby.'

'Yes. Well, you always wanted a younger sister. Aren't you pleased?'

'Pleased? It's *disgusting*!'

'*Why*?'

'It just is! And I'll have to babysit for it, won't I? For free!'

'I'm sure you won't. Your dad would never –'

'Of *course* he bloody would! He's got no idea about me – he doesn't give a toss about me! And how long have *you* known about this? I bet you've known all along. Oh, this is typical! Thank you both so much for bothering to tell me! Why didn't you wait till the bloody christening? Thank you very much!'

Now I knew why I'd been putting off telling her. 'Julie, I was just waiting for an opportunity to tell you properly. Honestly, I only found out myself the other day. Look, shall we sit down and talk this over?'

'Talk it over? Talk *what* over!' Sometimes she sounded so like Keith it was incredible. 'What is there to talk over? I'm going to have a half-brother or a half-sister – so what? Go away, will you – I'm busy!'

Mr Heslop was late in the following morning. He strode by in his damp raincoat, filling the air with pungent steam.

'It's HIV,' I said quickly.

His jaw dropped. 'Oh, God – how did you find that out?'

I explained.

'Oh, my God!' he said.

'The Andres have got a cast-iron alibi for the murder. I checked. But listen –'

'*Not now*! Chris, this is very serious, this thing with the Andres. I warn you, you're going to have to keep it zipped.' He made an explicit gesture across his mouth. 'I've been doing some checking, and I can tell you, this is one story there's no way we're getting involved with. Have you got that?'

'Yes. I told you, the Andres can't have had anything to do with the murder.'

'Good.' He shook his head irritably. 'You know, this Janet Cox murder is turning into a nightmare. First your little foray into breaking and entering – now this. It'll be a miracle if none

167

of us ends up in prison. How's your Millennium Centre piece coming along?'

Of course, I should have known better than to expect him to want to listen to my theory. I sighed. 'Fine, actually. I got lots of answers out of David Ormond. Do you want me to have another go at getting Councillor Draycott's views?'

'Yes. But be a bit more tactful this time, will you?'

I left him unpacking his lunch, collected some coffee from the machine, and went back to my desk. Just the thought of speaking to Councillor Draycott brought me out in a hot flush. I put it off for as long as I could, then rang his number. This time a woman who announced herself as his secretary answered. She said the councillor had left home an hour ago to attend a site meeting on Riddlesdown Hill to discuss the aesthetic effect on Tipping of siting a new TV mast there; he wouldn't be back till lunchtime.

'I see.' I was quite pleased really. I got out my diary. 'Well, I'd like to make an appointment to meet him for a short interview. I could manage any time tomorrow.'

'Really. Well, I'm afraid the councillor couldn't. The next slot I can offer you is – let me see – Thursday the twelfth of February at nine-thirty.'

'Thursday the twelfth! But that's much too far away! I need a comment for next week's edition!'

'Do you indeed! Well, take it or leave it!' snapped the secretary, who obviously shared her boss's view of press relations.

'Thank you. I'll leave it.' I put the phone down crossly. I was relieved at first – until I thought about it. If I was a man, Councillor Draycott wouldn't have dared speak to me the way he had the last time I phoned him. He also wouldn't have spoken to me like that face to face if I'd been blonde, twenty-seven, and partially wearing a miniskirt. Or would he? I wasn't really sure if he would, or if it mattered, but in any event I didn't feel like explaining any of this to the *Tipping Herald*'s readership.

I collected my still-wet umbrella, put on my coat, and hurried out of the building.

*   *   *

It had been raining hard since daybreak – the sort of rain that later in the day would send the weathermen into orgies of statistics – so I headed at top speed for Riddlesdown Hill. Tipping's councillors wouldn't spend long up there with their tape measures and calculators; they'd make a few notes, jot down a few measurements, then arrive at a quick consensus in the car park. I drove too fast up the boggy track to the foot of the hill, passing Councillor Ormond on his way down in a Shogun. He didn't return my wave – I don't think he could see me through the condensation gathered on both our windscreens. When I got to the car park it was deserted apart from a Volvo and a Land Rover. Two women dressed in full wet-weather gear were comparing plastic-wrapped maps under an umbrella, and a third was attempting to study the view through sodden binoculars.

At first I thought I must have missed Councillor Draycott altogether, but then I spotted him beside the Land Rover, short and squat and with shoulders like legs of beef after his years in the butchery business. He was wearing his trademark porkpie hat and carrying a black and white golfing umbrella, and he appeared to be about to depart.

I aquaplaned to a halt at the top of the track, leapt out of the car, and caught him with one foot in his cab.

'Chris Martin, *Tipping Herald*!' I exclaimed breathlessly, my hair already plastered unflatteringly to my scalp by thirty seconds of downpour.

Our conversation was to consist of short sentences shouted desperately into the wind.

'We spoke on the phone!' I began. 'I asked you for a comment on the Millennium Centre – remember?'

The councillor showed no sign of recognition or interest. He climbed into the driver's seat.

'Do you want to say something now?' I prompted.

'Huh?'

'There's going to be a major debate about the centre! Lots of people are upset they're not getting the riverside park! Do you want to comment?'

'What for?' He put his key in the ignition. 'Push off, I'm in the middle of a meeting!'

I got my arm in the way of his door.

'But people want to know what you think!'

'No, they don't! *You* want to know what I think! Get out of my way!'

I decided to try another tack. 'Look, I wrote most of that piece in the *Herald* about the centre myself –'

'Well, then, you've nailed your colours to the mast already, haven't you? *Clear off*!'

'– and now I need some balance –'

'Balance my arse!'

I managed to grab hold of his seatbelt and pull it out of the car. 'Councillor – is it true you plan to retire at the next election? Is it true you'd hoped to include a bowling green in your Millennium Park scheme and name it after yourself?'

His eyebrows beetled into a villainous frown, and for a moment, I thought he was going to slam the door on my arm. I'm sure it did cross his mind, but he was probably worried about the costs of a respray. I jumped back hastily and slithered out of the way.

Now he did slam the door, but his seatbelt hadn't retracted.

'Councillor!' I shouted, the adrenaline pulsing through my veins, as his door came open again for another attempt. 'All right – if you don't want to talk about the Millennium Centre – that's up to you! But what about St Martin's Court? You do remember St Martin's Court, don't you? It was on your ward! Why was it demolished? Was it unsafe?' The rain clouds were right on top of us now, but despite the gloom and even with half his face obscured by the hat I could see how startled he looked. He loomed over me, suspended on the door handle. 'I know all about St Martin's Court!' I yelled. 'I know about the Broxham system! Can you confirm that the real reason the building was demolished was because –'

But the councillor wasn't going to confirm anything. He slammed his door with gut-wrenching force, started his engine at the second attempt and slewed off out of the car park, deluging me in a tide of mud. I watched him bounce off down the hill on his off-road suspension towards the veil of cloud that hid Tipping. For a moment, I stood quite still in the pouring rain and wondered what on earth had come over me.

When I got home that evening, Pete was in the kitchen, washing up. He turned on me grimly.

'Have you seen this?' he demanded, presenting me with a baking tray encrusted with some sort of burnt-on brown substance.

It looked like pizza.

'It looks like pizza,' I said.

'And look at this – and this!' He ignored my revelation, and pointed out a pile of dishes on the draining board, four unwashed glasses, and a splatter of chocolate sauce down the front of the fridge. They all looked like perfectly ordinary dishes and glasses and splatters of chocolate sauce.

'Oh, come on!' he snapped. 'Even *you* must surely agree this is going too far! She's been on that phone for at least half an hour! She's only just gone up to her room. When I came home she was sitting on the stairs with the phone in one hand and some sort of pancake thing in the other – and you should have heard the language!'

'Ah. Well, she's got an essay to finish. I expect she didn't have time to wash up. You leave it, I'll –'

'Essay? Don't give me that! Look, it's not the washing up. I don't mind that –' He clearly did. 'I've done A levels myself! You don't pass them by spending hours on the phone discussing other people's love lives!'

This hit a raw nerve. 'I know, I'll talk to her, but she's a bit upset at the moment about this thing with Keith.'

At that moment the phone started to ring, and before I could stop him, Pete ran out to the hall. To my horror I realized he was going to *answer the phone*, a crime in Julie's eyes on a par with racism, vivisection and the wearing of floral waistcoats with matching blouses. Luckily though – or possibly not – she somehow got herself down the stairs and fastened on to the receiver like a terrier with a rabbit before he could get there.

'Oh, hi!' she exclaimed. 'Emma – I was going to ring you.

171

What happened with Ewan?' She covered the mouthpiece briefly. 'Go on, run along, Petie dear, it's for me!'

I really thought he was going to explode. 'Put the bloody thing down – *now*.'

Julie laughed. 'Sorry, Emma. What?'

'*Put it down.*'

Her eyes did a token roll. '*Ring you back,*' she hissed to the phone, and slammed it back on its cradle. 'What did you do that for? If you want to make a call you can use your bloody mobile, can't you?'

'Don't you talk to me –'

'You and Mum have both got your own bloody phones for people to ring you on! You won't let me have an extension in my room – I pay for my bloody calls – what more do you want? Just get out of my bloody face for once, will you?'

I had to say something, so I said, '*Julie,*' very ineffectually.

Somehow Pete managed not to lose his temper. The blood drained from his lips. 'Yes – I'll get out of your face,' he said tautly. 'Gladly. Nothing will make me happier, darling. But a year from now, when you're struggling with your mocks, and it's too late to do anything about it, don't you dare let me hear you've been whining to your mother about pressure. You know, if you really want to spend the rest of your life passing Tampax cartons past the till at Boots, you're on course for an absolutely brilliant career, darling.'

There was a long silence. I don't think any of us knew who'd won, or what might happen next.

'Er – why don't *I* answer the phone from now on while you finish your essay?' I suggested desperately. 'You can always ring people back later.'

Julie fled up the stairs, disappeared into her room and slammed her door without any regard for cliché.

'There,' said Pete innocently, when the sound of the nail varnish bottles falling off the shelf behind her door had ceased. 'That wasn't so difficult, was it?'

The phone rang again. This time I got there first.

'Is that – is that Mrs Martin?' enquired a female voice I didn't recognize. 'I been trying to ring you – was your phone off the 'ook or something?'

'We've been very busy, I'm afraid. *It's for me.*'

Pete went back to the kitchen.

'Oh, erm – it's about your *adinthe'erald.*'

'Sorry? About my –? Oh, about my *ad* in the *Herald*!' I snapped to attention. I hadn't expected such a quick response.

'I used to live at the Court when I was with me first husband. What's this all about then? Is there a reward or something?'

'Not at the moment.' I reached for a pen. 'But if you'd like to give me your name and phone number –?'

'Oh, no – I don't want to say me name.'

'All right.' I'd do dial-back on the phone. 'Look, I believe I'm right in saying that St Martin's Court was demolished in September 1982 – were you there then?'

'Oh, no, dear, they moved us all out first.'

'Oh.' I gritted my teeth. 'I see. Right. Well, what I'm trying to find out is *why* you were all rehoused. Was the building damp – were there cracks in the walls? Did it sort of – sway about in high winds?'

'Oh – erm, I dunno. Wouldn't that be dangerous?'

'It would! This is the point. You see, I think there may have been some sort of cover-up by the council of the real reason the building was demolished. That's what I'm trying to find out.'

'Oh, I see. But isn't it a bit late?'

I decided to ignore this.

'Well, they was nice flats – we liked them,' she said eventually. 'The only bad thing I remember is that it didn't half pen and ink in there when you come in after being out for a bit unless you left a window open. We was always complaining about it. It come in through the air vents – a sort of burning smell. Made you feel like you was choking.'

'Ah!' I wrote this down. 'Do you know what caused it?'

'Well, they said it was dust burning, but you don't know, do you? I sometimes think about it when you see these programmes on the telly about pollution and all that.'

'I see. So do you think this was why the council rehoused you, because of health risks?' I wrote down 'dangerous fumes from the heating system', followed by several question marks.

'I don't know really. People didn't worry about that sort of thing in them days, did they? We all signed the petition 'cos Mr O'Donoghue said we'd get one of them new houses out on the Barnwood estate if we did.'

I did a double take. 'I beg your pardon? What petition?'

'Oh, you know – like a letter, and everybody signs it. It had a bit at the top which said living in the flats wasn't like living in a proper community and we were all miserable, and that. You wrote your name underneath with your flat number.'

I was baffled. 'Are you saying you signed this petition asking to be rehoused because there was no community spirit at St Martin's Court?'

'Oh, no! We had a nice big meeting room and everything where they had a youth club. We all loved it there, but Mr O'Donoghue said this mate of his on the council said the Court was going to be knocked down anyway, whether we liked it or not, and people who signed his petition would go to the top of the waiting list for Barnwood. He said if you didn't sign you'd end up on that crap estate at Westway. So we all signed.'

I was now so excited I couldn't get my thoughts together.

'Who is this Mr O'Donoghue? Where can I find him?'

'Paddy? I don't know, dear. He used to be the supervisor at Edgeborough Park sports ground before all them sorts of jobs got privatized. He knew lots of important people. He had the keys to the clubhouse. Anyway, it wasn't right, my Bernie ran off with that trollop from the bookies, she'd got two kids, and –'

'Do you know Mr O'Donoghue's full name? Do you know where he works now?'

'Oh, no, I haven't seen him for years! I expect he was all right though after they went private. He was the sort of bloke always fell on his feet – do you know what I mean?'

'Yes. Look, could you give me your ex-husband's address? Perhaps he might remember –'

'Oh, yeah? I'm not having him get the reward! He got the bloody house on Barnwood, didn't he – just 'cos he'd got that trollop's two kids living with him. One of them kids of hers is *black*, you know. Look, I live in a council flat now – I don't want no trouble!' she said suddenly, and the line went dead.

I immediately dialled one-four-seven-one, but she'd with-held her number.

I went into the kitchen and told Pete, ending with the suggestion that someone, somewhere on the council had definitely connived at a cover-up over flaws in St Martin's Court and that it was only a matter of time before I found out who it was.

Pete put down his brillo pad, wiped his hands on a tea towel, smiled, and kissed me on the mouth.

'Congratulations,' he remarked. 'I knew you'd get there one day. This is what happens to all local reporters eventually – they finally reach the stage of being so *desperate* for a real story they start hallucinating bent councillors lurking behind every lamppost with plain brown envelopes stuffed full of money in their pockets. Go on, next you'll be telling me that hole at the end of our road is an undetected mineshaft.'

I was furious.

'That's not very fair! Look, all right – I know I've got no proof – yet – but I'm sure Lee Cox was blackmailing someone over something connected with St Martin's Court. You said yourself lots of councils got into trouble over system building – and I've already had one phone call in response to my ad! That's not hallucinating.'

He stopped smiling, put down the tea towel and hesitated for a moment. 'If I tell you something, will you promise not to be offended? The truth is, I think you're flogging a dead horse with this Janet Cox thing.'

'*What?*'

'Wait – hear me out for a minute. Look, I accept you're probably right about Lee being a petty hustler and a black-mailer. I think he's probably buggered off somewhere with his ill-gotten gains – there are other places in the world apart from Miami. But do you think it's really likely he handed Janet a *Beginner's Guide to Blackmailing* and his address book before he went?'

I got his point. 'No, but she went through his things with a fine-toothed comb a few days before she was murdered, she told me so herself. Perhaps she found Michael Irons's files.'

'Perhaps.' He shrugged. 'But I'm with the police on this

one. I think your friend Kerr-Dixon is the culprit. Look, you said yourself you couldn't be sure he was telling the truth if he gave you the time of day. I guarantee, by the end of the week the police will charge him and that'll be the end of the matter. Come on, let's have a drink, cheer us both up.' He opened the fridge. 'What do you fancy? Gin without tonic, Bacardi, South African Chardonnay?'

I frowned. '*Dave Ormond* took me seriously when I told him about St Martin's Court and the Broxham system.'

'Well, he'd have to, wouldn't he? The last thing a councillor wants is some reporter saying, "I told you so," when a block of flats ends up looking like a bad card trick. I think we'll go for the South African Chardonnay, it was on special offer at the wine warehouse. By the way' – he uncorked the bottle with a flourish – 'I finally got round to reading all your stuff on this new Millennium Centre thing. Jesus! It's way over the top for Tipping, isn't it? I think Dave's starting to suffer from delusions of grandeur. Where does he think this is – Basingstoke? The Watford Gap?'

'What do you mean? There's nothing wrong with Tipping. You've got to have progress!'

Pete muttered something about a second horse being progress, then poured the wine. Sometimes, he really irritated me. 'Oh well – I suppose Fairlands Leisure must think the place has some potential. They're a pretty ruthless bunch, the Fairlands Bellchamber Group. You know Bellchamber Hotels? Apparently they were desperate for planning permission for a site handy for the Channel Tunnel, so they took a bunch of councillors out to one of their hotels in the Canary Islands for a week, wined and dined them, promised them hundreds of local jobs at the top end of the industry – then, when the hotel was finally finished, it turned out to be part of their economy chain. You know, minimum staff, crap restaurant, no conference facilities –'

I felt a stab of alarm. Supposing it turned out that what Tipping was getting was an economy entertainment centre? Should I ring David Ormond and get him to double-check the small print? But before I could make up my mind on this, Pete said something that drove the idea right out of my head.

'Anyway,' he sighed, finishing his glass with one swallow. '*We* won't give a toss, because by the time the thing's built – if it ever is – you and I, darling, will be long gone.'

'Why? What do you mean?'

'Oh, come on, don't say you've forgotten? We agreed – as soon as Julie's off to university we're moving on to pastures new.'

'What pastures new?'

'Well, London, probably.'

I thought about this. Two years ago, when I was so desperate to fill myself up with Pete I'd have agreed to share an igloo with him at the North Pole without benefit of heating, I vaguely remembered a slightly drunken conversation about how great it would be for us to move on somewhere at some unspecified point in our lives.

I hadn't meant it for a minute. I actually love Tipping.

I changed the subject.

A couple of hours later Pete departed for the wine warehouse to see if they'd got any more of the South African Chardonnay on special offer, and I decided to seize the opportunity to make peace with Julie. I was on my way to her room with coffee and cake when the phone rang.

'I'm sorry,' I began. 'I'm afraid Julie's got an important essay to finish –'

'Mrs Martin?'

'Oh! Yes?'

'You put an ad in the paper – about Martin's Court?'

'About *St* Martin's Court, yes! Thank you so much for ringing. What I'm trying to find out is *why* the place was demolished after it had only been up for twelve years. You know – whether there was something wrong with it – or whatever.'

'I see. Do you want to meet then, and talk about it?'

'Yes, that would be great.' The voice was male, a bit on the rough side. I dropped my t's so as not to put his back up. 'Did you used to live there?'

'No, I didn't live there, but I know all about it. I've got something I want to show you.'

'Oh, wonderful! How about if you come to my office tomorrow?'

'No – it's got to be tonight. I've got to be in Newcastle tomorrow.'

'I see. Well, it's a bit difficult really –' Pete wouldn't be at all pleased if he got back from the wine warehouse to find a strange man sprawled across our sofa. 'Couldn't you just tell me over the phone?'

'No, I can't show you this over the phone, can I? You'll want to see it, believe me. I can be at the Total station on the bypass if you're interested. What car you got?'

'A dark-green Golf GTI –'

'So go on, what do you say? See you in twenty minutes, will I?'

Immediately about thirty very respectable reasons for not meeting a strange man at a petrol station late on a dark and windy winter's night lined themselves up for my perusal, but I almost as instantaneously decided to ignore them. This man had actual physical evidence in connection with St Martin's Court that he wanted to show me. Besides, I'd got my mobile, so if anything went wrong I could call for assistance.

'All right,' I agreed. 'I'll see you in twenty minutes.'

15

The Total station was still open when I got there, its forecourt
scoured by an east wind that now darted with sleet. I wished
I was at home with my feet inside my old tartan slippers, but
I pulled up beside a grey van and switched off the engine. A
flurry of ice crystals immediately settled on my windscreen
like predatory insects and then swept away over the car's
warm bonnet. I glanced at my watch: I was ten minutes
late, so he should be here any second. I guessed he must
be a council employee – or more probably *ex*-employee –
who had seen my ad and rung on the off-chance. I began
speculating excitedly about what he might have to show me.
An internal council memo detailing dangerous faults in the
structure of St Martin's Court? A note from someone high
up warning staff to keep their mouths shut? Whatever it
was I'd got to have it, and – I realized with horror – I'd
forgotten to bring any cash. Supposing he wanted payment
for the information? I reached for my handbag and tipped
out its contents. Fifteen pounds in notes and a few coins.
Then I remembered the five-pound note I'd stuffed into a
rear compartment in the corner shop yesterday. It was still
there, tucked inside a very garish-looking Christmas card I
didn't remember seeing before. I opened the card and held
it towards the light. 'To C,' it said, 'hope we can spend some
time together again soon when your not so busy. Love Mac D.'
For a moment, I was baffled, but then I had a quick flashback
of Cherie Bolt's desk littered with cards and files and my bag
lying next to them. Cherie had picked up my bag by mistake,
thinking it was hers – she must have stuffed the card into it
accidentally. Perhaps I ought to send it back.

Just at that moment a dark-blue Peugeot estate pulled up at the pumps and a man got out and started filling up with unleaded. He glanced over in my direction twice, and I returned the looks with raised eyebrows and an encouraging half-smile. Then he wrestled the piping back into place against the wind and ran into the shop, eyeing me over his shoulder. My heart began to pound. If only I'd thought of bringing the cash. Then I had a brainwave – Pete could be here inside ten minutes. I dialled his mobile. But he'd got it switched off; in fact, I now clearly remembered seeing it on the hall table next to the gas bill as I left. Feverishly I dialled our home number, but just as it rang for the third time the Peugeot driver emerged from the shop. I immediately disconnected the call and opened my passenger door. He stood on the step, his collar turned up, and stared at me. He looked all right – thirtyish, a bit scruffy – but you could never tell. I opened the door wider, letting in a blast of cold air. To my astonishment he now made a run for the Peugeot, leapt into it and started the engine. Then, as he swerved round the other side of the pumps, it dawned on me that he wasn't my contact at all, but a perfectly innocent motorist who'd popped out to fill up his car for the morning run. He mouthed an obscenity in my direction and drove off at high speed.

I wouldn't have minded, but his remark included the word 'stupid'.

I looked at my watch again. Nine-fifteen. That meant it was now *forty-two* minutes since I'd answered the phone at home, and the caller had said he'd be here in twenty.

At last I began to suspect that I might actually have missed him. Perhaps he'd waited for a few minutes, assumed I'd got cold feet, and given up.

I got out of the car and sprinted across the forecourt to the shop.

'Excuse me! Did you happen to notice if there was someone waiting out on your forecourt a short while ago?'

The assistant was about nineteen, with a nose-stud and a cold sore. 'Haven't seen anyone, except you. Are you filling up, or what? I'm supposed to keep things moving out there, you know? You'll get me into trouble.'

'What happened to the driver of the grey van?'

'Don't know – it's parked there. I think it's the boss's.'

I thought this over. 'So, you're saying *no one*'s been waiting out there at all.'

'That's right. Just you.'

I ran back across the forecourt. I wasn't quite sure about the boy in the shop, so I touched the grey van's radiator grille: sure enough, it was stone cold. I got into the Golf and dialled home again. This time I got the engaged signal. I rang Pete's number, and this, too, was engaged. Perhaps he was trying to ring me. I sat in the driving seat for a moment, puzzled and frustrated, and then I realized my feet were beginning to freeze and that if I didn't move soon I wouldn't be able to operate the foot controls. The call must have been someone's stupid idea of a joke.

I turned into our street too fast and almost immediately had to do an emergency stop. A queue of cars, including one with a blue light on its roof, was blocking the road completely, and there were men with powerful torches and fluorescent yellow jackets standing about on the pavements. I thought immediately of the elderly woman opposite who has weekly physio and a home help. 'Damn, damn, damn,' I muttered, 'this is absolutely the last straw,' but I got out of the car, ran up the road towards our house, and managed to assume a caring expression.

'Oh, dear!' I exclaimed. 'Can I help?'

One of the jackets turned his torch on me, and Pete appeared suddenly from amongst the throng. 'Chris,' he began tensely. 'You're not to panic, all right? Everything's OK. There's been a bit of an accident but *no one's been hurt*.'

'What?' I immediately panicked. 'What do you mean? What sort of accident?' He took my arm and I twisted this way and that, watching the shafts of torchlight slice off bits of darkness, turning them into broken shards of wood, a splintered tree, mud-churned grass. I began to get the picture. *'What's happened? Where's our house?'* I pulled away from Pete and my gaze alighted on a piece of torn, familiar fabric trodden into the pavement and a glittering trail of shattered glass –

'It's fine. Everything's OK, honestly. Chris –'

'We're getting it boarded, love –'

The fabric belonged to our living room curtains.

'It happened while I was out,' said Pete. 'Mrs Thing over the road says this lorry was going up and down trying to turn round and ours was the only house without cars parked in front of it. Bastard didn't stop. I told you, no one was hurt. Julie was –'

My stomach turned over.

'– Julie was a bit shaken and Richard happened to drop by so I sent her home with him. I didn't know how long you'd be. She's fine. It's just the downstairs front room, I'm afraid. It's a bit of a mess.'

Before he could explain I wrenched the torch out of his hand and shone it where I expected our house to be. At first I couldn't find it – or at least, I found it all right, but it didn't look like our house. Our front garden with its shabby fence and little rectangular lawn surrounded by straggly winter pansies had been replaced by a pair of enormous wheel ruts and lots of firewood, and as for the house itself . . . My hand flew to my mouth to stifle another scream. The house had a big hole in it where our living room window used to be. Upstairs, a light was on in the bedroom, and everything looked exactly as I'd left it, so part of me knew it was our house – but downstairs it didn't look like our house and another part of me kept thinking it wasn't.

I pulled away from Pete and started to run across the lawn, so I could see for myself, close up, even though I knew this wouldn't make me feel any better, but a policeman waylaid me in the middle of the pansy bed.

'You can't go inside, love. We don't know if it's safe. I'm afraid you'll have to sleep somewhere else tonight. We need an engineer to OK that front lintel. See?' He shone his torch helpfully along the upper windowframe, and made encouraging remarks about steel and stress, but I wasn't listening any more. My beam had just picked out something lying amongst the shattered remains of our glass-topped coffee table – two lengths of scaffolding pole, bound together with rope, and complete with heavy fittings on either end.

*   *   *

Wayne rang me first thing on Monday morning.

'What's this I hear about someone trying to run you over the other night while you were sitting at home minding your own business watching the telly? Don't tell me, it was a hit – you spelt someone's name wrong!' He roared with laughter.

I didn't say anything until he'd finished laughing. I'd spent the entire weekend waiting for the engineer to examine our front lintel, trying to fill out stupid forms for loss adjusters, arguing with an investigating police officer who kept telling me how perfectly normal it is for lorries to end up in people's living rooms, and having little run-ins with Pete, who'd been very impressed by Mrs Thing's tale of a lorry going up and down the road looking for somewhere to attempt a turn. And according to Julie, just before the crash, she'd come downstairs to look something up in the *Oxford Dictionary of Quotations*, and had only left the living room to answer a phone call – which had turned out to be my aborted call home. I was still having flashbacks about this.

When Wayne had got the message that I didn't think his remarks were funny, I said, 'Can I see you, please? I was going to ring you if you hadn't rung me. It's very urgent.'

'All right. Matter of fact I could be at the McDonald's on Church Street in half an hour. No, better still – make it Dino's. Do you know Dino's? It's –'

'Of course I know Dino's!' I put the phone down and reached for my coat.

Wayne was already there when I arrived. He stood up when he saw me.

'You look awful,' he said. 'Are you OK?'

'No.' I sat down. I was feeling sick and shaky – not least because I hadn't slept for two nights, but mainly because I'd decided I'd got no choice but to tell him everything, and that afterwards there was no guarantee where I'd be waking up the next morning. 'I've got something to tell you. I'm afraid it's a bit awkward, and you're not going to like it, but I've got to tell you because I'm pretty sure what happened to my house on Friday night wasn't an accident, and if I don't tell you and something else happens it'll be all my fault.'

Naturally, he laughed. 'Let me get you a hot chocolate,' he said, and shouted an order across to the girl at the counter.

This was the last straw. '*You* wouldn't laugh if it had been your house and your family,' I snapped. 'It was a *scaffolding* lorry! Have you forgotten what I told you about what happened to Lee Cox?'

He looked blank, but his smile wavered. I could tell what he was thinking: that my hormones had gone into overdrive. 'And what does your other half have to say about all this?' he enquired.

'Well, as a matter of fact, our daughter was very nearly killed in this so-called accident so he's pretty upset!'

'Christ! I didn't know. No one told me that. Jesus!'

And I don't know why, but it suddenly occurred to me that I'd referred to Julie as 'our daughter' instead of 'my daughter', and this seemed very important.

'I mean, *my* daughter – you know – Keith's child.'

'Oh – right.' He frowned. He was beginning to look worried. 'OK – do you want to start at the beginning? What's this thing that's all your fault?'

Our hot chocolate arrived, and while Wayne spooned off his froth, I told him the whole story, starting with my visit to Janet's flat, and encompassing the diary entries, Lee's attempt to blackmail Claire, St Martin's Court, Holly Cottage . . . The only part I left out was Stefan's HIV status, because Mr Heslop would have sacked me for sure if this got out. I finished up by pointing out that my 'accident' had happened on the very day my ad had appeared in the *Herald*, and the day after I'd had conversations with half a dozen different people in the council's offices on the subject of St Martin's Court.

Wayne stared at me aghast with his mouth open and chocolate froth on his upper lip. He looked like someone who has just discovered at midnight on Christmas Eve that his cold-water tank has burst, and that all those ads in Yellow Pages for emergency plumbers 364 days a year are not joking.

His expression turned cold and rather nasty. 'You are unbelievable,' he muttered, wiping his mouth. 'You broke into a murder victim's flat and tampered with evidence and now you calmly sit there and tell me about it. Have you any idea how serious an offence that is?'

I squirmed.

'Where is this bloody diary page now?'

'It's still there. I told you – I left everything exactly as it was.' He was much angrier than I'd expected. 'Honestly, I didn't break in. The key was outside the door. I just let myself in and looked round.'

'Oh, well that's all right then! How absolutely fabulous for you!' I had a horrible feeling my special relationship with DS Wayne Horton had just flown out of the window. He opened his notebook grimly. 'Go on then. I'm waiting. What did it say?'

I repeated the two names I'd seen on the diary page.

'And . . . ?'

'That's it, actually.'

'What do you mean? Am I missing something here? I thought you said it was this page that tipped you off to the blackmail plot?'

'Well, sort of – eventually. You see, the diary entry was written by Michael Irons, who used to be a property developer and ran a construction company. I think he gave Lee a tip-off – in return for a cut, of course. Well, all right – I don't know who they intended to blackmail or why, but look – the minute I start asking questions about St Martin's Court exactly the same accident happens to me as happened to Lee!'

'Hang on a minute. Let's slow down a bit, shall we? Where is this sodding building?'

'I told you, it was demolished nearly sixteen years ago, probably because –'

'Bloody hell! Come on then, give me this Irons bloke's address.'

I hesitated. 'Didn't I say? He committed suicide the same day Janet was murdered.'

Wayne sighed impatiently and glanced down at his notes. 'You've got bugger-all!' he snapped. 'You haven't even proved that either of the Coxes was blackmailing anyone. I don't know what you're on about.'

'But I told you! The moment I started asking questions about St Martin's Court –'

'Right – you know what this reminds me of?' he interrupted. 'That old chestnut about Germany and bananas and the illegitimate birth rate. You know – some statistician did a graph of banana imports into Germany and noticed that the peaks and troughs exactly matched the country's illegitimate birth rate.'

I thought about this. 'I don't get the point. What's the connection?'

'There *isn't* a connection. *That's* the point!' He looked very cross. 'Chris – if I didn't know better I'd think you'd been at the pharmaceuticals.'

This sank in, slowly.

'So you're not interested in any of what I've just told you?' I said finally, and I'm ashamed to admit it, but there were tears pricking at the back of my eyelids. 'You're not going to do anything to find this lunatic who makes hoax phone calls and then half demolishes people's houses in the middle of the night?'

He bristled. 'For your information I've got one call to make and then I'm going over to Tipping to ask for a copy of the report on your accident, and if it looks to me as if there's anything suspicious about it I promise I'll get CID involved straight away. I never thanked you for that tip-off about Trevor, so I owe you one.'

. . . *so I owe you one*. That sounded suspiciously like thank you and good night.

'But Wayne, please –'

'And let me point out one other thing. If somebody had really got it in for you you set yourself up good and proper at that petrol station. I hope that puts your mind at rest.'

I couldn't quite work out how he thought this would put my mind at rest, but before I could ask him, he said grimly, 'I don't think you understand the position you've put me in, Chris. I discussed evidence with you, I gave you tip-offs – I trusted you. OK, you say you didn't touch anything in the flat and I believe you, but there's no telling what kind of a spin a good defence brief could put on a story like this. We've had lunches together – you've paid.' He covered his face briefly with his hand. 'Believe me, if this ever comes out, my career will be beyond the help of Toilet Duck.'

I got his point. I began to feel really bad.

'And for your information – you're going to really love this – we've had a setback in the enquiry. No, three setbacks, as a matter of fact. First, that bloody grit in Cox's clothes turned out not to be the same as the grit they use on the steps outside Kerr-Dixon's flat. These so-called experts seem to think it's some kind of horticultural grit. Second, nobody came forward after the *Crimewatch* programme with anything of any bloody use – and third, Kerr-Dixon's done a runner. The day after the sodding *Crimewatch* programme.' He glanced up at the girl behind the counter, who was watching us. 'Apparently, no one knows where he is. Not even Trevor.'

I was glad I hadn't touched my hot chocolate. I would have thrown it up.

Wayne rose slowly to his feet. He said, 'Mrs Cox's flat has been sealed pending repossession by the building society. No one's given the go-ahead for it to be cleared, so this diary page must still be in there somewhere. It's probably a waste of time but since you've told me about it I'll have to take a look at it – provided I can dream up some bloody silly excuse for giving the place another going-over. Oh, and hang on, I almost forgot –' He was about to reach into his inside pocket for something. He hesitated with his hand in his jacket. 'If I give you this, we'll be quits – OK?'

A tear spilled out of my right eye and ran down my nose. I hoped he wouldn't notice.

'You asked me about Lola Champion. Right.' He pulled a folded sheet of paper from his pocket. 'She's got a whole little megabyte of computer space all to herself – soliciting, common assault, drunk and disorderly, shoplifting . . .'

I raised my eyebrows in surprise.

'You get the picture? At one stage her kids were on an at-risk register and we had to assist a social worker in taking one of them to a place of safety after the two older girls did the sensible thing and scarpered. This was all twenty years ago, mind, so I've only got what's on the sheet. Anyway, last

June we were called to an address in Ravenswood to investigate reports of a disturbance. It turned out your friend Lola Champion was punching the lights out of some woman.'

In the circumstances, I couldn't take much of this in. 'Why?' I asked finally.

'I don't know why. Some sort of domestic. No charges were brought against anyone and the papers were put away. Here – here's the woman's name and address.' He pushed a piece of paper into my hand. 'That's it – now we're even. Look, I'll give you a bell, OK?' he added. 'Take care.' And he nodded to the girl behind the counter and walked out without a backward glance in my direction.

I wondered how much worse things could get. I needn't have, though. I was soon going to find out.

I went straight back to the car and had a surreptitious weep into a tissue on the pretext of blowing my nose. I felt a bit better then, once I'd got it all off my chest. I repaired my face and opened up the paper Wayne had given me. It was part of a computer print-out listing complaints registered at Tipping police station on Friday, 20th June. It said, 'Name of complainant, Mrs Patricia Woollcott, 37 Hillside Close, Tipping.' The 'Nature of Incident' column just said 'domestic'. I knew Hillside Close. It was near Barrington Avenue, where I'd lived with Keith: a nice cul-de-sac of four-bedroomed houses, the sort of place you could stroll along on a summer evening when everybody had their windows open and all the TV sets would be tuned to *Today at Wimbledon*.

I didn't feel like going straight back to the office, so I took a familiar short cut to Hillside Close via Barrington Avenue, cruising slowly past my old house and taking in the strange curtains at what had been our bedroom window. This made me feel bad again, so I parked on one of Hillside Close's wide verges and reread the computer print-out to try and concentrate my mind. Then I got out of the car and made my way up the front path of Number Thirty-Seven. They had a tub of crocuses on their front step that were almost in flower.

The woman who answered my ring was in her mid to

late forties, and was wearing a very nice brown and black sweater I had once had my eye on in Marks and Spencer's.

'Mrs Patricia Woollcott?'

Her welcoming smile faded. 'Oh, not again. Don't tell me – social services!'

Naturally I was deeply insulted, since I'd had my hair done only last week.

'No. I'm from the *Tipping Herald*. If you can possibly spare the time I'd like to talk to you about an incident you were involved in with Lola Champion. I promise you, it's strictly off the record.'

'The *Tipping Herald*. Right, well, firstly I'm not Mrs Woollcott – *thank God* – I'm Elizabeth Harper. And secondly, I'd like to know why you're bringing all this up again after so long. Oh, *God*, Pat hasn't come *back*, has she?'

'Er –' She'd taken the wind right out of my sails. 'Mrs Woollcott's not here, then?'

'No, she isn't! She most certainly isn't! Look, you'd better come in. I want to get to the bottom of this!' She stepped back, holding the door wide, and looking anxiously beyond me to the street. 'If that woman's about to turn up on my doorstep again I'd like to know about it. This is my *home*. You don't want to have to wonder every time you go out what's going to happen at home while you're away, do you?'

Of course, this hit a very raw nerve. I think the right corner of my mouth went into spasm, just as she ushered me into her nicely appointed living room.

'What do you mean?' I managed, horrorstruck.

'Well, what do you think I mean? Coming home from work to find your house crawling with police – it's not very nice, is it?' She put on a pair of glasses and squinted at me. 'Hmm. You're a reporter, are you? I see. So what's going on? Why the sudden interest in Pat?'

I decided to come clean. She gestured towards a chair, so I sat down. 'I'm afraid the truth is I don't know anything at all about Mrs Woollcott. I was hoping to talk to her about an incident at an address in Ravenswood last summer and I was told this was where she lived. Would you happen to have her new address?'

'No, I would not! I could give you the phone number of social services if you like, but that's the best I can do. I don't want to sound callous, but that woman really did cause the most awful havoc in our lives and the less I have to do with her the better. You obviously haven't met her.'

'No –'

'Well, she's ill, that's the kindest way of putting it. Someone at the hospital told me she must have something called erotomania – whatever that is. I mean, I do feel sorry for her, but there are limits. I met her through Beginners' Italian and offered her a bed here out of the goodness of my heart – and this is what happens.'

I hesitated. 'I'm sorry – what, exactly?'

She looked irritated. 'Well, this thing with the solicitor, of course – Philip Chandler. She made a habit of it apparently. It was some doctor before him, so we found out afterwards from the social worker. I felt really bad about it because I recommended her to Philip Chandler in the first place – I even believed her in the beginning! I mean, she seemed perfectly normal and credible – quite a laugh really. I knew Mr Chandler was a widower, so why not? I thought it was all a bit of a whirlwind, but these things do happen.'

'Mrs Woollcott had an affair with Philip Chandler?'

Elizabeth Harper looked even more irritated. 'No, of course she didn't! It was all *in her mind*. She told me she was changing to another solicitor so they could start seeing one another romantically – and I was stupid enough to believe her. What can I say? I don't know what she thought she was up to. Apparently she used to sit in her car outside his house and take photos of him when he came to the window. She got herself barred from his office! I don't know – you feel such a fool, don't you? I defended her! I came home from work one day – I work part time at the hospital – to find her sitting where you are now with a policewoman. Apparently there'd been an incident at Mr Chandler's home and someone called the police.' She shook her head in disbelief. 'I even *encouraged* her to press charges.'

At last I was catching up. 'Against Lola Champion,' I remarked, nodding.

'No – not so much against her. She was the daily woman or something, wasn't she? Although she did give Pat quite a shiner! No – against Chandler, for the sexual assault. Oh God, I don't know how I could have been so stupid!'

'What sexual assault?'

'Don't you know? Pat said he put his hand up her skirt and fondled her. In his office, and again at his house. Honestly, in the beginning I had no idea she was making it up – she really took me in. I felt such a fool. Of course my husband never really liked her – he was *so* relieved when I finally asked her to leave. She used to spend *hours* in our bathroom every morning soaking in some dreadful herbal concoction. She said she couldn't use the shower in my sons' bathroom because it interfered with her PH factor.'

I was agog. 'So what happened? What happened about the assaults and everything?'

She shook her head. 'Nothing. Well, you can't get away with making up things about a *solicitor*, can you? Poor Mr Chandler! Apparently he could have had her charged with all sorts of things – forced entry, criminal damage, and I don't know what else! But he agreed to drop all charges on condition she dropped the sexual assault charge and undertook psychiatric counselling in another area. The social workers arranged it all.'

'I see.' I thought about this. 'Are you absolutely sure there was no foundation to Mrs Woollcott's allegations?'

'*What*? Well, of course there wasn't! God – don't start all that again! I'm surprised your colleague hasn't already told you all this anyway. Don't you talk to each other?'

'Sorry? My colleague?'

'Yes. The one who came here last summer to talk to Pat about Mr Chandler. I'm sure *he* wasn't taken in by her. We never saw anything in the papers, thank God!'

I was baffled. 'I beg your pardon?'

'Oh, wasn't he from your paper? The young, good-looking one with the nice car.' Sadly, she'd just ruled out everyone on the *Herald*. 'No – come to think of it, he said he was a freelance.'

'*A freelance*,' I repeated. Most of the so-called freelances in

Tipping were married women with school-age children who desperately staked out village fêtes in the hope of a toxic-jam scare. I had a sudden brainwave. I rummaged through my briefcase for the photo of Lee and Janet Cox and held it out to her, carefully covering Janet's image in case this confused the issue. 'Is this him?'

She studied the photo. 'Yes, that's him. Definitely. Pat was really excited after he'd gone. He taped her story, and he told her he was doing an investigation into Mr Chandler's private life – he *really* encouraged her. This was just about the time I was starting to get suspicious of her and I'd had enough of police and social workers turning up all the time. Poor Mr Chandler – I don't know how he managed to put up with it all.'

'I see!' I could scarcely contain my delight. Lee must have witnessed one of the incidents at Edinburgh House and tracked down Pat Woollcott; this was the proof I needed that he was a blackmailer.

I leaned forward eagerly. 'Mrs Harper, I know this is going to sound strange, but if it's necessary, would you be prepared to go to the police and identify this man as the person who came here and interviewed Mrs Woollcott?'

'Whatever for?'

'Well, it's a long story, but he's not a reporter. I think he may be involved in a blackmail plot.'

For once, she was speechless. 'Heavens,' she said finally.

I stood up and offered her my hand. 'Thank you so much for telling me all this. If Mrs Woollcott does get in touch with you I'd be very grateful if you'd ask her to contact me. Here's my card.'

Mrs Harper stood up too. She laughed hollowly. 'If Pat Woollcott gets in touch, I can assure you, you won't see me for dust!'

I hurried back to the car and climbed into the driving seat. I now knew I'd been right all along about Lee Cox. He was an opportunist blackmailer out for whatever he could get from whomever he came into contact with – ex-lovers, his own solicitor – anyone. Janet must have got hold of the tape he'd made of Pat Woollcott's story when she went through his house looking for clues to his whereabouts. If I'd agreed to help her find Lee, this was what she'd intended offering in return. I put my key in the ignition and turned it.

And then, something else occurred to me. Janet had tried to phone Chandler the week before she died and he'd left instructions with his staff that she wasn't to be put through. Perhaps she'd been trying to blackmail him with the tape. But if so, why hadn't he told the police? He was a solicitor – surely he must know that a blackmail attempt would be germane to a murder enquiry.

Unless, of course, he'd got something to hide.

I let go of the ignition key. Nothing had happened. There hadn't been so much as a chirp from the Golf's starter motor. I took the key out, waited a few moments, then tried again. Still nothing. Something was wrong. I reached for my phone to call the AA, but then I realized the rest of it: that my AA membership-renewal forms were sitting at home uncompleted just as they had been for the last three weeks, that the man we'd bought the Golf from had had a nasty smirk on his face as we drove off, and that I did not know the name or phone number of one single breakdown firm.

There was no one around, so I clung on to the steering wheel and screamed.

16

Almost two hours later, a breakdown van from Brown's Auto Repairs, a firm selected by Dawn from Yellow Pages, turned up and an engineer got out, grunted at me, and began poking around under my bonnet with a grimy fingernail. He had a sour look on his face and he wasn't interested in my explanation of what had happened, nor did he take up my offer to try starting the engine for himself.

'It's your electrics,' he said, wrenching irritably at a bundle of wires. 'See that? *That's* your problem! You should've said on the blower what model this is. You women – you've got no idea, have you? What did you get a car like this for if you don't know nothing about engines? I'm going to have to send for a tow truck and take it into my shop.'

'A *tow truck*? But I've got to get back to the office! I've got appointments!'

He shrugged. 'Should've thought about that before buying a heap like this, shouldn't you? You want me to have a go at starting it for you, do you? Well, you're paying for my time, love! All right, I'll give it a go,' he announced contemptuously, before I'd had a chance to express my wishes, and climbed grimly into the driving seat.

I stood back in despair, listening to him crank the ignition key. Then, everything fell silent.

After a few moments he emerged from my car with an odd grin on his face. Not the practised, sneering grin of a man who holds the power of life and death over your means of transport, but a strange, sickly grin a couple of degrees the right side of apologetic.

'You're in luck, love,' he said, baring his teeth unpleasantly as the grin reached dangerous proportions. 'Provided I've got the right battery on the van we should have you on your way in no time.'

'The right battery?' I followed him back to his van.

'Yeah. Of course, you'll still have a problem with your electrics, but you know where my workshop is, don't you? Pop her in sometime when you're passing and I'll get it sorted for you. Matter of fact, if you can leave her a bit longer I'll hammer out that dent on the side and do you a respray. At cost, to make up for the hassle.' He winked, then added earnestly. 'You should've said who you was – I could've been here an hour ago.'

'Oh!' I was surprised and a bit angry, but mostly flattered. This was the first time I'd ever been offered preferential treatment for being a *Herald* reporter.

I got back into the car and huddled in the front seat while he got things out of his van. And either I was suffering from early-stage hypothermia, or a warm glow of pleasure and pride was just beginning in the pit of my stomach. Things couldn't be quite so irretrievably bad after all; a breakdown engineer respected me. I pulled myself together and started tidying up the clutter on my passenger seat. On top of the pile was the Christmas card I'd found in my bag when I looked for cash in the Total station. Its inscription, 'To C, hope we can spend some time together again soon when your not so busy. Mac D,' stood out in heavy black felt-tip lettering, and an oily thumbprint now decorated its lower border. I thought about the thumbprint: it hadn't been there the last time I looked at the card. The breakdown engineer from Brown's Auto Repairs was now solicitously brushing imaginary dust off my new battery. When he saw me looking at him, he waved. So why on earth had Mr 'You women, you've got no idea, have you – I'll have to send for a tow truck' turned into Father Christmas after reading the inscription in Cherie Bolt's Christmas card? Then two things occurred to me at once. First, that since the card was on *my* front seat anyone reading it would naturally assume *I* was the 'C' Mac D hoped to spend time with – and second, that perhaps Cherie slipping the card into my handbag hadn't after all been an accident.

You don't pick up someone else's bag by accident and mistake their cosmetics for yours; you *know* what your bag feels like and what it smells like, even if it looks identical to someone else's. Cherie had reached for my bag and started fiddling with it quite deliberately – right after we'd talked about Lee and his mysterious disappearance. She'd been trying to tip me off. The only *mistake* she'd made had been to assume I was smart enough to recognize a tip-off when I got one.

I got out of the driver's seat and walked round to where a large backside was protruding from my engine.

'Mr Brown?'

''s'right, love.'

'Mr Brown, I'm Chris. You're being awfully kind. I just wondered why, really. Who is Mac D?'

He stood up suddenly, hitting his head smartly on the bonnet hood. 'Jesus! What you on about?'

'The Christmas card on my front seat. You saw it – and then you suddenly discovered you could fix my car. Why?'

He flushed angrily. 'Come on, love, I'm just doing my job – all right? I didn't mean no disrespect. I told you, if you'd said who you was on the phone I'd've been out an hour ago. I'm doing the best I can – all right?'

'Yes, of course.' I thought about Lee's boarded-up front window, and the scaffolding pole in the middle of my sofa. 'You wouldn't want Mac D to think you hadn't done the best you could for one of his friends, would you?'

He dropped his screwdriver. 'What're you talking about? Look – OK – forget my costs. You can have the fucking battery. I can't say fairer than that! Let me get on with my work, will you?'

At the back of my neck, something began to pound. Mr Brown was big and ugly. He smelt. 'Why?' I demanded, tremulously.

'What do you mean, why?' he muttered into my battery housing, and I watched his podgy blackened fingers grip a connector and wrestle it into place.

'I mean – you know – why are you being so generous just because you think I'm a friend of Mac's? Are you scared of him?'

He jerked round to look at me, and after a bit of fumbling in my handbag I produced one of my cards and showed it to him. 'I'm Chris Martin from the *Tipping Herald*. You know – the local newspaper. I'm hoping you'll tell me who this Mac is, so we don't have to – you know – run a great big story on our front page about how Brown's Auto Repairs fleeces women motorists.' I took two nervous steps backwards and ran into someone's gatepost. If Mr Brown decided to hit me and make a run for it, there was nothing I could do to stop him.

'Well, go on,' I squeaked, in a voice that was not my own, 'is he some sort of hit man? Who does he work for? Has he got a lorry? Does he drive his lorry into people's living rooms? If you don't tell me, I'll have to get on my mobile to my editor –'

'I'm not telling you nothing! I've got a wife and kids! You ask him yourself! Go down the fucking Anchor and fucking look him up!'

'The Anchor?' I got out my book. 'Where's that?'

By way of answer, he slammed down my bonnet. 'I'm warning you – you better watch yourself, missus, from now on! I'm giving you this fucking battery for fucking nothing. You do what you fucking like with your fucking newspaper!'

And he strode off to his van.

'*Wait*! Have you fixed my car?'

Before I could stop him, he'd jumped into the van and accelerated away with his rear doors flapping back and forth. I watched him go, then got into the Golf, held my breath and cranked the ignition. The car started first time. I sat in Hillside Close for the next few minutes, revving my engine noisily and reliving the moment when Mr Brown had dropped his screwdriver and offered me the battery for nothing. But after a while I started feeling a bit guilty about Mr Brown. I decided that when I got back to the office, I'd send him a cheque for the battery.

Mr Heslop was waiting for me by my desk when I got in, looking pale and worried.

'Are you all right? I only just heard! What happened? How come you're looking so pleased with yourself when you've just had half your house knocked down?'

'Because I know who did it – and why.' I reached for the phone to ring Wayne.

'Hang on!' He took the phone out of my hand. 'Are you saying this was deliberate?' He looked shocked.

'Yes. But it's all right, because –' I hardly knew where to begin. 'Because I've had a tip-off. It's all to do with Janet Cox and St Martin's Court and the ad I put in. Ah – I meant to tell you about the ad – you'll be getting a bill.' From the look on his face, he'd already had it. 'Anyway, as I'm sure you'll agree, it was worth it, because I've been given another tip-off about a man called Paddy O'Donoghue who used to work for the council and who should know all about the St Martin's Court thing.'

'I see.' He didn't look as if he did. He let go of the phone. 'Well, as long as you're all right, that's the main thing. And you definitely know who did this?'

'Yes – well, *almost* definitely. Or at least, I think I know the name of the person who was *paid* to do it.' I thought for a moment. 'Of course, I'm not sure if the person who was responsible for the scaffolding poles is the same person who was responsible for murdering Janet, because there are quite a few things I haven't got to the bottom of. You know –' I hesitated. Something had been nagging away at the back of my mind ever since my conversation with Cherie Bolt, but so far I'd managed to avoid bringing it out into the open to look at it. 'You know – I'm beginning to think Lee Cox may have been murdered too.'

Mr Heslop gave me an odd stare and went back to his office. This was a relief. I hadn't wanted him to agree that Lee Cox might be dead.

I immediately dialled Hudderston Central and asked for Wayne.

'He's only just got into the office and he's gone straight in to see the super. I'm DC Bennet. Can I help?'

'Yes, I'm sure you can!' This was excellent. Wayne must have called in at Tipping as promised and was now referring the matter to a higher authority. 'I'm Chris Martin from the *Herald* –'

'Oh, yes, I've heard of you –'

'– and I was talking to Wayne this morning about an incident at my house. Could you tell him I've had a tip-off and I've got a name.'

'OK. Shoot.'

'Well, I've only got a first name, I'm afraid. It's Mac – Mac *D something*. I got the tip-off from a Mrs Bolt at Radley's Road Haulage, so –'

'I see. Well, don't worry, love, we've heard of Mac D. A nasty piece of work he is, I'm afraid. Couple of convictions for ABH and a suspected GBH on the file. Calls himself *Mac D Knife*. Get it? It's a joke.'

I didn't think it was funny.

'Has he ever murdered anyone?'

'No, not that we know of.'

This was a relief at any rate. 'Would you happen to know if he's got a lorry?'

'He's a lorry driver.'

'I see. Well, the thing is, if someone was to go out and inspect his lorry right now – someone from forensics – I'm sure they'd find evidence on it. Wayne knows all about it. Could you get him to ring me as soon as possible?'

'Will do. Cheers, love.'

I put the phone down, reached for the phone book, and started looking up O'Donoghues. There were lots of them – thirteen O'Donoghues, one O'Donogue, and two O'Donohues.

It took me the rest of the morning to ring them all, and it wasn't a very salutary experience. Only my very last call, to a Mrs P. L. O'Donohue, offered a whisper of promise.

'Sounds a bit like my father-in-law, dear,' she said, after my sixteenth attempt at describing a man called Paddy who had once been supervisor at Tipping's sports ground and lived at St Martin's Court in the early eighties. 'But I'm not sure really. I *think* he used to live at the Court – you mean that place that was knocked down? But he was never supervisor at the sports ground. Not Paddy.'

'Oh.' I was now desperate. The name must not be *O'Donoghue* at all. It must be O'Donald, or O'something else, and I was going to have to start all over again. 'Are you *sure*?'

'Oh, yes! He just cut the grass, that's all.'

'Ah! At the sports ground?'

'Sometimes, I expect. He worked for the Parks Department. He was caretaker at the bowls club for a while.'

'At the *bowls club*?' I thought about this. 'About sixteen or seventeen years ago?'

'Could have been. You never know with old Paddy, mind – he exaggerates a lot.' She sounded like a nice woman, the sort of person who makes her own shortcrust pastry and says, 'poor little love,' to children who cry in supermarkets. 'Why? What do you want old Dad for?'

'I just want to speak to him. I'm ringing from the *Tipping Herald*.'

There was a moment's incredulous silence. 'What – the newspaper – the one that does the Quicksaver ads?'

'Yes, that's right. Could I have a quick word, do you think?'

'Oh, he's not here, dear. He lives with my sister-in-law.'

'Well, could you give me *her* number?' I grabbed a pen.

'Oh, no, I couldn't do that – she's gone ex-directory.'

'I see. Well, I really do need to speak to him – it'll only take a few minutes. By the way, I've got his name as Paddy – what do *you* call him?'

'Dad,' she replied unhelpfully. 'Mary would kill me if I gave out her number. Tell you what, I'll ring him, and get him to ring you! What's your number?'

I gave her my name and number. 'Could you make sure it's today? It is quite urgent.'

'Oh, that's all right, dear. I don't suppose he'll be working in this weather. I'll ring him now.'

Five minutes later, the phone rang.

It wasn't Paddy O'Donohue. It was Pete.

'I've got some bad news, I'm afraid,' he said. 'I've got to go to Toulouse.'

'Oh – what for?'

'Oh, some bloody silly thing to do with the World Cup.' He hates football. 'Actually, I'm ringing from the airport. They've already called the flight.'

'Oh!' I couldn't think what to say, except, stupidly, that I didn't want him to go.

'I shouldn't be gone more than a couple of days – I'll ring you, OK? You'll be all right?'

'Of course I'll be all right!'

'OK. Actually, the thing is –' He broke off, and I could hear the public address system announcing the last call for his flight. 'Christ, I'll have to go. The thing is, Chris, I didn't want to worry you, but this business with the lorry – *OK, OK, I'm coming* – Look, I haven't got time to discuss it but if anything else happens you're to go to a hotel and put it on the card. All right? You got that?'

I felt a bit shaken. 'Well – all right, but actually –'

'Have to go. I love you. Bye . . .'

I put the phone down and stared at it for a moment. I was quite shocked to think that Pete was worried. He hadn't said anything. I made a mental note to be much nicer to him when he got back.

I gave Mrs O'Donohue until four o'clock, then rang her again.

She sounded a bit aggrieved. 'I've left your number with my sister-in-law, that's all I can do. Dad was in bed. I'm not ringing again.'

'Oh dear – is he ill?'

'He's getting on a bit. He's got his back.'

'I see. Well, look, I'm sorry to be a nuisance, but I've got to go out now, so if I could *possibly* give you my mobile number – if you could be kind enough to ring it through to him –'

She agreed, reluctantly, to do so, but just to be on the safe side I left a post-it note at reception with instructions that if a Mr O'Donohue rang, his number was to be taken down and put on my desk.

Wayne hadn't rung either, but I hoped this was because he was busy organizing Mac D's arrest.

Mrs Champion answered Philip Chandler's front door and I immediately stepped back and held my big handbag at the ready.

'He's not here,' she said, peering at me first over, and then through, her glasses, before I'd had a chance to ask her anything. And this time she didn't smell of brandy. 'He's in London at the hospital and he won't be back till eight or nine.'

I kept the handbag ready to deflect blows. 'At the hospital? Why?'

'His daughter had her twins six weeks early. They had to take them up to the Children's Hospital and put them in incubators.'

'Oh, I see.' I steeled myself. 'Well, actually, I wanted to ask you a couple of questions, if that's all right. Do you remember me, Mrs Champion?'

'Yes.' She shuffled from foot to foot in a gesture of contrition. 'You're that woman from the paper. Mr Chandler told me about you.'

'Did he? What did he say?'

She made it clear she thought this a particularly stupid question. She gestured towards the foot of the steps where Philip Chandler and I had stood and talked. 'Well, he said it was all right you coming here. He said you weren't batty!'

'Oh, I see.' I began to have doubts about the whole enterprise. 'Mrs Champion, when the other woman came here, the batty one last summer – what happened exactly?'

'What – when the police had to come and everything?'

'Yes. But before that. What happened before the police arrived?'

She looked hostile. 'What do you want to know about all that for? Mr Chandler knows what happened! He knows it wasn't my fault. I told him what happened, and he spoke to that policeman for me. He knows what I did!'

'Yes, it's all right, I didn't mean that. I meant what happened with the *woman*. Did Mr Chandler invite her into the house? Did –'

'He most certainly did not! He told me never to let her into the house – she wasn't welcome here!'

'What *never*? I mean, before this incident, did –' At that moment my mobile phone let out a sudden and alarming trill, and I somehow wrong-footed myself reaching for it and only just managed not to dive headlong over the top of the rockery. 'Oh, my God! Hallo – this is Chris Martin!'

'Chris? Is that you? It's Dave, here. Dave Ormond.'

'Oh.'

'Oh dear, you sound disappointed.' He laughed. 'Look, Bill Heslop just told me about your accident and I'm ringing to see if you're all right.'

'Well, that's very kind of you – and actually I'm fine but I've got someone with me at the moment.'

'Ah. OK. In that case I'll leave you to it.'

'Were you ringing about what we discussed the other day?'

'No. Just to see if my favourite reporter was OK.'

I studied a semifrozen clump of aubretia through the gloom and realized I quite fancied Dave Ormond.

'Well, I'll give you a call another time,' he said, and rang off.

I put my phone away. 'I'm awfully sorry,' I said, blushing slightly. 'That was Councillor Ormond.'

'Oh, *him*!' Her derision sounded heartfelt.

'What – you know Councillor Ormond?'

'Yes. Jumped-up little prat! Got no manners. I used to work on his mum's smallholding, feeding the chickens and that, when I needed a few bob. He never even gave you the time of day.'

'Oh.' I did my best to digest this piece of information. 'I'm sorry – what was that you said about Councillor Ormond's mother?'

'What? Oh, I wouldn't say anything against Jean. She was a nice friendly woman, she was. Had a smallholding on Gooserye. They lived on Harewood Common, the pair of them, in one of those little cottages they knocked down when they built the new road. He thought he was too good to go out and get himself a proper job. He used to go off with his rucksack on trips but he always came back when he ran out of money. Used to sit there under the trees smoking that cannabis stuff till he was out of his mind! Still, I shouldn't say anything, should I? Me and Tom used to go through a bottle of brandy a day, and it's all the same, isn't it? I went through a very bad time with Tom. A very bad time,' she added, gazing off speculatively into the gloom. 'Mr Chandler says it doesn't do to dwell on the bad times, but sometimes you can't help it, can you?'

'No. Of course not,' I agreed. Mrs Champion must be thinking of some other councillor: Dave Ormond's mother couldn't possibly have kept chickens for a living. Perhaps I ought to treat anything Mrs Champion said with more than a pinch of salt.

I decided to give up on the Pat Woollcott incident. I got out my photo of Janet and Lee instead. 'Do you recognize either of these people, Mrs Champion? Have either of them ever come here to see Mr Chandler?'

'What do you want to know that for?' She took the photo, removed her glasses, peered at it, and thrust it back at me. 'Don't know. Don't think so. I think I'm going in.'

'All right – just one last question.' I followed her into the porch. 'I know this is going to sound strange, but would you happen to remember where Mr Chandler was on the evening of Tuesday the twentieth of January, between six and eight?'

She stared at me with her mouth open, her breath slowly misting up her glasses. 'Well, of course I remember where he was. He was at the hospital – we had to call him home from his office in the middle of the afternoon. That was the day the twins were born. Look, I've got a polaroid.' She produced a black and white photo of two tiny babies side by side on a white sheet, their faces tight shut and tubes attached to them with sticking plaster. 'Gemma and Victoria,' she said proudly. 'I'm going to be able to sit for them when they get older.'

I turned the photo over. On the back someone had written, '20 January 1998, 18.15'. I wasn't sure if this meant Philip Chandler had an alibi or not, but I made a note of it anyway.

'*My* girls are dead,' said Mrs Champion suddenly, as I started out of the porch.

'I beg your pardon?'

'They're dead. No one believes me, but they're dead. They wouldn't have left me. They would've come back – they were only teaching me a lesson. They wouldn't have gone just because of Tom hitting Sally that time. I used to hit them but they never minded. They would've come back!'

'I see –'

'God giveth and God taketh away. As you sow, so shall you reap!' she boomed, and retreated into the house.

I went back to my car, switched on the internal light, and made a note to run Lola Champion's name through Archive and see what it came up with. Then I sat for a moment with the light still on and the window open to dry up the condensation seeping down the windscreen. I wished Wayne had rung to tell me what was going on. I got out my phone and thought of dialling his number. Then, in Ravenswood's almost total, serene silence I heard a car engine start into life somewhere out on the road. I put my phone away and waited for it to pass, but it didn't, so I started the Golf and moved down to the end of Philip Chandler's drive. The lights of a stationary vehicle were glimmering through trees just beyond the corner, so I gave up waiting for it to pass and pulled out into the road. I decided that in the morning I'd phone Philip Chandler and ask him straight out if Janet Cox had tried to blackmail him. I was too tired to think about it now.

I stopped at the end of Ravenswood to turn right, and at this point I think I half noticed that there was a car close behind me with its lights on full-beam. It followed me out on to the main road and across the mini roundabout into heavy traffic, sticking to my bumper like glue. And I wasn't sure, but now I thought I remembered a white car tailgating me across the mini roundabout on my way to Ravenswood half an hour ago. I glanced in my rear-view mirror again. It was hard to tell, but I was fairly sure this car was white, too. Still, it was the rush hour. Tipping would be replete with white cars. I put it out of my mind, accelerated towards the lights, and tried to work out whether to go straight ahead towards the dreaded one-way system, or left towards the station bottleneck. It was a difficult choice, and at the last minute, just as the amber flicked to red, I changed my mind and made a sharp left without indicating and drove off before anybody could take down my number.

It must have been about half a minute before I realized that the white car was still behind me. Which meant it must have jumped the lights too – on the red. Now I began to worry. I tried to remember my journey from the office to Ravenswood. There'd been a white car parked next to the wheelie bins in the *Herald* car park with a man sitting in it, smoking. I put my foot down, but there was nowhere to go, and I still wasn't sure if I was imagining things or not. Then I thought of something. Just up ahead on the left was Horseshoe Crescent. If the white car followed me along Horseshoe Crescent and back out on to the main road again, I'd know it was following me. I steeled myself to make the turn fast without braking so as not to alert my pursuer, left it to the very last second, then skewed the car into Horseshoe Crescent with a skirl of burning rubber. I was almost certain he wouldn't be able to change direction in time, even if he wanted to, but just before the first bend I looked in my mirror – and there he was, about twenty yards behind. I began to panic. He was accelerating. I made for the bend, misjudged it badly, and with a crack like a bullet my wing mirror impacted on something red on the left. I braked, swerved, wrenched the steering wheel to the right, and pulled away with shards of glass from a nice red Toyota's wing mirror clattering over my back window. I didn't even think about stopping. If I could reach the main road before the white car came round the final bend I could go either left or right and he wouldn't know which.

I slammed to a halt at the junction, which was solid with traffic. I'd half made up my mind to go right and head back to the one-way system, but I could see at a glance there was no chance of that. Desperately I indicated left and nudged forward. I edged bravely in front of a BT van – but it was too late. Out of the corner of my eye I caught sight of the white car skidding out of Horseshoe Crescent and forcing its way in behind the van.

Whoever he was, and whatever his reasons, the man in the white car was following me – and not only that, but he knew now that I knew he was there.

17

Five minutes later I was out in the country, with bends and
trees and road signs lurching out of the darkness on all sides.
In my panic I'd made things worse by getting in the wrong
lane and missing the station turn-off. Of course, I knew what
I ought to do now – I ought to lead my pursuer to the nearest
police station – but I couldn't think where the nearest police
station was. I was heading straight for the main Tipping to
Hudderston road with its ugly orange lighting and nonstop
traffic and police speed traps. I put my foot down and jumped
across to the fast lane, ignoring volleys of hoots and flashes,
held the accelerator to the floor and drove up the back of
a BMW so close I could read the words 'Man-size tissues'
on the top of the Kleenex box the owner kept on his back
window. There was a Shell station coming up. I could pull
in and reach for my phone, but of course he might get to
me before I could dial 999. Was there any possibility at all
that a petrol station attendant would notice a customer being
stabbed in front of his pumps? I wished I could make up my
mind. The white car was still behind me, still with his lights
on full-beam. The Shell station was approaching fast and I
was in the wrong lane and I couldn't make up my mind. All
I knew was, I couldn't take this. In the end, I didn't think
about it at all. With the speedometer veering towards eighty,
I slewed across two lanes in front of God knows how many
cars and headed straight for the pumps.

I don't know exactly what happened next. First there was
a grinding bump as I hit the approach road at the wrong
angle, then there was a 'Diesel only' pump charging at me,
and then there wasn't. Lights spun round and things crashed

into one another and my car deodorizer snapped off its string and slapped me in the eye. The car came to a shocked halt. It stalled. All I could think of was that the pump might explode at any minute. I ripped off my seatbelt and staggered out, hands up protectively. But there wasn't an explosion. In fact there was no smashed diesel pump spewing out oil, just two men clutching petrol nozzles blinking at me in astonishment, and yards of courtesy handwipe blowing about the forecourt. For a moment, I was too dazed to think. I'd knocked over two wastepaper bins and flattened something plastic, and I felt like apologizing or explaining to someone, but no one looked interested. There was also no white car in evidence. I got back into the Golf. It would be silly to call the police now. I took deep breaths, started the engine, and headed back on to the road.

I drove straight home, left the car in the road and ran up the front path. There was a light on in Julie's room and I could hear the phone ringing. I fell on it, praying it would be Pete or Wayne.

'OK,' said a voice. 'So you've got a fast car and you know how to drive, but remember – I know where you live.'

He put down the phone. I hadn't even had time to decide whether it was the same voice that had called me out to the Total station.

Julie appeared at the top of the stairs, looking soft and pink in her bathrobe. I couldn't speak, but she didn't seem to notice.

'Who was that?' she demanded.

'Nobody. Double glazing.'

'Oh, right. What's for tea?'

As soon as I got to the office the next morning I went straight to my desk, rang Hudderston Central and asked for Wayne. They put me through to a youngish-sounding WDC who said that Wayne was on leave for a couple of days.

I tried not to panic. 'What about DC Bennet?'

'DC Bennet? He's got someone with him at the moment. Perhaps I can help. What's it about?'

'It's Chris Martin from the *Herald*. Could I hang on for

DC Bennet, or could I ring back for him in a few minutes?'

'Chris Martin from the *Herald*. Hold on, I'll see.'

There was a long silence, during which I rehearsed my description of last night's drama exactly as I'd intended to repeat it to Wayne. Then the same woman came back to the phone.

'Mrs Martin? I'm sorry, but DC Bennet won't be available this morning. He said to tell you that if it's about the incident at your address in Tipping, you should ring the investigating officer at Tipping police station whose number I believe you already have.'

'I should ring Tipping –' I got a sort of cold feeling at the back of my neck. 'Look, I think there's been a misunderstanding. Couldn't I just speak to him for one second. You see –'

'I'm afraid you're really going to have to ring Tipping, Mrs Martin.'

'But – wait! DS Horton was going to investigate this *personally* for me. He's a *personal friend* –' Suddenly I got the message. The cold feeling ran slowly down my spine and seeped under my shoulder blades. 'Thank you very much, I'll ring Tipping,' I said sharply, and put down the phone.

I rang Tipping.

The officer in charge of investigating my 'accident', PC Lyons, listened sympathetically to my story, punctuating it occasionally with, 'Yes, madam', 'I see, madam', and 'Oh dear, madam', at appropriate points. When I'd finished, he said, 'Did you happen to get the vehicle's registration number?'

Of course, I couldn't believe he'd said that. 'Its registration number! Look, I told you, I was doing between fifty and eighty miles an hour most of the time – if I'd tried to read his number I'd be dead! Look, first this man half demolishes my house, then he lies in wait for me and tries to force me to kill myself –'

'Now hold on a minute! As I understand it there was no communication whatsoever between you and this driver – isn't that right?'

'Yes, that's right. There wasn't at the time, but afterwards he –'

'Well, madam, in this kind of instance, it's best not to rise to provocation.'

I immediately exploded. 'But I *told* you he laid in wait for me outside my office! He followed me across town, he waited for me while I conducted an interview – I *had* to try and shake him off! I *told* you, this man has been paid to intimidate me!'

'I see. Well, I've got a note on the file here which says you've alleged a Mr Terence MacDiarmid is responsible for the damage to your property. Are you also alleging that this Mr MacDiarmid was the driver of the vehicle you say harassed you yesterday? Can I ask what is the nature of your relationship with Mr MacDiarmid?'

There was now a pile driver working overtime in my right temporal lobe. I tried to take in what he'd just said. 'Terence MacDiarmid – I'm sorry, you've got a *note on the file*? Does that mean you haven't been out and impounded his lorry yet?'

'No, madam,' replied PC Lyons, in a deeply patronizing tone. 'I'm afraid things don't work quite like that. Now, what I'm going to suggest is that you pop down to the station for a chat sometime during the next couple of days so I can go through all this with you. Sometimes people react differently to the trauma of accidents – we have a list of counsellors here. In the meantime I'll send you our leaflet on how to handle so-called road rage incidents . . .'

'OK! Fine! Just forget it, will you!' I slammed down the phone.

I took my coat off, hung it up, and sat down. The pile driver was still working, but I was quite calm, because I knew exactly what I'd got to do next. I'd made up my mind about it at four in the morning, when the wind had been trying to get its fingers under the boards at our living room window and some phantom kept making footstep noises on the stairs. I'd decided that if push came to shove I was not the stuff of which heroes are made. Push had now come to shove, and I was going to do the sensible thing. I got out my notebook with Mr O'Donohue's daughter-in-law's number in it, tore off the number, screwed it up, and tossed it into the wastepaper basket. I tore up my copy of the St

Martin's Court ad, my notes on the Broxham system, and the transcript I'd made of my phone conversation with the ex-St Martin's Court resident, and I threw these away too. Then I rang Dawn.

'Dawn, if anyone calls for me about my ad, or if Mr O'Donohue rings – tell them I'm no longer interested.'

'*What*? But I've got this *urgent* post-it note here somebody's stuck on my monitor.'

'I know. I'm sorry.'

She sighed heavily. 'All right then. But I've got a Philip Chandler on hold down here.'

'OK. Put him through.'

While Dawn worked her switches, I got out the list of people on the council I'd either phoned or written to about St Martin's Court.

'Mrs Martin? It's Philip Chandler here,' he said. 'I believe you were trying to get in touch with me last night? Mrs Champion seemed rather concerned about some of the questions you asked her and I thought perhaps I should put things straight.'

'Right –' I wasn't in the mood to be tactful. 'Well, I've been given information that both Lee and Janet Cox tried to blackmail you over a certain matter and I was wondering if you'd like to comment on that.'

There was a long silence, and I could almost feel him reaching for his latest copy of *Slander: Law Society Precedents in Practice*, or whatever.

'I beg your pardon?' He sounded shocked. 'Over what certain matter?'

'Pat Woollcott.'

The silence resumed for a moment.

'Pat Woollcott?'

'Yes. I wondered why you didn't report Janet Cox's approach to the police. After all, if –'

'Pat Woollcott,' he interrupted. 'You think someone would want to blackmail me over Mrs Woollcott. Where did you get your information from, Mrs Martin?' He sounded very angry.

Wayne. Oh, God. 'I'm sorry, I'm afraid I can't possibly say – but it wasn't anyone on your staff, I do assure you.'

'I see. Well, I can't compel you to reveal your source of information, obviously.' He waited for me to say something but just at that moment I couldn't think of anything appropriate. 'Mrs Martin, I hope you realize you're making some extremely serious allegations here. Let me elaborate. Firstly, you're alleging that the circumstances of my dealings with Mrs Woollcott might give rise to blackmail; secondly you're alleging criminal activity on the part of Mr Cox, who – I might remind you – is still technically a client of mine; and thirdly you're alleging that I've failed to cooperate with the police in a major investigation. I don't want to be unhelpful, but I'm sure you'll realize that from a legal point of view if I answer any of these allegations, I could be placing myself in an extremely difficult position if any future legal action should arise concerning either myself or other persons. I suggest you consult your legal department. Good morning to you, Mrs Martin.'

I had no idea what he was talking about. I decided this was probably legalese for you're barking up the wrong tree without a paddle and I don't give a stuff, but I wasn't really sure.

'I see. Well, thank you for ringing back.'

He rang off before I'd finished, and I sat staring at the phone trying to blot out images of the moment yesterday evening when I'd walked innocently down the front steps of his house in Ravenswood while Mac D Knife sat waiting for me just out of sight beyond the trees. Of course, I knew that if he'd really wanted to, Mr Knife could have bashed me over the head or carved me up in Philip Chandler's drive without Mrs Champion noticing a thing, and I suppose I should have taken heart from this, but that's not how my mind works.

I didn't want to think about it any more, so I turned on my monitor, typed in the Archive password, and initiated a search on the name Lola Champion while I looked up phone numbers for the people I'd contacted at the council. By the time I'd completed the list, Archive had whirred its way impressively through its paces and found two references.

I called up the first one. It was on a page dated 29 December 1971, when the *Herald* was still in its old format. Under the headline: 'Christmas Disturbance', the story read: *Police were called to the Star Public House on Christmas Eve, following reports of a disturbance. It is understood that a member of staff and one customer were slightly injured by flying glass during what has been described as a marital dispute. Thomas and Lola Champion were subsequently bound over to keep the peace.* This was at the bottom of page three, which in those days was the *Herald's* 'Crime Notebook' page. I called up the second item, and found myself looking at an oddly familiar photograph of a man with enormous sideburns wearing the mayoral chain of office. At first, I couldn't think where I'd seen this photo before, until I read the item beneath: 'Suicide verdict' – the story of Miles Anthony Lloyd's suicide at Holly Cottage. I stared at it, confused. Archive must have somehow recycled an old instruction – did this mean the programme had crashed? But then I spotted Lola Champion's name highlighted at the foot of the screen, in the centre of a short item headed 'Girls Found'. It said: *A spokesman for Tipping police announced yesterday that Tina and Marie Champion, aged 19 and 20, who were reported missing by their mother, Lola Champion, of The Meadows Caravan Park, Gooserye, last Monday, have now been contacted by police. It is believed that the girls, who were last seen at Pan's Disco last Tuesday evening, and whose bicycles were spotted in the railway station car park at the weekend, left home after a dispute with their stepfather, and are staying at an address in London. Mrs Champion was admitted yesterday to Manning Green Hospital and her two younger children are being cared for by social services.*

I was intrigued. Manning Green Hospital (now defunct) specialized in the treatment of various addictions and minor mental disorders. Sadly, they'd obviously failed to cure Mrs Champion of her alcoholism, if that was what she'd gone in there for. But could there be some sort of connection between Miles Lloyd's suicide at Holly Cottage and the Champions' domestic crises – or was this just an odd coincidence?

I reread the 'Girls Found' item. All I could think was, poor Mrs Champion: drunk and disorderly, an abusive husband . . . Whatever his motives might have been, in taking her up as his 'good cause' Philip Chandler had saved her from a miserable life.

Mr Heslop arrived, so I followed him to his office.

He peered at me intently as I leaned in his doorway. 'Are you all right? You don't look very well.'

I had a horrible feeling if he started being sympathetic I might cry.

'It's this St Martin's Court thing,' I blurted. 'I've got to drop it.'

'Why?'

'It's a long story. It's awful! Last night when I left here something terrible happened – I don't think I can talk about it now. That ad – I'll pay for it myself –'

'No, no!' He leapt to his feet. He hates reporters crying in his office. 'Don't think about it. You go and get yourself a coffee and take your mind off things. Whenever you're ready – tomorrow – next week – my door is always open.'

'Thank you, Mr Heslop. But it's OK for me to drop the St Martin's Court story for now?'

'Yes, yes. Of course it is. We've got much bigger fish to fry.'

By the end of the afternoon, by which time I'd phoned round half a dozen bemused council workers and told them on no account were they to process any of my requests for information on St Martin's Court, I was feeling a lot better. Then Julie rang.

'Mum? Have you been trying to ring me? I think there's something wrong with our phone. It's rung five times in the last half-hour, but when I pick it up, it just clicks and goes dead.'

I know it's a cliché, but a shiver really did run down my spine. I ignored it.

'Oh, for goodness sake, it'll be one of your friends messing about!'

'No, it isn't! My friends are not little babies! I've done dial-back and it says "caller withheld their number".'

'Well, it would say that, wouldn't it?'

'It's *not* one of my friends.'

'Are you sure?'

'Yes. I'm ringing BT –'

'Wait –' She was about to hang up. 'Julie – look, wait a

minute!' I had a sudden, horrible flashback of Janet lying under the polythene tent in her red jacket and torn tights. I tried to dismiss it, but it wouldn't go. 'Look, I've been thinking – why don't you go and stay with Richard and Becky for a while? You know – till the window's mended?'

'What?'

'Why not? Becky can help you with your French.'

'Oh!'

'Go on – get a few things packed – now. I'll arrange it.'

I put the phone down. I was trembling. This wasn't fair. I'd *dropped* the story. *They* – whoever they were – ought to know that by now. I'd phoned everybody I could think of and told them so. Who had I missed? Of course – I'd missed Paddy O'Donohue. Frantically I rummaged through my wastepaper basket, retrieved Mrs O'Donohue's number, and punched it into the phone. I had to do it three times, because I kept transposing numbers.

Finally, she answered.

'Oh, Mrs O'Donohue, thank God I've got you! It's Chris Martin from the *Tipping Herald* –'

'Is it, indeed! Well, will you please stop bothering me! My father-in-law is an old man! If he doesn't want to talk to you there's nothing I can do about it. I've given him your message and –'

'Look, Mrs O'Donohue, it's desperately important you give your father-in-law *another* message. Will you tell him I've *dropped* the story on St Martin's Court! Have you got that? I've dropped the –'

But she'd hung up. I dialled her number again, but her phone was now off the hook. This was hopeless. If I couldn't get my message through to the right people I wouldn't be able to get Mac called off. I suddenly realized with horror that I'd told Dave Ormond – and that Dave Ormond would probably have made his own enquiries of all kinds of people I couldn't know about, possibly mentioning my name. I could of course ring him and ask him for a list of all his contacts, but somehow I had the feeling that things had already spiralled out of my control. And there was no telling what tool of the construction industry might turn up next in my living room if I couldn't get Mac's contract cancelled.

I stared out of the window for a moment. And then, of course, it came to me. I'd got it all wrong. My best course of action would not be to drop the story, it would be to pursue it to its bitter end – fast. If I could only find out who was behind the St Martin's Court cover-up and present the evidence to the police, I'd be safe.

I sat still and listened to the pounding in my head. I'd told Councillor Draycott. On top of Riddlesdown Hill, I'd told Councillor Draycott. I thought about this. The remains of my St Martin's Court notes were scattered all over my desk. My gaze fell on the crumpled print-out of our story on the Court's opening. I picked it up. St Martin's Court was built on the Broxham system, it said, which Councillor Draycott was *proud to have been instrumental in introducing to Tipping*. I pulled more notes out of the bin and pieced them together. I found the biographical note on Councillor Draycott. He'd served as mayor of Tipping from 1983 to 1986. Would he still have got elected if one or more of the residents of St Martin's Court had been asphyxiated by fumes from its central-heating system?

I ran down to reception and caught Dawn on her way out through the swing doors.

'Dawn, did anyone ring for me about my ad?'

'What?' She looked incredulous. 'I thought you said you didn't want to speak to anybody about it?'

'I know I did, but I've changed my mind. Did anyone ring?'

'Oh, *God*!' she snapped. 'No, they didn't. Do you mind? I'll miss my bus!'

I let her go, ran back upstairs, and dialled Councillor Draycott's number. It rang four times, and then his voice said: 'Councillor and Mrs Draycott are unable to speak to you. Leave a message, or ring back. Message ends.'

'This is Chris Martin from the *Tipping Herald*,' I announced, after the beep. 'I want you to know that I am not dropping the St Martin's Court story! Have you got that? *I am not dropping the story*! My editor has got all the details so you're wasting your time! You're not getting away with this!'

18

Julie was unnaturally quiet while we drove to Becky and Richard's.

'Is everything all right?' she asked, as I hustled her up the footpath with her suitcase.

'Of course it is.' I retrieved Becky and Richard's front door key from its not particularly good hiding place under a flower pot and handed it to her.

'Oh, good,' she said. 'I just wanted to be sure. Pete's in France, is he?'

'Yes. Toulouse. Give me a ring if you've forgotten anything.'

'I will.' She went in. 'By the way, I don't really hate Pete, you know. He's just a bit of a pain sometimes. Sometimes I actually quite like him. I mean, it'd be a bit boring if we were always on our own – and of course if the exams go OK and I'm off to university next year . . . Oh, well – bye!'

I was halfway home before this had sunk in. The last time I'd bundled Julie off to stay with relatives at short notice she'd come home to find that Keith and I had split up. Tomorrow, I'd find some way of straightening things out. Not that I could do anything about her going off to university, of course . . .

I went into the house, found the phone book, and looked up entries under the name MacDiarmid. But there wasn't a T. MacDiarmid. I rang the Anchor instead.

'I want to speak to one of your customers. It's urgent. His name is Mac D.'

'I think Mac's gone. Hang on.' The phone banged down. *Gone*? Gone where? My stomach turned over.

'Yeah – you missed him. Want me to give him a message?'

'*Where's* he gone? When will he be back?'

'Dunno. Won't be tonight. He's making another delivery on Tyneside. Who is this?'

I was so relieved that for a moment I couldn't speak.

'You still there? You want to give me a message, or what?'

'No. I have to give it to him myself.' A little ripple of adrenaline tingled in the back of my neck. I'd still got a buzz from the message I'd left for Councillor Draycott. 'Can you give me his home number?'

'Bugger off! I've got customers. Mac'll be in tomorrow at six. Come in then and give him your own sodding message.'

'Oh, but I don't actually want –' It was too late. He'd disconnected me.

I woke up with a shock the following morning to discover that a) I was still alive, and b) it was broad daylight and ten to nine. I had slept right through my alarm, set for seven-thirty. I leapt out of bed, washed, dressed, downed coffee and extra-strong paracetamol, and ran out to the car with a half-eaten banana clenched between my teeth. As I started the engine I realized I'd forgotten to comb my hair, put on lipstick, or check my top lip for stray hairs, but it was too late now to do anything about any of this. I wanted to catch Mrs O'Donohue before I went into the office, and I had a horrible feeling she was the sort of person who'd be up at the crack of dawn searching the greengrocer's for perfect mushrooms for her steak and mushroom pies.

I gritted my teeth and got into a line of bad-tempered, first-gear/second-gear traffic. The O'Donohue residence was in a narrow street of Victorian semis not far from the railway station, and when I got there the whole area was still bumper to bumper with late commuters. I pulled up on the pavement outside the house and rattled the door knocker tentatively.

No answer.

I spotted a bellpush and pressed it with a nervous finger. In the constant grumble and whine of the traffic, I couldn't tell if the bell was even ringing.

The door wrenched suddenly open.

'Mrs O'Donohue?'

'Yes?' She was breathless and bleary-eyed in a dressing gown, in her late fifties. A small dog was yapping in the background.

'I'm Chris Martin from the *Herald*. I'm terribly sorry to have messed you about –' And I knew immediately that this had been the wrong thing to say, because her face stiffened. I got my knee in the way of the door just in time.

'Look, I know I said I wanted to talk to Mr O'Donohue and then I changed my mind and said I didn't – but now I do. I'm really awfully sorry, but if you could just give me his address I won't have to bother you any more.'

'He doesn't want to talk to you!'

'Why not?'

'Go away!'

'*Please*! Look, I don't want to go into the details, but I'm really worried that someone could get hurt. I think it could be me –' She suddenly swung the door wide and closed it hard on my knee. I withdrew instantly, wincing.

The door slammed shut.

Passers-by in cars were leaning out of their windows staring at me, but I couldn't afford to be squeamish about this. I bent down and lifted the letterflap. 'Mrs O'Donohue – listen! All I want is to talk to your father-in-law for five minutes. He doesn't have to meet me in person if he doesn't want to, or sign anything – but I've just *got* to speak to him!' By now I'd given up on the stiff-upper-lip thing, but it was no use. There was complete silence inside the house. 'Look, I'm going to put my card through your door. *Please* give me a ring.' I posted my card through her flap and went back to the car.

I pulled out into the road. I'd give Mrs O'Donohue an hour, then call her again. The traffic was still heavy with mothers returning from the school run, and I got as far as the multistorey car park behind the station before everything ground to a complete halt. I took the Market Street detour and this was solid, too. It was now half past nine. I reached for my mobile and dialled David Ormond's number.

'Hallo, it's Chris here. I'm sorry to bother you but I need to ask you something urgently.'

'I see –' I'd caught him in his gym. I could hear the thump

of someone's feet on the treadmill. 'Is this about St Martin's Court? You're still keeping on with that, are you? How's it going?'

'It's going very well! I've found out that there were choking fumes coming out of the air vents, and that some of the residents were bribed to sign a petition asking to be rehoused! But that's not what I'm phoning about. What I want to know is, did you tell anyone else I was investigating St Martin's Court?'

'I'm sorry?' The thumping in the background halted abruptly.

'Oh, I'm sorry, you're busy.' I was beginning to think I'd made a mistake in phoning. His voice wasn't as friendly as usual. 'It's just you said you were going to check whether there were any more buildings in Tipping built on the Broxham system and I wondered if you had.'

There was a short silence. 'Yes, I have and there aren't.'

'Oh. So – who did you actually check with?'

'Well – look, I can't go into all that now.' He was beginning to sound rather cross. 'I've got to get ready for a meeting. Come over and have a drink one evening if you like and we'll talk about it. Give me a ring later.'

'OK. I'm sorry.'

The traffic moved off, and we wound round the corner in second gear before coming to a dead halt again outside the electricity board building. I wished I hadn't phoned Dave Ormond. Sometimes people give you all the wrong vibes. I was forty-three and happily married, but if I was perfectly honest, I'd have to admit that I'd imagined the councillor's helpfulness had stemmed from his appreciation of my knees. I shivered in embarrassment at this thought. In the distance I could now see the actual site of St Martin's Court – the Belfair House office block and multistorey car park that had replaced it – and suddenly I had a vision of Market Street as it used to look sixteen years ago. In fact, Market Street had been an almost exact replica of the street where Mrs O'Donohue now lived; cramped terraced houses on both sides of the road snaking darkly into the distance, a run-down corner shop here, a sub-post office there. The area had been mostly residential, apart from a couple of shabby builders' yards at the top end. Now it was high-class commercial. Whoever built the prestigious office block on the St Martin's Court site must have made a huge leap of faith.

Somewhere up ahead a light changed, and we moved on in close procession until it changed again, by which time I was sitting outside Belfair House admiring its glass atrium, attractively tiled floor and marble-faced columns. In estate-agent speak, Belfair House was luxuriously appointed and handy for the station and the town centre. And suddenly, something happened inside my head. The word 'Belfair' swam round in a circle so that it joined up with itself and became 'Fairbel'. It kept on dancing for a bit, as though it was trying to tell me something, and then I thought – Fairlands and Bellchamber. The Fairlands Bellchamber Group.

I met Mr Heslop on my way in to the office.

'You still look a bit tired,' he said.

I ignored this. 'Are the Fairlands Bellchamber Group into property development, do you know?' I asked.

'I don't know. Why? Have a look at their literature – there's a whole mountain of it in the stuff the council gave us. Must go – meeting with the bank.'

I ran up the stairs two at a time and got out the stuff Dave Ormond had given me about the Fairlands Bellchamber Group. Sure enough, there was a Bellchamber Properties plc listed as part of the group.

I rang them.

'I wonder if you could tell me if your company built an office block in Tipping about fifteen or sixteen years ago and called it Belfair House?' I enquired.

The Australian woman who answered said she had no idea, but she put me through to someone in public relations who, after a bit of umming and aahing, said she'd got an artist's impression on her wall entitled Belfair House, which she understood depicted the prototype for several office blocks that had been built in the South East in the early eighties.

'Can you confirm whether one was definitely put up by you in Tipping?' I persisted. 'With marble columns and a sort of glass front?'

'I don't know, but it sounds right. Why don't you check with your local council?'

I thanked her, hung up, and dialled Mrs O'Donohue's number.

She answered straight away.

'Hallo, Mrs O'Donohue, this is Chris Martin. Don't hang up!'

She hung up.

I immediately redialled, but of course her phone was off the hook. I imagined the poor woman, cowering in her tiny darkened hall, afraid to answer her own phone. I didn't want to, but I'd have to keep on trying. Keeping one eye on the stairs in anticipation of Mr Heslop's return, I rang Councillor Draycott instead. At the very least I wanted to know how he'd reacted to my message.

'Hallo,' said an elderly female voice. 'Councillor Draycott's residence. Can I help?'

'Yes – I need to speak to Councillor Draycott right away, please.'

'I'm afraid they're away. They went to Barbados at the weekend.'

'Barbados!' I felt a stab of alarm. If I was a prominent local councillor, and I'd hired someone to maim or kill a newspaper reporter, I'd go to Barbados too. 'Was it a sudden decision?'

'It was a surprise late Christmas present for Mrs Draycott.'

A surprise late Christmas present.

'When will they be back? Will they be in touch to pick up their messages?'

'I don't know. I only come in to water the plants.'

I began grimly sifting through my mail. Two postcards had arrived from different departments of the Borough Council. Despite all the desperate phone messages I'd left yesterday, they were acknowledging my requests for information on St Martin's Court. Neither gave any indication when the information would be available, but one gave a number to ring for enquiries.

I rang it.

'Look, I'm awfully sorry, I'm afraid there's been a misunderstanding,' I lied. 'One of my colleagues mistakenly rang you yesterday to say we didn't want the information we asked for, but I'm afraid we do – and we need it today.'

She put me on hold.

'I'm sorry,' she said, after several verses of 'We Are Sailing', 'but the information you've requested has to come from files which are now in storage. Your request has been logged and you'll be contacted by post as soon as we've managed to get hold of the files for you. If it's really urgent you could always send us a first-class stamped addressed envelope –'

'What? But this is the *Tipping Herald* –'

She plugged me into another verse of 'We are Sailing' without comment, and at that moment Mr Heslop walked past with a doughnut. I disconnected her and ran after him.

I told him the whole story, piece by piece, starting with my run-in with someone I could only assume was Mac D on the dual carriageway, my suspicions of Councillor Draycott and my attempts to track down Paddy O'Donohue, and concluding with a slightly toned-down version of the message I'd left on Councillor Draycott's answerphone.

Mr Heslop turned a sort of apple-white.

'You see, the thing is,' I went on, 'it's going to take ages and ages to get any information out of the council – we may never be able to get it – but we could short-cut all this if we could find some way of persuading either Paddy O'Donohue or Terry MacDiarmid to tell us who paid them.'

I waited for the *some way of persuading* to sink in. His frown deepened.

'Well, it would be an investment, wouldn't it? To save man-hours. Look, somebody must have paid Paddy O'Donohue to take up the petition at St Martin's Court. I'm now certain that Lee Cox and Michael Irons – and probably Janet Cox as well – tried to blackmail someone over St Martin's Court, and Lee Cox got a scaffolding pole through his window – *I* got the same thing. Janet Cox is dead. Someone must have paid for all this. If we could find out who, it would be half the battle. It would save hours and hours of going through old files and council minutes and things.'

He picked up his doughnut in its greasy bag and dropped

it in the bin. 'You know perfectly well that financial inducements are out of the question.'

'But why?' Surely he could see I was desperate. 'I haven't
met this Paddy O'Donohue yet, but he's an old man! An
all-expenses-paid weekend in Bournemouth would probably
do it! What else do you suggest?'

'Chris, I've told you before – there's no substitute for good
old-fashioned journalism. Look, even if you're right about
this – what was it? – Broxham system thing, and frankly
–' He shrugged so theatrically that a stack of files on the
corner of his desk was toppled by a flying elbow. 'Oh,
damn it. Frankly, even if you're right, this man's statement by itself is worthless. We'd still have to come up with
proper evidence before we could run the story. It could
take years, and to be quite honest, while we're on the subject, I wouldn't have thought this Mr Big of yours – be he
Councillor Draycott or not – would bother to have anyone
killed to stop it coming out, if that's what you're suggesting.' He reached for the files. 'Half the electorate would
probably have died of old age before you'd got to the bottom of it.'

I waited till he'd picked up the files. 'Yes, but you see, I'm
not sure about this Broxham system thing any more. I'm
beginning to wonder if maybe it's not the St Martin's Court
building itself we should be looking at – it's the building that
came *after* it. You know, Belfair House.'

'What about it?'

'Well, it's a really nice building, isn't it? And now, it's in
a really good area, but *then* that area used to be rubbish!
Whoever decided to redevelop the site after the Court was
demolished made a very lucky choice, don't you think?'

He stared at me for a moment. He was getting the point. He
got up and pulled open the bottom drawer of his old green
filing cabinet.

'We can soon sort this out,' he said, extracting a plan and
spreading it across the files on his desk. 'Tipping Town Plan,
1977. Here we are – here's St Martin's Court. It's just inside
the pink area – residential and commercial – see? Whereas, as
you can see, the rest of Market Street is pale blue – residential

only.' I nodded, even though I couldn't quite make out which street was Market Street.

'And,' he went on, opening up another plan with a flourish. 'On the 1987 plan, if we look, we can see that the whole of Market Street has now gone red. *Commercial*. He frowned over the map. 'Hmm. I see what you mean. Whoever bought the St Martin's Court site in 1983 must have had vision.'

I peered over his shoulder. 'I'm pretty certain Belfair House was built by Bellchamber Properties.'

'Hmm,' said Mr Heslop again, thoughtfully. 'Your theory being that Bellchamber Properties bought the site cheap, and someone on the council got a backhander to influence what would be in the next town plan, thus improving the area and enhancing property values. The petition and inducements to residents of the Court were so no one would put a spanner in the works by protesting, is that it?'

I hadn't even thought of this. I nodded.

He sighed and pushed the plan away. 'It's a neat idea, and I can't say I like Councillor Draycott any better than you do, but I can't see him compromising his position for money. I expect you know he used to own a very successful chain of butcher's shops and he's not short of a few bob.'

'Actually,' I heard myself say, 'I wasn't thinking of Councillor Draycott. I mean, Councillor Draycott isn't the one promoting the Fairlands and Bellchamber Millennium project, is he?'

He stared at me in such outraged astonishment that I immediately began to wonder if I was suffering from sleep deprivation or premature senility or both. 'I know – I know it sounds ridiculous. But have you ever wondered how Dave Ormond manages to afford trips abroad, huge sapphire rings – a private gym – and God knows what else – on what he makes from the Harewood Garden Centre?'

'Well, he's – one of the *Ormonds*, for God's sake! He doesn't *need* to live off what he makes from the Harewood Garden Centre. He told me once he started it off as a hobby – he only keeps it going out of loyalty to his staff.'

'But *is* he one of the Ormonds? Someone told me the other day his mother had a smallholding on Gooserye. Councillor

Ormond apparently spent the seventies unemployed wandering about with a rucksack – and smoking cannabis. Are you absolutely *sure* he's one of the *biscuit* Ormonds?'

'Well, of course he is!' Mr Heslop was almost speechless. 'Unemployed and wandering about with a rucksack? People like Dave are never unemployed – they simply take time out to consider their options – and why not? *A smallholding*? Whoever told you all this nonsense must be out of their tree!'

This was of course a pretty fair description of Mrs Champion. I bit my lip.

He began to put the plans away. 'We've got absolutely nothing to go on,' he said, thoughtfully. 'Nothing at all. But all the same, if one of our councillors took a backhander from these Bellchamber property people, you can bet your boots he'll have taken backhanders from other developers as well. There could be something in it, and if we knew where to look –' I could see he was tempted. 'All right, this is much against my better judgement, but if you can buy O'Donohue's story with something that won't stand out like a sore thumb on your expense sheet –'

'Thank you, Mr Heslop!' I leapt up before he could change his mind. 'And what about this – if I can get a statement from Mr O'Donohue – or if I can get some other kind of proof – will you let me take someone else with me to the Anchor tonight to confront Mac D with the evidence?'

He gave me an incredulous look. 'Are you mad? Don't push it!'

I decided not to. I turned to go. Then I thought of something. 'Mr Heslop, on Monday evening, Dave Ormond phoned me to ask if I was OK after the accident. He said you'd told him about it. Did you?'

He looked blank. 'I've no idea. I think I rang him about the Chamber of Commerce dinner. If he said I told him, I must have done. Oh, come on – you're barking up the wrong tree with Dave.'

I went back to my desk, got my coat and started to head for the stairs, but then I had a brainwave. Mr Heslop was right; if Dave Ormond was one of the biscuit Ormonds he wouldn't need to take backhanders from property developers. I dashed off a fax to our search service requesting a copy of David Ormond's birth certificate on their super premium service, which would mean it should arrive by five o'clock this afternoon. I would have a hard job justifying the super premium, but I'd worry about that later.

It was midday when I got to Mrs O'Donohue's house. The afternoon was grey and overcast, there were lights on up and down the street, and you could see the flicker of television screens and coal-effect gas fires. All the windows of Mrs O'Donohue's house were tightly curtained, but I wasn't put off by this, because everybody now knows that when the press come knocking at your door you close the curtains so they can't get their zoom lenses into your bathroom. I rang the doorbell and tapped gently on the door-knocker. I'd got my cheque book in my pocket.

After a few minutes one of Mrs O'Donohue's neighbours, a large woman with a washed-out complexion and overstretched leggings, wrenched open her door aggressively and stared at me.

'Clear off!' she bawled. 'I know who you are. We've heard all about you! You ought to be ashamed of yourself, upsetting Pauline like that! Go on – clear off before I call the police!'

'Hang on a minute! You don't understand.' I pulled out my cheque book. 'I want to pay the O'Donohues' expenses. Could you just call through the door and tell them for me? Go on, please – it's very important!'

She came out and planted herself on the step. She had the sort of thighs that require planning permission.

'Look,' she said. 'I don't know what all this is about – it's none of my business. Pauline's been a good neighbour to me, right? If you don't clear off I'm going to set my dog on you.'

'But I only –'

'And it's no good you banging and hammering on that door, 'cos they're not there – right? Pauline's on her own with two grandkids to look after and you've hounded her out! I hope you're proud of yourself!'

227

She went in and slammed her door. I didn't feel proud of myself at all. I felt quite sick with shame, but at the back of my mind was an indelible image of the moment on the Tipping to Hudderston road when I held my breath and waited to be obliterated by a diesel-pump explosion. I lifted her letterflap and shouted through it.

'Please tell Mrs O'Donohue I'm sorry. I'm going now, all right? I'm sorry to have bothered you, but I'd be very grateful if you could ask Mrs O'Donohue to give me a ring when she comes back. Thank you.'

I went back to my car, turned the lights on full-beam, and drove off noisily. I was sure Mrs O'Donohue was in. She had to be. I waited till I was out of sight of the house and then pulled over and counted to fifty – just time enough for Mrs O'Donohue's neighbour to relay the news of my departure and go home. Then I turned round, drove back and found another parking space about six cars down from the O'Donohue residence. I made myself as comfortable as I could while I waited for Mrs O'Donohue to tweak a curtain or put out a milk bottle. If she really wasn't in, I had no idea what to do next.

It was half past four when I finally gave up on Mrs O'Donohue and went back to the office. I couldn't wait any longer, or I'd miss Mr Heslop. When I arrived at my desk a faxed copy of Dave Ormond's birth certificate and a large bill were propped up against my monitor. There was also a faxed press release from the police stating that Daniel Kerr-Dixon had been arrested early that morning at an address in Brighton, and was currently being questioned in connection with the murder of Janet Cox: a further announcement was to be expected shortly. I gritted my teeth. Despite everything, I still couldn't help feeling just a bit sorry for Daniel. I spread out the birth certificate and examined its splotched surface. It showed that David Andrew Ormond had been born to Neil and Jean Ormond of One Harewood Cottages, Harewood Common, on 12 December 1948. Neil Ormond's 'rank or profession' was given as 'District Manager'. District manager? I thought about this. To begin with, I was all for going into Mr Heslop's office proclaiming, 'There you are – Dave Ormond can't be one of the Ormonds – his father was a district manager!' but then I realized that the term district manager meant absolutely nothing at all. Neil Ormond could have been the district manager of anything – including some branch of Ormond Biscuits. *One Harewood Cottages.* This didn't exactly sound like the address of a mansion, but names can be deceptive. A girlfriend of mine was once invited to a party at One Baron's Mews, Kensington and went expecting it to be a bedsit – but that's another story.

I was back to square one.

19

'I've got another idea,' I said. 'How about if we go to the Anchor and tell Terry MacDiarmid we've got evidence and we're going to the police? He might agree to make a statement.'

Mr Heslop snapped his briefcase shut. 'No. I told you – no. We don't do things like that here. We'll have another go at finding this O'Donohue bloke. Perhaps we can get at him through his employment records. Leave me the details and I'll get on to it first thing in the morning.'

'He used to work at the sports ground. At the bowls club,' I added significantly.

'Right. Look, you've obviously had a rough time. Why don't you go and stay at a hotel for a couple of nights? I'm sure it's only a matter of time before the police sort things out one way or the other. Do you want me to help you find one? Here –' He selected a book from the shelf. 'This is a bit out of date, I'm afraid, but it'll give you an idea. I can certainly recommend the Park View, but it's a bit pricey.'

I waited till he'd gone, then put down the hotel guide and looked up the street directory. The Anchor was on a back street down by the river and, purely on the basis of its location, it didn't look like the sort of pub the writers' circle would pick for their annual social. In fact, it looked more like the kind of place that would be full of men who didn't clean under their fingernails and women in spangly tops; there'd be fruit machines and a juke box whose repertoire ran the full gamut from 'Stand By Your Man' to 'Suspicious Minds', and the air in the ladies' loo would be stiff with hairspray. In a place like that I'd stand out like a sore thumb. I glanced at my watch: it was just after five-thirty.

I got my coat. As far as I knew, Terry MacDiarmid had only seen me twice, both times in the dark, wearing this coat. I took off the coat and ran downstairs to the ground-floor cloakroom. I was beginning to get the germ of an idea. Last summer a temp had left behind a short silver-coloured plastic raincoat no one had quite had the heart to dispose of. I put on the raincoat, hitched up my skirt, and studied myself in the mirror. I was beginning to look like the sort of woman who wore false nails and made loud remarks about men's bottoms. I applied mascara, some old blue eyeshadow and a trowelful of lipstick. Then I dowsed myself relentlessly with hairspray until my hair was standing on end like the bristles of a loo brush. I did a slow twirl in front of the mirror, and the words 'desperate old tart' came immediately to mind.

I wasn't sure if I could do this. I was now halfway towards being the sort of desperate old tart who'd pay to have her ex-lover's legs done in. But halfway might not be enough.

I ran back upstairs and got two pads of post-it notes, one pink, one yellow. On the pink one I wrote 'Councillor David Ormond', and on the yellow one 'Councillor George Draycott'. I tore the pages off, folded them in half carefully to stop them sticking to each other, and pushed them into the raincoat pocket. Somehow, if I decided to go ahead with the plan, within the next thirty minutes I'd got to make up my mind which one of them was behind the St Martin's Court scandal and quite possibly Janet's murder as well.

I got to the Anchor at ten to six. The pub was a small, single-storey building, overshadowed on one side by a giant furniture warehouse and on the other by mountainous heaps of old tyres in some sort of breaker's yard. The car park was empty. To begin with I parked carefully on the forecourt under a streetlamp, but then I thought better of it and moved to a discreet space in a corner next to an old Escort propped up on bricks.

Mac might not recognize me, but he would certainly recognize the Golf.

I almost lost my nerve again at this point. A slow drizzle

was whispering against the windscreen and the broken pub sign silhouetted against the dim orange sky looked like a gallows. Even with the hair and the raincoat and the mascara I didn't look the part. He'd see through me; I'd end up in a crumpled heap behind the wheelie bins with several teeth down the back of my throat. I wished I'd brought some sort of weapon – the paper knife from the top drawer of my desk, perhaps – but it was too late to think about this now. I took deep breaths, then tried to practise reaching surreptitiously for the switch on the cassette recorder concealed in my handbag, but I couldn't do that either. And I wasn't sure if I should take the cassette recorder. If he heard it click on and off, he'd guess.

By the time I opened the door to the bar, minus the cassette recorder, my heart was pounding so hard it hurt.

The barman looked up.

'A large gin and tonic, please,' I whispered, above the pounding. The bar was completely empty. Suddenly a tidal wave of relief swept over me – after all this, he wasn't even here. 'Is Mac in?' I enquired, crossing my fingers tightly in my pockets.

He poured me the drink without comment, took my ten-pound note, and shuffled across to the till.

I waited for him to come back with the change. 'Is Mac in?' I said again.

'Does it look like it? You the one that phoned yesterday with the message?' He was in his fifties, the sort of barman who looks as though he crawls out of the nicotine-stained woodwork at opening time.

'Yes.'

He raised one eyebrow almost imperceptibly and gave me a lethargic once-over. 'Oh,' he said, unhelpfully.

I couldn't make up my mind whether this meant, 'Oh, well, he'll be in in a while,' or, 'Oh, well, you're wasting your time,' so I picked up the drink, went over to a sagging bench seat, and sat down. I was beginning to sweat, so I opened up the plastic raincoat and fanned myself with stale air. Then I got the horrible feeling that an open plastic raincoat might give out entirely the wrong kind of signal should any customers arrive, so I did it up again. Four minutes oozed by in a silence broken only by occasional outbursts of the barman's bronchitis. Then suddenly, just as I realized that I desperately needed the loo, the bar door opened and a short fat man in a donkey jacket walked in. I knew Mac couldn't possibly be a short fat man in a donkey jacket, so I got up and went out to the loo.

When I came back, there were three new customers at the bar, and the short fat man was sitting at my table. He had a double chin and pale, delicate-looking skin.

I towered over him and sweated into the plastic rain-coat.

'Mac,' he said softly, extending a small fat hand. 'You got some sort of message for me, have you, my darling?'

I sat down awkwardly, too shocked to worry about my skirt riding up. Perhaps there was some mistake: this man was *five foot five*. Reluctantly I gave him my hand and let him shake it.

'Well, it's – I was recommended to you. To do a job.' I wanted to be sick. I couldn't bring myself to say it. 'A job – you know. I've got money.'

He looked calm and relaxed. He was drinking tomato juice on ice. 'Well, that's a good start, my darling. What did you say your name was?'

I cast round desperately for inspiration, and my gaze alighted on an English Tourist Board calendar incongruously displayed beside the dart board, January's picture being a view of slick-looking boats in a harbour.

'Marina,' I said tentatively.

'Well, go on then, Marina, I'm listening.'

I took a large gulp of gin without much tonic. What if there'd been some sort of ghastly misunderstanding and this man thought I wanted him to lag my ceiling joists? 'It's – it's my boyfriend, actually. He's – you know – He's dumped me, and I was wanting to – you know – pay him back.'

'Oh dear, Marina, I'm sorry to hear that. It's a hard old world, isn't it? But the thing is, my darling, I don't know you, and I don't work for people I don't know. I know that may seem strange to you, but in my line of work I like to be careful.'

I thought, so much for the ceiling joists, but he wants *references* . . . 'Well, I'm a friend of Cherie Bolt's. You know Cherie, don't you? She told me all about you.'

'Did she?' He didn't look very pleased about this.

'Oh, well, only that you could help me – I mean, nothing personal. The thing is, this man has really hurt me, and I want him to be hurt too.' I hesitated so there could be no mistake. 'I thought perhaps – something *terminal*.'

'*Terminal*.' He appeared to study the table top for a moment. 'Well, Marina, it's been nice meeting you, my darling, but I don't think I can help you. There's something wrong about you, Marina.'

'What?' And I hadn't even worked out where all the exits were. 'What do you mean?' I squeaked.

'What I mean, my darling, is that I don't think you know what you want. This boyfriend of yours – he's gone back to his wife, has he? Or he's taken up with somebody younger – tut, tut. All your life gone down the drain, oh dear. I understand how you feel, but for me to top someone for you I'd have to know you better than I know my own brother. And it wouldn't give you the satisfaction you want, believe me. Topping people doesn't do anybody any good except the fucking police. They love it. It gets them in the papers.'

I felt a stab of alarm at the word 'papers'.

'I see,' I said shakily. 'So you won't help me?'

'Not if you want someone topped. That's not my scene, Marina. Do you want to consider some other options? I could make your boyfriend very sorry – I could maybe even bring him back into line, you never know. You want to think about what he's got he wouldn't like to lose. Maybe he likes to exercise – maybe he's got a nice car. I don't know – you tell me.'

I took another gulp of gin. He was giving me the creeps. 'How much would this cost?'

'Well, that depends. Let's say – five hundred up front. Could be another three or four hundred to come – depends what you want done.'

I wished to God I'd brought the tape. 'Well, I could give you the name now, but I'd have to get the money later. Perhaps – perhaps you could just damage his house for starters –? He's very fond of his house.'

'No problem. Want to give me the name?'

Suddenly, I realized that both post-it notes were still in my pocket. I'd just about settled on giving him Councillor Draycott's name, mainly because of the trip to Barbados, but I'd forgotten to sort out the notes. 'But it's someone quite well-known locally,' I protested, wondering if I could get both pieces of paper out of my pocket and palm one of them without him noticing.

'That's all right. Give me the name now and I'll meet you in a week for the downpayment.'

He was staring at me expectantly, waiting for the name. I reached into my pocket.

'I've written it down.' My fingers closed over a small folded square of paper. I tried to feel for the other one.

'Come on, my darling,' said Mac. 'We're not going to get very far if you're not sure.'

It was no good: I couldn't find the other piece of paper. I handed him the one I'd got and he took it without looking at it and held it under the table. 'Well done, Marina. Now, you don't ever come in this pub again,' he said. 'You give me your phone number and I'll ring you.' And then he looked down at my piece of paper. I heard the faint lisp of the adhesive parting and the crackle of the fold snapping back. He looked up at me, and his expression was impenetrable. 'I won't be a minute, Marina,' he said, and he got up and went out through the door marked 'Gents'.

I sat quite still for a moment, waiting for him to come back. This wasn't what I'd meant to happen at all. What I'd meant to happen was for him to open up the piece of paper with my chosen name on it, and to react with obvious anger or shock or alarm – at which point I would immediately have grabbed my mobile and dialled nine-nine-nine. Did this mean that the whole thing had been a waste of time? Or did it mean I'd given him the wrong name, and the other name – whichever it was – was the right one?

I was by now in too much of a state to work this out or to care. As soon as Mac returned I'd give him a false phone number, promise to raise the money, and get out of here as quickly as possible. The bar was filling up now, mainly with men in oily overalls. Two more customers came in while I waited, ordered Guinness, watched the barman pour it, paid their money, counted their change, and sat down. An old man with the shakes put on 'My Way' on the juke box. I began to panic – what could be taking Mac so long? The room filled with swelling violins, Frank Sinatra got to his second chorus – and it slowly began to dawn on me that he wasn't coming back. I stared at the Gents door. It had begun to swing slightly in a cross-draught.

Which could only mean one thing. The Gents had a back exit. And if my geography was correct, that back exit must open directly into the corner where I'd parked the Golf.

I took in my breath and held it, wondering what to do. Then the hairs at the nape of my neck began to tingle and I couldn't take any more. I leapt up and ran out of the bar, knocking over Mac's glass on the way and spilling tomato juice over the carpet in a ghastly scarlet splatter.

The car park seemed to be deserted. I approached the Golf cautiously, my hand to my mouth, but the flickering streetlight didn't at first pick out anything out of the ordinary. The car looked exactly as I'd left it; no one was crouched in it waiting for me, nor – and I took a detour to check – was anyone lurking behind the old Escort. But then I noticed something: across my bonnet, catching the light like thousands of tiny stars, were the shattered fragments of a pane of glass.

Mac D had picked up a brick and thrown it through my windscreen. Whichever name I'd given him, he'd taken one look at it, suspected a set-up, and walked out of the pub. And the presence of my Golf in the car park had confirmed it for him.

By now, my heart was threatening to burst out of my ribcage, but I had to know. I reached into the pocket of the raincoat and squirmed my fingers into the sticky plastic. Right at the bottom was a sharply folded square of paper. I pulled it out.

It was yellow.

Mr Heslop looked totally flabbergasted.

'You did *what*? You gave this – this *criminal* Dave Ormond's name and address and told him to consider the options? *Oh, my God*! Do you want us all to end up in prison? I don't believe this! I've known Dave for years. The Ormonds used to own half this town and they could buy it back again any time they wanted. I've been to his house for dinner! It *can't* be Dave! He wouldn't need to take backhanders from property developers. It doesn't make sense.'

'It does if he's not really part of the Ormond family. Perhaps he's a distant cousin or something, cashing in on the name! Look, I've got a copy of his birth certificate here – he was born at One Harewood Cottages. Look!' I waved the birth certificate at him triumphantly.

His smile faded. 'One Harewood Cottages. Well, perhaps that's –'

'It isn't. I didn't think of it last night, but this morning I came in early and checked with the Land Registry – Harewood Cottages was a terrace of farmworkers' cottages. They were demolished in 1979 to build a roundabout – just like Mrs Champion said.'

Mr Heslop set his jaw. He picked up his phone and pressed his secretary's extension. 'Karen. Get on to Councillor Ormond right away and tell him I can't make the lunch tomorrow . . . No, I don't care what reason you give, just cancel it. Thanks.' He put the phone down and stared at me blankly for a moment. 'This is just to be on the safe side,' he said. 'It doesn't mean I'm swallowing your version of events. Who knows why this Mac bloke walked out on you? Maybe he saw through you right from the start –'

'He didn't. I know he didn't!'

'You've got no proof. No proof at all. The whole thing is just speculation. Your blackmail theory – St Martin's Court – all of it.'

'What about Paddy O'Donohue and the petition?'

Mr Heslop seemed to be having a hot flush.

'All right. There's some sort of case for somebody to answer there, but let's not jump to conclusions.'

I turned to go. 'There's one other thing, Mr Heslop. When I was negotiating with Mr MacDiarmid last night he assured me he doesn't commit murder for people unless they're his brother.'

He shuddered. 'I'm very pleased to hear it. So?'

'Well – Lee Cox is missing, and *someone* killed Janet Cox, didn't they? That grit that was found in her clothes – did you know it was *horticultural* grit?'

'What?' He stared at me in astonishment. 'Oh, for God's sake!'

I left him chewing indigestion tablets, and took David Ormond's birth certificate back to my desk to double-check his biography on our computer. Sure enough, the entry was quite unequivocal: *David Ormond is a descendant of Matthew Ormond, the founder of Ormond's Biscuits*. These notes would have been quoted from repeatedly whenever Dave Ormond got himself into the news; if he wasn't descended from Matthew Ormond, he'd have had plenty of opportunities to say so. I called up the entry for Ormond, Matthew. It ran to pages and pages, and there was no mention of Councillor David Ormond as a descendant, but this was hardly surprising since the entry hadn't been updated since shortly after the biscuit factory closed in 1964.

Suddenly, I had a brainwave. *The Ormond Arms*. I hadn't been there for years, but I remembered it as a nice old-fashioned pub with comfortable leather seats and chunks of cheese and onion on the bar on Sunday lunchtimes. It overlooked a recreation ground where Keith used to play cricket. And the walls had been plastered with Ormond family portraits, black and white photos of amdram productions at the Ormond Theatre – and a handpainted rendition of the Ormond family tree. I had a feeling it was now an Auntie Sally's Restaurant, but I was sure they wouldn't have got rid of their Ormond memorabilia. I grabbed notebook and phone and went out to the car.

It was still only ten-thirty when I arrived at the Ormond Arms, so they weren't open for business, but fortunately a delivery lorry had just arrived so I wouldn't have to bang on the door to try and attract attention. It was one of those big container lorries advertising the Auntie Sally chain, and it had a lurid picture of an apple-cheeked old woman plastered across its rear doors. As it happened, I had once followed such a lorry for fifteen miles along the A281 at thirty miles an hour, and had got to the stage of wanting to do the most unspeakable things to Auntie Sally, so when a man emerged from beneath her jolly striped skirt hem I wasn't at my most amenable.

'*Tipping Herald*!' I shouted, leaving my car skewed across the forecourt. 'Would you let me into your bar, please? I need to look at something.'

'Blimey – that bad? You ought to carry a hip flask, love.'

'It's not for a drink. I told you, I need to look at your family tree.'

'At my *what*?'

'At the Ormond family tree.'

He still looked blank, and I directed his attention contemptuously to the pub sign. It said, 'The Badger and Bullock'.

I began to get a bad feeling about things. I pushed past him through the open door, where a horrendous sight greeted my eyes. Gone was the heavy wood panelling that had once adorned the walls; gone was the faded photograph of Matthew Ormond that had frowned down on the clientele from above a prim tiled fireplace; gone were the views of Tipping as seen from the old Ormond biscuit factory. Over the bar, where the Ormond family tree had been etched proudly in gold on a mahogany plaque, hung a life-size effigy of Auntie Sally riding a bicycle with a bunch of plastic carrots draped across the handlebars. I rushed over and tried to look up her skirts, in case the plaque was hidden beneath them, but there was no sign of anything apart from more polystyrene vegetables.

'Where's it gone?' I demanded. 'The Ormond family tree – what have you done with it?'

'The what?' There were now three of Auntie Sally's employees lined up in the doorway, open-mouthed in their blue, red and yellow striped uniforms. 'Can I help you?' enquired a woman wearing a badge marked Katrina, in a menacing tone.

'Yes! There used to be a sort of plaque thing with the Ormond family tree on it hanging up over the bar. It's very important I have a look at it. Could you get it for me, please?'

'What's an Ormond?' asked the man who'd recommended the hip flask.

Katrina sighed. 'Look, we're in the middle of a delivery – you'll have to come back later. This is an Auntie Sally's! We're not allowed to have anything on show that's not part of our marketing. Sorry.'

I was horrified. 'So what have you done with all the old stuff that was here before? Haven't you still got it?' I stared at their blank faces. 'But *somebody* must know what happened to it! All the photos – what about the photos and the pictures? Did they go to the museum or something?'

Katrina shook her head, but one of the others piped up, 'I think there used to be some horse-brasses and stuff in a box in the store but I'm not sure if somebody from the brewery nicked them.'

'Oh, God! Please could someone show me the box?'

'Well, it's very inconvenient!' snapped Katrina. 'The store's outside, where they're unloading the stuff –'

Before she could change her mind I ran out of the bar, weaved round a pallet load of Auntie Sally's homebake pies, and followed the delivery man into the store, which was piled from floor to ceiling with crates and packages displaying the Auntie Sally logo. At the back behind an old snooker table was a battered cardboard box packed with dusty pictures. I pulled one out, and Matthew Ormond, thin of face and fair of hair, stared back at me severely from behind his handlebar moustache. I struggled to release more Ormonds, some with bigger and better moustaches. Dave Ormond didn't seem to bear much resemblance to any of his alleged antecedents, but this was hardly incontrovertible evidence. When I'd removed all the pictures from the box, all that was left were two pieces of wood thick with dust and nicotine. I pulled these out too and rubbed at one of them with my sleeve. It had a smooth lacquered surface and neatly chamfered edges. Excitedly I butted the pieces together, and soon realized I was looking at the bottom part of the Ormond family coat of arms – the part with the tree. Matthew Ormond, born 1801, died 1885 – father of Matthew, Richard, Elizabeth, Arthur – Matthew Junior, married Florence, Richard, married May . . . It went on and on, in tiny gold lettering edged in black, ending with Flight Lieutenant Edward Ormond, killed in action in 1944. I sat back on my heels in despair. They'd stopped updating the family tree four years before David Ormond was even born. I tucked it under my arm anyway, and was about to leave, when I realized something. David Ormond might be too young to have his birth recorded on the tree, but his father wasn't. I got down on my knees again and went carefully over the tree; altogether there were five Matthews, two Richards, and three Arthurs. There were definitely no Neils – nor, for that matter, was there a Jean.

I ran back to the car, and tossed Matthew Ormond and his family tree into my boot. I still wasn't sure whether I was pleased by this development or not, but I rang Mr Heslop to tell him the news.

'He's gone out,' said Dawn. 'He'll be about half an hour.'

'Well, if he comes back tell him I need to speak to him *urgently* and I'm on my way in –'

'All right. By the way, there's a fax floating around for you. Did you get it? It came in during the night. If you haven't had it, it must have gone back to the post room.'

I disconnected the call, started the car, and began trying to get off the forecourt. Then my mobile rang.

For some reason I expected it to be Mr Heslop. I answered it eagerly. 'I'm glad you've rung back! Mr Heslop, you'll never guess what I've just found. I'm on my way in with –'

'Hallo? Chris? Thank God I've got you at last. I've been

trying to reach you all morning. We need to talk urgently.
Are you in the Tipping area? I could meet you in the Dolphin
Centre in half an hour. Can you make it?'

It was David Ormond.

20

I let go of the pedals and stalled the engine.

'Er – actually, I'm on my way into the office for a very important meeting.'

'I see. So where are you now, at this moment?'

'Now? I'm outside the –' Oh, God. 'I'm – I'm –'

'Come on, Chris, we really do need to talk. Bill won't mind waiting. I'll meet you at the coffee shop in the Dolphin Centre. There are one or two things we've really got to sort out.' His voice, even electronically distorted, was so friendly and soothing that for a moment I forgot all about Mac D and the mess in my living room, and I remembered how much I'd once liked him.

I thought quickly. I'd still got the tape machine in the car somewhere, loaded with a fresh cassette.

'All right.' I wasn't at all sure what Mr Heslop would say about this. 'I suppose I could. Did you say the Dolphin Centre?'

'Yes. You know the little café there, with the tables outside?' said Dave. 'I'll meet you there in half an hour. Great.'

I made it to the Dolphin Centre in fifteen minutes, found a parking space in the multistorey, and went into the Ladies to get ready. My head was beginning to throb just thinking about Dave Ormond, so I took some paracetamol. I had a strong feeling he wouldn't want me taping our conversation. Just to be on the safe side, I decided to conceal the machine in my pocket. I checked it over, gave the batteries a rub, and voice-tested it. Then I combed my hair, put on lipstick, and got in the lift and descended to the little square on the ground floor where the café is to be found.

Dave Ormond was already waiting for me at a table.

He looked grim. He got up as I approached.

'Sit down,' he said. 'I've ordered two coffees. I hope that's all right? First I want to say –' A mob of teenagers swirled past us into the HMV shop next door. 'First I want to say how terribly sorry I am, Chris. This has all been an awful error of judgement on my part.'

'Sorry?' I sat down.

'Oh, come on, let's not beat about the bush. I had a phone call last night. I know you know exactly what I'm talking about. Look, what that thug did to your house was unfor-givable –' The café was packed with mothers and toddlers, and screams echoed up into the glass roof. He had to keep raising his voice above the din. 'All I ask is that you let me explain before you decide what to do.'

'What do you mean, before I decide what to do?'

'Well, let's talk it through. I told you, I deeply, deeply regret the business with MacDiarmid. All I can say in my defence is that I thought you'd put two and two together, get the message and back off. I thought in the long run this would be the best thing from everyone's point of view. You can't imagine how I felt when Bill told me about your daughter. Look, let me tell you about the Court first . . .'

At this point I recovered myself enough to put my hand in my pocket and switch the tape on.

'You mean St Martin's Court?' I prompted, for the benefit of the machine.

'Yes. You remember it, do you? It was a monstrosity, wasn't it? I can remember driving up Market Street soon after I'd been elected, and seeing it there, and thinking, God, what an eyesore! Why on earth do we have to put up with something like that in our midst just because it seemed like a good idea a few years ago? There were all these pokey little terraced houses on either side of the road, a builders' yard piled up with old bricks with nettles growing out of them – and I thought, somebody ought to do something about this whole mess. Where are our coffees – I ordered two coffees ten minutes ago,' he added, to the waitress who had just sloped by with a cloth. 'So I mentioned this to a chap I'd been at school with who was a land buyer for a major company –'

'Bellchamber Properties,' I muttered, pointedly, again for the benefit of the tape.

'Er – yes.' He hesitated. From the HMV shop, the sound of Radiohead suddenly pounded around the glazed-in square. Dave Ormond raised his voice. 'Look, Chris, I know it's the caring, sharing nineties now and things are different, but this was the greed-is-good eighties. Believe me, it was a whole different world, people thought making money was smart, and not only smart but *moral*. Don't you remember? In fact, there wasn't much alternative. Honestly, if I'd suggested spending public money on making the Court more aesthetically acceptable and improving the housing stock in Market Street, what do you think would have happened? There'd have been arguments and committees and more arguments – and in the end we'd've knocked down a few houses and built the multistorey in their place and St Martin's Court would be there to this day.'

I wasn't sure I got his point.

He frowned tensely. 'This isn't easy for me, you know. My friend, whose name I'm not going to give you, needed some brownie points with his company. Bellchamber Properties were actively looking for sites in the South East at the time – and obviously if a buyer could negotiate a low price for a good site it wouldn't exactly do him any harm on the promotion ladder. As I've already explained, Tipping desperately needed another multistorey car park. I discovered that Bellchambers would be happy to provide some of the building costs in return for a high proportion of contract parking which would benefit their building users – it was just a question of my friend putting in the right bid at the right time and no one objecting.' He let this sink in. 'Honestly, what we did was being repeated up and down the country without anybody thinking twice about it. All I actually did was to persuade a few people that the scheme was right for Tipping – which I sincerely believe it was.'

At that moment our coffee arrived in those unappetizing brown plastic tubs suspended over cups. I didn't say anything, and I ignored the coffee.

'With hindsight it looks very wrong, I admit that,' he went on, 'which is why I think it's in everyone's interests for the whole thing to stay buried. If it all comes out it won't just be me who has to answer for it – everyone on the council will come under scrutiny. We'll all look like a bunch of hicks – is that what you want? Look, who's to say that some of the things we're doing now won't look pretty shitty a decade or so into the next century. The truth is you can't second-guess history. I *believed* in what we did, Chris – I admit it may have been slightly unethical, but I honestly don't think even now that it was immoral.'

He'd almost got me convinced. Almost, but not quite. 'Are you asking me to believe you didn't get anything out of this *personally*?' I demanded. 'And what about the people who lived at St Martin's Court? They *liked* their flats. You made them move –'

'Oh, they did very well, they've got no complaints! Come on, these people are *council* tenants, for God's sake. They can't even cope with simple lease agreements – they've already put their fate into the hands of various authorities – they *expect* to be harried from pillar to post.' He fiddled irritably with his coffee cup and spilled hot water on to the table. 'Don't waste your sympathies, Chris. And of course I got something out of it personally. I got the kudos of having been instrumental in setting up a deal that was very good for the town only a short time after I'd been elected.'

'Oh, really?' It's amazing how quickly you can change your opinion of someone. I was by now beginning to dislike him with a quite frightening intensity. 'Come on – roughly how many other land buyers did you go to school with?'

His winsome smile vanished. 'That's a very nasty allegation. Do you really want me to answer it?'

'Yes! I know you lied about being a member of the Ormond family. I've got proof –'

'No, I didn't!' He affected to look indignant. 'For your information I have never claimed to be a member of the

Ormond family – although as a matter of fact my great-grandfather was a first cousin of Matthew Ormond.' He was beginning to get angry, and I knew I'd hit a sore point. 'It's not my fault if other people jump to conclusions. It started at school – my classmates assumed I'd got vast amounts of cash sitting around somewhere, waiting for me to come of age. I got tired of denying it. They all thought I lived in one of those big houses on Harewood Common and that I was too stuck-up to invite them round. Your paper should have done its homework properly. Ask Bill when you get back to the office. Ask him to dig out the very first piece that appeared in the *Herald* when I was standing in the 1980 elections. Then look at the byline.' He smiled slightly. 'He should have checked.'

'Oh!' Mr Heslop would have a fit. Literally. 'Well, *you* should have put the record straight! You let people think you were some sort of – of rich playboy! How do you manage to live the way you do on the money you make from the garden centre?'

'Good heavens, do you want to look at my books or talk to my bank manager?' He had now completely regained his cool. 'Why? Are you accusing me of taking backhanders? Is that what you think? Because if so, let me repeat – I didn't get one penny out of the St Martin's Court deal. Oh, no – I tell a lie – there was an all-expenses-paid day out at Ascot for me and my first wife!'

I was now so angry I didn't care what I said. I clenched my fists on the table, knocking the plastic tub off my coffee and sending it spinning to the floor. 'I don't believe you! If that was true – why did you hire Terry MacDiarmid? You paid him to threaten Lee Cox – and me – and Michael Irons, too, I shouldn't wonder! And what about Janet?' My voice rose to a squeak. 'It was you – you met her in that layby, didn't you? You couldn't get your hired thug to do it for you, so you met her yourself, and then you lured her to the garden centre and killed her! And what happened to Lee? Is he buried somewhere under one of your greenhouses?'

His mouth dropped open. He glanced uneasily at several women at the next table whose mouths had done likewise.

Then he pretended to laugh. 'For God's sake, Chris, you can't be serious.' He flashed a disarming smile at the women, then turned back to me with his teeth gritted. 'You're over-wrought, for God's sake. Look, I *never* met this Cox woman, and I've absolutely no idea where Lee is at this moment. Besides, as you very well know, I was several hundred miles away from Tipping on the night Janet Cox died.'

'I beg your pardon?'

'My trip to Honfleur, remember? We discussed it.'

'Oh.' I thought about this. 'And you can prove that, can you?'

He shook his head angrily. 'Come on, this is ridiculous! I don't have to prove anything. I'm telling you, you're quite wrong about this. I can understand you being upset, and thinking the worst – I deserve it – but really! Look, the truth is this – Lee Cox turned up on my doorstep last summer and demanded two thousand pounds not to go to you people with a wild story about me taking a bribe over the sale of the St Martin's Court site. He didn't have any proof of any wrongdoing because there was no wrongdoing to have proof of!'

I was beginning to get the horrible feeling I'd jumped to too many conclusions. I glanced down nervously at the trail of spilt hot water on the table top.

'Listen, Chris – I'm telling you the truth. Cox said a property developer friend of his had heard something on the grapevine sixteen years ago – they'd put two and two together between them and thought they could make a bit of money out of me, that's all. Of course I should have just ignored them or gone to the police, I see that now, but Cox was an irritating little sod – he kept ringing up and annoying Carol – so in the end I asked Mr MacDiarmid to take care of him for me. And before you say it, the answer is no – I don't make a habit of employing men like Terry MacDiarmid to take care of people who irritate me. I'd heard of him through an acquaintance of an acquaintance and it seemed like a good idea at the time. I paid MacDiarmid to warn Cox and his friend off, that's all – just warn them off – and it worked. In fact, it was because it worked so well on Cox that I thought it would be an easy way out with you. Easier than having to sit down and tell someone I admire that I made a stupid mistake when I was young and inexperienced.' I met his eye reluctantly. 'I'm *dreadfully* sorry, Chris. Is this making any kind of sense? Am I putting your mind at rest?'

I had to admit to following his logic, but the truth was, I hated him. I hated him for lying to me, for the trauma he'd put me through – and most of all for making me like him a lot more than I should have done. 'I'm not sure,' I said finally.

'All right.' He nodded. 'If I was to offer you some form of compensation – would that help?'

I frowned. 'What sort of compensation?'

'I don't know. But you could at least let me pay for the damage. Oh, excuse me.' He reached into his pocket suddenly. 'That's my pager, they want me in a meeting. Well, they'll just have to wait. Look, ask me anything else you like. I really want to get this cleared up.'

I racked my brains for a moment, then shook my head. 'I'd like to think about it all for a while, if you don't mind,' I said stiffly.

'Of course. Fine! Give me a ring at the farm any time. And of course, if Bill's not happy about anything I'd be glad to talk to him too.' He stood up and offered me his hand. He smelled of Gucci aftershave. I hesitated, then shook the hand.

As soon as he'd disappeared from sight in the direction of the High Street, I bolted up the emergency stairs to the car park, taking the uncompromising concrete steps two at a time. I leapt into the Golf, rewound the tape, and pressed 'play'.

'. . . *St Martin's Court*?' my voice crackled back at me, sounding oddly nasal.

'*Yes. You remember it, do you? It was a monstrosity, wasn't it . . .*'

I switched off the machine triumphantly. Dave Ormond sounded a bit nasal too, but he was instantly recognizable. I reached for my phone and tried to dial the *Herald*, but the wretched thing wouldn't work inside the car park. I started the car and raced for the exit. Perhaps Dave Ormond *did* make enough out of the Harewood Garden Centre to finance his luxury lifestyle; perhaps his only real crime had been to espouse the ethics of the eighties a bit too enthusiastically: I'd got it on tape – Mr Heslop would have to decide. I was on the spiral ramp, going much too fast, when my phone suddenly started to warble. I swerved to a halt at the barrier and grabbed it.

It was Dawn.

'I've got two messages for you,' she said. 'Your husband called, he's on his way home, and this woman with a speech impediment rang.'

'What woman with a speech impediment?'

At that moment the driver of a Cavalier behind me started pumping his horn. I dropped Dawn on to the passenger seat and pulled out into the street. It was five minutes later before I managed to stop the car at a bus stop.

I rang Dawn back.

'What woman with a speech impediment?'

'I don't know. I asked her twice but I couldn't get the name. Anyway, she said she wanted to see you urgently so I did one-four-seven-one and got her number. Can you write it down?'

I reached for a pen and wrote it down. I decided I had never seen or heard the number before.

'I don't think I know this woman,' I said. 'I'm on my way in to see Mr Heslop urgently. Do you think you could ring the number and find out what it is for me, please? Just tell whoever it is I'm busy today and I'll call them later. And don't let Mr Heslop go to lunch until I've spoken to him.'

'He says he's not going to lunch. He's not feeling well. See you then.'

I was almost back at the office when she rang again.

'That number – it's Radley's Road Haulage,' she said. 'But the woman who answered the phone didn't know who'd rung us so I couldn't give her your message. Sorry.'

'Radley's Road Haulage?' Cherie Bolt didn't have a speech impediment. 'Are you sure? And she said it was urgent?' I don't know why, but I felt a slight prickle of alarm. 'All right – change of plan. I'm on my way to Radley's Road Haulage. Bye.'

The sun was shining from a clear blue sky when I got to Radley's Road Haulage, glinting off the windscreens of the trucks parked in lines on the tarmac. I ran straight up the stairs to the office.

'I've come to see Cherie Bolt. It's Chris,' I demanded of the woman in front of the *Full Monty* poster.

'Sorry, she won't see you. She's not well.'

'Yes, she will. She rang me and said she wanted to see me urgently.'

The woman suddenly came out from behind her desk in pit bull mode.

'I told you, she's not seeing anyone today – she's got flu. You can make another appointment, or I can get Len up from maintenance. What's it going to be?'

At that moment Cherie's door opened. I caught a brief glimpse of her wearing something white, then she stepped back into the office and held open the door. I took this to be an invitation.

'Thank you!' I sidestepped the pit bull and followed Cherie into her office. Then I remembered she'd got flu, and hovered discreetly in the doorway. 'I believe you tried to call me at the paper?'

She was wearing enormous dark glasses, white housecoat, a white turban-style scarf arrangement, and holding a bundle of tissues theatrically to her nose. She looked as if she'd just stepped off the set of *Sunset Boulevard*, and I allowed myself a little inward groan of contempt: I would never go in for such histrionics, even if I was sixty and caught pneumonia.

'Shut the door,' muttered Cherie, her words understandably muffled.

I came in and shut the door.

She faced me across a small square of carpet littered with trodden-in staples, her legs apart in an oddly aggressive stance.

'*You bitch*,' she hissed, venomously.

'I beg your pardon?'

'You bitch. Come over here. Come *on* – come over here! I want you to take a good look.'

Nervously, I stepped forward.

'Thank you,' said Cherie. She slowly removed the glasses and lowered the tissue, and immediately the Forte Posthouse's full English breakfast I'd had that morning reasserted its half-forgotten taste in my mouth. Something had happened to her right eye. It had disappeared completely beneath a welter of puffed, livid flesh topped off by two pieces of eyebrow, both oozing redly, and her nose and upper lip had coalesced into one hideous entity. I think one of her front teeth was missing.

'Oh, my God, how on earth did this happen?' I gasped. And then I realized how it had happened, and when, and why, and I wondered very briefly if she knew (it was obvious she did) and – and I hate to admit this – if I could bluff my way out of it.

'Don't be stupid. Thank you very much!' She backed towards her desk. 'You stupid cow – what did you think would happen if you started giving my name out? Shall I tell you about it?' She was breathing spasmodically in small, painful gasps. 'My doorbell rang about eight o'clock last night. When I answered it, I thought he was paying me a social call. Then he called me a bitch and hit me. I fell over, so he picked me up. I'm quite tough really – it took some time before I passed out.' Slowly she circumnavigated her desk and sat down. 'Satisfied? Just as well he was still fond of me, or I'd really have been in trouble,' she added, without a hint of irony.

'Oh, my God! Look, let me take you to hospital! Please – you ought to have x-rays or something. I'm so sorry! I had no idea anything like this might happen!'

Cherie ignored this.

'You are so stupid,' she said. 'I pointed you in the right direction. I told you I didn't want to get involved. Don't they teach you anything in journalism school?'

I didn't want to tell her I hadn't been to journalism school.

'I thought you people had contacts! I thought if I gave you a name you'd know what to bloody do with it!'

'I'm sorry. On the *Herald* it's mostly – you know – lost cats and stuff –'

'*Christ*! Hand me those keys.' She indicated a large bunch of keys in the centre of her desk. 'Come on! I don't want to lean forward, do I?'

I pushed the keys towards her.

'I'm going to give you something,' she said. 'I didn't give it to you before because I didn't want *this* to happen. I had a bad bloody feeling about you and I was right, wasn't I? Now I just want whoever's responsible to pay. I can either give this to you or I can send it to the bloody police myself anonymously. Do you know how much it's going to cost me to get my nose put back? I only had the last set of stitches out a month ago! But get this – if I give this to you I don't want you coming round here *ever* again asking more questions or sending the police round to ask questions – if that happens I'll see to it you get exactly what I got last night. Except that by the time they've finished putting you back together your face'll be stitched up like a pair of Nike trainers!' She was deadly serious. 'Have you got that?'

I had absolutely got it. I nodded.

'Good. Because I mean it. Just one glimpse of a uniform on my premises and you'll be getting a knock on your back door.'

She selected a key, unlocked her desk, and produced a fat manila envelope done up with brown sticky tape. She pushed it towards me.

Just for a moment, I considered refusing it.

'What's in it?' I asked nervously.

'*Oh, Christ*!' She snatched the envelope back. 'It's Lee's bloody insurance policy, isn't it? Suit yourself. I'll put it in a jiffy bag and send it off myself. I'll get one of the drivers to post it in Wales or some other bloody dump! Well, go on, piss off!' she added, and a small blood clot landed on her desk with the 'piss'.

I tried not to watch the blood seep into the folds of her tissue as she dabbed at it. 'I'm sorry. It's not that I don't want it – his insurance policy? What do you mean, exactly?'

'Oh, come on, what's the matter with you? You think I'm talking about Scottish Widows or something? These are copies of documents Lee tried to use to blackmail someone – I thought you knew all this. Look, I'm not stupid, I wouldn't have touched this with a bargepole' – she picked the envelope up by one corner and shook it vengefully –' but he *promised* me he was dropping the whole thing. He said he'd sent all the originals back like he'd been told and he only wanted me to have this because if ever he was going down for the third time with a lump of concrete round his neck he'd like to know someone had copies to send to the police.'

'Oh. So why didn't you send it to the police when he went missing?'

'Oh, come on, missing's not dead, is it? I told you, I tried to find the bugger, then I forgot about it till you turned up. I'm not his bloody mother! Look, he gave me this the day after the so-called accident to his house – he said he'd put the originals in the post. I didn't ask him if he'd got a thank-you letter. Then, at the beginning of September, when I'm in the middle of a meeting he suddenly turns up out of the blue and asks for the envelope. I told you, I was bloody furious with him for coming here and pestering my staff. When I came out of the meeting the envelope was back on my desk and he'd stuck it down with more tape so I know he must have opened it. That's all I know. He left me a note with it that just said, "See you".'

I reached eagerly for the envelope and started prising off the brown tape.

'No – you can take it and *piss off*!' said Cherie, wincing slightly at the effort of raising her voice. 'I've got work to do.' She put on the glasses, straightened her back, and suddenly, apart from the nose, she looked almost her old self. 'If I wanted to know what was in there I'd already have looked, wouldn't I? Well, are you going, or do I have to get Len up from maintenance? You won't like Len – he's got halitosis.'

I muttered another apology and opened the door.

'One more thing,' said Cherie. 'Just remember – that lot out there think I've got flu.'

I backed out into the main office and shut her door, levering up a corner of the envelope as I did so. I didn't dare pull out its contents, but I could see what looked like a bundle of photocopies of some old typed documents. In the dim interior of the envelope, it was possible to make out the words 'Harewood Farm' underscored with a manual typewriter.

I hurried across the computer room without a word to the pit bull or to her assembled, whispering colleagues, none of whom was making any pretence at working.

If Cherie thought her staff had swallowed the flu story, she was wrong.

21

Mr Heslop was sitting at his desk surrounded by empty paper cups.

'I think you may be right,' he said unhappily. 'About Dave. I managed to track down a P. D. O'Donohue who used to work for the council's Parks Department.' He paused. 'He now works at the Harewood Garden Centre – has done since 1984. Apparently he travelled first class to Dublin two days ago to stay with a cousin.'

I heaved the dusty plaque and the portrait I'd found at the Badger and Bullock on to Mr Heslop's desk without comment. I put the tape and the envelope on top of them.

'This is a tape of a conversation I had with Dave Ormond this morning, where he admits to being responsible for the damage to my house, and to being blackmailed by Lee Cox, and he offers me compensation for the damage. The rest of it is complete *crap* though.'

Mr Heslop looked mildly shocked, because I am known at the *Herald* for my moderate language. His hair was sticking up in spikes where he'd been running his fingers through it all morning. 'Oh my God, oh my God, oh my God,' he muttered, miserably. 'This is so embarrassing. I don't know how I'm going to live this down.'

I couldn't wait any longer. I opened the envelope and tipped out its contents. 'There! Copies of invoices from a firm called Irons and Black Construction Limited for work to Harewood Farm in eighty-three and eighty-four. You see? Erecting the garden centre shop and buildings, adding a wing to the farmhouse. Here's a copy of the original specification –' I waved a fat sheaf of A4 at him. 'It's addressed to Councillor

David Ormond at Harewood Farm but there's a copy to somebody at Bellchambers. There's even a photocopy of a cheque signed by somebody at Bellchambers – see?'

He seized the envelope. 'Bloody hell – where did you get these?'

I hesitated. 'They were Lee Cox's. Michael Irons was one of the directors of Irons and Black of course, and these are copies of the papers Lee Cox used to blackmail Dave Ormond. But I absolutely *can't* tell you who I got them from.'

He got up and took them to the window. 'Nineteen eighty-three,' he muttered gloomily. 'Harewood Farm was a dump of a place before he had it done up – *Damn!*'

He slumped back into his chair and we both stared bleakly at the strew of papers and the old photograph on his desk. The atmosphere in the room was grim.

'You don't look very pleased,' he remarked bleakly, after a pause. 'I'd've thought you'd be over the moon.'

'I'm not – I made a terrible mistake. This person who gave me the tip-off about Terry MacDiarmid has been badly beaten up because of me. I feel really awful.'

'Do you? Well, in my experience people who are able to supply tip-offs about thugs are usually keeping bad company in the first place. That's not your fault.'

I hadn't thought of this. I began to feel slightly better. But only very slightly.

'But I'm no nearer finding out who killed Janet – or what happened to Lee. Dave Ormond says he was in France the night of the murder.'

'Does he, indeed?' Mr Heslop's knuckles on the edge of the desk were white. 'Well, since he's spent the last twenty-odd years lying about who he is and where he's been I think we ought to take that with a very large pinch of salt! I swear to you, I'm going to nail that bastard if it's *the last thing I do*,' he added, and got up and contemplated his old green filing cabinet thoughtfully. 'I don't know, but I might have a few things in here –'

At that moment I noticed my phone was ringing, and I left him and went out to answer it.

It was PC Lyons from Tipping's traffic department.

'Good morning, Mrs Martin. This is a liaison call to keep you informed of progress regarding the incident you reported to us recently. Is this a convenient moment for you?'

'Yes – go ahead.'

'OK. Well, our officers are actively pursuing the matter, but it appears that to date no new material has come to light. As soon as there's anything concrete to report I will personally be in touch again.'

I waited. 'Oh – is that it? But what about what I told you about Terry MacDiarmid? Have you questioned Mr MacDiarmid?'

'We haven't been able to ascertain Mr MacDiarmid's whereabouts, I'm afraid.'

'So did you examine his lorry?'

'Oh, no, madam. We'd need a search warrant for that.'

I gritted my teeth. 'Right. I see.' I cast about for a suitably terse rejoinder, but Pete appeared suddenly at the top of the stairs, so I just said, 'Thank you very much for ringing,' and put down the phone.

Pete was carrying a bag marked 'Duty Free' and a sticky-looking box bearing the name of a patisserie in Toulouse. He offered me the box.

'Hallo, darling. Nice quiet week?'

When he'd sat down, I told him what had happened.

First he looked shocked. Then he looked angry. 'Christ,' he said. 'What's the matter with you? What's the matter with *Bill*? You went to meet this hit man *by yourself*? Didn't you think about what could have happened?'

Then, when we'd both calmed down, he said, '*Dave*? What a bastard! I'll kill him!'

Before I could comment, Mr Heslop emerged from his office, looking tense. He saw Pete and did a double take.

They exchanged routine pleasantries.

'It's a bit of a bugger, this thing with Dave,' Pete said. 'I always thought he was a personal friend of yours.'

'Yours too.'

Pete laughed humourlessly. 'Not me, mate. It was his credit account at the Star I got on with. So where are you up to exactly?'

Mr Heslop shrugged. 'We're getting there. It seems his mother died in 1978 so he must have used whatever she left him as a downpayment on Harewood Farm. I don't know where the father is. The rest is history. We all swallowed the whole performance, hook, line and sinker. Oh – and this Millennium Centre thing, if there's a sweetener in the pot I think I know what it might be.' He opened up a map and spread it across my desk. 'The old library site. It's in a fantastic position, not far from the Forte Posthouse and access to the A3. I suspect that if all this had gone ahead as planned, in a year or two when the old library was so rundown nobody cared any more, Fairlands Bellchamber would put in a bid for the site and Dave would make sure they got it.'

We all stared at the town plan, and for a moment, it felt just like old times.

'Oh, and by the way, this is a complete waste of time,' he added, tossing my tape cassette towards the rubbish bin. 'It's Radiohead. I know, because my youngest son is a keen fan. Where did you record it? At a rock concert?'

'*What*? What do you mean?' I dived for the tape.

'Oh dear –' said Pete, sympathetically.

'The music comes on after about half a minute and what with that and the nursery-school outing – Anyway, at least we've still got these,' he added, flourishing the copy invoices. 'Don't worry about the tape – I'm sure we can get him with these. They're dynamite!'

I pushed the tape into the machine and pressed 'play'.

'Actually,' said Pete. 'I hate to put a spanner in anybody's works but these are *copies* of copies. Come on, Bill, you know the score. You need to get hold of at least some of the originals. These are *fifteen years old*, which means they're outside the taxman's six-year rule and Bellchambers would be quite within their rights to have destroyed them. You try to put a story together with nothing but these as evidence – even if you can get it past the *Herald*'s brief – and Dave's team will have you for breakfast without bothering to spit out the pips.'

Mr Heslop and I stared at one another in horror.

'Oh, go on, Bill, you know all this as well as I do. They're dynamite, but they're dynamite that's well past its sell-by date. What was it you used to say to me – there's no short cut to good journalism? I daresay you will get the bastard eventually – I certainly hope you do – but not with these.' I had a nasty feeling Pete was enjoying this. 'You have to get up very early in the morning to pin anything on the Dave Ormonds of this world. You practically need a smoking gun.'

At that moment a strangled chord whined from my cassette recorder. I switched it off.

'Right,' said Mr Heslop briskly. 'Well, we'll see. Have a look at this then – see if you can tell me what it is.' He unfolded a sheet of paper and glanced at it. 'This was in the back of the envelope but I can't make head or tail of it.'

He held out a photocopy of a quarto-sized page of lined paper covered in densely packed, backward-slanting handwriting and splotches of black ink. At the top, it said, 'Melly College, 15 June 1976. Please post.'

I took it. 'What's Melly College?'

'Well, I don't know – I thought *you* might. I can't read the wretched thing. As I said, it wasn't attached to the rest of the stuff – it was folded up in a square at the back of the envelope. I thought it might mean something to you.'

I did my best to decipher the first two lines. '*Dear Norman*,' I read aloud. '*Dear Norman, I'm addressing this . . . this letter to you because I know you were in when I rang this morning but you wouldn't speak to me, and this is my last . . .* I held the letter at arm's-length and tried again. '*. . . my last opportunity to . . .*' Oh, God! . . . '*to tell you what I think of you . . .*' It didn't seem worth it, so I gave up and tossed the paper to one side. 'Melly College – Could that be a horticultural college, or something?'

Mr Heslop looked as if he was too depressed to care. 'I don't know. See what you can find out. I'm going out for a sandwich. Nice to see you again,' he added curtly, to Pete.

'Same here,' muttered Pete, and he nodded and reached for the photocopy. He put his head on one side to look at it. 'Hang on. This isn't *Melly College*. Those aren't l's – they're t's. and the o's and a's and e's are almost indistinguishable. I think it's something *Cottage*. It's – didn't you mention to me a *Holly Cottage*?'

I reached for the letter and examined the signature. '*Miles*!'

'Who the hell's Miles?'

'Miles committed suicide – at the cottage!'

Pete looked totally blank, so I filled him in. He picked up the letter and read it aloud.

'*I can repeat your letter from bitter memory, even though I burned it the day it came. "Based on a totally unsympathetic main character who could not possibly engage the sympathies of an audience, your play lacks insight into human nature . . .*'

Pete broke off to laugh hollowly, having received several letters from publishers along similar lines. Then he went on:

'*. . . So where do you get off saying this is constructive criticism? I was always there for you when you needed me, Norman. I always had my hand in my pocket. Do you know how much you still owe me after that last year at . . .*' He broke off. 'I can't read that bit, it's covered in ink blots or something. Hang on –' He moved on to the next paragraph. '*So now let me tell you this. I had a little accident last week with a couple of girls from the village. They were two pieces of shit I picked up at the station – you know the type. They were ready for anything and they needed somewhere to doss because they'd been thrown out of the house by their stepfather. Anyway, they stayed two days and I did the business with both of them and I was getting sick of them.*' Pete swiftly raised and lowered his eyebrows. '*We did some stuff and I was going to take them to the station and get rid of them, but then the younger one passed out, and the next thing I know she's choked on her own vomit and she's pissing herself . . .*'

I began to feel sick.

'Oh God,' said Pete, holding the letter at arm's-length as if to distance himself from it. 'This gets worse.' He went on, '*Anyway, it wasn't my fault but the other one – Marie or Tina, I don't know which was which – started screaming and crying, and she was going to get in my car, which is new, and drive to the hospital even though she can't drive and it was too late so there was*

*no point. I hit her, Norman, and once I started hitting her I couldn't
stop because I kept thinking of you, and the play, and I wanted to
knock her brains out. But these girls were nothing, Norman.* He's
underlined the word "nothing". *Their mother is a drunken
prossie who doesn't give a toss about them and God knows who
the real father* – he's put an "s" in brackets – *was-oblique-were.
Everybody knows the little tarts were on the run and their friends
think they went to London. Of course the mother made a fuss and
called the police, so I rang her up yesterday and said I was from
the Met and that the girls had been found in a dosshouse in Notting
Hill and didn't want to come back . . .'* He paused. 'I can't read
the next bit. It's all blotched. Anyway, then it goes on: *. . .
until last night when my so-called tenant, who incidentally is just
like you and thinks he can turn up here when he feels like it and
not bother about such niceties as rent, spotted a stain on the cellar
steps I'd forgotten to clean up. I told him one of the girls had a bit
of an accident with a syringe and it was nothing for him to worry
about, but I don't know if he believed me and he's not the sort you
can trust. Even though he knows the mother and that no one will
believe the old tart I think if the police start asking questions he'll
get all cosy with them and to hell with me despite all I've done for
him. He's worried about his reputation and his future prospects. I
can't face going to prison. What have I got to live for? I've thought
about it and thought about it and as far as I can see there's only
one way out. So goodbye, Norman, I hope you have a nice life
and think of me often. Without you, none of this would have been
possible.'*

He dropped the letter on the desk. I picked it up gingerly
and studied it. If you believed the letter was genuine, it was
obvious now what the black splodges were.

'But there isn't a cellar at Holly Cottage!' I exclaimed,
after a moment's thought, and was immediately overcome
with relief. 'The letter must be a hoax!'

'Don't be silly. It can't be a hoax. Does it sound like a
hoax? Remember what you told me about Holly Cottage?'
He looked shaken. 'You said somebody approached this
developer guy wanting the place *razed to the ground* –
remember? Well, I don't know where *this* has come from,
but I'd say there's a cellar there all right.'

I stared at him in horror.

'Where is this place? Who owns it?'

'An Australian woman. She bought it after the suicide –' I reread the instruction at the top of the letter. 'It says "please post", but there's no address or anything. I don't get it. What happened to this tenant? Why didn't he tell the police? The police must have gone to the cottage to attend the suicide. Why would the tenant cover up a murder he didn't have anything to do with?'

Pete picked up the patisserie box and the 'Duty Free' bag. 'Well, if you ask me, Miles Lloyd got it wrong. I think this tenant was prepared to do anything to protect his career and future prospects. Come on. Get your coat.' He started for the backstairs.

Suddenly my brain began operating at 800 r.p.m. I grabbed my coat and followed him down the backstairs. 'Wait, Pete, I've just realized. This was with Lee Cox's papers – the ones he was using to blackmail Dave Ormond. He must have been blackmailing the *tenant* for his part in the cover-up.' Pete disappeared round a bend in the stairs. I ran headlong after him. 'What if you're right? What if there *is* a cellar there, and the girls are buried in it? Do you think –'

'I told you, I don't know. Let's go.'

When we got to Holly Cottage, thick cloud had closed in over the sun and a dank silence reigned beneath the pines. Mrs Sutton came to the door under several additional cardigans. She obviously had no recollection of meeting me before, and I didn't know what to say.

'It's about your cellar,' I said finally.

'I'm afraid we haven't got a cellar!'

Pete ignored this. 'Could we have a look at your kitchen, love? We need to know if you've got a cellar. Where do you keep your coal?'

'In a shed round the back. We haven't got a cellar. Are you from the coal merchant's?'

'No, we're not from the coal merchant's. And I'm sure you have got a cellar.' He handed her the patisserie box which he'd carried on his knee all the way from Toulouse. 'Here

– try these. You'll like them. I can soon tell you if you've got a cellar . . .'

He sidestepped her as she puzzled over the box, crossed the hall to the kitchen and made straight for the cupboard with the kilner jars in it. Then, despite Edward Sutton's protests, and before I could say anything to stop him, he wrenched open the door.

He caught the ironing board just in time.

'There!' exclaimed Mrs Sutton triumphantly. 'You see?'

Pete shook his head. 'No – I still think it's here.' He rapped smartly on the painted wooden panelling at the back of the cupboard. 'My aunt's got a house just like this one in St John's Wood. These old houses always have cellars. Someone's blocked it off.'

I shuddered involuntarily.

'Look.' He pointed at the floor. 'The brick floor butts up against the back of the cupboard instead of the cupboard back butting on to the bricks. See? I think this is the first step at the top of stairs leading down into a cellar.'

'Are you sure?'

'No – not sure enough to want to risk dismantling the back of this bloody cupboard and finding it isn't.' He thought for a moment. 'My aunt had a sort of a trap-door thing outside where the coal was delivered.'

'Oh, my word, all our coal's in the shed!' wailed Mrs Sutton.

'Don't worry, love – you put the kettle on.'

We raced round to the side of the house.

'Pete, don't do this – let's get someone!'

'What – and look like idiots if we're wrong? Look – what about under those holly bushes growing up against the kitchen wall?'

'Holly bushes!' That was putting it mildly. A great mountain of foliage tumbled around the foot of a sizeable tree.

'Yes. Come on, you've still got that spade and the gardening gloves in the back of your car from when we went to that dig-your-own-Christmas-tree place – get them for me, will you?'

I got him the spade and the gloves and watched as he

attacked the Suttons' holly bushes. For a while, the sound of the spade clinking against a brick wall, his grunts, and the scratch and thunk of falling holly branches reverberated through the clearing. I sat on a rotted tree stump with my back to him and tried to work out how a copy of Miles Lloyd's confession/suicide note could have come into Lee Cox's possession. The answer had to have something to do with Michael Irons and the redevelopment plans for Holly Cottage, but somehow, it still didn't quite make sense.

The sound of the spade stopped. At the top of the tree in front of the Suttons' kitchen a squirrel made faint swishing noises as it skittered from branch to branch, vaulted into the void over their patchy lawn, then disappeared amid a tangle of birch trees. For a moment there was complete silence.

Pete put a hand on my shoulder. His face was covered in little red weals where the holly had scratched him and sweat was dripping from the end of his nose. 'Do me a favour, go back to the car and get a phone.'

'Why? Is there a cellar?'

'Yes. Go on – get the phone and ring the police. It's too dark down there to see anything properly so if I'm wrong I'll just have to look like a tit. This place is giving me the creeps. It looks as if somebody's scratched two bloody crosses on the floor.'

22

Pete rang his editor again at half past four, just as Marjorie Di Carlo turned up accompanied by two constables, unaccountably clutching a ledger entitled 'Hardings – Inventory of Property'. On the muddy track outside Holly Cottage the number of parked cars was gradually increasing, and now included a Three Counties Radio Land Rover and refreshment van. A unit equipped with some sort of special device for investigating the cellar floor was expected to arrive at any minute.

'. . . Well, until we know if there *are* any victims – What? . . . No, only this mysterious tenant's letter,' Pete said, to the phone. 'Obviously they tried the electoral register and the only name on it was that of this Miles Lloyd guy . . . Well, I don't suppose it was an official tenancy . . . Say again? . . . OK, hang on.' He covered the mouthpiece. 'He wants to ring the owner and get a reaction to the investigation. Have you got the name, Chris?'

I decided I was probably already in enough trouble for telling the police how I'd come by the letter: Julie's boyfriend had a pair of Nike trainers, so I knew what my face would look like if Cherie Bolt carried out her threat. 'It's in the office – but I don't think the police would like it if I gave it to your editor.'

'What? Oh, come on! She's going to ring in and get it,' he said to the phone.

I snatched the phone from his hand. Sometimes he goes too far, and I was feeling pretty overwrought. 'No, I'm not. I appreciate your help on this, but I don't work for your editor. I'll ring the woman myself! If your editor wants the story, he'll have to negotiate with Mr Heslop!'

I ran back to the car, manoeuvred it out of the mud, and drove back to Tipping. To be honest, I'd had enough of Holly Cottage. I didn't really want to be there when the cellar floor came up, even though I knew I ought to be. If I could get back to the office, track down a phone number for Mrs Gladstone through her solicitors, get her to talk to me, and be back at Gooserye inside the hour, it would be a minor miracle. I double-parked the Golf by the fire exit, ran up the backstairs two at a time and got the file out of my drawer. There was no sign of Mr Heslop, so I didn't have to waste time explaining. The whole journey had taken twenty minutes.

Pete rang on my mobile while I was still looking up the number for International Directory Enquiries to get Mrs Gladstone's solicitors' phone number.

'Forget the owner!' he said excitedly. 'A man has just turned up with a sensor thing and he says there's definitely something buried under the cellar floor. They're going to start digging!'

'It'll only take me a few minutes to –'

'No, forget it! Since you flounced off, I chatted up this agent woman, and to cut a long story short I can tell you it's the middle of the night in Brisbane and they're not answering their phone. You'd better get back here now.'

'All right,' I agreed reluctantly, dropping my note about Mrs Gladstone's solicitors back into the file. Then I noticed something. There was a *second* note with Mrs Gladstone's solicitors' name on it taped to my monitor. 'Pete, wait –' I said. 'There's a –'

'Get back to me later!'

I put down the phone and pulled the note off the monitor. 'Urgent fax', it said, 'to the *Herald* reporter. Reference your letter, apologies for the delay in replying due to Mrs Gladstone being currently too unwell to correspond. Regarding your query, we are not aware of any recent proposals to redevelop our client's property. What is the reason for your interest? Please let us know if there's anything we should be aware of. Meantime, we suggest you contact Mrs Gladstone's UK agents, Hardings of Tipping, whose address follows.' Underneath the address was a scrawled signature, followed by a handwritten postscript: 'Regret we were not involved in the attempt to sell the property in 1987. This was proposed by Mrs Gladstone's nephew, who is Mr Philip Chandler, of Ravenswood, Tipping, and whom you might wish to contact in this regard.'

Philip Chandler? I reread the postscript, twice. Then I redialled Pete's number. Alison Carter had said she'd had to take an ironing board into the office to press her boss's suits because he was living hand to mouth in various digs . . . Could one of those 'digs' have been Holly Cottage? Could Philip Chandler have persuaded his Aunt Violet to buy Holly Cottage for the sole purpose of preventing a future purchaser from poking around in its cellar and finding the remains of the Champion girls? The thought gave me the creeps. If Chandler had been Miles Lloyd's tenant, it meant he'd looked after Mrs Champion all these years knowing full well what had happened to her daughters. In fact, the more I thought about this, the more sense it made in an awful kind of way. Philip Chandler must have nearly had a heart attack the day I asked him if he knew anything about Holly Cottage.

I stared at the fax in a daze and tried to piece the story together. At first, it seemed to fall into place quite easily. The police wouldn't bother looking very hard for two runaways who'd told their friends they were going to London, and Mrs Champion had believed this story too at first. Besides, she had her own problems. Philip Chandler must have hoped the tragedy could stay hidden for ever, and he'd almost got away with it. But what I couldn't understand was why Michael Irons and Lee Cox had bothered messing about investigating Chandler's personal life – and risked getting telegraph poles through their windows – if they knew all along what was under Holly Cottage. It didn't make sense.

And of course, if only I'd taken up Janet Cox's offer of a 'hot story' on Philip Chandler, perhaps she wouldn't now be on someone's embalming slab.

Pete's number wasn't responding. I glanced at my watch. It was now ten past five, and Tuck Woodford & Chandler's offices would be closing in twenty minutes. I ran down the backstairs, leapt into the Golf, started up the engine and swerved past the queue at the exit with my hand on my hooter to the disgust of the entire Accounts Department in their Fiats, but I didn't have time to worry about this. I edged out on to the street with my lights on full-beam, lurching recklessly into a tiny gap and ignoring a barrage of furious horn-blowing.

It was already past five-thirty when I finally approached Edinburgh House after a nightmare of stop-start driving. Stranded behind the lights at the bottom of the hill, I could see that Tuck Woodford & Chandler's car park was already half empty. If I'd missed him, I'd have to go through the whole thing at Ravenswood while Mrs Champion watched *Neighbours* in the granny flat. The lights changed to green, the traffic edged forward two car spaces, and the lights changed back to red. A man came out of Edinburgh House's front entrance and crossed the car park. A tall man, silver-haired and distinguished. He got into a car. The lights changed again. This time I managed to squeak through on red, but only to come to a dead stop the other side of the junction – and now there was a black BMW waiting to turn left out of Tuck Woodford & Chandler's car park. I was sure it was Philip Chandler's, and there was a gap coming up for him to slide into. Without stopping to think, or to indicate, or to hoot, I floored the accelerator and leapt forward across the carriageway towards the car-park entrance, just as the BMW driver – who was engaged in looking the other way – started to pull out.

Of course, I knew exactly what was going to happen next, but there was nothing I could do to prevent it.

Philip Chandler jumped out of his car and ran round to inspect the damage. I got out too. He recognized me.

'What on *earth* do you think you're doing? *Look* what you've done!'

Briefly I wondered if colliding with a person who's about to be arrested on charges of murder, perverting the course of justice, and God knew what else, would invalidate one's motor insurance. I stepped boldly into the gap between our crumpled front wings.

'Mr Chandler – I've come here to tell you that I know you murdered Janet Cox and I know exactly how and when and why!'

'*What*? Oh, don't be ridiculous! You really must stop making these absurd allegations, Mrs Martin, or I'm going to have to report you to someone. Where are your insurance details?'

'To hell with my insurance details! I've seen the letter from your flatmate, Mr Chandler.'

'*What*?' Fleetingly, but only fleetingly, his expression froze, and he looked as I imagine a butterfly must look when it feels an impaling pin go through its body and knows it's all up. Then his face relaxed again and he said calmly, 'I beg your pardon? What letter?' as though querying an administrative detail with a member of his staff.

'The suicide note from your flatmate – the letter Michael Irons and the Coxes tried to blackmail you with. Didn't you know there were more copies? I've got the one Lee kept for insurance. I suppose you thought Janet had the only copy.'

He stared at me for a moment, and I stared back. Then he turned on his heel, walked back to his car, and reached in for the keys. I followed immediately.

'Where are you going? Haven't you got anything to say?' He started towards the building. I cut him off. 'I've got it right, haven't I! You tricked Janet into coming to your house and you killed her while Mrs Champion was drunk or watching television in her flat! The grit on her clothes – it comes from your rockery, doesn't it!' Suddenly I thought of the missing piece of Janet's brain, and Mr Tiggywinkle gorging himself on something dead on the rockery.

I halted in mid-manoeuvre.

Philip Chandler looked furious, as though he could have killed me too on the spot. 'You think you're very clever, don't you, Mrs Martin? Well, believe me, you don't know the half of it!' he snapped and sidestepped me neatly.

I sprang after him. 'I most certainly do! Where's *Lee Cox*, Mr

Chandler? What did you do – did you kill him too?' I shouted, but then I let him go into Edinburgh House, because I'd just realized with horror that my car was still on the road with its door open and the engine running. I dashed back and reclaimed it from the midst of a small group of delighted onlookers who – through a strange twist of irony – clearly imagined they were witnessing a road rage incident. Then I moved it just inside Tuck Woodford & Chandler's car park and rang Pete. This time, he answered.

'Philip Chandler was the tenant,' I announced breathlessly, before he could say anything. 'I'm at his office. Listen, he killed Janet – tell the police to check his rockery!'

'*What*?'

'I haven't got time to explain now, but I think he killed Lee too. Did they find any bodies?'

'We're expecting a statement any second but they're taking down spades and plastic bags and things so it looks like it. Wait! About Lee Cox. There's something –'

'I can't! Get here soon!'

I disconnected him and ran back to Edinburgh House. Two girls were putting their coats on in reception. I ignored them and ran up the main stairs, clinging to the impressive mahogany handrail and panting for breath. At the top of the stairs several doors led into offices cluttered with lever-arch files and stacks of documents bound up with different-coloured tapes. One of the doors was closed. I made for it.

Philip Chandler was seated at his desk, holding a phone to his ear.

'I have nothing at all to say to you, Mrs Martin. Will you please leave these offices,' he said tautly, and he disconnected his call impatiently and redialled.

I ignored this. 'What have you done with Lee Cox?' I demanded. 'The police are excavating the cottage – they'll be here any minute. Where's Lee?'

His face turned as white as a bleached bone. 'Don't be ridiculous. I'm making a phone call –'

'He threatened you with the letter and you killed him! How did he get hold of the letter?' At the back of my mind, something belatedly clicked into place. 'Wait a minute – the burglary at the cottage!' I gripped the edge of his desk excitedly. 'It was Lee who burgled the cottage – that was how he got the letter! He went up to the attic. He stole jewellery and pictures –' But I still didn't quite get it.

'Charles? Hallo. Philip,' said Chandler, to the phone. His voice sounded oddly tremulous. 'I wonder if you could give me Richard Sefton's number. I've got a bit of an emergency . . .'

'But that was last *June*! If Lee got the letter from the cottage last June –'

'Yes . . . I need a good criminal man . . . Fine, thanks a lot . . .' Chandler put the phone down suddenly and stood up. And he was surprisingly tall when standing. I retreated slightly, but I wasn't going to give up.

'Mr Chandler – please – I've already got half the story. Why don't you tell me what you did with Lee Cox's body?'

'For your information, Lee Cox is alive and well and living the life of Riley in South Africa.'

'I don't believe you.'

'*Sun City*, the last I heard. What do you think, that I'm some sort of mass murderer?' He was breathing heavily, as though he'd just spent several minutes on a running machine. 'Really, Mrs Martin, do you read horror comics in your spare time? I didn't murder Mr Cox – I bought him off. I agreed to sign over to him some of my late wife's holdings in South Africa on the understanding that he took the next available flight out and that if he or anyone else ever came back for more I'd go straight to the police.'

'Oh, yes? So why didn't you go to the police when Janet approached you? Why didn't you buy *her* off? Or haven't you got any more relatives with overseas holdings who could've helped you out!' I added sarcastically. 'First there's your Aunt Violet in Australia, then your wife's South African –'

'Now, hold on, you don't know the first thing about it!' He was beginning to get angry. 'I worked hard to get where I am. No one gave me handouts. Do you want to know the truth? The truth is that those girls were rubbish, and Mrs Champion doesn't know how lucky she is. Where do you think she'd be today if it wasn't for me!' He sat down again and leaned forward. I could see the little marks on his stiff white collar where his chin had rubbed against it. 'What difference would it have made to anyone's life if I'd gone to the police and told them about those girls?'

I considered this, but he didn't wait for my response. 'I'll tell you what difference it would have made. It would have been the end of my career! You haven't got the faintest idea what things were like in those days, have you?'

I was flattered. 'I have, actually –'

'Do you honestly think I'd've spent one night under the same roof as that lunatic at Holly Cottage if I could have avoided it?' he interrupted, little red spots appearing on his cheekbones. 'I had my mother in hospital, I had fares to pay to and from County Durham every other weekend, I had appearances to keep up. I was on the verge of getting engaged to Anne. And if anybody at Tuck Woodford had known what went on at Holly Cottage I'd have been out of the firm on my bloody ear!' Just for a moment, his accent slipped back to Darlington. 'I always knew one day Miles would go too far – I lived in dread of it – but when I came home from work that day and found him lying there with his head blown off – when I read that letter he'd written to his friend at the BBC – it exceeded even my worst nightmare. He'd been threatening to kill himself ever since he had that stupid play rejected – sitting on the floor with the shotgun in his mouth threatening to pull the trigger and laughing at me when I begged him not to. I don't care if you believe me or not but to begin with I didn't even read his bloody notes and I didn't know anything about the girls. All I could think was that I'd have to call the police and that they'd go through the place with a fine-toothed comb and find drugs and pornographic material and God knows what else, and that everything I'd worked for would fly out of the window. Do you think Messrs Tuck and Woodford would have still offered me the partnership after my name had been dragged through the gutter press?'

'But –'

'Well, I wasn't going to take the chance. I stoked up

the boiler and burnt every suspect substance – every herb, every little bag of white powder I couldn't identify – all his magazines. I tidied the place up and made it look respectable. I read his notes while I was waiting for the police to arrive. I had to go out into the garden to throw up. I couldn't even bring myself to go back into the house, much less look in the cellar. I knew enough about criminal law to know I'd probably destroyed vital evidence and made myself an accessory –'

'Now hold on!' I was outraged. 'You're trying to say you didn't know what happened to the girls, but that's a lie! I told you, I've read the letter! The main reason Miles Lloyd killed himself was because he thought you were going to the police!'

Philip Chandler shook his head. The colour was almost drained from his cheeks. 'No. That's not how it was. I came home that night and there was blood on the cellar steps and a chair broken in the kitchen. I knew he'd had a couple of girls to stay for a few days – everyone knew the Champion girls. They were always full of themselves, out for whatever they could get. I thought there'd been some sort of drunken fight and he'd thrown them out. There was quite a lot of blood, I was afraid someone might have ended up in Casualty and that the police might get involved. I never imagined for a minute that he'd killed anyone – not till I read the letter. All I said to him was that if the police turned up on our doorstep asking questions I wouldn't lie for him.'

Downstairs, there were loud voices in reception.

I couldn't make up my mind whether to believe him.

'I was in shock,' he went on. 'I put the note in my pocket and waited for the police to arrive. They had a quick look round, and their medical officer announced that it looked like a classic case of suicide while the balance of the mind was disturbed. Miles had written another letter, you see, to his mother, blaming *her* for everything, including his failed writing career. They went through the motions and then just took away the body and left me to clear up the mess.'

The commotion downstairs rose to a crescendo and then subsided to a dwindling murmur of voices, so I decided it couldn't have signified the arrival of the authorities. I frowned.

'I see. So you calmly blocked up the cellar, got on the phone to your aunt, and suggested she might like to buy a property with a couple of very quiet sitting tenants.'

'Don't be ridiculous!' he said again. 'You don't know a thing – those were the worst weeks of my life. I picked up the phone twice to call the police but I couldn't go through with it. The Woodfords had insisted I move out of the cottage and into their guest room until I could find something more permanent, but Miles's mother sent me a letter anyway via her solicitor in Jersey informing me that my tenancy had no legal standing and that she intended to sell – the cottage was in her name apparently. That was when I thought of my Aunt Violet – who, incidentally, has no children or dependants and who declined to contribute a penny towards providing medical care for her only sister. She'd been talking about buying a house in the south of England with easy access to what she apparently regards as London's cultural scene to retire to. I thought she'd ask me to handle the purchase, but I never heard a word from her. Eventually I believe she put in a bid for the cottage two days before it was due to go to auction. As for blocking up the cellar, I got a carpenter in to do it. I went to the cottage one evening after work to meet him and borrowed the money to pay him from the firm on some pretext – it was the only thing I could think of doing. I told him there was a damp problem, and he advised having the cellar filled in with rubble and getting a proper damp-proof course fitted. If I could've afforded it, that's what I would have done, but I couldn't.'

The building was now completely silent. 'So what did you do with the letter? Why didn't you destroy it?' I asked.

He gave me an exasperated look as though I was one of his juniors. 'Look, I had lived in a property where two suspicious deaths had occurred. The letter at least proved I didn't take part in them. I had to keep it. I fully intended to put it in a bank deposit box where nobody except me would have ever had access to it, but as I told you, the

Woodfords insisted I went to stay with them the very day after the tragedy, and I didn't want to take it with me there. I put it in the back of an old picture in the living room just as a temporary measure. Well, the cottage was empty, I still had a key, Miles's mother had told the police she was too unwell to come to England and she wanted his body flown back to Jersey for burial – I thought it would only be for a matter of days. But at the time I was assisting in a very difficult litigation, I was in court every day, and I simply couldn't get to a bank during banking hours to sort out the formalities.' He pushed his hair back distractedly. 'The court case dragged on and on, and then I had to go to South Africa with the Woodfords to meet Anne's relatives – it had all been arranged and I couldn't get out of it. Naturally as soon as I got back, I went to Holly Cottage and tried to let myself in, but the agents handling the sale had had the locks changed and everything padlocked because there'd already been two break-ins. Some of Miles's hooligan friends, no doubt, looking for drugs,' he added, bitterly – and I began to feel almost sorry for him. 'Well, I called on the Suttons a few days after they moved in. I told them I was a relative of their landlord and I needed to retrieve a valuable picture. I was taking an awful risk, but I had to do it. They let me in to have a look round, but I couldn't *find* the damn picture! All I could think was that it must have been stolen during one of the break-ins – I just had to hope and pray that if anyone ever found the letter they'd think it was some sort of joke. In fact, apparently, according to Lee Cox, the picture was in the attic the whole time.' He broke off, breathing heavily. 'Now, I've told you what you want to know and I'd like you to leave my office, please – I have an important call to make.' He picked up his phone and began dialling with shaking fingers, misdialled and tried again. 'And by the way, you can't use any of this – or your paper will be in contempt.'

'But I don't understand!' I protested, reaching out to grab the phone from him and not quite having the courage to do it. 'I don't understand why Lee Cox broke into the cottage in the first place. Why did Michael Irons –'

'Oh, for goodness sake!' He slammed the phone back on its

cradle. 'Use your intelligence! I told Irons in 1987 I wanted the cottage completely destroyed down to the last brick as quickly as possible and the cellar filled in with concrete, and I offered him an extremely lucrative deal. Obviously he smelt a rat. I think he thought I'd got several filing cabinets full of incriminating documents in my cellar – hence the burglary – but when Cox couldn't find any documents – or a cellar – they turned their attention to my private life. You know the rest. Cox only found the letter in the picture much later, when he'd given up on my private life and he was preparing to sell the frame to a dealer. Now, will you please leave?'

I shook my head resolutely. 'I can't leave. I'm waiting for the police. And you still haven't told me what you did with Lee's body or what happened with Janet.'

'Oh, you're waiting for the police, are you!' He began to look angry. 'Mrs Martin, you and other riff-raff like you have ruined my life. There are two small children on their way home from hospital at this very moment who are going to have to be told some day that their grandfather is a murderer. Isn't that enough for you? I *have* told you about Mr Cox, at length – if you don't believe me that's up to you. And as for Mrs Cox – that woman was greedy and rude and a liar. The day I met her I'd spent the afternoon waiting to find out whether my grandchildren would live or die. She said on the phone that her husband had told her everything about me and that she'd got the evidence, and that if I wouldn't meet her to discuss it I'd be reading about it the following day in the papers. Well, her husband had sworn blind he hadn't told anyone else about the letter, not even Irons, with whom he said he was no longer associated, but I panicked. I agreed to meet her where she suggested – in the layby – and she demanded five thousand pounds in cash. Of course, I should have gone straight to the police as I'd threatened and admitted the whole thing – but she said she was desperate for money, and if I gave her five thousand pounds immediately I'd never hear from either her or her husband again. Well, I was overwrought. I offered to pick up as much as I could from cashpoints and meet her later at my house. Then, when she arrived, she said five thousand wasn't enough – not for someone who could afford a house like mine. She said she wanted ten thousand. I told you, I was tired and emotional and I'd had enough. I'd missed my granddaughters' birth thanks to her – I'd had to leave the hospital to meet her – and I suddenly felt very angry. I picked up the brass umbrella holder that used to stand in my porch and I ran after her and hit her over the head with it – twice.' He closed his eyes, and his head jarred slightly, twice, as though he was reliving the moment. 'But Mrs Martin, that isn't the worst of it. I've destroyed myself and my family for nothing, because when I opened her handbag afterwards to look for the letter – do you know what I found?'

At that moment, the door to his office opened noiselessly and a young constable with acne stepped nervously into the room.

We both ignored him. 'What?' I prompted.

He chuckled mirthlessly. 'Nothing, Mrs Martin. Absolutely nothing.' He stared blankly at the constable. 'Well, unless you count a tape-recording of her husband talking to Pat Woollcott about that woman's pathetic allegations.'

There was silence.

'You mean, she hadn't got a copy of the letter? Are you saying she didn't know anything about what had happened at Holly Cottage – the only thing she'd got on you was the Pat Woollcott story?'

Philip Chandler gritted his teeth and didn't answer.

'So you killed her for *nothing*!' I repeated, aghast. 'She only had the *tape*!'

The constable stared from one to the other of us nervously. He cleared his throat. 'I'm sorry, sir, but I've had a radio message. Are you Mr Philip Chandler, the solicitor? I don't know what this is all about, sir, but I've been instructed to remain on these premises until the arrival of a superior officer. If it's all right with you, sir, I'll just wait outside the door until my sergeant gets here . . .'

Pete poured water on to a teabag and prodded it gingerly with a teaspoon.

'You sure this is all you want? You don't want anything stronger?'

I held my head in my hands and moaned. 'I feel awful! It was so stupid of me –'

'Oh, go on, it's only the headlamp! I've done much worse things to my cars. We'll get it fixed in no time.'

I moaned again. I hadn't meant the Golf. I'd meant that brief moment on Philip Chandler's rockery when Dave Ormond had called me his favourite reporter and I'd allowed myself to think unchaste thoughts about him. 'I didn't mean the car. I meant something else –' I hesitated, agonizing over how to put it.

'Yes?' He frowned. 'Do you mean accusing Chandler of being some sort of homicidal maniac and murdering Lee as well as Janet? Come on, it wasn't your fault, you were all psyched up! I did try to tell you the police had tracked Lee down to a flight to Johannesburg, but Chandler's hardly going to sue you for slander in the circumstances, is he?'

'No. Actually, it's something else. Something really awful to do with someone I thought was a friend.'

His smile wavered. Then he said, 'Oh – Detective Sergeant Horton! I see. Well, don't worry about that, he can take care of himself. Give him a few weeks and he'll get over it.'

'But I didn't mean Wayne. I meant –'

'– And you'll have made young Kerr-Dixon very happy. They released him an hour ago without charge. Hang on, I'll get you something to put on – it's bloody freezing in here!'

He ran up upstairs to get my dressing gown. When he came down he tucked it carefully round my shoulders and dealt with the tea.

'There you are. Now what's up?'

I thought better of it.

'It's nothing. I just don't want to do this any more. You know – reporting. Linda Thingy from the *Advertiser* was right – it's awful, I hate it. I don't want to spend my time finding out all these bad things about people. I want to do something positive. Listen, I was thinking –' Suddenly it came to me in a flash. 'Look, I'm not old – not really. I'm only forty-three

– other women do it all the time. It's going to be quite the thing in the new millennium apparently, older parenthood. We could have a child of our own!'

'What?'

For a moment, time froze. Pete's right eye twitched and I could tell his whole life was flashing before him including the part he hadn't had yet – and that he wasn't sure he liked it.

'Ah,' he said finally. 'Well, well. What a thought. You know, in an ideal world that would be a great idea. In an ideal world you and I would have half a dozen children with my looks, your sweet nature, my wit –'

'Your modesty –'

'Yes. Right. Precisely. But in an ideal world you and I would have met twenty years ago. I wish we had, but we didn't, and we've both already done parenting and it was never my best thing. I'm being honest now.'

'I know, I know you are, but it doesn't matter, really. Your best thing is being you and I'd really like to have your baby.'

'Thank you. That's very sweet of you.' He kissed me. 'And I really love you, too, but I'm just not sure if it's a good idea. I think we ought to think about it very carefully before we come to a decision,' he added.

We stared out of the kitchen window at the distant lights of the Stag House office block, and watched them twinkle gently through the rain pattering down the glass.

'Do you?'

'Yes. I do. I really think we ought to think about it very, very carefully,' he said earnestly.

But I knew we never would.